OVERDUE

LIBRARY SYSTEM RESET
BOOK ONE

K.T. HANNA

Book Cover by Illustration by Marko Horvatin
Typography by Inorai
1st edition 2024

For Luke
And knowing just the right questions to ask

1

DISTORTION

The world shook with all the vigor of a wet dog.

There was no better way to describe it.

Quinn looked up from the desk, startled by the movement, only to notice that no one else had even budged. Odd enough, but it wouldn't be the first time she'd suffered vertigo and thought the world might be surreptitiously ending.

She waited a few more moments before shrugging and flipping to the next page in the course catalog. Declaring majors was never fun. She'd heard enough grumbling about it over the years. Now it was her turn, and she had to agree.

How did they expect nineteen- and twenty-year-olds to decide what they wanted to do for the rest of their lives? And how was she supposed to tell if what she was choosing even had a hope in hell of getting her the sort of money she'd need to survive?

Taking a deep breath, she centered herself.

Mom always told her it was better to do something you loved as long as you could put food on the table.

Which was all well and good, but if Quinn had any say in it, she also wanted to travel overseas, have some nice vacations. The bare minimum wasn't an option.

Even taking all her future wishes into account, Quinn couldn't shake the constant feeling that library sciences was the way for her to go. She'd loved books since she could remember, in this deeply attached sort of way. And no matter what she tried, she couldn't escape the desire to work with them, despite the current economy.

She still remembered falling into magical worlds through the pages of books she secretly read by flashlight under the covers. Those worlds always gave her a sense of peace.

Maybe if she did something along the lines of information science and systems? That might work. She stared at the page, raising her pen to her lips and nibbling on it absent-mindedly. Of course there was an online catalogue, but this way it felt like a tangible choice. She liked the feel of the paper in her hands. It grounded her.

More weighted.

"Although..." she muttered out loud. "What sort of job would I even get with those qualifications?"

"You talking to yourself again?"

The voice startled Quinn, and she glanced up, squinting against the light pouring in the window. A smile crossed her face. "Hallie. Good to see you too."

Her quasi-friend shrugged. They'd shared a couple of the same classes the first year of college, but Quinn wouldn't exactly call them friends. Frankly, she wouldn't really call anyone a true friend. She'd left those at home when she crossed the country to get as far away from her foster parents as possible. Not that they hadn't kicked her out the moment she turned eighteen. After all, she didn't bring them income anymore and they needed the room for someone who wasn't a legal adult.

Distance was preferable. Just in case.

Still, Hallie was nice enough even if she never took her classes seriously. The other girl flopped into the seat across from her and opened her course catalog too. "Any ideas?"

"You know picking a career path isn't like using my lecture notes, right?" Quinn quipped, raising an eyebrow. Hallie hadn't precisely cheated off her, but she had on rather frequent occasions borrowed her notes, rarely taking her own. In a way, the girl had sort of cheated herself.

Hallie stuck out her tongue in that super mature way. "I know. Don't remind me. I was thinking maybe a business major. Or something."

Quinn tried to make her smile encouraging. "A business major leaves room for a lot of possibilities."

"Yeah. I should probably leave my options open." Hallie sighed, and then leaned over the table and asked, "So, what are you going to do, then?"

Quinn glanced at her. "Well, I'm leaning toward something to do with libraries, probably library sciences or computer systems. All about books, really." It was probably time she gave into this strange urge she constantly felt around books.

"Oh." Hallie let a few seconds of silence lapse. "But wouldn't libraries disappear... eventually? Even our textbooks can be digital these days."

This time, Quinn paused. That was a super accurate observation, and she knew, deep down, that it was realistic too. So why in the seven hells was Quinn considering something with limited longevity? No matter what she flipped to, her brain pulled her back to this.

Probably misinterpreting Quinn's silence, Hallie continued on. "Well, I mean, I guess if it's something you feel passionate about. Right?"

Quinn sat back and gave Hallie a long look. There was something different about the girl today. She seemed mostly serious about choosing a career and to actually have it sorted out for herself.

At that moment, Quinn envied her. So, she just shrugged and gave Hallie the best possible response she could think of. "It's probably a good idea to pick something we're not going to be miserable doing. Make sure it's something that we can at least love a little bit if we have to be doing it for the rest of our lives. You know, and make money. Find that happy balance."

Her own advise was based on the wisdom she vaguely remembered her mother telling her before her mom died. But those weren't nice thoughts, and she didn't really want to think about them at all.

Luckily, Hallie smiled and nodded. "You know, you're right. Screw the business major. I'm not going to be a business major. I'm going into theatre."

Quinn laughed softly, mindful of their location in the library and not wanting to make too much noise. The librarian here could go on the warpath sometimes. "That suits you much more than some stuffy office. I think you're going to do fine."

That was when the world shook again.

And it didn't stop.

Everything around Quinn shook—the tables, the bookshelves, even the people. Vibrations spread across the entire area, climbing up her spine until her teeth tingled.

The people around her trembled in a way that made them appear flimsy, intangible, like stop-motion cutouts. Their movements were stilted and stiff, yet none of their expressions changed. It was like they didn't even notice.

They wavered around like warped images on an old-fashioned television with bad reception. They flickered in and out, black and white, static interference, there one moment and gone the next. It was as if no one near her actually existed. Like everything was being broadcast solely for her.

Quinn jumped up from the table, her course catalog falling to the floor, suddenly winking in and out of existence along with everything else in the room. She held her hands up in front of her face, checking to see if she too had become weirdly intangible. But her hands were just their same pale shade of boring.

Alarmingly solid.

The library walls rippled like waves on an ocean as if the walls were made of rubber. The glass-paned windows crackled like someone had flicked them and shattered all the glass, replacing it with cellophane. Yet any movement on the floor beneath her sounded as if she was breaking even more glass. Like a car driving over windows.

Overhead, the chandelier that hung down in the main lobby of the library entrance to the left of her table warped and fizzled. Electric sparks shot out, disappearing in the rising hum all around her. White noise made her eardrums ache right through to her jaw. From the pain, she thought for just a moment that blood was trickling out of her ears. But her fingers came away dry.

If this was vertigo, it was one hell of an episode.

She tried to take a step forward but stumbled to her knees. Pain shot through her forehead as if she'd hit the table—which she should have because it was there—but she didn't remember making contact. Now the table was gone, yet there, ethereal, as if it wasn't actually tangible.

"Hallie?" she called out, but the only answer was a strange buzzing through the air, like a swarm of hornets about to attack her.

Darkness spread throughout the library, reaching for her like the fingers of shadows. They extended toward her, through the book-cases, past the books, through the walls and the windows, through the people who should have been there, who were there moments before, but now were just static images in her mind. Ever lengthening in their desperate attempt to reach her.

The roar of hornets buzzed around her head while smokey tendrils yearned toward her.

Shadows, closer now, reached for her, bending, twisting, churning almost, like something under the water trying to emerge and grab her. The floor began to warp, cut through by static lines of black and white.

Her entire surroundings went dark, and the ground beneath her heaved violently once more.

And then, just as suddenly as the violent tremors started, they stopped.

Silence hung heavy in their wake.

Slowly, Quinn calmed herself. Even if calmed might be a tad over-selling it. She did, however, stop outright hyperventilating. She chalked that up as a win and looked around, taking stock of her predicament.

The library was empty. No books were scattered anywhere. There weren't even books on the shelves. The shelves themselves had morphed into the wall in twisted ways that should have broken the wood or at least made it crack. But it was smooth, very wall-like, resembling something out of a seriously warped dream.

Quinn couldn't quite get her mind around it, not like the way the table in front of her had somehow become a floor. Smooth and sort of spongey. She could almost feeling it bracing to bounce her again...

Looking around, she took in everything.

From the darkness and severe lack of windows, to the cavernous ceiling she could tell reached far above her despite the lack of illumination. She gulped and closed her eyes for a count of twenty before opening them again. But nothing had changed.

She definitely wasn't in her university library anymore.

The windows were gone, replaced by a strange wooden material on circular walls all the way around the massive area. As far as she could see. It wasn't like that horrible 70s paneling that was in vogue so many years ago. No, the walls here reminded her of the beautiful trees in the forests of Europe, of those huge redwoods in California.

Majestic and mighty.

Ancient.

The air around her felt stagnant, as if no breeze had graced this glorious wood for more time than she could perceive. The cavern stretched out in front of her. Even if she couldn't see it properly, she knew that much.

A pure sense of vastness.

The absolute silence was weighted and heavy. There was no whisper of even a breeze from the ceiling fans that should be going full blast in the tail end of the hot summer months like it was now. There was no noise coming from anywhere and there were no people in her vicinity.

Hallie had disappeared along with everyone else. Quinn's course catalog was gone too, along with the choices she was making for the rest of her life. For just a moment, Quinn wanted to collapse. She'd spent days, months, her whole life on this fruitless future quest. And now she was going to miss the deadline. Now it was all gone.

Gone.

Because this place wasn't her college campus. It wasn't anywhere she could even remotely identify. Maybe she had been knocked unconscious by the edge of the desk, but there was no pain in her head, so she didn't think that likely. Given that... why the hell would a course catalogue and major choice even be remotely important right here, right now?

Anymore.

She wanted to sit there on the floor that she couldn't identify in this unfamiliar, almost alien area that she'd ended up in and pause and stop and just breathe. Maybe she'd fallen asleep. Maybe this was a dream.

She pinched herself and it hurt.

Like, that-was-going-to-bruise-tomorrow sort of hurt.

Okay, so probably not unconscious, and maybe not a dream. She obviously wasn't lying there with her head on her hands on the desk. Maybe she'd been knocked out. As far as she'd been able to see there had been debris all around... and flying books. Perhaps one of those hit her in the head and she passed out. Except that pinch should have woken her even in that event. Yet another unlikely conclusion.

So if this wasn't a dream, what was this?

Gathering up courage, she looked around trying to get a better sense of where she was. It was extremely dark with nothing but a dull, greenish-blue glow to the whole area. The soft light suffused the area, lending it a more relaxing atmosphere despite the circumstances she'd yet to figure out.

As much as she tried to look around, she couldn't discern anything. She could make out shapes in the distance, but they were shrouded in shadows. At least the latter weren't moving anymore.

It was like the whole area was an optical illusion trying to trick her into believing something was there when it wasn't. She took a few steps forward and it was like the floor moved with her, similar to an escalator that she couldn't see, except it stopped when she stopped, mirroring her actions.

"Hello," she called out and the sound echoed back to her in the way it does if you're standing in a mountain range. Where the sound just bounced off every single mountain in the area. But she wasn't in some hilly region, she was in what seemed like... a wooden cavern.

Now she was getting a little pissed off. Whisking her off to who knew where, and who knew how... and no one was answering?

"Hello!" she called out again, more insistent this time, and received no response. She stomped her foot on the ground, getting really irritated, but the action fell flat with nothing but a dull thud to show for it. "That's enough, you've had your fun, what is this?"

Because it was either a really, really bad dream she was not waking up from, the world had in fact come to an end, or somebody had kidnapped her. Maybe it was a prank. Why would somebody kidnap her? She'd never offended anybody on college campus. Hell, she'd barely spoken to anybody on college campus.

It wasn't like they could ransom her for her inheritance.

She took another breath, calming her nerves, and this time tried to keep the irritation out of her voice when she spoke. "Okay, if this is a joke, that's fine. Just tell me so I can get out of here and get home. I've only got till midnight to declare my major."

Another several seconds passed without a sound. Taking another few steps forward, she realized her footfalls didn't make a sound. Almost as if the ground swallowed every single movement. And only when she spoke would it echo back at her.

Just when Quinn was about to speak again, a light flashed in front of her eyes, like a holographic screen. It appeared in front of her moving as she turned her head, and a voice resonated throughout the chamber, even though it sounded like it was in her head. The words it spoke scrolled across her vision.

Projected energy expenditure exceeded.

Stand by for emergency protocol.

Emergency Power Mode Override Activated

The sound echoed through the wood-lined cavern she found herself in and the subtle glow changed from bluey-green to red. The holographic words disappeared.

And once again, the world shook.

2

ALARM

THE RED GLOW SUFFUSED THE AREA, LIKE A THIN VEIL OF MIASMA drifting over the ground. If it weren't for the low blaring alarm trying to burrow into her ears, it'd almost be beautiful.

Quinn had to stop for a moment to let her thoughts catch up with her. The alarm faded into the back of her mind in a neat partition of concentration. She'd learned to shut out the noise of her foster siblings early on. This wasn't too different on that level.

But she couldn't quite wrap her awareness around what was happening otherwise.

The way the alarm honked reminded her of geese in flight when they took off in their flocks. The timber of the walls all around her reminded her more and more of old Californian redwoods, with the way the intricate knots played with each other, and the grain of wood brushed in the same direction consistently.

A humungous, old, living tree.

Frankly, it was lovely, even under the blood-red alarm flashing light.

But the light did allow her to notice one thing she hadn't seen before. Just out of the corner of her left eye, she thought she saw something move and turned to look. She wasn't expecting what she saw.

For several seconds she just watched.

It wasn't alive, not in the traditional sense that it was a creature, anyway, she thought, despite the thrum that seemed to echo through the ground to her from the strange trunk that stood in the middle of the room. That was the only word she could come up with for it. There was a decidedly uneven and ancient air about it. The wood was so old, it was almost smooth grey, sort of like metal.

Perhaps it was petrified.

That's when Quinn craned her neck to look up at the alarm-illuminated ceiling far, far above her.

It was at this point Quinn finally realized she seemed to be standing under the boughs of a tree. Except there weren't leaves or branches as such, but more a massive trunk in the middle of a cavernous room apparently made of wood.

There was a softness to the room like it could nurture whatever was in it. Cautiously ignoring the full flashing alarm, she made her way directly to that center. That was it. This was where that underlying hum came from. Its warmth increased the closer she got to it.

It was whatever the alarm was protecting.

Core was a much more fitting description than trunk, even if the latter was eerily accurate as far as appearances went.

It was difficult to tell why she took those steps, but something about it lulled, soothed, and even calmed. Frankly, it felt like it was calling out to her, not quite whispering her name. It wasn't exactly like memories or voices in her head, but there was still that element of familiarity.

Despite the existence of the alarm, Quinn felt no real sense of urgency. More that this alarm was indicative of the overall lack of power in the vicinity. To warn people of the severe absence of energy.

Perhaps.

The ancient tree core was much farther away than it seemed, and whatever these emergency protocols were that it put into place, they hampered her every move. Time felt fluid, yet she had no idea if it had been several minutes, hours, or days.

There was a foggy sensation to all her thoughts.

This whole setting, from being whisked away to essentially being in a cave or cavern, was so far-fetched that she again considered the possibility she was passed out somewhere in a hospital wing. Maybe she was actually in a coma after the earthquake that seemingly demolished her university library and couldn't be woken with a simple pinch.

But she'd worry about that later.

The floor's sponginess continued to stand out to her. Sort of like one of those kid's playgrounds with the matting meant to protect them as they fell. Only this version of didn't actually feel safe.

It was as if roots were deliberately standing in her way and the ground was a soil that could suck at her feet and keep her in place. Maybe that was one of the protocols, maybe this whole alarm was set just to protect this tree, or well, the tree that was not a tree but felt like a tree.

This was all making less and less sense.

Maybe she had taken a hit from the table and thus her thoughts were truly hampered.

Air whooshed by her suddenly, and in the space of a blink, it stopped.

She found herself right next to the trunk, to the well of sound that vibrated through her entire being. And the room, it seemed, had stopped moving. Upon closer inspection now, it definitely wasn't wood as such. There was a faint woodsy smell about it, but its scent was colder, like stone.

This tree was never going to be firewood. The trunk was so wide and huge in circumference that her arms would only reach a fraction of the way around if she tried to hug it.

It also didn't appear to be natural; there were lines running through it, these beautiful faint blue fluorescent lines that ran barely under the surface like glowing veins. Upon closer inspection, they flickered in and out, sort of like when everybody and everything had appeared before when she was standing in the college library.

In fact, the harder she looked, the more those lines appeared vein-like or perhaps even similar to circuits as they flooded through the tree, and up the core of the trunk. Suddenly, as she looked up, she saw two bright, bright blue dots staring right back at her.

It took a few moments for her to register that they were, in fact, eyes and not just some glowing something else. Especially once they blinked at her, very slowly.

Not dots.

Definitely eyes.

She blinked back.

Had she fallen down the rabbit hole? Was this a Cheshire cat? Before she could say anything or do anything, a creature leaped down, much larger than any cat she'd anticipated.

Its back stood about thigh height to her paltry five-foot frame and felt much larger than life when it landed on the ground. Quinn stumbled back in shock. She gasped, and may have let out a small scream, but couldn't exactly hear it because the alarms were still blaring.

She was going to be cautious and say that she didn't scream anyway, because really, who screams when a massive cat that's probably the size of a large dog jumps down from God knows where because it's not a tree and that wasn't a branch?

"It's good that you can keep your wits about you," said a voice that really didn't sound like it was happy with anything she'd done ever, nor would it ever approve of any action she'd ever take. "That's enough staring now. Would you rather take a picture? It'll last longer."

It was all Quinn could do to not just stand and stare and catch flies. To be more precise though, that's exactly what she was doing. She just couldn't tear her eyes away from the creature. No one was going to believe this. She reached into her back pocket for her phone.

"What are you doing?" the voice asked, a hint of incredulity in the tone.

She stuttered, lowering her phone hand. "You said to take a pic—"

"Not literally!" it snapped.

She hurriedly put the phone away.

"What are you looking at?" The indignant voice was even worse than the first time it spoke. But maybe there was something else in that tone. Another sentiment that she couldn't quite latch onto. A bit of caution. Perhaps some bone weariness?

"You can talk," she said, realizing quite how awkward that sounded the moment the words left her lips, especially considering it had already spoken to her three times. But it was a fricking talking feline.

"Of course I can talk, how else would you understand me? You don't have access to telepathy yet."

To distract herself from the scathing retort sitting on the tip of her tongue as well as the fact that this cat mentioned telepathy, Quinn looked at the creature in front of her. She was mistaken. It wasn't a cat per se. It seemed to be a lynx, maybe? Perhaps that was the right one? A caraval? No, it was a lynx, definitely. Except it wasn't any color she'd ever seen. It was this glowing, deep purple that was almost black and had black stripes.

But maybe they weren't stripes. If only she could get a little closer to see just what those things were because they seemed to move, to twist around its body.

"Excuse me? Do you mind? It's rude to stare."

It was only then that Quinn realized how far forward she'd been leaning to try and get a good look at the creature. Despite the almost overwhelming urge to pet it, to reach out and run her fingers along what she was pretty sure looked like script woven into those stripes, she managed to resist by channeling her embarrassment instead.

"Oh, I'm sorry. I'm really, really sorry. I just, you just, I suddenly, and I'm here..." She pointed at the lynx and gestured all around her, feeling quite helpless.

The creature stared at her which did nothing to alleviate the awkwardness of the situation since it said nothing.

And then it blinked.

Once.

Slowly.

Did it talk to her? Or had she imagined that? She must have hit her head really hard because this was all even more fantastical than falling down a rabbit hole. So Quinn shut up. Because the stare the lynx was giving her could have cut ice.

The thing was, Quinn was starting to feel less intimidated and more very irritated. Especially if this was all something just playing out in her head. "You know, you could be nicer. I have no clue where I am. I could be dreaming for all I know, and you're just some figment of my imagination. Figments of my own imagination should definitely be a lot nicer to me."

The lynx blinked at her with those massive eyes that were not the right size for a creature that big. They were far larger, almost like anime eyes. Well, except for the fact that they didn't twinkle happily or magically. They seemed pretty angry too.

"I am not a figment of your imagination," the cat spat out. "I am Links."

A giggle escaped Quinn. Her first reaction was to clap her hands over her mouth, but another chuckle escaped her. She couldn't help it. "Lynx. Your name is Lynx. Seriously?"

"Yes, seriously. What's wrong with my name?" There was this indignant undertone to the words that just set Quinn off even harder.

"Lynx. You're in the shape of a lynx. Not exactly original."

"Well, you're not exactly original," the lynx said, or Lynx said, a little bit flustered. "My name doesn't necessarily relate to my shape. But that's beside the point. You shouldn't be worrying about dreams. You should have realized what this is."

"And how do you propose I realize what this is?" Quinn said, suddenly complete and utterly exhausted. Her sense of time was skewed, but she knew without a shadow of a doubt, that she'd been in this place a lot longer than it seemed.

All of a sudden it was like her energy was gone. In contrast the lights surrounding the trunk seemed to have grown slightly brighter and she could feel a headache coming on. "Why don't you try explaining to me what's happened? Because obviously, I'm in a cavern of some sort with an electrical tree, or whatever this is. And I'm quite sure this is nowhere near my university campus."

"It's not an electrical tree. We don't use electricity here. We don't need to. Or we didn't need to. We're in emergency power mode right now." Lynx sounded sort of sad, and Quinn felt a little bad that she had teased the feline so much.

"Okay, so if you don't use electricity, how do you power things?"

"Through magic, of course. What did you think the blue veins and lines are? I'm quite sure the packet explained everything in detail." Lynx's impatience had returned full force.

"I thought it was electricity," Quinn said, shaking her head as if she might jolt her hearing a bit. There's no way he could have said what she thought he just said. "Wait a second, did you just say magic?"

"Of course I said magic. I'm a talking feline. How did you think that was possible?" Lynx practically spat the words out, obviously annoyed. "Surely you can't be that dense. Of course magic exists. Maybe not in your world…"

He took a moment, shaking his head and very obviously pressing down his urge to yell. "Anyway, that's why it was pure luck that we found your magical signature. I guess it's no wonder it's taking you time to digest the facts. You haven't experienced magic before."

Just that statement almost made her blood boil. "Oh, we've heard of it. All right. But nobody believes in magic. We have technology for that sort of stuff. We developed it ourselves."

It wasn't until after she'd made the statement that what Lynx said really sank in. Earth didn't have magic? Her world? And something about a packet? What the hell was that cat on? Wait a second. She was having a literal conversation with a cat. The last thought stopped her in her tracks and only Lynx's yelling brought her back out of it.

"Are you even listening to me!"

Quinn cringed. "Sorry, my brain was catching up. You can't just throw around 'oh, by the way, magic is real' and not expect a person to react." She spoke slowly, glancing around the cavern again, taking it all in. It definitely didn't feel like home, even though she wasn't sure how she could tell that. Even so, she quelled the rising panic she could feel emerging and focused on what Lynx was saying.

"Fine. I guess I'll repeat that. But only once." Lynx cleared his throat. "Anyway, it's partially because your world is starved of magic. But I digress. I'll talk to you about that later. First of all, we need you to synchronize before the Library disappears."

"Say what? Synchronize me? What the hell is going on?"

Lynx actually paused and looked up at her, a brief flash of confusion evident in his expression. It mixed with the annoyance so she couldn't be quite sure of anything, but she thought she saw a sliver of doubt in his eyes. "Wait, what do you mean, 'what's going on'? Did none of the information get through to you?"

"Information? You call this garbled listing of all the impossible you're giving me *information*?" Quinn pinched the bridge of her nose, suddenly very aware of the increasingly volatile encroaching headache.

"No. I did everything I should have. I set everything up. Initiated all the correct protocols. While the transition was in progress, you should have received a bundle of information highlighting the situation here and your place in it." There was a general air of confusion around the cat now.

"What do you mean transition? I was sitting studying my course catalog and talking to a friend." Quinn even managed to feel a pang of regret at Hallie having disappeared while she scolded the cat. "Everything went static. My friend and everyone else around me warped. I think some glass might have exploded, but I'm hazy on that. I stumbled and am pretty sure I smacked my head on the table. Then it was dark and black and I was here. After which the alarm went off. The only information I received before encountering you was that the system had used too much power and emergency protocols had been engaged."

That's when Lynx started muttering. Quinn could barely make out what the cat was saying under its breath.

"But that doesn't make sense. We sent the packet through. She should have known. She should have come here at least with some knowledge about what..."

Quinn planted her hands on her hips, her small amount of

patience evaporated. "How about you just tell me and we can stop wasting time."

"Of course, that's... I'm Links. I am a manifestation of the entirety of the Magical Library of Everywhere. And you are our next Librarian and last hope."

3

CORE

QUINN BLINKED AT HIS LAST STATEMENT, RATHER SKEPTICAL ABOUT THE whole thing despite wanting to believe she wasn't dreaming. "I'm your last hope?

"Literally. Our last hope of getting a Librarian for the Library," Lynx nodded for emphasis.

Quinn shook her head still not quite parsing his words. "The magical library of what now?"

But Lynx didn't seem inclined to give her an explanation. Instead, the cat sat down and curled its paws under its front, looking at her with a quizzical expression on its face.

While it literally sat like a loaf.

It was all Quinn could do not to comment on its peets disappearing.

Finally, after what seemed like an age, Lynx spoke. "The Magical Library of Everywhere. Also known just as the Library. I understand that your world doesn't have magic, but you were supposed to get all of this information in the time it took you to get here. This is how it works regardless of the background of the individual. It's always worked like this. It should have uploaded into your brain and given you a generic understanding as soon as you were recognized by the system."

Quinn hugged herself for a moment, took another deep breath, and tried her best to keep her voice even as she steadied herself. "First up—you should be asking people for permission to load stuff into their brains. And secondly, I already told you I didn't get a packet. Explain where I am and what the hell you mean by connecting me to a system before we disappear. That sounds like some dodgy cyberpunk b movie stuff? Just what the hell do you mean?"

This time, the cat just gestured with its paw and patted the ground, and Quinn reluctantly sat down next to him. Not too close, though. "Okay, it seems I'll have to catch you up to speed, but it won't be all the information you need. And we have to do this as fast as possible."

"Why do we have to do it fast? It seems to me fast is an extremely good way to leave out very important things." She raised an eyebrow.

Lynx paused for a second and gave one nod. "That is valid, but as you can see we have been reduced to Emergency Power Mode. We don't have the time to explain everything in detail. The basics is all I can do. For now."

"And this synchronization will supposedly extend the time we have?" She eyed him and the red flashing glow all around them warily.

Lynx nodded once more.

"Fine." Quinn crossed her arms and watched him, still ignoring the sound of the alarm in the background. "But at least give me something. This is all... a lot. How is it even possible that I'm your last hope?"

"If I knew how it was possible, I could have reversed it and we wouldn't be having this conversation because I'd never have had to go into low power mode in the first place," Lynx started off snappily, and then sighed again. He really seemed to be frustrated. "I couldn't find a compatible signature even before shutdown and that's been..."

For just a second he paused, and his eyes churned and flickered strangely until a pinpoint of bright blue appeared ever so briefly in the depths of each iris. "Four hundred sixty-eight years and fourteen days. Yep, that's it. That's the statistic I needed."

19

"How did you pull that number out of thin air?" Quinn raised an eyebrow.

"It wasn't thin air, it's part of my database." Lynx grimaced at Quinn's blank stare and continued. "Because I'm the Library, or I'm the manifestation of the Library and thus completely interconnected with the Library, just like you will be once you amalgamate with the core."

"Wait, wait." She shook her hands out in front of her body. "Are you saying that I'm going to turn into you?"

Lynx actually laughed. It was a full-throated belly laugh. "No, no, you will stay you. You just… that connection, can you feel it? Do you sense it? Can you hear it humming? That's the Library. It's got a wavelength you should be able to detect. And when you connect, you'll be able to feel it and hear it and understand it more and more as it powers up. Help it get new knowledge. Help it replenish its magical supply. Let it give magic back to the universe. Because right now, it's running on almost empty."

Quinn listened. She had heard that hum. It was low and comforting and safe. It thrummed through the floor, right up through her spine. Sometimes it even set her teeth on edge. It was a sensation she'd thought was just nerves. But on reflection, it didn't feel bad, but instead welcoming.

For just a moment, the alarm seemed to blare louder, and then it receded again.

Was that really the Library? It was there; she could truly sense it, just like Lynx said. She reached her hand forward, hesitantly, placing it against the trunk or core or whatever the hell it was called. The material under her hand felt nothing like what she'd expected. It was cool to the touch, not rough like stone, though—it was smooth. She could feel it tugging at her consciousness. Sense it was magical. It was like everything she'd ever wanted in one place. There was a hitch to her voice when she spoke next.

"Does that mean this is my Library?" she asked, her voice barely audible above the alarm.

Even though she couldn't see his face, she knew Lynx was smiling.

"Technically. As long as we prevent complete shutdown, there's so much we can do. We can find the Combat Branch. We can unearth the Horticultural Branch. We can rediscover the Culinary Section, the Bardic and Musical division, the Alchemical and Medicinal Branches, the Crafting Branch. You don't even understand. We've lost so, so much."

"You're moving a little too fast for me. All of that is confusing."

"Sorry." He seemed to mean it, too.

"So if I don't do this." Quinn paused. "Then no one can get magical Library books?"

Lynx stopped her, shaking his hand. There was a mild expression of panic on his face. Like he didn't want her to misunderstand. "Magic exists, and people with magical affinities can use magic, which is practically everyone. The Library is like a focal point. It helps you focus, it helps you get better and stronger. The more you know, the more power you have, as long as you understand it too. But we don't have time for more of an explanation. Not right now."

Quinn barely resisted the urge to snap at him. "Look, we need to *make* time for this. I don't understand this connection you keep saying I have to make."

"We'd have more time if you'd just connect now," Lynx retorted.

"Hey, there's no need to be sarcastic with me. You realize you pulled *me* here. You're asking me to do something I didn't agree to. You just yanked me through a bloody wormhole or whatever it is, and you just expect me to be okay with connecting myself to a computer?"

"It is not a computer," Lynx corrected her. "The Library, the... listen, I'm sorry. I realize this must be overwhelming and really difficult to understand. You've already got your hand on the core. Can't you feel that? You have to connect. If you don't connect, then there's nothing."

"You mean like, nothing for me to do but go back home, right?" Quinn glanced at Lynx, but could already tell from his expression that that was not what he meant in the slightest. "Wait, you mean everything right where we are will be gone?"

Lynx nodded. "Yes. Completely and utterly. Everything you've ever known will cease to exist."

She drew in a breath and let herself feel the hum again, that flickering lifeline right beneath her skin. It reached out to her tentatively, like it knew she was confused and uncertain. Maybe its caution could be enough?

Lynx cleared his throat. "Look, I get that you need to know a lot of stuff, but I promise that we will fill you in as soon as the connection's been made and the power drain halted. Can you do that much? Can you accept that?"

Quinn didn't know what else to do. She obviously wasn't going home anytime soon and definitely not if she suddenly winked out of existence. She hadn't hit her head that hard, and she was pretty sure she wasn't in a coma, and this was unlike any expectation she'd had of being transported into a different world.

Isekai anime had a lot to answer for.

What was she supposed to do?

It took a lot of courage to speak what she needed to, but she managed. "Fine. Connect us, but I'm going to hold you to that promise."

4

LIBRARY

THAT WAS ALL THE ENCOURAGEMENT LYNX NEEDED. HE GUIDED HER second hand to join the first, about shoulder-width apart, against the smooth, cold surface of the trunk. His touch was cool and almost wispy, like it was made out of compact smoke.

She could feel the grooves beneath her hands that might have been grains at some stage.

As soon as both her hands hit the surface, the lights throughout the tree began to illuminate, resembling veins or maybe circuits on a motherboard. It was beautiful yet terrifying as she felt a brief surge of power fire up through her, right through her body, to her brain, lighting up her own veins under her skin like Christmas tree lights strung around a bright star.

However, when she opened her mouth to comment on it, it felt as though her veins were on fire. Instead of speaking, she screamed. It obliterated all other thoughts in her head, leaving only the fiery rush of everything, and all of it at once.

There were planetary alignments and stars in skies she'd never seen before. Star systems she'd never heard of, despite her passing interest in astronomy. There were continents with creatures that roamed them as if out of some fantasy book. Floating islands littered skies with rivers falling down into nothingness.

She could have sworn it was pulling memories of video games, only the images were never quite accurate, and always different to what she'd played.

Maybe if she jumped off one of those floating islands, she could fly to the next. Images of massive cities floating in space encased in huge clear domes. Ships on water, through the stars, in bathtubs.

The images continued to assault her brain, inundating her with sensations.

Sounds.

Smells.

Sights.

Suddenly, she was pulled back into the branches of the core she was connecting to. She could trace all of those ley lines right through to the core of the tree itself. She chafed at that word because it wasn't entirely accurate. *Tree* was the only thing that could explain the roots and branches. She'd come up with something eventually.

And all the while, pain tore through her veins, threatening to rip her apart.

Down through the roots and into the vastness beyond, the ley lines or magic veins ran. They gathered in pools of... power, perhaps? Except right now there was nothing but muddy and congealed dregs in the bottom of them. The nodes were withering away, having not been filled for so very long.

Desperation and despair clung to every forgotten and neglected crevice.

Cracks appeared where magic had leaked out, entering the world in a wild form. But she could see the outline of everything that had to happen in order to fill the pools back up. In order to return things to their former glory. All she had to do was let it happen.

No. That wasn't right. What she had to do was let the Library in and allow the flow of power to continue again.

For it to wake the Library up once more.

Suddenly, without a shadow of a doubt, she knew she was the right person. Everything about her could connect seamlessly with these ley lines, with this magic, with the core, and with all these tendrils of magic. She might not understand everything yet, but she did feel the connection.

All she had to do was fix the Library, retrieve all the overdue books, and reopen it to the people who needed it again.

She just had to gather, treat, and spread the magic. That couldn't be too hard, could it?

With that simple thought, the core opened up to her. It was a well of knowledge so profound that it hurt as it entered her mind. The Library system did so many different things. It serviced worlds, and encountered dangers, but most of all, it echoed the utter thirst for knowledge she'd been trying to grasp when choosing her major back on Earth. How did that seem so long ago now?

Information poured into her brain faster than she could process it.

None of her past mattered anymore, because she was here now, and she'd found the Library she'd been searching for. Being a librarian had been the exact right vocation for her. Just, strangely enough, not in the way she'd assumed. It was perfect, oddly on the nose considering where she found herself.

It had always been a part of her.

The core still thrummed beneath her hands, but now there was less franticness to it. She could feel the all-consuming panic of the Library abating. While there was still an underlying sense of urgency, it was duller than it had been.

You have a connection to the Library of Everywhere's Core. Potential Librarian, do you accept this connection?

The words flooded her vision, dancing all around her. The options of Yes and No floated with it.

She directed her thoughts toward the *Yes*.

A bright light flashed all around her. Brighter than anything she'd ever seen, and yet it didn't hurt her eyes. Instead, it felt all-encompassing, gentle, and welcoming.

For now, the Library had found its Librarian and the next steps could begin. It was enough to scale back the panic ever so slightly.

There was so much power all around her, but just out of reach. The information in it was so much clearer, so purposeful. So uniquely fitted to her. And so many tasks she'd have to undertake.

She couldn't just run and jump; there were steps to take first. Things she'd have to do in order to replenish power reserves and gain access to the full interface. She wasn't even quite sure how she knew all of this.

Finally, she noticed that the alarms had dimmed, and she allowed herself to blink. Lynx stood against the tree, leaning there with his arms crossed, watching her. There was a very cat-like grin on his face.

"See. I knew you'd fit."

"Nothing that you told me prepared me for this." She removed only one hand and felt a small pang of loss, even as she gestured vaguely all around them. Her breath caught in her throat, because the sense of belonging was overwhelming.

"Yes, it did. I explained it very well, thank you very much." He lifted his nose haughtily for just a moment. "You are what the Library needs. You synced with the Library, and now we can go about restoring it."

Quinn held up a hand stopping him short. "No. I've linked to the Library now. You owe me a summary. I'm waiting."

"I get it, I get it." Lynx took a breath and began. "To simplify it as much as I dare: the Library you're sitting in is the distributor of all magic. Everywhere. In the universe. All around us."

That took Quinn aback. Even though he'd mentioned the Library multiple times, it still didn't feel like one. "This looks more like the bowels of a tree than a library."

"Well, that's because we're in what you'd probably call a basement. In the control center. And it's not a library, it's *the* Library." Lynx reached out and gently nosed the petrified tree trunk next to them. It glowed briefly at the contact, like it could tell he was there.

Quinn raised an eyebrow in disbelief, and ignored his little barb at the end. "A library that has a control center. What do you even mean by that?"

"Because, like I said, it's the Magical Library. One of a kind. I think that hit on the head you mentioned on the pull through caused the information transfer to malfunction. This would be so much easier if you just automatically knew things." Lynx studied her, a frown on his face.

Quinn had the grace to blush. It was still fuzzy on how she'd hit her head when the world appeared to be dissolving around her, but over time she began to feel a dull throbbing. Odd that it hadn't been immediate.

Lynx shrugged and continued. "For a very brief understanding that doesn't go into intricacies at all: Everyone has a magical affinity. If you read a book within your affinity, and understand the knowledge you absorb, you gain the power within. There are a few other requirements, but that's the gist of it. Once you've gained the knowledge, you have to return the book. The Library has existed this way for countless years. Millenia. Eons."

Lynx paused, a troubled look on his face, though Quinn was really worried about the fact that she could tell that a lynx had a worried look on its face because it was a lynx. It was a cat. She truly must have knocked her head badly.

"Stop looking at me that way," Lynx said somewhat defensively, perhaps even a little flustered. "I can manifest into other things, too, you know."

A whoosh of air brushed past Quinn's ears ruffling her hair in the process, and suddenly, in place of this beautiful, purple cat, was a child. A small child, about the same size, about the same mass, with dark black hair that had rings and rings of... were those runes engraved into it?

Maybe that's what was on the cat's stripes. Then, there was another gush of wind, and it changed again, revealing what appeared to be a type of owl. It was massive, and its wingspan brushed the ceiling and touched the floor, yet it didn't appear to touch the trunk.

Before she could say anything, there was another shimmer in front of her. This one made the air around her vibrate, and a flash of light caused her to close her eyes for a moment. When she opened them again, an adult several inches taller than Quinn, around five feet seven or so, stood directly in front of her.

She scrambled back and stood up, but the purple hue told her who it was, even if her eyes didn't want to believe it. "Are you... are you a hologram?" she asked incredulously. "You look so—so real."

Lynx chuckled, and the tone was a little deeper. He was even taller now, maybe closer to six feet, and his hair was purple-black and shoulder length. But his eyes were these purple orbs with no sclera, and just deep and fathomless, limitless.

Like she imagined the darkest regions of space.

Easy to get lost in if you looked too close.

She shivered.

"I'm not a hologram as such. I'm a... you would call me a manifestation. I'm the Library. The Library is me, but I'm also myself. I evolve frequently because I have to."

Quinn just nodded, unsure of what else to say.

"So, as you've probably gathered," Lynx began, "you are not on your world anymore."

Quinn just looked at him, at the fathomless eyes, at the rune-written hair, and nodded. "Yeah. Yeah, I got that."

At least Lynx had the good grace to laugh. "I hoped you would. Otherwise..." he trailed off, a confused expression crossing his face ever so briefly. "Anyway. The Library is technically located in the system of Gregari. You won't have heard of it. Your world hasn't discovered these universe designations yet."

"Okay." Quinn mulled that over in her mind. It sounded about as far-fetched as she'd expected. Still, she was trying to keep an open mind which was difficult with so much new information trying to overwhelm her senses. "Go on."

"Well, the Library is everywhere. And anywhere. All the time. And none of the time. It's infinite. And much bigger on the inside."

"That's been used before." She snorted at her own joke, but his blank expression told her he didn't get it. Clearing her throat, she continued. "It's a library building. How can it be much bigger on the inside?"

Again, Lynx laughed. "You're inside the Library right now. And it has no actual physical address. It's in a dimensional pocket all of its own. It functions on mana, energy, and magic. And it pulls in the energy and magic from all of the books, and from all of the patrons. All of the excess. It fuels and cycles and purifies that mana and sends it back out into the universe. Through ley lines, through nodes, using its core to replenish the magic of the universe through the knowledge and the books in the Library. That's a bit of a simplification, but it'll do for now."

Quinn wondered what Lynx would consider complex if this was the simplification. If the Library really was as big as Lynx said, then it made no sense that it would only have one Librarian. Something had to have happened. Quinn could only hope that Lynx was actually going to tell her.

Since she'd just taken on the job and all, maybe she should have asked about hazard pay first.

"Okay, then," Lynx said and sighed thoughtfully, his brows scrunched together as if he was trying to figure out the best way to phrase what he was going to say. "The Library has existed since the dawn of time. I've been here almost as long. All of the knowledge has been gathered over time. It didn't exist until it did. And then it was cataloged in the Library. Anybody who needs to use the Library will find a door leading to it. As long as the door can be opened, you can enter it. It can fit in a tree, it can fit in a floor and be a trapdoor. It can fit on the side of a building. The Library and its knowledge, and therefore its power, is there for everyone."

Lynx paused, and a sadness came flowing off him in a strange, aura-like way. She leaned forward expectantly, wanting to know more. It was like listening to a storyteller, sort of.

Lynx smiled, a little sadly still. "I can see why you were picked. You're the right one. Your affinities are so very strong. But that's just it. All of a sudden, where we had so many librarians before, a master librarian of course, and then multiple librarian assistants to the master librarian, you don't understand how big the Library is. It's..."

And then he paused, because nervous laughter had overcome her and she couldn't stop.

"Of course I don't know how big it is." She laughed, clutching her stomach. She couldn't help it. It wasn't just amusing. There were so many nerves right there. A little bit of fear, and trepidation. She was terrified. How could any of this be real? She'd just connected to a damned mythical super computer and a shapeshifting cat was telling her its history.

She pinched herself, sobering up a little, but still didn't wake up in her bed.

"Go on, go on," she said, struggling to remain serious. "I'm sorry, I'll not laugh again."

Lynx inclined his head. "I get it. This must be overwhelming. And I bet even the information package, if it had loaded properly, wouldn't have assuaged all of your fears. This is very big, especially coming from a world that doesn't utilize the Library."

He watched her for another moment and then continued. "The Library has branches. You won't... you won't see them yet. Because they're—for want of a better word, and to go in line with your world—they're offline, and they can't be brought back online until we get the system set up to receive. How could I say this?"

He paused like he was trying to figure out the best way to make her understand. "The Library needs to go back online, and it needs to enable its systems again, to retrieve any lost tomes or codices, grimoires, the knowledge in general, to get all of its power back. So, like I said earlier, we need to restore the Library."

"And just how are we supposed to restore the Library? How do I get—" But that was as far as she got.

Blinding images assaulted her. Of overgrown gardens, rotting food, and torn books being devoured by creatures she couldn't identify. Pain ripped through her like she'd never experienced and she clenched her eyes shut. As if someone was flaying her skin from her body and it wasn't until her other hand left the trunk of the core as she fell to the ground, that the assault on her mind ceased.

5

CONNECTION

THE OVERWHELMING SENSE OF DISORIENTATION FINALLY ABATED. QUINN was relieved to find that she hadn't actually passed out, though the pain was so intense she thought she might have. Slowly, she cracked one eye open. When nothing happened, when no vertigo hit her, when nothing assaulted her senses again, she carefully opened the second.

A simple tree stood in front of her. She was on all fours to stop herself from falling all the way down. Lynx squatted next to her, a look of panic on his face.

"Are you all right?"

Librarian Connection Established

Status: Tentative

Future Synchronization Required

Quinn shook her head to clear the words, a mistake as the headache began pounding as soon as she moved. She sighed and angled herself to fall on her butt as gently as possible by twisting to the side. And then she willed the words away, and they finally disappeared. "No, I'm not, but I will be."

"Well, that's a relief. I haven't ever linked with someone from Earth before, and I was kind of worried," Lynx said, running a hand through his hair. It flickered slightly in the corner of her vision, raising more questions in her mind.

Quinn counted to five in her head before she realized she was suddenly too angry and looked at him anyway. "You're telling me you didn't know if this would work?"

Lynx shrugged. "I was *pretty* sure it would work because you had the right signature, but your physiology isn't something I'm an expert in yet. There are differences. So there could have been something... "

"Seriously? There could have been *something*. Are you shitting me?" But she held up her hand when he went to speak and took a deep breath. "It's done now. Don't ever pull that crap again, okay? I've been through enough. But it's fine, this is... " Quinn paused as words flashed across her vision.

No, it wasn't quite words, more like script. Slanted, cursive, not quite decipherable. She blinked, trying to focus on each individual cluster of lettering, but she couldn't quite grasp it yet. The headache wasn't helping either.

The pounding behind her eyes only intensified, and she massaged her temples.

"You know," Lynx started and almost stopped when he noticed her pointed glare. "You have to accept the information and that headache will go away. Right now you're stopping the floodgates of knowledge."

"Wait, I can see the Library information just like that? No touch-screen needed?" But she already knew that answer because of the script telling her she was a tentative Librarian or whatever had flashed in front of her eyes. Touching the core had done more than she imagined. "Did I just power the Library back up simply by touching that trunk?"

Lynx chuckled. "That's not quite how it worked, although I do understand the theory of electricity that runs on your world."

Quinn leveled a stare at him. "I'm so glad you find my homeworld amusing, but I did ask a question. Did what I just did power the Library up?"

Lynx at least had the grace to look a little bit ashamed. "Well, you've asked more than just one question. But yes, it did. You linked.

There is no touchscreen needed; all that's required is that you stop fighting the connection."

"Connection?" Quinn paused and closed her eyes briefly, still massaging her temples. Let the information in, eh? Counting to ten, she began to relax, pushing all of the fear and confusion as far away as she could.

First of all, she began with reasoning. She was, indeed, in a huge-ass room that was now lit. Simply touching the console or whatever that trunk had been did that much. She could accept that. The evidence was right in front of her.

Like an on switch.

So the next step was to relax as much as she could and let the Library know she was ready to accept it.

Emergency Power Mode still in activation.

Rudimentary Library transfer activating.

Emergent Librarian receiving in

3

2

1

She forcibly lowered her shoulders and just let the information flood in. The sheer onslaught surprised her and left her gasping for air.

"That's it. This initial flow won't happen again. You'll be fine." Lynx's voice was soothing, and he gently patted her back with just the right amount of reassurance. Surprisingly solid for what she'd assumed was a hologram. As she began to breathe deeper, he continued.

"It's now able to gather ambient mana from you and use your energy reserves. I mean, *I'm* now able to gather ambient mana from you."

Maybe he thought that was reassuring, but it really wasn't. Quinn paused, pushed herself up straight and opened her eyes, regarding him questioningly. "From me? I have mana?"

"Well, yes, you have a magical signature. Of course you have mana." He said it like it was the most obvious thing in the world.

"Oh." Quinn thought that over for a second. "Like in a video game?"

"Well, we don't use video games because we have magic. But I guess, from references... " His glowing eyes flickered momentarily, "Yes, from reference, technically like a role-playing game."

"Oh." Quinn was a little taken aback, but she'd already accepted the fact that she had come to a completely different world, and now she had connected to a tree-core-computer-library-console thing.

So sure, why wouldn't she have magic?

There were probably dragons around here somewhere too.

"Well, just give me a few." This time she tried to focus on, well, it wasn't a screen, it was more just like information in a sort of heads-up display that slowly appeared in her vision. One of her foster parents had had this fancy BMW with a heads-up display that fascinated her. Sadly, she'd never been allowed to drive it, but she had seen it once, and that's kind of what all this information was like.

Anything she looked at, a feed of information flashed across her vision. She looked at the core, and it simply said:

Library System Core - console accessible

She wondered if she asked it to give her more details, like what it was made out of, but even as she had the thought, it popped up in front of her.

Petrified World Tree Core

"Wow, okay." She was right. It was petrified wood, and that explained absolutely nothing.

On a whim, she glanced at Lynx and willed the system to bring up information on what he was. After a split second, it listed him as

Links: Category F Manifestation - Library Core Manifestation - Duration Infinite.

Oh, it was spelled differently. She frowned. Still, he reminded her of a cat. She was sticking with Lynx.

"You know," Lynx drawled, "you could have just asked me. I would have told you. I'm an open book. Quite literally."

It was like he was waiting for her to laugh, and she couldn't help but give him a small grin. "That was a really bad dad joke."

He pouted ever so slightly. "Will you explain to me what a dad joke is?"

Quinn laughed. "Well, it's more like stating the bleeding obvious. Jokes that aren't necessarily funny but kind of make you laugh anyway."

Lynx nodded thoughtfully.

Quinn changed the subject. "You can read my thoughts?"

"Not yet. But I can see what I display for you when you pose a query." He grinned at her.

"Ah." She mulled that over.

Lynx flashed her a smile and said, "Well, do you need me to explain anything? Right now it's easier for me to do so, to preserve what power we can."

"Isn't this you who's explaining things to me with words in front of my eyes?" Quinn asked, extremely confused now. If he was a manifestation of the Library and was an infinite manifestation of the Library, then couldn't he already see what she was already seeing and knowing?

Wow, did that make him like a library god? She was getting very, very confused.

"I can see the Library's end of things. I can't see yours. You're not—you're not a part of the Library; you're an addition to the Library. And like an annex, I can't read your mind. We're not fully integrated yet. Just because I can see what your thoughts are bringing up doesn't mean I necessarily understand the why. I could explain things better if I did. And I can only process and hear those thoughts if you, well, if you're specifically directing them to be answered by the Library." Lynx paused as if waiting to gauge her response.

"Oh." Quinn couldn't help but feel relieved. "Then all my thoughts are still my own unless I'm specifically directing them toward you."

"Yes, technically. Exactly. It's kind of like directional telepathy at the moment."

"Sure," Quinn said, digesting that as well. "Telepathy. Why not? I've got mana. I've got magic. I'm connected to a magical library. Great. Why not telepathy too?"

Quinn stretched her arms out, trying to relieve the inherent sore-ness in her body, not to mention to give her something else to focus on.

Lynx had been staring at her, his lips pursed. Then he clucked his tongue in triumph. "Do you think you tend to rely on sarcasm as a defensive mechanism?" he asked, and she could tell he was genuinely curious.

"It's definitely a defensive mechanism. Thank you so much for pointing that out."

"And now I've offended you," Lynx said, but it was phrased more like a question. "I apologize. This will take some getting used to. I haven't had company for a few centuries. It's odd having someone else to speak to."

Quinn shrugged, feeling slightly uncomfortable. "Well, that's okay. Everything will be fine. I just have to figure out how to use the system."

"That's easy enough. You just ask it what to do. Ask me to make you a to-do list. I can show you everything." Lynx sounded smug.

"I don't suppose you've got any food, do you?" Quinn really needed some food, because she was starving. If she judged time correctly, it had been at least a day since she'd last eaten breakfast.

Maybe even longer, if her stomach cramps were anything to go by.

A shadow passed over Lynx's face. "Oh, yes, food. We can definitely do some food, I think. I think we have some roots, some vegetables. Is that okay? I mean, you're organic, right?"

Quinn just looked at him. "Yes, I'm organic. Have you had non... no, I'll ask that later. I can eat roots and vegetables as long as they're not, you know, toxic."

"Of course, they're not toxic," Lynx said, waving her away. "We're not going to keep toxic vegetables on the premises—at least not in the kitchen, anyway. At least, I'll make sure they're not toxic to humans. Of course the alchemical annex has toxins, but that's still sealed."

Quinn cocked her head to one side and chose to let the latter comment slide. "You've had non-organic Librarians before?" She was so curious.

"Of course. Library Assistants to be more accurate. There are a lot of different species out there." He sounded quite proud.

"But you're not organic, are you?" She considered him carefully.

"Look, that's neither here nor there. I don't need to breathe. I don't need to sleep. I don't need to do a lot of things, and yet I can do them all. But what I do need to do is get you to help me with the bookworms." He smiled.

"Help you with the bookworms?" Quinn asked, not understanding at all. "Aren't bookworms a good thing? I mean, I think they'd be a good thing."

Lynx just looked at her, shock evident on his face. "Bookworms are very important and have to be carefully handled. As long as they're maintained, they're a necessary thing. I mean, you can't just let them go rampaging through any book dust they want to. The residual magic is going to destroy their insides and make them absolutely useless for the night owls."

"Night owls?" And it was suddenly very, very clear to Quinn that they were having two completely separate conversations.

It appeared that Lynx realized the same thing because he stood there, just looking at her, blinking very slowly. "Damn it. I keep forgetting I need to recalibrate the Information package. Let me get a start on that."

His eyes grew distant for a moment and then he grimaced. "That's going to take longer than I'd like. But anyway. I know what bookworms I'm talking about. What do you think a bookworm is?"

Quinn just sort of shrugged and said, "A person who reads a lot of books."

Lynx actually laughed. It would be closer to a guffaw because it was like a super huge belly laugh that just reverberated throughout the cavern. He wiped his eyes that were dry of tears anyway, even though she was pretty sure he hadn't laughed that hard and looked at her again.

"A bookworm feeds off magical residue. It's a worm, you know, like the ones that grow in the ground. Do you guys call that something different than the wiggly things that, you know, help fertilize the earth around us?" He asked, curiosity winning out.

Quinn shook her head. "No, we call those worms earthworms."

"Okay," said Lynx, "that's something we have in common. So earthworms are very distant cousins of bookworms. Bookworms are much smarter than earthworms. I mean, bookworms have affinities to specific types of magic, just like humans do."

"Wait," Quinn said, "humans have different affinities to magic. How many different affinities to magic are there?"

Suddenly a massive amount of information flowed up in front of her face, and she had to close her eyes. But it didn't matter because the information was still there like it was drawn on the back of her eyelids. She'd have to figure that out later.

This was getting really bizarre.

Lynx poked her shoulder.

"Hey, stop trying to fight the connection. Let's just get the bookworms out of the way. You can figure out the rest of the Library later."

"I still need to eat." She took a deep breath. Focus. She needed to focus. "Okay, so what do you mean by affinities?"

He sighed like he just wanted to go fight worms. "All different magic has different affinities. There's earth, air, fire, water, spirit, electricity, and, I mean, you name it, there's an affinity for it. There's mind magic, there's physical magic, telekinesis, telepathy, like everything. Anyway, all the books will give off different, I guess, vibes." He paused, deadpan stared at her, and wiggled his fingers like an entertainment magician before continuing. "And different frequencies of the different magics that are used. Got me?"

Quinn nodded, fighting the urge to laugh at his finger wiggle while trying to process it all. It was a lot of information. "Yeah, okay, I've got it so far, I think."

"Good, we'll work with that," Lynx said and continued. "So basically, bookworms have their own affinities and so they'll gravitate to cleaning up any excess magic residue, or dust, which is currently a problem in itself because the Library needs all the magic it can get. But while there was no one to take care of the worms and the books, and as I had to manage everything, they got a little out of hand."

"What do you mean they got out of hand?" Quinn said.

"Maybe it's just better if I show you."

"You show me? Are they, like, have they gotten big? Are they like a dog now?" She tried to coax the answer out of him, not entirely certain why he didn't just tell her everything at once.

Lynx just looked at her, cracked his neck a bit, and sounded slightly uneasy when he finally spoke. "Well, the smaller ones are. See, it's been a few hundred years since I could take care of them properly. Without the golems to help me, it doesn't matter how well I can technically multitask."

"Golems?" Quinn said, trying to stop her mind from reeling.

"Oh, sorry." Lynx batted that away like it didn't matter. "I'll get to that. We need to go take care of the bookworms and you're not going to like how we're gonna have to do that."

"And just how are we gonna have to take care of bookworms?"

"Well, we're gonna have to kill the really big ones. And when I say we, I mean you, because I'm technically incorporeal and I can't really help at all."

Quinn stopped because she was sure she'd heard him crack his neck earlier, plus his hand against hers had felt smokey but real. "You said 'technically incorporeal.' What do you mean by 'technically'? Does that mean you can sometimes be corporeal?"

Lynx sighed. "Yes, but it takes a lot of effort. And when I say effort, I mean power, which the Library doesn't have to spare right now. So pulling on any extra power will drain the Library more and thus quicken its demise. Which, until we get everything sorted, is not an option. Now, follow me."

Quinn followed him through the dark cavern, past all the beautiful, dimly mint-green glowing branches and veins that suffused the entirety of the room she'd been in for the last... well ever since she'd arrived.

She had no idea how long that had been. They went up a spiral staircase that didn't seem to want to end. It was probably two stories?

Maybe three stories? She had never been very good at judging that sort of thing. And there were no landings to give her definitive stopping points.

And then they finally made it up to the top.

Quinn gasped.

The Library spread out in front of her. She lost all ability to articulate anything at all. It was huge. It was massive.

And it was totally wrecked.

6

WRECKED

QUINN STOOD AT THE FRONT OF THE ORNATE, MASSIVE LIBRARY, staring at the wreckage before her. She breathed out her exclamation, "What the *hell* happened here?"

Lynx glanced at her, a dusting of irritation in his expression. "You haven't been listening to a word I've said, have you? I told you. Over hundreds of years, the Library lost everything. It lost all its Librarians; many of its books are missing. It has had nothing but the dregs of power for centuries. This isn't just the work of bookworms, this is the work of neglect, the work of whoever decided that the Library should wither away without Librarians."

But it really didn't matter what he was saying, because Quinn was distracted by the sheer magnitude of the interior of the Library. It didn't register. There was dim lighting overhead, probably a lot brighter than it had been before she'd touched the core. It added a modicum of light and allowed her to take in most of the room, or the building...

Frankly, she wouldn't be surprised if she found a lost city in these walls.

The sides ran deep, and she couldn't see past a few feet into the shadows. There was no real sense of danger in here, but there was something sort of ominous, underlying whiffs, scents of things she couldn't quite place, which was odd, because her sense of smell had always been heightened.

She'd always had somewhat of a super sniffer.

In front of her stood a massive wooden desk. But that wasn't quite an accurate description. It appeared to be a desk, but there was a lot more to it. The thing stood almost five feet tall, because she could look over it, but it pretty much came up to her eyes.

At one stage, this monstrosity had been beautiful. Carvings of trees blossoming into books, with words strung across like leaves blowing in the wind. It gave her an odd sense of motion, not quite like vertigo, but instead, it had a smidgen of safety.

It smelled like the blues of freedom on the surface of a lake, with reeds blowing in the wind.

That's where it became apparent that the desk was part of a platform that oversaw the Library.

She tried to analyze it, and the good old Library came to the rescue.

Check-in Counter.

Level: Administrator Access Only

Status: Damaged 20% Operational

For some reason, the summary made her feel a little sad. She turned her attention away from the desk.

Beyond it, there was nothing but gloom. Nothing but dully lit areas, with massive bookcases rising up to the ceiling, and books scattered absolutely everywhere. An eeriness hung around beyond the safety of the entrance. Yet it beckoned to her, like it wanted her to solve its problems.

The desk itself, though beautiful, was damaged. There was something about it that had faded, and it wasn't just the weathering of time. She moved slowly around the desk and found a couple of steps that led up onto the platform within it. She stepped tentatively inside, unsure of why, but once she was in there, it felt like she'd come home.

Even though dust tickled her nose, there was no scent of decay.

That in itself was surprising. Decay crept into everything, from wood and food, to just being alive. But this place felt right.

Ancient in a way that transcended her current understanding.

The desk was safety. The rest of the Library... that was currently debatable.

She turned to look over the back of the desk and peered deeper into the Library. Some of the gloom seemed to have abated. Before her stretched a long path, edged by massive wooden columns, and she realized that the bookshelves that went up to the ceiling only went up to the ceiling of the first floor, or ground floor, because above it, all around the sides, was another floor, with more bookshelves, going even higher, and pillars that rose all the way up.

It was difficult to see much above seven or so feet though.

There were carvings low down on the pillars, and they reached up into the gloom. Even though she was fairly sure she could see the second level connecting them. The light just didn't reach far enough for her to identify anything with accuracy.

The level she was on, was like a veritable treasure trove of, well, dilapidated furniture, books that had been upturned and scattered. Some books were creased down the spines in such a way that she was fairly sure they were broken. She'd always tried not to leave a mark on spines when she read a new book.

She shuddered seeing the spines cracked beyond repair. It was wrong.

Otherwise, the Library was devoid of any life other than her and Lynx. Apart from an odd sound she could hear through to the back, something distant and unappealing. Lynx stood silently next to her, his hair deep, deep purple, with those strange black runic accents, and he watched her. He watched her with an expression of curiosity and contentment on his face.

"Are you done gaping? We don't have all day," he said, but there was no admonishment in his tone. In fact, he seemed more amused than put out.

Quinn nodded. "It's a lot more run down than I thought it would be. I guess I didn't really understand when you said it was ruined."

"Well, it's not an actual ruin yet. How about we see if we can save it?" His eyes sparkled in a way she didn't think a projection should be able to do.

Still, though.

Magic, right?

Quinn didn't have to consider any other options. Even the meager possibility of bringing this Library back to its former glory? It made her skin tingle with excitement. "I think restoring the Library is a really good idea."

"Well, it's a good thing you do, because you're kind of obligated to now that you're linked to it." He grinned somewhat impishly. "Otherwise, I'm just going to annoy you until you do."

"Oh great, like the big brother I never wanted." Quinn rolled her eyes.

"You really have a penchant for sarcasm."

"Yeah, learned it from my mother." Saying that made Quinn feel a little melancholy. But she wanted to clear one thing up. "Just so we're on the same page. I've helped you out, and I'm linked, but I'm choosing to stay and help. Don't make me change my mind."

Lynx watched her for a few seconds, his brow creasing in thought. "Understood. I'll have to hope you don't change your mind."

Quinn nodded as the gravity of the exchange hit her. She'd left Earth behind? Seriously? Was she actually okay with that? Not that she'd had super close friends, or any family to speak of. If she was going to get a fresh start with a career, it may as well be somewhere where nobody knew her at all. She clapped her hands together and grabbed onto all the determination she could muster.

She'd deal with all that other stuff, later, when she had to. "Okay, so what do I do? Where do I step on these bookworms?"

Lynx laughed. "Yeah, so stepping on them is not going to happen, because I think you forgot the fact that I told you they were bigger than small dogs."

She turned and blinked at him, running all their conversations back through her mind. "Oh, that's right. So where are they?"

Lynx gestured toward the darkness-obscured end of the Library. The part where the weird sounds were coming from?

Quinn gulped. "Oh, is that them?"

"Yep, that's them."

She listened to the sound of... munching? Or sucking. "Are they, like, devouring the books?"

Lynx shrugged his shoulders in a way that told her it wasn't quite accurate, but that she was pretty close, and he couldn't think of a better way to tell her.

She paused for a second realizing he hadn't told her what he was thinking, but that the connection with the Library somehow relayed the spirit of the information. "Okay, so tell me about bookworms, then."

Whether the Library misunderstood her deliberately, or she had just directed her thoughts well enough, information popped up in front of her face with images of bookworms. They were really, really cute. Maybe three or four inches long? A little fatter, more like a caterpillar than the earthworms from back home, but not quite. And they had rings of color around each end. They were this sort of steely grey and not brown at all. "Oh, wow, they're actually quite cute."

Lynx snickered. "Yeah, when they're not trying to rip your face off or devour your magical books or steal the remaining energy from the Library."

"You sound a little bitter," Quinn said.

"Well, they're supposed to help. Because of them, I haven't been able to feed the night owls properly. There have been no magical quills for..." He paused. "Okay, you don't need to know that until we can actually do something about it. We're in a huge time crunch right now. So I just need you to trust me to tell you things when you need to know them. Okay?"

Quinn narrowed her gaze at him, not overly happy with being kept even somewhat in the dark. "You'd better tell me *before* I need to know things."

He nodded emphatically. "I will, it's just a lot, and I have to prepare a different variation of the guide for you to absorb too. Our time right now is limited, though not as drastically as it was when you first got here. It won't be once we get everything done. First things first, bookworms need to be dealt with."

Quinn realized how much effort this was going to involve. There was so much information, so many encompassing changes that would affect her and how she lived her life.

What even was her life going to be? She paused, took a deep breath and glanced at the information that was still sitting somewhat distantly in her vision. She whirled it forward and gave the summary a quick read-through.

Bookworms

Required ingredients in Magical Quill creation. Also excellent at soil fertilization for magical herbs.

Danger: When left unattended, Bookworms can become engorged. Salt is the best weapon against an engorged bookworm. It should sap moisture from the creature, leaving it relatively helpless and able to be picked up.

"Okay, well then do you have salt?" She turned to ask her guide.

Lynx looked at her and a slow smile spread over his face. "Salt is probably the one thing I have a lot of. It doesn't really go off or bad or away. But keep in mind, the information you have is relevant for mildly engorged bookworms. You won't be able to pick up the ones we need to get rid of."

She shrugged, trying not to retort with something like "who's a salty little Library, then?" because that would do neither of them any good. "Slugs dry out with salt, stands to reason a worm will too. We could make a salt gun, even."

"A salt gun? You're funny and you didn't even know it."

"You know I didn't mean it like that," Quinn said. Salt barely even sounded like assault, but she had to admit it was a wee bit funny.

"Anyway, let's go get some salt, kill some worms, and then we'll be scot-free to go and eat and clean up the Library."

"Well, aren't you just a positive ray of sunshine?" Suddenly, Lynx transformed back into his cat form, and he stretched out one paw after another, shaking it off like he needed to stretch. Except he was a little bigger than he had been the first time she saw him, coming clear up to her hip now.

"You know, a talking cat is super weird." She peered down at him.

"Well, I may be a talking cat, but I can also be a talking human, or if you really need me to be, I can be a talking alligator." He managed, somehow, to waggle his massive lynx eyebrows. "This form, however, may allow me to use my claws if the bookworms decide to get more violent than I'm anticipating."

Quinn was taken aback. "Do you really think that's possible? Do you think they'll lash out at us?"

Lynx shrugged, which looked liquid smooth on a cat. "I mean, wouldn't you want to stop something that was draining all your life-force away? If they attack us, I'm going to rake them with my claws."

"Sounds like a plan," Quinn said, even if she was not sure about that at all. Her stomach grumbled, and for a second she regretted thinking of fighting worms first. Hunger pangs were no joke.

Lynx picked his way delicately through the refuse on the floor, which was mostly books and pieces of furniture. Quinn followed, picking her way through just as cautiously. There were more book-cases than she'd realized, lots of desks, chairs, and tables. Everything was haphazard, some of it was broken, and all of it was extremely untidy.

Loose pages fluttered around the main hall. It had a dilapidated, dejected feeling to it, and there was a smell of staleness about it, a sort of sadness underlying everything. Even if she closed her eyes briefly, she could sense a stagnant smidgen of hope. Maybe that was related to her arrival, coming here, connecting, and having all this information flung into her brain that she still needed to process.

"Where are we?" she started to ask, but it was quite obvious where they had gone once Lynx stopped. They were in a kitchen of sorts, more of a break room. There was what looked like a magically powered cooler, like a refrigerator perhaps, but it was off. And then there were gardens, like terrariums, most of them overgrown.

She really hoped that wasn't where the food Lynx had spoken of earlier was going to come from, but she had a nauseating feeling that it was. Even if the vegetation was slightly rank on the nose, there was hopefully something good in there if he thought she could eat it.

Lynx rummaged around in the cabinets after transforming back into his human shape and pulled out a large box of salt. "There we go. How about we see if your idea holds any water?"

"That's not going to hold water with salt, is it?" And she had to stop herself from laughing at her own joke. Lynx just raised an eyebrow and walked out with her.

"Not turning back into a cat?' she asked cheekily.

"No, don't have opposable thumbs in that form. Need them to hold the box," he answered her matter-of-factly.

She laughed. "I thought you weren't corporeal. Isn't holding that box taking up energy?'

He paused. "Yes and no. It's just a box. I'm not trying to force anything. I just created a solid platform in the shape of my hand. That's it."

"Oh" was all she could say, because she really didn't understand at all. She didn't like that he was withholding information from her, but she understood. He needed her to be functional. Too many questions and too much information at once might overload her. As she understood it, they needed something drastic to restore power to the Library.

Then they'd have all the time in the world for her to melt down every now and again at the sheer magical nature of the place.

They picked their way through to the dimly lit back of the Library, where the rejuvenated light had yet to reach. It was dark and dank; it smelled musty and earthy and sort of melancholy.

There were two short steps up onto a new floor with more books. It had railings on either side of the large entrance stairs with more ornate carvings.

But she did not expect to be greeted by one very silent, massive worm standing—or worming or whatever they did—directly in front of her.

This thing came up to her waist. It was round, and it squelched as it slowly moved its attention to her. It was maybe six to seven feet long, tubular in shape, and its strange matte grey coloring was over-laid with what might have been iridescent rainbow-colored rings around the mouth. Except there were splotches of other colors that dimmed the original outer ring. Like something had infected the true shade of the beast.

If the creature didn't appear to be so bloated, there would have been ridges all along the body. The face wasn't a face like she was used to but had only a mouth and no discernible eyes. Its ring of color was oddly stretched and contorted. It had a paper scrap hanging out of its mouth, and dust particles clinging to its once-shiny body. Energy pulsed softly around it.

Quinn couldn't say quite how she knew that, but she did. The flash of knowledge jolted through her brain and appeared directly in front of her as if she'd punched it into an internet search bar.

"This is an engorged bookworm?"

Engorged Bookworm

Status: Alert

Health: 100%

"Yes. Yes, that's precisely what these are." Lynx's mouth opened in an unnaturally wide grin and he tossed what appeared to be a broom in her direction. "That's your weapon for now."

"You're kid—" But that's as far as Quinn got. Because the worm she'd thought was looking at her sniffed the air.

As if it had finally fully sensed her presence, it turned slightly and focused on her, and opened its gorging mouth. Teeth rimmed all around the circular opening. Sharp and jagged rows of them. The creature raised itself up several feet on the hind section of its body and roared out a squelching, guttural challenge.

7

BOOKWORMS

THE CREATURE IN FRONT OF HER WAS JUDGING HER. QUINN COULD FEEL it in her bones, not to mention her white-knuckled gripping fists as she tried to stave off her own fear.

The bookworm chewed—sort of, anyway. Its mouth opened and closed, but she was sure she could hear those teeth grating against each other as its mouth moved.

And it contemplated her. Moreover, it felt like the creature was focused on the damned broom in her hands. All of a sudden, she had this distinct urge to shoo it away and shake the bottom of the broom at it, but there was a part of her absolutely certain that wouldn't be effective.

Just as she was sure the monster had dismissed her, just as her muscles relaxed from the tense grip she had on her broomstick... the massive creature launched itself at her.

Despite how cumbersome the worm appeared to be, it was surprisingly agile. Like a thick vine twisting in midair, it changed direction with unnatural ease, coiling toward her with a rapidity that took her by surprise.

How did a worm even jump like that? It wasn't like it had legs!

She swung out widely with the broom. Truly more of a flail, if she was being honest with herself. But newly minted broomstick battling book lovers couldn't be choosers. "Throw the damn salt!" she yelled out as she thrashed with her makeshift weapon.

Somehow, she managed to catch the creature off guard so that it threw its body weight off-kilter where it hit the ground awkwardly. Judging from the jolt to the floor, the thing weighed a ton.

It slouched over, though Quinn couldn't quite tell how she knew that it was slouching. She tiptoed toward it, not quite believing that she'd gotten lucky enough to do it true harm with that one hit.

Which basically meant it was faking it.

Since she wasn't sure how intelligent worms were or how they breathed, especially not larger-than-human-sized worms, Quinn decided that her best course of action was caution.

Well, that or running away, but since she had no idea how to get out of the Library, and the place seemed her best bet to get to anywhere anytime soon... she chose the former.

Caution, however, was only useful when the other elements cooperated. Which, she found out in quite short order, the bookworm had no intention of doing. In the meantime, Lynx was making it rain salt. She could only hope he wasn't using all of it on one worm.

Just as she was about to prod it with the broomstick once more, the bookworm opened its massive maw again, but this time a high-pitched squeal emanated from it. The sound pierced her ears so badly it felt like someone had put her head in a pot and hit it with a metal ladle. It made her wonder if she'd perhaps perforated an eardrum.

A split second later, despite the pain in her head from the noise it was making, she realized that she had to shut the creature up. Because it didn't sound like it was in pain. It was calling for aid.

With speed born of sheer desperation, she hefted the broom up in the air and brought the rectangular wooden head crashing down right on top of what might have been the head of the worm.

If she didn't have the ends mixed up.

Quinn wasn't sure what she was expecting. Unlike some of the kids she grew up around, she'd never tried to explode a worm before in her life. She had no idea how the flesh of a worm reacted when it encountered a more solid object attempting to bash in its flesh.

Taking into consideration the fact that the worm in question was, indeed, several hundred times the size of your average earthworm, the result was unexpected.

Its skin was oddly elastic.

The most noticeable thing was that the shrill shrieking sound cut off. There was a second's pause, as if the entire universe stood still.

Followed by the forceful squelch of the heavy wooden floor brush biting into the soft flesh of the worm and effectively exploding through it and then outward. The strike carried through in such a way that it tore the soft flesh open and allowed the not-insignificant insides to splash out with the brutish force of the strike.

Bookworm guts splurted everywhere.

Massive globules of marginally shriveled-up gelatinous body exploded all over the entire area.

It got into Quinn's hair, all over Lynx, and splashed over some of one of the Library pillars, where it dripped down to settle on the floor as the worm fell to the ground convulsing from the shock.

Quinn blinked, highly concerned with the very messy turn of events. "What..."

But she didn't get further.

Lynx shifted slightly, causing himself to appear briefly transparent, which got rid of the goop on him. Then he solidified again, this time in a far more corporeal manner and grabbed the broom. Pushing down with brute force, he severed the worm in the middle, before shrinking back to his usual density.

Engorged Bookworm defeated

Magical Density dissipating proportionately

Experience Gain: Allocated into Energy and Mana capabilities

Quinn had no idea what the Library was on about there, and shook her head, leveling a stare at Lynx. "I thought you couldn't kill these yourself." Quinn's voice came out flatter than she'd expected, which was probably good since she recognized that his seemed highly suspicious.

Lynx sighed. "I shouldn't right now because it takes too much energy. Energy the Library is in desperate need of right now. But if we didn't kill that thing straight away, it was going to regrow its head and one more summoning call and we'd have been goners. Didn't you hear that noise?"

"The screaming sound that tried to implode my eardrums? That super pleasant sound is a noise?" Quinn didn't think she was entirely successful at keeping the sarcasm out of her voice, but in her defense, she wasn't trying to.

Lynx ignored her blatant irritation. "Then next time act like it. Everyone knows you have to kill worms completely. You can't just let them go all hydra on you."

About to correct him that not everyone knew how to kill massive magical bookworms correctly, Quinn blinked and changed her focus. "Hydra?"

"You know, cut off a head, another grows back. Have to cut..." Lynx rolled his eyes. "Never mind. Anyway, looks like the first thing we need to find you are some books on basic combat, the first of which should be on how to hold a weapon in the first place."

She grabbed her broom back and glared at the man. "Look. You called me here. That's on you. It wasn't like I was barely surviving on the streets. I was in a perfectly good home, where I didn't have to know that cutting a rabid bookworm in half was going to make it grow more or again or whatever..."

"It's not rabid," Lynx corrected her. "It's engorged."

"Engorged, then!" Quinn really had to respect that smooth change of subject. It truly was well done. "It's a library. Just what is a worm going to eat?"

"It's a bookworm. I'd think that was self-evident."

"Explain it to me like I'm five. I have time. I don't need magic to run." It was a bit of a gamble for Quinn to say that, but it was at least partially true. All she needed was food. A fact which her stomach was none too gently reminding her of right then. "I would say this falls under the need-to-know category, since there are more of them."

Lynx actually rolled his lizard-like eyes *and* *tsk*ed beneath his breath. She could practically see his need to get stuff done five seconds ago and his logic warring with one another. "Fine, but we don't have all day, you know."

He patted the small step that had led up to the worm, and waited until she sat down before he said anything. "Bookworms are an important part of any magical library ecosystem," he began.

"Wait." Quinn interrupted him. "There are more magical libraries?" She looked around incredulously.

"Yes, and no." Lynx paused for a moment. "Technically—sort of. But I'm answering your initial question and not a drop more. The other portions of the Library are something to worry about when we have enough power to keep the main part afloat. I'll start an exchange at this rate. You do a thing I need you to do, and I'll explain one thing to you."

Quinn mulled that over for a moment before squinting at Lynx. There was obviously a catch to the whole thing, but she wanted the information, so this was probably her only real shot at that. "Fine. Deal."

Yep, Lynx looked smug. Quinn would figure out why later.

"Bookworms, when they're functioning optimally, absorb the overflow of specific magical essence that spills from a tome, book... whatever you want to call them. It's not the same as magic or mana, but more like a sense of the type of magic specifically. Sort of like flavoring." The lynx paused, allowing Quinn to take in the information.

Although most of it went completely above her head, she sort of got the flavoring of magic. She nodded for him to continue. She was following enough of it to record it and piece it all together later. That's how she got through half her history assignments in high school.

"The bookworm is necessary to prevent a book's magic from stagnating or overflowing. Both of which can spark minor explosions

54

when utilized by a less-than-experienced magic user. They're also sort of a vacuum for any dust that gathers in that specific type of magic signature. If you mixed all the dust of different magical signatures in an actual vacuum, that would be bad."

Lynx paused for a second, as if getting his train of thought back on track. Then Lynx sighed. "As you can probably imagine, with the Library not functioning at optimal capacity, the bookworms have sort of gone rogue. They've consumed far more than they should ever have been allowed to. Mostly because they've had to. Without the pruning the Librarians have always undertaken, they've just... well... gorged themselves."

"Oh. The poor things." Because it actually made some sort of sense to Quinn. She suddenly got it and just as quickly felt extremely sad for the poor creatures. They were mostly just doing what they were made to do, but it got out of control. "Can't we just like—wave a magic wand or something and get them back to normal?"

Lynx snorted. "The engorged ones? No way. They're too far gone. Also, magic wands are a social construct in specific worlds, but we'll get to that at a later date. There's no way to shrink them back to something smaller from their current size. When they're still relatively small, we might be able to save them. But like this? No, sadly, these ones have to be exterminated. They've stretched their own magic properties far too thin. They're a danger to every single being and book that encounters them. Not to mention to themselves, too."

"Oh," Quinn said again. There was something about the whole thing that made her inordinately sad for the creatures. They'd just been doing their job but because no one was there to help take care of them, they had to die now. Maybe there was something to being this Librarian or whatever it was.

"Okay then." She mulled the whole situation over in her head. "What's the best way for me to help get this under control?"

For a moment, Lynx just looked at her, like he was figuring out how to phrase all the subsequent information. It made a cold ball form in the middle of Quinn's stomach.

"There's eighty-seven of these guys," He cocked his head to one side like he was reading an invisible screen of some sort. "Actually, eighty-six now that are in the danger zone. It could increase before we get you prepared to fight them."

"Prepared?" She wasn't sure she liked the sound of that, even if smashing them with a broom hadn't been the best solution. "How do you mean *prepared*?"

Lynx reverted back to his feline form, leaving the salt box on the floor. He glanced at the broom with what could only be described as a smirk. "We need to get you an actual weapon, and have you learn some basic combat skills."

"Combat? I thought I was supposed to take care of books." Fighting and reading were so vastly different, it made Quinn nervous.

"Can't do that if they're all destroyed, can you?" Now it looked like Lynx was raising his eyebrow at her.

She grumbled out her response. "I'm not really the fighting type. I thought this was all about magic?"

"Follow me." He totally ignored her question and led her away from the entrance to the bookworm lair, and through to another portion of the Library she hadn't realized existed.

Nothing was well-lit. Bookcases loomed up all around the sides of every area they passed like ghosts of better times past. All she could tell was that so many of them were far too empty of books. Something she hadn't expected in a library. And it made her want to know why it was like this.

Who abandoned this place and why on not-Earth would they have left it to waste away like this? How did it happen? All things she needed to hear from Lynx once they got through this first set of stuff.

"Here we are." Lynx sounded a little relieved. Like this was something he'd hoped would be there was actually still there because he hadn't checked it in a while. It appeared to be less of a Library section and more for the things involved in living. But it was dusty and dirty.

"Where is here apart from this super old and sadly deserted Library?" Quinn realized she sounded a little defeated. Which wasn't what she'd aimed for. It also wasn't her personality. She frowned. "Why do I feel down?"

Lynx cast her a sad smile. "Ah, I was hoping it would take longer than this."

"What would?"

"It's the distance from the core. Or, I should say, it's the distance from the core while the Library is in a state of Gloom."

"Gloom." Quinn stood her ground and crossed her arms. It sounded like something out of one of her fantasies... oh. Well. Perhaps she shouldn't be so mocking considering where she was standing right now. "What is Gloom?"

"The mood? The lighting? Gloomy. It's a state of feeling down in the doldrums. Of hopelessness creeping in. With the Library in such low power mode for so long, it can't stave off the darkness like it usually would. There are some downsides to being our own little pocket-dimension, after all." Lynx's tail split all of a sudden into several different tails all indicating different directions as if to make a point, before it amalgamated back into a singular one. "Anyway. It seeps into you and supplants hope in a gradual manner. Being aware of it should help."

"Thanks for the heads up."

Lynx sighed and motioned for her to stop for a moment. "I should apologize. I'm doing this all out of order. Generally, when I have a new Librarian to train, I have others still working here. I'm not the one to train you. I'm just an addendum. Usually, the Library isn't in such a sorry state when you arrive, and you're already keyed into your magic and how the magical world works. This..." He gestured vaguely around the entire library. "It's but a shadow of what it should be."

"It's okay." Quinn nudged one foot against the other as she looked down at the ground. She felt oddly touched by his admission. "I'm a pretty quick learner. So, what say you feed me whatever you have, and we'll get to work resetting the bookworms so you can use them to feed the night owls?"

Her guide laughed. "Yeah. That sounds like a solid plan. I apologize for getting ahead of ourselves." He flickered for a moment and returned to the human form, bowing in front of her. "I welcome thee,

Quinn, to the Universal Library of Gregori. May you help me reset the system."

Quinn smiled. " Excellent, but first, we eat." She bowed back with a flourish and followed him as he headed back to where the kitchen area had been.

Finally, Lynx stopped in the little kitchen, right next to a table. He dusted off the surface with his hand before pointing at the seat for her to sit on the bench beneath it. Wordlessly he moved over to one of the more overgrown terrariums and fiddled about with some of the plants. Frankly, she couldn't see him anymore, and the brush and stems wiggled as he did whatever it was he was doing from the opposite side.

She shrugged and sat down at the table.

Or at least, she tried to.

Just when her butt should have hit the seat, the piece of furniture was suddenly not there. Instead, Quinn plopped onto the ground with a rather sudden drop, the shock of which reverberated through her tailbone.

"Ow!" she called out. Her tailbone always hurt sharply whenever she was unceremoniously dumped to the ground because that's how tailbones worked. And this was no exception. Quinn struggled to stand up as the shooting pain distracted her.

What she didn't expect was the high-pitched squeal that met her ears while she was trying to stand up and she turned rapidly trying to find the bookworm that had followed them. It took a moment to register that the sound was slightly different.

"You don't just sit on someone you don't know. How rude! Where did you learn your manners? What do you think this is?"

Looking down, Quinn noticed the bench was... well... it was hopping around with the front portion of it raised enough that those two of the legs were off the ground. While its back legs bent as if they had knees, and waved the other legs around like hands.

She felt like she'd fallen into an animated movie.

Thankfully, there was no mouth. Not one that she could see at any rate.

"What are you looking at? How dare you ogle me. You're just a commoner and I am timeless. You must respect me!"

Quinn blinked and then rubbed her eyes.

Nope, she definitely wasn't seeing things.

The furniture was talking.

And it seemed to be quite irate with her.

8

CORRIDORS

THE BENCH CONTINUED TO HOP UP AND DOWN LIKE IT HAD BEEN greatly inconvenienced while Quinn tried to get her thoughts neatly lined up. Who was she kidding? Nothing about any of this lined up any which way she tried to put it.

Reaching up to the opposite upper arm, she gave herself a hefty pinch. An "ow!" escaped her involuntarily, regardless of how prepared she'd been for it. And pinching herself was only proving to give her lasting bruises now.

She'd already linked herself to this core thing and endured pain for it. Been splattered in worm guts, and talked to a cat. This was definitely a reality. Perhaps not the one she was used to, but it was real. So why couldn't she seem to accept it as such?

She was still gaping at the seat and trying to figure out how to deal with what appeared to be a sentient piece of furniture when Lynx returned.

"Oh, well. That's unsurprising." Lynx surveyed the scene in front of him and snorted back a laugh.

Not taking her eyes off the still angrily trembling bench, Quinn added her own sarcasm for good measure. "I'm so glad you're not surprised. Because everything about this world has, of course, made complete and utter sense to me."

Which was, of course, was the wrong time to look at her guide and see that he wasn't, in fact, a simple human replica at that moment. No, he'd managed to grow an extra set of hands enabling him to hold a glass, a water jug, and two plates. Obviously, he'd never waited tables as a part-time job or he probably wouldn't have needed more than two hands to begin with.

Even so, she gaped at his added appendages.

Lynx actually laughed. It sounded like a cross between him having trouble breathing and a squeaky door hinge. "Dottie. Stop it."

The bench, however, seemed even more insulted. "Now you side with this interloper, Lynx! How could you? You're being so…"

But Dottie didn't get to say anything else, as a pulse of pressure rippled very subtly across the space.

"Fine," the bench blustered in a much more subdued tone. "But I want it on record that I don't approve!"

"You can sit now." Lynx motioned to the suddenly quiet bench as he shuffled over with the bowl held by one of his two extra hands. "Furniture will be one of the first things the Library can reproduce. But for now, we have what we have."

Quinn simply sat down, trying not to just drop her weight onto the poor bench that had been so mortified by her taking a seat. She had to try her hardest not to stare. "Thanks," she said as Lynx put the meal down in front of her.

Glancing into the food bowl, she suppressed a sigh. She guessed drive-thrus weren't a thing here. This food didn't exactly look appetizing, and if truth be told, her appetite had mostly fled along with the bookworm goop that was still in her hair. It was stuck to the loose curls that refused to be tamed by any number of messy buns or ponytails.

But her stomach betrayed her and rumbled anyway. There was nothing for it; she did need to eat. She stirred the lumpy liquid and peered into it. It looked like carrots, and maybe some steamed potato and something that looked like rice, but she wasn't so sure about it.

But then she looked back up to see Lynx standing there, expectantly, like a real boy again—sans extra hands.

She had to ask. "You just had four hands, and you were, like, tangible." Okay, so it was a statement and not a question. She knew what she'd seen. For someone who kept harping on how much power the Library didn't have, he sure was using it.

"Yes, I did. Can't you grow an extra pair when you need it?" Lynx managed to deadpan the question so perfectly, Quinn almost laughed even though she noticed that he didn't add any comment about being solid. She filed it away for later. He seemed extremely deft at not answering questions, so much that she had to wonder if he didn't know how to answer some of them.

Quinn looked down into her food bowl and chuckled. "Well, no. No, I can't grow extra limbs. But I know a lot of people who would like to." With that, she finally raised a spoonful of the food to her mouth. She blew on it, making the steam clouds waft away, closed her eyes, and put it in her mouth.

She was surprised by the saltiness and a little bit of a savory undercurrent that she couldn't quite place. It smelled like home in a way, like one of those dishes that your mom or grandmother would make for you on a rainy day when everything else seemed to be going wrong. At least like they made for her before they died in that horrible car accident, anyway.

"This... this isn't bad," she said, surprising herself. It definitely tasted a lot better than it looked.

Lynx laughed, but there was a hint of pride in the tone. "Great. It's good to know that you thought I might poison you."

Quinn smiled but forwent a quip of her own because frankly, her stomach was cramping from hunger. Now that she'd given it a taste of food, there was nothing for it but to finish the rest of it. She also thought it best not to ask the Library to define what it was. Best to just enjoy it.

She shoveled spoonful after spoonful into her mouth, pleasantly surprised that the savory sensations increased with each bite. They compounded and made it just a dance of flavors on her tongue, sort of like a milder version of roasted vegetables and grains. Just with so much more.

She guessed the grains were like wild rice. It looked like the type of expensive rice that came in tiny packets in some of the stores back home. There was a hearty aroma underneath all of it, this earthy, amazing taste. Warm, comfortable. Yeah, it was just right.

For a moment she felt like Goldilocks, having found the perfect porridge.

All too soon it was gone, and she scraped the spoon around the bowl, making sure she got the good of it all. And then she leaned back.

"Hey now, hey now, don't do that!" the bench beneath her grumbled. It seemed Dottie's mood hadn't improved since her first little outburst. "You can't just go using me like a couch and leaning back like that. You'll overbalance me. Then we'll both fall and I could break!"

Quinn laughed at the visual, which seemed to infuriate Dottie even more, and the bench went on a tirade, practically quivering with rage beneath her. "And now you're laughing at me? Do you take nobody else's feelings into consideration? What an impertinent child!"

"Hey," Quinn said, her mood suddenly soured. She pushed herself to stand, staring down at the insulting bench. "I'm not a child, and you guys called *me* here. You pulled me here away from a potentially decent future and plopped me in the middle of all of this without asking or checking to see if it was something I wanted to do. So stop it with the attitude and be happy I'm not copping one."

There was silence for a moment. Quinn glanced to the side and could see that Lynx actually seemed mildly uncomfortable at her words despite them all being truth. Dottie, on the other hand, was trembling ever so slightly. Quinn could feel it against the back of her legs.

"She doesn't have all the information, does she?" The bench angled the question toward the Library manifestation. Lynx shook his head, and the bench seemed to sigh.

"I see. I apologize. I was out of line." Dottie sounded contrite, and the trembling must have been nerves, not anger this time.

Quinn sighed and reached down to pet the bench before pushing away from the table even though she really could have eaten another five bowls of that stuff. "That's fine, but seriously, sometimes you need to think before you speak. You might not have the full story." Quinn cringed at the fact that there were echoes of her foster parents in there. Maybe she really was growing up.

She'd been transported to another world. There was no safety net anymore. Her small inheritance wasn't hoarded in a bank here waiting for her to turn twenty-one soon. She had no backup. Nothing. Heck, she wasn't even sure of what passed for currency in this world. Was there even currency?

Lynx cut in before she could go too far down that rabbit hole. "At least we got you fed. Hopefully enough to belay the hunger a bit. The grumbling was starting to disturb me. It was so loud I couldn't think straight." His eyes sparkled in a non-human, sort of electrical outlet way, but at least the humor reached her.

"Well," Quinn said, clearing her throat. "Whose fault is that? You pulled me here before I got to eat for the day, and then wrangled me into synchronizing with the core system thing, and even made me fight a damn monster—all before feeding me. Universal hospitality is nothing to rave about." She could swear that she heard squelching off in the distance that sounded suspiciously bookworm-like.

A sudden well of trepidation formed in her gut. "We're gonna have to do something about those worms, aren't we? I mean, like now. I can hear them from here. Should I really have stopped to eat? I mean, aren't they just growing and devouring more and becoming larger and worse and..."

Lynx cut her off. "Hey, they've been doing this for centuries. It's taken a while for them to get this far. Before we go back, you're going at least need to know how to swing a broom."

"A broom. Is that really the best weapon you have for me?" Quinn crossed her arms, still expecting Dottie to pipe up at any moment.

"As I've mentioned, the Library is only minimally functional right now." Lynx looked uncomfortable with that last statement.

"But you keep solidifying anyway." Quinn squinted at him, trying to get a read on what he meant. He blushed at her last comment but in a more embarrassed way. She had to remember that Lynx wasn't actually human, and therefore, it was difficult to get a read on an entity that technically was a library.

She shook her head and held up her hand so he didn't say anything else. "Look, I get what you mean by the Library is only minimally functional right now because we just rebooted it and it doesn't have power."

"Actually," he cut in, "it's not quite rebooted yet."

She shot him a glare and continued like he hadn't spoken. "The grids have to load, or power up, or insert your magical spell here, or whatever you guys call this power structure you have, but it seems to require something other than power." She paused, waiting to make sure she'd been following correctly.

Lynx nodded, and she could almost see the thoughts flying through his brain. How was he going to explain this to her? "The library has many different divisions. There's magic, alchemy, medicinal, combat, and several more. The portion of the Library we currently have has the basics of everything except for magic, which is its only advanced subject. It only has complex magical tomes, or it should have. That's a tangent we'll come back to. Combat, for example, is something we only have the very basic introductory elements of, and some of those are overdue library books and thus not where they belong. So we don't actually have access to that knowledge right now in order to give it to you. Do you understand what I mean?"

Quinn shook her head, noticing that Dottie was trembling again in a weird sort of anticipatory way. "Well, I don't understand what you mean, but it seems that Dottie thinks she can probably explain it better."

"I can! I can!" Dottie said, sounding excited to actually be able to contribute after her weird faux pas from earlier. "Since you're the Librarian, any book you absorb from your magical affinities becomes your knowledge, and as long as you understand what you're reading, it becomes your power."

"Wait, wait." Quinn pinched her brows with her fingers. "Wait, I don't... so knowledge is power, basically. You're telling me if I read a book and believe and understand what's in it, then I can use that as a form of magic?"

"Well, you're simplifying it a little bit," Lynx said. "That's not quite how it works. You have to have the correct affinity, and taking in the information and processing it into a form that requires you to put it into practice even though you're aware of the technicalities does require a modicum of the Library's functional magic, yes."

"So technically I'll use... innate magic to learn this stuff?" Quinn tried to wrap her head around the ramifications of that.

Lynx grimaced. "I mean, you're a part of the Library now, and thus you do have access to magic. But with the state we're currently in? You need more power; the Library needs more power. In order to get your magic and thus generate more power so the Library can get more power, you need to learn from your magic."

"All righty, then," Quinn said, rubbing her temples while trying to absorb all the information. Power was an overarching theme it seemed. "But the basics are absorb a book, learn a book, understand a book, gain magical access to abilities. Correct?"

"Well, only the Librarian can absorb the magic... technically," Lynx muttered. "If you want to make it sound easy."

"Maybe you should let it sound easy," Dottie said haughtily.

Lynx raised an eyebrow at her. "You've certainly changed your tune."

"Well, that's because she treated me with the respect due to me, and because you never gave her the information."

Lynx barked out a laugh. "Yeah, well, the information scrambling isn't something I controlled and we both know you're not due anything. You're being insufferable."

"Well, at least I've kept you company this whole time." If Dottie had a proper mouth, she would have been pouting.

But it seemed Lynx was being particularly stubborn. "You didn't have to, you know. I have other furniture I can talk to."

"Guys," Quinn interrupted. "Look, I think it's great that you're communicating, but we have a lot to do right now. I need to understand how to fight enough so I can go squish those worms there without simply flailing a mop around. We can start getting the Library on track again if I can defeat them, right? Isn't that the whole purpose of me being here?"

Lynx had the grace to look somewhat contrite.

"You're right," he sighed, which was, you know, a feat in itself, considering sighing while talking was like multitasking. But then Quinn guessed he was sort of a computer in a roundabout, magical way.

"Okay, getting back to magic. You said there are basic books here, basic skills, right? And that the Librarian absorbs them?"

"Yes. Only the Librarian absorbs them. Occasionally correctly affinitied assistants too." Lynx nodded.

Quinn popped that information on the backburner. "Won't I have to learn all of the basic skills in order to master any of the magic in this place anyway?" Logic. No matter the circumstance, logic was usually a safe bet.

Lynx's eyes did that weird distance thing again, and he nodded. "That's true. There are only a couple of introductory fighting texts available. We'll start with those. Come on, follow me."

A thrill of excitement ran up Quinn's back. She'd dabbled some in martial arts and never really got the hang of it, but she'd always been fascinated by any sort of book or drama or television show that gave her the opportunity to witness fighting, to imagine fighting. Maybe she'd be good at it.

Well, if the broom was anything to go by, she probably wouldn't be.

But still, it was worth a try.

She hurried after Lynx, who strode away with complete and utter purpose. They dodged through strewn books, ripped-out pages, bent furniture, broken furniture, and other furniture that skittered out of the way as they approached.

Bending down to grab a book, she started when Lynx snapped. "Don't touch the books before you know how they work!"

Pulling her hand away, Quinn decided she'd talk to Dottie about that later. Maybe inadvertently getting the bench on her side had been a good idea.

Still, she followed Lynx past the hall entrance where she could hear bookworms munching away at magical dust motes or whatnot, and down a small side corridor instead. The walls of which felt like they were closing in, it was that narrow. The wood had become scratched and worn and nothing like the faded beauty that was in the entrance hall or the rest of the Library.

In fact, an eerie sense of abandonment lingered in the hall. She hugged herself and rubbed her arms to maintain some warmth because all of it seemed to have bled out of this section of the Library.

The Gloom was real here.

A smell of mustiness permeated the whole area, not like the low and earthy smell in the rest of the Library or the slightly pungent, mildly disgusting smell that existed where the bookworms were.

No this, this felt like something was angry and festering and old, very, very old. Still, she pushed on and finally, Lynx stopped in front of a door at the end of the narrow hallway. He turned back and looked at her.

"Okay, you wanted to fight, right?" It almost felt like he was speaking in code.

"How else are we gonna get rid of the bookworms?" She tried to keep it lighthearted as the aura in this hall was anything but. The Gloom was thick here.

"I know, you're right," he said. "I just wish we had more time to take care of this. Hold your breath for a few seconds; you're going to need to."

And with that, without any further preamble, he opened the door and the gust of wind that tore out of that room threatened to blow everything away.

9

ABSORPTION

QUINN BARELY MANAGED TO GRAB ONTO A PIECE OF TRIM IN TIME TO stop herself from getting swept away by the wind that buffeted out of the room beyond. She'd never used such a death-grip before in her life.

Even Lynx had to brace himself. Maybe it was her imagination, but he appeared to flicker ever so slightly. Perhaps magical interference or something. Quinn wished she knew more than she did.

It felt like an eternity but was probably only a few seconds long. Yet it left Quinn gasping for air.

"Why didn't you warn me about that sooner?" she asked, still panting to get her breath back.

Lynx blinked at her. "Oh, right. Sorry. I didn't really think. It was a seal I didn't have the power I needed to deactivate. I'll have to get used to this corporeal thing. It's amazing what a few hundred years without a human, or at least a solid person around, can do."

Quinn crept closer to the door, ignoring the utter lack of consideration from her guide. She filed the fact that his visage had flickered away. There was plenty of time to go over that later. She peered into the room. It was much smaller than she'd expected, with far fewer books.

"This is an odd addition to the Library," she said, slowly looking around. It was highly obvious that it had been added on at some stage in the far distant past. Even the wood on the floor was worn in such a way that, if she'd been barefoot, she probably would have gotten splinters in her feet. It was old and dilapidated and not cared for in the slightest.

"Why is it so broken?" she asked, turning around slowly to see all of the bookcases, some of which had splintered shelving, some of them literally cracked in two, or worn in such places that it appeared about to crack with the slightest force. She could almost count the amount of books in this room. Maybe a hundred or so?

For a room with fifteen bookcases, that wasn't much. Most of them were empty. And there was a window, but it looked like it was boarded up. No light streamed in. She wondered where that might even lead to.

Still. "Lynx, are you going to answer me? I mean, this isn't exactly what I thought we'd be coming into when you said I'd learn to fight." She quelled the panic. Just because it didn't look like a training room, didn't mean anything, right?

Lynx didn't respond. His eyes were far away. She stepped closer to him, looking at his face from probably a foot away, the closest she'd been to him since she arrived. And that was when she noticed that his eyes really were more lizard-like than cat-like, and not human-like at all. They had a slit and a weird, jeweled membrane over them. It lent an iridescent hue to the purple-black of his eyes. She shook herself so she could focus again.

"Lynx." She snapped her fingers in front of his face, and he suddenly blinked.

"Sorry, I had several settings that I had to check. The Library has begun to slowly recharge. Things are just not all where they should be... yet."

There was a small smile playing at the corner of his lips, and Quinn felt mildly accomplished. She might desperately want to know how it was recharging, and just how she facilitated that. It was something she could ask the Library later. Right now, she needed to learn to fight before the bookworms got bigger or multiplied. "Look, that's great, but tell me what I need to do. There's nobody else here who can help me."

He looked contrite again. He was actually very good at that. It was like he'd had practice.

She gestured out at the room. "Spill. What is the story behind this room? Why is it so..."

"Wrecked," Lynx said. "Finished, broken, dilapidated, run down. Take your pick. A few hundred years with nobody to maintain it, with nobody to use it. We came through one of the connecting corridors. Usually, this would be the antechamber for the combat wing. Right now, it's more like a storage room for the very basics. That's all we've got to go off."

Quinn wanted to scream and tell him to stop trying to coddle her, stop trying to protect her or whatever it was he was doing. Instead, realizing that learning to fight was important, she swallowed that down to save for later and turned to glare at him, crossing her arms as she looked him dead in the eyes. "Can't you just let me use magic? I can take care of it lickety-split that way!"

Lynx started to laugh; the sound echoed strangely in the small, broken room.

She got exasperated with him and had to calm herself to speak. "Why are you laughing? Don't just laugh at me. Try explaining instead."

That sobered Lynx up a bit. "I'm sorry. I just... you can't use magic on bookworms. Didn't you listen to anything I told you about them?"

Quinn scrunched her brow, trying to remember. "Well, they feed off ma—oh. So you're telling me if somebody uses magic to try and kill a bookworm, it's just gonna absorb it?"

"Yes and no. If you use magic that is its affinity, then it will absorb that magic. But if you use magic of an alternating or a different frequency, type, or affinity, it could do one of many things. It could empower the bookworm. It could enrage the bookworm. It could explode the bookworm all over you."

Quinn gulped at the visual. "So basically what you're saying is: we don't use magic to kill bookworms."

"Precisely."

"Okay, got it. That's all you had to say about it."

"Well, now I've explained. That's what you asked for." Apparently, Lynx could be pedantic when he wanted to be.

Quinn couldn't argue though, so she continued on as if nothing had happened. "That could have been a really bad rookie mistake. Make sure to tell me things that might seem obvious to you. Teach me to fight now. I don't care if it's with a stick or a mop or a broom or a desk. We need to get those bookworms under control."

"I know," Lynx said. "But you don't have any magic abilities yet. So it shouldn't be a problem."

Quinn watched him as he moved toward one of the far bookcases. He reached up a couple of shelves and grabbed a very old and tattered book before pulling it down. He then crouched on the floor and patted a spot in front of him. Quinn took another deep breath and walked over.

She could put up with this. The way he sometimes treated her like an afterthought. After all, he'd been alone for a long time.

This would help give her the power needed to kill the worms, to feed the owls.

Oh my God, how was this her life now? Taking a deep breath, she spoke as evenly as she could, ignoring the butterflies of doom in her stomach. "Okay, fine. So what do I do? Crouch. Kneel. Sit. What do you want?"

"Just sit down comfortably enough so that you can read the book."

This seemed odd. How did they have time for this? "You seriously want me to sit and read a book right now? You can't just plug that into my head."

This time, it was Lynx's turn to take a deep breath. Did he even need oxygen? Quinn had so many questions. So many questions that weren't pertinent to getting the Library up and powered right now. But damn, maybe she could do an equal parts exchange with him.

"Quinn, are you listening?"

"Oh, sorry. I just... can we do an exchange of information? I'll ask you a question, you'll give me an answer, and then I'll do some of the work you want me to?"

Lynx looked at her, blinking rapidly. Maybe he was accessing information. Magical beings seemed eerily similar to computers in some ways.

"Equal parts exchange. I thought we were sort of doing that already," he said, like he was testing the words out. "I'd say I owe you one, so what question do you have?"

"I want to know... just... do you need to breathe? Are you like a shape-changing species? Are you—what are you?"

Lynx smiled. It was a small smile, but the expression actually seemed to be genuine.

"Well, I'm a manifestation of the Library, perhaps *the* manifestation would be more accurate. It uses some parts of mana, knowledge, and projection. I think your world called it a holograph, but it's not quite accurate because I can manifest tangibly depending on the amount of magic expenditure. This makes me a unique being, and I evolve outside of the Library, but at the same time as the Library. I do not require oxygen, but I do attempt to mimic the life forms around me. Does that answer your question?"

Quinn just sat there and gaped at him. "Mostly," she said, because to be honest, she wasn't exactly sure if she understood even two-thirds of what he just told her, but he had answered her question, and she could process that information on her own time.

Now it was her turn. "Okay. I just read through the book and that's it?"

"Yes." He handed it to her, and she crossed her legs, spreading it out in her lap, and began the long and arduous task of reading the book. Except after a few minutes of not having turned more than a couple of pages, Lynx reached out a hand and placed it on the book.

"What are you doing?" he asked, obviously perturbed. It was like he'd never seen someone read a book before.

She looked at the book and back at him, wondering if she needed to demonstrate in a different way. "I'm reading the book."

"But you're the Librarian. That's not how *you* read a book. You just *read* it." He said it as if it was the most obvious thing in the universe.

She cocked her head to one side and said, "That's what I'm doing. I'm reading each word of the book. That is how you read." She wondered if perhaps something had malfunctioned when she connected to the Core. Lynx was behaving oddly even for a magical manifestation.

"No. I'm sorry." Lynx paused for a moment like he was mulling over how to explain something to her. "Okay. I need you to spread both hands, actually, wait, open the book up into the middle, spread both hands, one over each side of the book palm down, and place them just above those pages."

"Okay. Fine," she said, spreading the book over her knees, she placed each hand on one side of the book. "I just don't see how suddenly—"

A screen flickered in front of her, or maybe it was just a picture. She wasn't sure. It was like a 3D structure of the book that reached down and through and spread throughout her mind. And the moment she let herself connect to that progression, knowledge flooded through her. It was like the wind spread out of the room when they first opened it. It went all through her mind, all through her body, right down through into her veins.

They were on fire, but a different type of fire. It was like windburn and cold and ice. And suddenly, she knew; she just knew how to hold a sword.

Basic Swordsmanship for the Beginner
Access Level: Highest
Knowledge: Granted and Assimilated
Practical aptitude ready

"What even?" She opened her eyes and blinked up at Lynx. There was a lot she wanted to say, but the only thing she could think of was "Whoa."

Her head felt as though it was filled with cotton candy. There was a strange taste to it, like clean linen suffused with raspberries, with a sort of tang, perhaps lemon. The smell was fresh but fiery, yet maybe with an underlying odor of sweat. She blinked again, looking at Lynx, who seemed extremely expectant in the way he leaned forward.

"So," he asked, "how do you feel?"

She couldn't answer that quite yet. She closed her eyes, put her hands on the book's pages, and tried to process what she'd done. There was intrinsic knowledge embedded into her now. She instinctively knew how to hold a sword, how to block with a sword, how to swing a sword. These were just extremely basic things, but already so much better than she'd ever been with that broom. She could tell without even having to pick up a sword. But where was she going to get a weapon from?

She opened her eyes. "Is this what you meant? The Librarian reads by absorbing knowledge?"

"To a certain extent," Lynx said. "Basics like this will require very little practical study and provide a solid foundation. You should be able to learn the foundations of absolutely everything in existence. Which is a little unusual, to be honest. It'll be a huge overload at first, but the Library should help you begin to recognize the full extent of what you can absorb, what you can process, and what your brain can hold. You'll be surprised." He smiled. "What do you think?"

She grinned at him, thinking that being unusual wasn't a bad thing. "You know, I think we need to get me a sword."

This time, Lynx chuckled. "Don't you think you're getting a little ahead of yourself there?"

"Maybe," Quinn said, "but you just gave me a book on how to use swords, so what else am I supposed to do? I can't use a broom like a sword; it doesn't have the same weight ratio." She paused. "Wow, that sounded like I really know what I'm talking about."

This time, Lynx laughed. "Well, you technically do, you just need practical experience now."

"Wait, so the knowledge isn't going to just make me an expert in whatever I've read about?"

"Of course not. This magic just provides the avenue to mastering an ability. You'll have to fuel your knowledge with the power of mana so that it makes it so that you have the power to execute the skill that you've just learned. You've got to build muscle and memory for the things you master." He actually sounded quite kind while instructing her. Not as flippant as he sometimes appeared.

Quinn squinted at him. "You say that like I'm supposed to understand it inherently."

"Well, you should. You're the Librarian now."

"Great. I'll take that under advisement then, shall I?" She took a deep breath, knowing that he didn't deserve her to snap at him. Apparently, it wasn't just Lynx's fault; it was the Library and the magic and the way the universe worked. "Give me a sword so I can practice and we can take care of the bookworms. Then I can make more food so I don't starve to death."

While she'd been talking, Lynx had moved over to another of the bookcases. He was frowning as he rifled through them. Most of them had broken shelving and books that were falling apart. It was like the magic in the Library had gotten so low that there was nothing left for it to maintain things this far out from the core.

She only hoped that what they were doing would help because, at this rate, nothing was going to survive. Which, if she believed the magical Library she was standing in existed, then it also meant that she would perish along with the universe.

"Here we go," he said finally, gripping a wooden short sword in his hand.

It was a training sword, or at least that's what she gathered from reading the book. Its edges were pointed but not exactly sharp, although enough force should help rectify that with something as soft as the bookworms.

Information still overlapped and ran rampant in her mind, but her body seemed to know exactly how to hold the hilt as she grabbed it. "The hilt of a sword. It's not a handle. Learn something new every day," she muttered under her breath.

Lynx only raised an eyebrow in her direction.

Despite herself, Quinn was actually feeling pretty good about the knowledge in her head. She made a couple of swings in the air with it before tsking under her breath. "Okay, I think, I think this can work, but like, am I supposed to hit you? I mean, there's going to be no resistance because you're incorporeal."

"Give me just a second." He glanced around the room. "I'll have to. I think I'll have to use the winch to get it to rise up since my level of control here is mostly nil. I'm just going to have to make do manually."

"Make do with what?" Quinn wanted to know. She watched him skeptically, still feeling the weight of the sword in her hand, trying to get used to it. It wasn't very well balanced as far as she could tell. While she wasn't sure how she knew that, the fact that she did filled her with excitement.

But it was definitely better than the broom.

She watched as Lynx pulled out a handle at the back of one of the bookcases and wound a winch. A definitive creaking accompanied the action, and the floor opened slowly. What looked like an extremely old and dusty combat dummy rose out of the floor.

"This is different," she said, eyeing it critically. It was old but in better condition than the rest of the room.

"It's a training dummy. Whack it a few times so you get the feel of the sword." Lynx crossed his arms and stood back against the wall to watch.

Quinn obliged. She whacked it a few times for good measure on the arms, on the body, on the neck, on the head, dancing around, getting a feel for moving with the weight of a blade in her hand.

Well, the weight of a wooden blade in her hand, anyway. It was smooth and much lighter than a steel sword would be. All she had to do was reference the stances she'd read about and her body moved of its own accord. Eventually, it would all probably feel like second nature if she practiced enough.

"Just how much can I learn this way?" she asked, a spark of excitement in her gut.

As Lynx was about to answer, there was a tremble, a rumbling that shuddered through the floor and right up into her very bones. She could feel the way the Library groaned, the way the magic darted around, and the way the mana twisted.

If even a novice like her could tell, then something was very wrong.

1 0

WORM FOOD

THE RUMBLING TURNED INTO SHAKING AND WAS SO INTENSE THAT SHE almost lost her footing and had to adjust in order to keep her balance.

"What was that?" she asked, hoping Lynx knew.

His eyes flickered again like he wasn't entirely there. This time, however, he multitasked better. Even though his voice was distant, he answered her question. "That's coming from where the worms are. Their energy is fluctuating. They seem to be absorbing more mana than they were earlier. It's like…"

She gulped, instinctually knowing why, "They're absorbing the magic from the one we killed, aren't they? That seems so clever. I didn't think the bookworms would be sapient."

Lynx shrugged, his focus still not entirely on her. "I can't be sure. They *shouldn't* be sapient, but they have been running rampant for a few hundred years. Anything's possible. But this is not good. It's also not impossible that because the Library suddenly has a smidgen more power. They're trying it draw on it too."

The room shuddered once more. This time, some dirt fell from the ceiling, along with fragments of wood that had splintered off from overhead and from the bookcases. Even the training dummy started to shake.

"We need to move now," Quinn said, feeling a sudden impetus to act, despite practically quaking where she stood. That was complete and utter nerves. She was scared. She prided herself on rarely being scared of things. She'd been through a lot in her young life, losing her parents, and being thrown into the foster care system.

But she'd always looked out for herself. This wasn't just about herself anymore. This was about the survival of a universe's magic. For some obscure reason, she even thought about Dottie the little bench with an attitude.

Not to mention the fact that, if Lynx was to be believed, Quinn was the only one capable of doing anything at that point in time. "Come on, then. Let's get there. Let's go. I need you to guide me there. This place is still a labyrinth to me."

In response to her comment, the Library popped a map up in front of her eyes, as if it was trying to be helpful. She waved it away.

Lynx flashed her a quick grin, even though she could tell he was worried, and they took off.

Quinn pushed herself past her fear and into movement. They headed out down the same dark and dingy hallway. The sense of foreboding followed them like a bad smell, like rotting vegetation. The earthy undertones had strange vibrations to them. It was like this lingering, overpowering need for control.

It stank like regret.

She paused, getting her bearings. Lynx pulled farther ahead of her and led them off to the left, to where she'd killed the first worm. In hindsight, it probably hadn't been a good idea to leave the corpse of the creature lying around. But you live and you learn.

Quinn steeled herself, trying to ignore the shaking that continued underneath her feet, trying to ignore her own quivering nerves. They sped toward the source of the disturbance as fast as her legs could carry her and stopped right in front of the section they'd been in scant hours before.

Just beyond the corpse were at least half a dozen of those damned bookworms. She'd always thought bookworms were a good thing until she came to this world, where of course, something that used to be an awesome nickname for herself and her friends was now something evil.

Fan-freaking-tastic.

She took a deep breath, centered herself, and let the images from the book flood her mind. Quinn gripped the sword in her left hand, trying to figure out which hand would be best to use. She was technically ambidextrous, even if she sometimes favored her left. She could use both, right? Maybe that was something she could use to her advantage. Either way, those bookworms weren't just sitting there devouring dust anymore. They were focused on her.

Three of them sprang for her at once.

The first worm lunged at her, much like the original one had, only this one lacked the same power. It flopped over and rolled, which was lucky as it allowed Quinn to evade the other worms launching themselves in a similar fashion. She ducked and rolled, bringing her wooden sword down in the very center of the first bookworm. It squelched and then burst audibly as the sword ripped through the flesh. It splashed over everything in a five-yard radius.

Especially her hair, and her hands. Oddly enough, it didn't slick down her grip, which was a blessing in disguise as the other two worms dove for her as well.

She managed to round off rather clumsily over the one she'd just split in two, narrowly avoiding a hit from what she thought was a green-ringed bookworm. A part of her mind stashed away the color of the rings for later reference, but she couldn't afford to let her attention wane.

The overabundance of magic the worms had consumed rendered their coloring suspect at best. So the information was likely tainted anyway.

Unfortunately, while trying to figure it out, she rolled right into a pile of goop, which was slippery and offered no traction for her feet. In desperation, she flailed her sword in the air and accidentally managed to impale the worm currently lunging at her. She sliced it along the underside before extricating herself barely in time. Worm guts slushed down next to her, coating her right leg.

Leveraging herself up, she leaned against one of the bookshelves, panting and trying to regain her equilibrium. This whole fighting thing was not as easy as reading about it in a book.

And the smell of rotting corpses and vegetation made her gag reflexes work overtime.

"A little help here," she said, sounding angrier than she wanted. Not to mention, opening her mouth to speak let some goop fall into it. It clung to the roof of her mouth, making her stomach churn in response. She literally had to turn her head and throw up.

"Watch out!" Lynx yelled, his voice booming through the space. He threw out a cascade of salt, doing what he could to help without draining too much energy from the already emergency-powered Library.

Quinn barely twisted away in time. Some of the weird gelatinous substance that expelled from the worm attacking her hit the book-shelves and slid down. It was black, sludge-like, and quite simply gross. But it appeared to be even stickier than the initial stuff she'd been hit with. Avoiding it moved even higher up on her list.

She took another breath and lashed out with the sword again, but this time she only nipped the head. She knew that she'd have to cut the creature in two if she was going to prevent it from splitting into multiple worms.

Diving forward once more, she wielded the blade and finally brought it down on the center of the worm's body, eliciting an airy gasp from the creature. The sound made her hesitate before she could get the sword all the way through, and the two pieces writhed beneath her hands.

The very movement caused Quinn to panic, and she hacked away at the worm with something close to a frenzy until it was indeed in two pieces again. Sadly, there was no reprieve because she could see more worms inching their way toward them, and this time there were more than just three.

"How am I supposed to deal with all of these? All of them at once?" she gasped out, her chest heaving with the exertion.

Lynx looked around, glancing at more boxes of salt to the right.

"All I know is we have to kill these. I'm sorry, this has gotten way out of hand."

"You don't say," Quinn muttered, trying to scoop some of the worm guts off her body that had accumulated during the fight. It made moving more difficult because it clogged her ability to maneuver. She decided not to bring up him saying we have to kill them. The salt he strategically threw slowed them enough that she could deal with them so far.

All she could do was knuckle down and flail about with her little wooden sword, desperately wishing the edges were sharper. Luckily, worms were very soft even in their engorged state, perhaps even more so considering they were pretty much just a sack of food and innards.

But those were the last inquisitive thoughts she managed to have before the onslaught.

Worm after worm came, leaping at her, jumping higher than anything without legs had a right to do, screaming at her. And when she cleaved them in two, they quite literally poured their guts absolutely everywhere.

All over the floor in a sea of sludge, caking her clothes in the pungent, mucus-like film. She had to move further into the corridor to face all of the worms head-on and to avoid the massive pile-up of worm parts that was starting to accumulate at the front of the corridor.

If she wasn't careful, she was going to trap herself back there with the rest of the worms which, in her very humble opinion, was not a good thing. All she could hope was that the Library had some way of taking care of all the carcasses when she was done.

Her arms ached, her shoulders burned, and she swapped arms whenever the one she was currently using felt like it was about to fall off. Her thighs felt like the muscles she knew and the ones she'd never realized she possessed were all about to explode with overexertion. Not to mention her back was aching in ways it shouldn't at her age.

The book might have taught her the technicalities of sword fighting, but it had done nothing to prepare her body. Understanding the drawbacks of the Library system was not the epiphany she wanted while battling engorged bookworms.

"You've got this," Lynx said from his place of observation in the bookcases. He'd changed back into a lynx once he threw out a scattering of salt. Since his claws were much more effective weapons, he occasionally dove into fights as well, but only when his cleave could make a definitive difference. He didn't draw extra energy from the Library for nothing.

After solidifying his form so that his claws would make contact with the worm bodies, even for just a few seconds, he would flicker so much that Quinn had to tell him off.

"You need to stop doing that. If you flicker out of existence, who am I supposed to talk to, and who is supposed to help me?" She panted out the words, not used to this much physical exertion. At least there was a brief lull in attackers.

But that's as far as she got because a worm larger than any of the dozens of others that she'd seen so far came into view, slithering through the remnants of its brethren. The master worm was probably four times as large as the others, and there was no way her tiny sword was going to cut through any part of it.

Wormzilla

Status: Maximum Engorgement

Danger Level: High

Maximum Mana Density: Leaking

Great. Now the Library chose to be helpful and only succeeded in making her more nervous.

"Get out of the way!" she called out to Lynx, belatedly remembering that it wouldn't matter because he could probably just blink out of existence. She, on the other hand, could not.

Thankfully, she slipped on some of the worm guts underneath her foot and managed to completely avoid a strange whirlwind attack from the bossworm. It's body cycloned. It was the only way she could describe the movement of it twisting in rapid circles standing on one end.

Something flickered in the corner of her vision, but she was too busy concentrating on the sight in front of her. She didn't have to see any more information to understand it was hellbent on killing her. Every portion of her body ached, but there was no choice other than to push through the pain and the knowledge that this wasn't going to be easy.

From the corner of her eye, she saw a stick flying at her.

No, it wasn't a stick, it was a broom. Catching it deftly with her left arm, she was now dual-wielding a broom and a sword, which seemed comical until the worm suddenly appeared in front of her with some sort of short-range teleportation move that none of the others had possessed. She instinctually crossed the sword and broom, barely holding the creature at bay.

She didn't even think she'd be able to fit her arms around this thing's neck. It was massive. And her left shoulder groaned under the pressure.

Quinn managed to cut a large slice off it as she darted out of the way after pushing back, but it wasn't nearly enough to decapitate it or even render it slightly immobile so that she could hack away at the middle of its body. She didn't know what to do.

Her weapons were subpar and her energy levels were flagging dangerously.

"Lynx, there has to be some other weapon, something sharper, something bigger, something... stabbier?" She rolled out of the way yet again and came up panting. She was not a super fit person. Hell, this was not what she had been aiming to do after learning to fight.

This wasn't a set of mathematical equations that she could easily calculate her way through. Right in front of her was a literal monster trying to kill her, and it was doing a bang-up job so far.

Her left arm throbbed so much that there was little feeling left in it. That was going to take some work if this ever got done. The rancid smell all around her made her sick to her stomach, and she wished she'd have got this done *before* she ate food. Before this, she'd never regretted eating in her life.

The creature reared back and screamed out a guttural noise that sounded like chains grating against each other. Its head flailed around with such speed she realized it must have been similar to that whirl-wind attack from earlier.

But she didn't move in time, and the massive head impacted her chest so hard it knocked the wind out of her and sent her flying all the way into one of the bookcases across the room. Books rained down on the ground around her, and she couldn't breathe. She gasped in air, guts, and muck. Her body ached. It felt like she'd been crumpled against a concrete wall.

And then the worm was back, there, looming over her like a death knell.

11

WORMZILLA

GIANT WORMS WERE A THING OF NIGHTMARES, BUT GIANT ENGORGED bookworms looming over her when she couldn't even move were something even worse. Every part of Quinn's body pulsed, each nerve on edge even as the creature rose up on its hindquarters—or hind section was maybe a better term—and screamed at her again. If it had arms, they'd probably be beating its chest like a gorilla.

As it was, the creature appeared oddly snake-like despite it being a worm. As if it was a *very* hungry caterpillar.

It was strange, the calm that came over her, even as she attempted to grip the sword in the hand that appeared to have lost all of its strength. The broom fell out of her grip while she was flying through the air. If she looked at what she just coughed up, it would probably be guts mixed with blood.

Her blood, because her insides felt more than just bruised. She wouldn't be surprised if she was bleeding internally.

Everything slowed down around her as if somebody had just recorded the entire scene on a slow-motion camera and was playing it back to her. Even the bookworm's movements were exaggeratingly slow. Little bits of her life flashed before her eyes, but not like she'd expected it to before her death. They talked it up really big, to be fair, you know, your whole life flashing before your eyes in the moment before you die.

Like a veritable saga.

This was proving to be a very, very long moment.

So long, in fact, that she found it a little easier to breathe now, and her left hand even twitched. Fine, it wasn't holding a broom anymore, but there was still life in it. More strength than she'd had a portion of her moment ago.

Quinn rolled her shoulders, or tried to. Any movement still felt like a colossal mistake. The pain shot through her chest, but that's when she realized that this wasn't actually slow motion. Her life wasn't flashing before her eyes in some sort of ultimate showdown prior to death. Her pain traveled at a completely and utterly normal speed.

Something had slowed the bookworm's movements to a crawl. The creature moved as if it was trying to swim through glue. It screamed again, and even though the sound was about the same frequency and around the same speed as it had been previously, she could tell it was also full of frustration because its body was impeded.

Which meant it gave her time to get her bearings. It gave her time to build up some strength and to figure out some sort of strategy to maybe, you know, not die on her first couple of days in a different world.

As many mangas and webcomics as she'd read on the subject, this wasn't how the protagonist was supposed to go. Unless she wasn't the protagonist and she'd gotten it all wrong.

Still, she sucked it up and groaned as she moved. A grating sensation ran through her left shoulder, and she really hoped it was just dislocated and not broken. It would hurt like hell putting it back in place, but hey, that was better than a break that she didn't know how to treat in a magical world.

Even slowed as it was, the worm still inched toward her far too fast for Quinn's comfort. She scrambled out of the way, barely making it, drawing air into her lungs. She looked around for Lynx, but he wasn't there. He wasn't anywhere. She pushed down the mild panic that rose at his absence. Not once in her life had she ever needed someone else to save her. She wasn't about to start now.

Regardless of how much fear and fatigue were trying to convince her otherwise.

Quinn managed to slip and slide through all the guts and body parts, falling occasionally as the boss worm continued to move like molasses. She had no idea when that state of being would end, so every second counted, now that she'd rid herself of her mind fog.

Finally, she managed to get herself propped up against a table. A table that didn't move out of her way in indignation and thus probably wasn't sentient. She glanced around.

Suddenly, Lynx flickered into view.

"Here." He placed something on the table, and she could tell that he was paler. Almost transparent. Hell, she could see the table through his body.

And she could see the machete. That *was* a machete that he just put down. Rusted and on its last legs, but it looked like it still had an edge and was much sharper than her current weapon. Plus, it was vaguely sword-like.

Quinn was willing to try anything at that point.

Anything on a last-ditch effort.

"You've got this!" She heard Dottie's voice and she looked towards its origin. The bench was standing upright on what would appear to be its hind legs with its stubby other legs reaching toward the worm. It was as if Dottie was controlling it.

Okay, that was too bizarre. Quinn was gonna have to have a long talk with that bench if she ever managed to cut this bloody worm in half.

Compacting all the remaining energy she had, Quinn gripped the machete as hard as she could with both hands, discarding the wooden sword to the ground. Her left hand was too weak to do anything on its own anyway.

Then she launched herself at the snail-paced moving worm that was slowly turning toward her. She sailed through the air, both hands gripping the machete's handle as she brought it down on the midsection of the creature with a resounding, squelching, shuddering slash.

The machete, despite its rust, tore through the skin as easily as through butter. It was far more effective than the wooden sword she'd been hacking away with. A fleeting thought about a book on machete fighting crossed her mind, but it vanished as soon as the machete hit the ground beneath the massive worm.

Each side of the creature began to shudder, spurting goop, guts, blood, and viscera everywhere. The ground beneath it shook so violently that even more books began to tumble from the shelves once again.

Landing awkwardly, her right leg gave out beneath her. Quinn scrambled back as fast as she could, an inexplicable premonition warning her of what was about to happen.

Suddenly, the two halves of the worm's body began to shudder even more violently, right up until the moment they exploded.

However, the shower of worm guts she expected didn't rain down upon her. Looking up, Quinn registered that Lynx had cast some sort of barrier around the massive creature. It flickered out of existence just as she noticed it, and she realized that Lynx's light was starting to wane. He had clearly drawn on far too much power.

Turning to her, he smiled wanly. Even his voice flickered in and out like static as he spoke. "You know, that took a lot more effort than I was expecting," he admitted. "I think I need to recharge now."

And then he was gone, leaving Quinn alone in a sea of worm guts.

Alone, that is, unless she counted the talking bench.

Wormzilla - Defeated

Status: Deceased

Danger Level: Neutralized

Mana Status: Dissipating

A strange wave of power suffused the air all around her. It wasn't actually visible, but more of a scent and sensation. It felt like this strange resistance to the air around her, and smelled like a whirlwind of colors and flavors all wrapped up together into something not entirely unpleasant, despite the number of carcasses in the vicinity.

The aura emanated from the worm corpses and rushed through the Library like a tidal wave of fresh air. On second thoughts, it moved *into* the Library, because it very obviously remained contained within.

Even her own body felt a sense of rejuvenation from it. It lifted her mood and washed away some of the smaller aches and pains. And ever so slightly, it appeared that the Library itself gained some measure of vibrance.

A thought occurred to her.

Perhaps the magic the worms had devoured was released upon their death. With no other worms to take it off them, it dissipated back into its original host. Quinn just hoped it would help replenish the Library stores. Maybe that way Lynx could recharge quicker too.

Of course, she had no idea if that's how it worked.

Quinn sat there trying to muster enough energy to move, simply gaping at the emptiness around her. She'd been left to her own devices, and the pain was starting to catch up to her.

Her body ached in ways she didn't even know were possible. There were parts of her torso she hadn't even realized existed. Scrapes, cuts, bruises, and the gods knew what she'd done to her left arm. But she was alive, and the worms, by the very obvious pungent aroma around her, were dead. That was a win situation, right?

She went to pinch herself but paused. The guts of all her worm victims adorned her body in multiple pungent layers. She didn't need one more bruise to tell her she was awake.

She'd thought that if she pinched herself enough she'd wake up from this decidedly odd dream. But she wasn't waking up, and she was bone tired. Maybe she could fall asleep in this gelatinous sea of viscera. Surely just a nap wouldn't hurt?

"Now come on, love," Dottie said, her tone very mothering, pulling Quinn out of her contemplations. "Let's get you up and get you set, and we can probably help you get to the bathing room."

It took several moments for all those words to sink into Quinn's brain. "What? This place has a bathroom?"

"Of course, it has a bathroom, dear. It's the Library. We've had

Librarians before. Organic ones even! All you organic creatures need those bathrooms. I'll take you to your quarters." Dottie laughed softly and muttered something about visitors to the Library and their ways.

Quinn ignored it in favor of digging out more information. "Wait, quarters? I get quarters?"

The bench appeared a little flustered as she answered. "Yes, yes, of course. We're not uncivilized. We can hardly have you sleeping on one of the benches can we? I can only accompany you to the staircase, though. I'm not very good at navigating stairs, but I'll see if I can coax the Library."

Quinn paused and looked at the bench, who appeared to be very apologetic about the way she had treated Quinn initially and really did seem to be trying to step up and help take care of her in Lynx's extremely sudden absence. Quinn wasn't about to look a gift bench in the mouth and decided to give the seat the benefit of the doubt.

"Okay, Dottie, just tell me what I need to do."

"Perfect. Give me a moment. Let's figure out how to move you and help get you doctored up, shall we?" There was something about the way Dottie spoke and the way she sort of fussed around her that reminded Quinn of happier times, way back when her grandmother had still been alive and her parents had still been there.

Memories truly could hit at the worst of times.

"Now, let's get you sat up, okay?" And Dottie motioned with one of her very bendy bench legs.

It struck Quinn just then that this bench was not only sapient but could kind of bend herself into variations of her shape. Yet another question to file away to ask later. At this rate, Quinn was going to have a very large list of things she needed answered.

"Hey, Dottie?" she asked, and realized it even hurt to draw in enough breath to speak.

Maybe she'd bruised her lungs or something. This was not good. She needed more power. There had to be a way to gain more abilities and make things less dangerous for her. If there were killer engorged worms in the Library itself, there was no telling what else she'd encounter outside of it.

"Now don't you overexert yourself, dear," Dottie said, and there was actual worry in her tone. Quinn tried a wan smile and just shrugged, which again was a very bad idea. Her shoulder protested the movement with a distinctly huge amount of agony.

She ground her teeth together to prevent herself from crying out. "How are we going to get me up those stairs?" Because being completely honest with herself considering the way her vision was blacking in and out, walking probably wasn't on the cards right now.

"Yes, that does pose a little bit of a conundrum," Dottie said, and suddenly there was a strange sort of scooter thing there.

It reminded Quinn of a dolly, but it was flat and had a handle sort of like those shopping carts that you got at those big-box stores. It was much easier to leverage herself up onto the platform that was only a few inches off the ground instead of trying to walk or clamber her way into a wheelchair. It was difficult enough to maneuver with only one functional arm.

It seemed to be made of something that seemed hardier than the plywood the base of these were often made out of, and Quinn settled herself as comfortably as possible trying not to pant too loudly. The little wheels provided for smooth rolling, and Quinn couldn't tell how it was being moved as she lay down on the pallet. But the motion was soothing, almost relaxing.

"Are you okay down there?" the voice asked her, with an accent similar to British that wasn't quite there yet.

"I'm fine," she answered, not quite daring to think that it might be the trolley talking to her. It could be the several bashes to her skull that she'd taken during the Wormzilla battle making her hallucinate.

The bench was trotting after them, and Dottie seemed to be oddly pleased with herself. That was another amazing, observation because Quinn had no idea how she could tell that the bench was actually pleased with herself without the bench speaking, which Dottie was not doing right then.

"Yes," Quinn answered slowly to reinforce it for herself, "I think I'm doing about as well as can be expected."

There was a little bit of a chortle from the trolley as it pushed her

through the Library and toward the front desk where she had originally entered with Lynx.

"I think you're a little bit confused, aren't you?" it said, again in that
weird accent that was oddly lulling. "Yeah, I guess it is sort of under-
standable. Well, don't you mind, we will figure out a way to help you
get up those stairs into your room, and then I promise you there's a
couple of us up there that can help take care of you."

Quinn wasn't quite sure how to process all of this. She felt like
she'd been taken to a fairytale castle with talking furniture,
shapeshifting holographs, and magical death worms.

The closer they got to the stairs, the less she could keep her eyes
open. Quinn could feel her head lolling to one side, and the aching in
her body wouldn't subside. All she wanted to do was close her eyes.

Despite how hard she fought to keep them open, she lost in the
end. Her last thought before she fell unconscious was that perhaps it
wasn't the best idea to fall asleep in a library full of magical things that
weren't all necessarily friendly toward her.

12

ACTIVATION

THERE WAS A POUNDING IN HER HEAD, SIMILAR TO THE KNOCKING AT A door. No, that wasn't accurate. It was more like one of those big old iron knockers pounding at a door with a resounding boom.

"Quinn."

Yes, that *was* her name. She was pretty sure that was her name. Everything hurt. Everything was chasing her. There was a sea in front of her of guts and blood and vile-smelling black entrails.

She gagged.

She gagged again.

"Quinn, wake up."

Suddenly, she was sitting upright in a bed that was surprisingly soft, with no true recollection of how she got there. There was only a vague recollection of two voices arguing with a third about turning into a ramp just this once?

None of that made sense.

Not to mention that the light was far too bright for the splitting headache trying to separate her brain from her skull. This dream was strange. There was a purple-tinged person standing in front of her and...

"Lynx?" she asked and wished she hadn't spoken because now the word was bouncing around inside her agonizing skull.

"Quinn, I need you to wake up."

"You're looking particularly solid," she said to him. However, why wouldn't he be looking solid was another valid question. Fragments of memories began to piece themselves together as she slowly came out of her daze.

"The Library." There was a hint of excitement in Lynx's voice, and Quinn couldn't quite decide whether the sound and pitch change made him sound different.

"Slow down," she said, and her voice came out croaky and dry like she hadn't had water in a month. "Just let me breathe."

She squinted up at the still definitely purple-tinged manifestation of the Library as all the bits and pieces finally clicked back into place. Perhaps Wormzilla throwing her into that bookcase hit her head harder than she realized. The whole concept of where she was and what had happened felt distant.

Was it all a dream?

She didn't think so. Hadn't she already tried to pinch herself awake multiple times?

But this room was new. Finally, she gave it a good look. This room was grander than anything she'd set foot in in her entire life. The ceilings went up, probably twenty feet tall, with columns of stone adorned with beautiful carvings and gorgeous deep purple drapes.

"The Library really likes purple," she muttered out loud. It was easier to put the words together outside of her head. At least out in the open they weren't alone in her skull, bouncing off the sides, like a pointed triangle that was trying to kill her.

"Quinn, I need you to snap out of this. You need to get downstairs to the desk."

She squinted up at him again. "First up, make the light go away so I can think. Second, what desk?"

Lynx scowled briefly. It was the first time she could remember seeing him visibly irritated. But he did move to close the curtains tighter before speaking again. He was fast too, almost like a flash of light himself. "The front desk, silly. I need you at the check-in counter."

"Check-in counter? That desk is the check-in counter?" It suddenly all clicked into place for her, and a wave of excitement washed through Quinn.

"Yes, like a library, a check-in counter. You know. Pretty integral to the operation of things."

"Well, it's not obvious since my world is largely digital now," Quinn muttered. With a sigh, she rolled her shoulders and realized that her left arm wasn't hurting as badly as it had before she went to sleep. It was still stiff and a bit sore, but she'd been sure it was dislocated earlier. Now, however, it was definitely back in its socket.

This was very strange; her entire body was still sore, but not in the agonizing way it had been before the dolly took her up the stairs.

"How did I get here?" she asked, glancing around to try and find the cart and the bench.

"That's not important right now. The Library took care of you." Lynx's eyes gleamed like he'd been reignited somehow. "The worms contained enough magic so that when they died it dissipated back into the Library and managed to replenish some of the reserves. It's finally rebooting."

"That's a good thing, right?" she said to him, still uncertain about everything she'd witnessed. Had she really absorbed all of that information from a book?

"Quinn, I need you to focus." Lynx bent down next to her and looked her directly in the eyes. "I need you to get up. You're healed enough to move. I need you to activate me."

That was actually enough to get Quinn out of her own head. "You need me to activate the Library?"

"Yes, I'm running on emergency power and everything I do is currently restricted. I require the Librarian to assist me. You're the only one who can activate me." There was a tiny undercurrent of pleading in his tone.

This time, she moved out of bed quicker than she thought possible and realized that her clothes were still, in fact, caked in worm guts. At least they smelled slightly better.

"I'm getting changed first." She held up a hand when he went to protest. "No. I refuse to walk around in stiff, worm-guts-decorated clothes. And the sheets will have to be washed."

Lynx sighed, practically vibrating on the spot, and nodded at the wardrobe over the other side of the room. "Clothes are in there."

Quinn scanned through them, pursing her lips. It wasn't ideal. But there was a T-shirt blouse sort of thing, and a pair of pants that would do. She quickly ducked into the bathroom, barely let the water touch her skin before she changed, making a note that she'd get a real shower and wash her hair as soon as possible. Lynx didn't seem to be in a waiting mood.

She pushed her long, dark, encrusted curls up into a bun and glared at him for being so impatient. "Get my jeans cleaned. These pants are itchy. You and I are gonna talk after this," she said grimacing as each movement made reminded her she'd fought a giant bookworm.

"Well, of course, we're going to talk. There's lots we have to cover, including all of the stuff that I need you to help me get the Library to do." Lynx most definitely wasn't paying any real attention to her or her demands.

"I'm serious, Lynx. Do whatever magic the Library needs to get my jeans clean. Do it now."

This time he looked at her, surprise entering his gaze. "Done. Sorry. I'm just having trouble believing that after so long..."

And he headed down the stairs.

She followed him, glad dashing down the spiral staircase didn't result in more injuries. "What? What can't you believe?" Quinn asked him.

"Well, it's been so long. I didn't think I was ever going find anybody to fill the role. It took centuries to find you, and frankly, it was a last-ditch effort on my behalf to scan beyond the worlds we service. I would never have found you if your signature hadn't suddenly been so loud. I was mostly resigned to just winking out of existence and taking viable magic with me." He was chattering so much, it sounded like nervous excitement.

Maybe she could coax some of the need-to-know information he'd been withholding from her. She wondered if he realized he'd just admitted that he almost ceased to exist. Considering the amount of details she didn't know, everything she did in this place was like going in blind.

Chatty Lynx was ideal.

"So the Library's connected to all magic?" she asked as she set foot on the main floor of the Library.

"Without the Library, magic is wild and unpredictable and almost impossible to harness." He paused close to the desk and frowned as he fiddled with some of the filigree carvings. "The Library acts as a safety filter of sorts so that anyone anywhere can access magic or magical items as easily and safely as possible. But not everyone can wield magic deftly. It's a fickle thing. It can read each potential user like an open book. A lot of people resent that."

"Oh," she said, mulling over everything he'd given away.

"Only the Librarian can literally absorb the books. But everyone with the correct affinity can read and understand the information the books impart. They can all read them the way you were trying to initially." He grinned and motioned them over to the massive wooden desk she'd first seen yesterday.

Quinn climbed up into it because she had no idea what else she was supposed to say to a manifestation of the Library who almost died. Plus, she really needed to absorb everything she'd heard. That the Library was so integral to the existence of the universe was now firmly set in her mind.

She felt an odd twinge in her chest at the thought of losing something as magical as the Library, even if she'd only just found it. For some reason she felt closer to him, or more accurately, the Library, than anybody in the last several years since her parents died.

Clearing her throat, she looked around the area. There was clearly enough room for several people at the check-in desk. "Anyway, what am I supposed to do?"

"Place your hands on the console," he said, a small, smug smile emerging on his face.

"Oh." She looked over the desk properly this time. There was nothing like a computer screen or anything that she would have expected from her earthen days. However, there was a definite shiny surface with indentations right near the front of it. She placed the heel of her hands in those marks and spread out her fingers, feeling the cool and smooth sensations of granite beneath her.

Suddenly a strange whirring sound echoed through her ears. Her headache seemed to recede into the very background of her being while something bigger than her took over.

A screen flickered to life in front of her, not just in her vision, but actually in front of her and sort of accentuated by what she was seeing. She knew instinctually that somebody else wouldn't see this screen the way that she did because it was connected to her. It ran through her and she could feel the way the energy thrummed inside of her. It made her flesh tingle in an extremely odd sensation that was neither pleasant nor unpleasant.

It just was.

As if a power current was running through her body at low voltage.

Words flashed across the screen and through her head, and she knew unconsciously that these words would only make sense to her or to anybody whom she relinquished some form of control over it to. Anyone else would see gibberish.

Library system initialization complete.

Library system reboot?

Yes or *No.*

"I guess we're hitting yes," she mumbled under her breath, but even as she reached out to touch the area the words were in, it was already activated. All she had to do was think toward it.

Suddenly a bright light swept throughout the Library. It ran from the screen like a scanning beacon all the way up and over and then back through the rest of the Library.

The red light seeped into the pores of everything, including herself. It felt hot and invasive.

It happened so fast that she only blinked twice before the screen alerted her anew.

Library system complete: emergency low power mode.

Records synchronizing.

Borrowing ledgers synchronizing.

Staff synchronizing.

Librarian designation: Quinn, h-human, Librarian, 19 years. Ability access: one skill. Magical affinity: 99.99998% compatible. Highest compatibility probability. Access to all library features including:

One Links A542 Edition Category F manifestation. Links activated - Duration Infinite. Full mode on. Access Infinite Library Archives.

Resources synchronizing

...

...

Error

Error

Error

Division Branches sealed. All Secondary Branches sealed.

Main branch lacks assignments.

Incomplete book retrieval

Incomplete bookworm rejuvenation chambers. Status: remnants

Night owl status: Hibernation

Silverfish status: Lost

Compatibility with System: Librarian Override Permitted

Golem status: Zero

Helper status : Zero

Furniture status: Analysis underway

Assessment Protocol Enabled...

Result: Dregs of Power, Resources, and Inventory.

Assessment: Assigning relevant duties

New missions generated:

1. reinstate bookworms

2. reinstate night owls

3. recover silverfish

4. produce replacement tomes

5. produce new magic tomes

Number one priority: *retrieve overdue library books*

Current count: missing 18042

Retrieval listing in order of importance. Books must be recovered or balance is lost.

Quinn blinked at the words scrolling in front of her. They spoke in her head at the same time, in a sort of almost robotic, lilting voice. Like it was trying to lull her into a false sense of security.

But of all of those words echoing through her head, ringing in her ears, eighteen thousand and forty-two was the loudest.

"What does this mean, Lynx?" she asked, still processing the fact that the Library itself was very computer-like, even if it wasn't technically chips and wires.

She glanced over at Lynx who hadn't answered. He seemed to be practically vibrating on the spot. He appeared more solid than he'd ever been before, and there was a new light to him, like life had literally been breathed back into him.

Lynx turned to her, that abnormally wide grin spread over his face again. "The Library has been closed out of necessity. No one got to return their books before we had to close the doors. There are so many overdue books out there. When the Library was functioning at peak capacity, we had thousands of visitors a day. Hundreds of thousands sometimes, depending on what was going on." There was a hint of pride in Lynx's voice.

But Quinn could only focus on numbers right now. "How would hundreds of thousands of people fit into this library?"

He glanced about with a vague air of surprise and gestured all around them. "Well, this part of the Library is the main branch, you see, and there are annexes and other branches. You know, like the one we found your sword text in. Usually, that hallway wouldn't be as narrow or as dank or as broken, and when the power returns, everything will begin to revitalize and rejuvenate. Then we'll have to retrieve the books that we need to unlock the other divisions and branches. I mean, you get it right? It's a whole thing."

Quinn put her hands on her hips and looked away from the heads-up display in front of her. "No, Lynx, actually, I do not get this. You're saying this is just a small portion of the Library?"

"Yes, this is the magical portion of the Library. The one that contains the actual magical codices, tomes and whatnot." He laughed, and it was such a refreshing sound.

"So, there are other divisions of the branches—I know this—and they will expand and have more information than just the beginning books like this one does." Every time Quinn thought she was starting to get a handle on this whole "magical library kidnapped me and pulled me into another world" sort of thing, something else came up.

"You are the Librarian." Lynx turned to her, all his smiles gone, a serious air about him. "It's your *job* to retrieve all of the tomes, codices, and other books. Those from this section that contain magic knowledge themselves. Right through to alchemical texts, horticultural guidelines, culinary books, musical instruments and texts, and even magical weapons that were borrowed and not returned before the closure. And that's just the tip of the iceberg, as you'd say!"

"Oh great," Quinn said dryly, heavy sarcasm leaking into her tone. He was far too excited about all the work ahead of them or ahead of her as it seemed. "All I have to do is go out and tell people to kindly give me back the Library items they've borrowed and we can reopen everything?"

"Well." Lynx grinned. "It's a little more complex than that."

"Isn't everything here?" Quinn muttered.

Suddenly, the console beeped in a long, drawn-out tone, interrupting their discussion.

Tome Retrieval Importance Listing:

Dire: *Must be recovered within the specified timeline to enforce actual recovery of all Library Systems.*

DeKarlyle's Thesis of Spatial Distortion

Mantis Leaf's Advanced Combat Strategy

Tarlegish's Dichotomy of Herbal Evolution

Quinn glanced at it and could practically feel the blood draining from her face.

Time remaining for retrieval completion:
71 hours, 59 Minutes, 50 Seconds.

13

TIMING

THE COUNTDOWN TIMER STEADILY COUNTED DOWN. QUINN GULPED and felt panic rising in her gut as she stared at it. She pointed at it, knowing for a fact that Lynx could see it too since he was the actual Library incarnate.

"Why is there a timer that makes no sense whatsoever?" She was very proud of how steady she managed to keep her voice even if it was slightly squeaky.

Lynx focused on the timer, giving no outward indication of his state of mood, and shrugged. "I mean, it's pretty self-explanatory to me. You have less than seventy-two hours to retrieve those three items so that the Library can recover strength."

"Why are you emphasizing you as in me?" she asked suspiciously.

"Because I can't very well go with you to do this. I'm only just gaining my equilibrium back, and there is far too much for me to do. Power needs to be allocated efficiently and precisely, and that doesn't include enabling me corporeal form strong enough to leave the Library right now in its time of need."

Quinn held up a hand to belay any further words from Lynx. "Releasing all of that magic from the worms back into the Library's atmosphere significantly replenished some of the very drained reserves. Am I correct?"

"Yes. I really appreciate you doing that—"

She didn't let him get any further. "I'm so glad you're appreciative. How about I take that with me when I'm getting myself mauled by whatever's out there while I try to retrieve your books?" Quinn was doing her best to keep her tone even, but she didn't think she was successful.

"That was a huge help," Lynx began, but balked slightly when he really examined her face. "I mean, you've already done so much…"

It was very obvious by this point that Lynx had no idea how to speak to someone he'd just dropped into the thick of it. His eyes took on a brief distance again before he cleared his throat and spoke again.

"I cannot yet leave the confines of the Library. I require certain magical levels to be reached in order to maintain any sort of corporeal form outside of its direct influence. And right now, some of the more intricate systems are still rebooting. I'm sorry. I truly can't do anything about this."

His tone was soft and somewhat contrite like he actually meant each word he was saying.

"I get that. But… you could have at least let me eat before you made me reboot the damn Library. Now we have a huge time crunch. I need a shower to decrust my hair. I need to eat. All of that's going to diminish the time we have left to find the books. This is not okay, Lynx." She fixed him with her most withering gaze, almost wishing it worked.

Instead, he just squirmed uncomfortably. Another very human gesture on his behalf.

Quinn glared at him briefly, resigned to the fact that she'd likely only extended her own life a few days because she was almost completely certain she'd die on this book hunt. But, what was she going to do? Go curl up in a corner and wait to die anyway because the Library would end up shutting down after all?

She sighed and pushed some stray strands of hair out of her face.

"None of us, including myself, would be alive if you hadn't stepped in with the machete, so maybe I can give you a small pass for now."

"Thank you," he said, his voice sounding more subdued than he'd been earlier. "I should be able to find some things to help you on your journey."

There was a pause, and it was pretty somber and filled with what-ifs. Only then did Quinn realize quite how close she'd come to just not existing anymore while battling the worms. It was a sobering thought, and it drove a need in her, a need to discover more about the Library, to understand what she was going to be doing here and to find more power. Because just knowing how to wield a sword wasn't enough.

If she was going to cut it in this strange magical world, she needed more power, and she literally had it all at her fingertips. What could possibly be better than that?

"Bear with me here. The crux is: I need to go and retrieve like eighteen thousand books?" she asked a little incredulously yet suddenly resigned to the fact. "Starting with these three that seem to be hugely important?"

"Putting it simply, yes." He still seemed extremely apologetic.

The timer continued to count down.

She squinted at Lynx. "How about you put it not so simply, then? Also, why an arbitrary three days?"

Lynx hesitated for a brief second before obviously deciding against holding anything back for now. "Because the Library currently has the right levels of power to reabsorb and categorize those books. If it falls too low on power, then even if we get those books back, we will have to revitalize the Library more before we can actually use them to their full extent. And that's going to take a lot longer than it would if we can specifically get those three books in time. Without them, the odds of getting the Library back to its full potential becomes close to impossible."

"That's all you had to say, you know?" She frowned. Her shoulder was still sore, but her hand felt fine when she made a fist. Her scalp felt ever so itchy. Then a thought hit her. "Okay, so the three books are our key. Like starting the ignition? Are we going to tidy this place, or maybe you could get started while I go get your books?"

"Of course! This place is a wreck right now. Once we've got the books back we'll be able to reinstate some golems." He paused as he accessed other information. "Then we can take care of the book-worms that didn't get engorged and put them back in working order, and the night owls, and find silverfish, and..."

"Wait," Quinn interrupted him. "Golems?"

"We can make golems to help us with shelving and sorting and cleaning and assisting visitors." He blinked at her, his reptilian eyes somewhat disconcerting as they flickered. "Oh. Golems aren't a thing in your world. Sorry. They are pretty useful here, and we'll be able to get one of the supervisors as well. But..."

"Books back first. Priorities. I've got it." Quinn sighed, and her stomach rumbled again. She groaned, not wanting to bother with the stew yet. Instead, she pushed on. "I don't understand any of the other things you said either. Why do we need night owls, and silverfish, and bookworms, and whatever you just said? What does all that have to do with anything?"

"You need those three things in order to create new magical tomes." He said it in such a way that Quinn almost felt inferior for not knowing.

She shook her head to clear those thoughts. "We can create our own magic?"

"Of course! Magic evolves all the time. What did you think happened? That there are just a finite amount of spells and that nobody ever experiments and comes up with new stuff? That's just ludicrous, Quinn." He actually laughed.

"Do you know what, until two days ago, would have been ludi-crous, Lynx?" Quinn said, and didn't wait for him to respond, sort of ticked off by his attitude. She gestured all around them. "This. All of this. Magic and everything. This isn't real in my world. So I am sorry if I need things to be spelled out a little bit more clearly for me."

"Ouch. I was being insufferable, wasn't I?" Lynx asked, looking a little uncomfortable with himself.

"Yes, I believe you were being what we would have called a jerk in my world." She crossed her arms and fixed him with a glare, her temper only mildly subdued.

"Sorry, this has been duly noted, and I will do my best to not be an insufferable jerk anymore." He actually sounded sincere.

"I'm gonna hold you to that," Quinn said. "Now, I guess I have to go get books. But what if someone wants to return the books they borrowed a while ago, or even if someone wants to borrow a book now? How will people know that the Library is here? How will they know it's active again?"

"Well, that's pretty easy. Anybody who wants access to the Library can gain access to the Library, as long as they're aware of the Library. This means that anybody who's aware of magic and has a magical signature—which is most people, by the way. Your world is a more unique one."

"Lynx, don't tangent." Quinn suppressed a sigh at having to redirect him.

"Yes. Good idea," he said without missing a beat. "Anyway, most beings will be aware of the Library. And so, any of them can come back or come and borrow books. However, we can also lock the Library to all or specific entrants at any given time, which we'll have to do once it's open since we won't be fully operational yet. It's proven quite useful in such cases of plague, or even like this where we didn't know who was friend or foe. The unsealing of other sections can wait. We need to get the main branch online first, tidy up, and fix everything before actually opening to the public."

"Why did it unlock just before, then?" She glanced toward the doors about thirty feet away, expecting them to spring open at any moment.

The timer in the corner of her vision ticked down ominously. Quinn shuddered.

Lynx shrugged. "I needed to briefly scan outside of the Library in order to get approximate locations for all of the tomes and books it's missing. Usually, the system would just tap into and search from the leyline standpoints, but right now they're down to the dregs and magic just hasn't been working properly for the last few hundred years."

"Makes sense," Quinn said, not thinking it made any sense at all. Magic was going to take some getting used to. She turned to the console and studied it again. "Finding the books that can return the Library to its former glory is our number one goal, right?"

"No choice, really. I analyzed the content we have here, and nothing that fits the initial power markers we need to address is left here. I can't process what is necessary without those books..." Lynx frowned as his voice trailed off.

"What's wrong?" Quinn knew something had to be out of the ordinary or he wouldn't be making that expression.

"Just that *DeKarlyle's Thesis of Spatial Distortion* will be tricky to retrieve. Kajaro can be very... difficult when he wants to be. Pretentious might be a better word. He's determined to crack space-and-time distortion and he'll stop at nothing to achieve it. While it appears he still hasn't broken through that barrier in our absence, I'm unsure he's going to want to give the tome back. Not to mention, he's never been the greatest fan of the Library."

A flutter of nerves assaulted Quinn. She didn't like the sound of that. But there was more to focus on. "The other two books though? Like I can probably pop in and go, 'Hi! I'm the new Librarian. Give me your four-hundred-and-sixty-year-old overdue Library book back and I'll waive the fee if it happens in the next sixty seconds?'" She could hope, right?

Lynx actually chuckled. "No, that's probably not the best way to go about it, but they'd likely get a laugh out of it. And if you're going threaten a fee or fine, you'll have to already have it in mind."

"Shouldn't I charge fines for these ones? If the Library's been closed, it was hardly other people's fault they haven't returned the books, right?" It made sense to Quinn, but she was talking to a Library manifestation. Perhaps Lynx felt different.

He shook his head. "I'm not saying that. What I'm saying is that you need to know what you're going to charge ahead of time. Or at least have a couple of options available. For right now, anyway. As we power up, the Library connection to you will increase to the extent that it'll give you options in the field and then you won't have to come up with them yourself. Frankly, sometimes power-hungry people with grey motivations need harsher punishment for harming a tome than those who are genuine."

"Great." *Because that's not cryptic or totally subjective at all,* she thought but didn't add. "So we should probably lock the doors from entrants until we have the Library back in some sort of working order, right?"

"Wait. I was sure I already did that." Lynx surveyed the Library beyond the desk. He cringed slightly and nodded. "Why didn't it work for me? Damn it, we have to lock them. At least until we get it tidied and have a larger energy reserve. Opening dimensional doorways isn't cheap on the energy. I doubt many people are paying enough attention to the tomes they have from us that they'll notice the Library is back online."

"Will the borrowers still be alive?" she blurted out, the sudden thought hitting her. Her scalp felt like it had dirt trying to burrow into it. She needed that shower now.

Lynx shrugged. "Most of them should be. Hopefully the others have been passed down. A Library book from the Library of Everywhere is quite special no matter what the subject matter is."

Quinn nodded. How had potentially immortal beings become a part of her daily conversation? She breathed out a long breath to calm herself and then looked back at the console with its larger-than-life list still unwavering front and center. "Do I just direct my thoughts to set a lock on the door? How does that work?"

"Right. If you want to interface with the interface..." Lynx laughed at his own joke, then continued, "Anyway, sorry. If you want to interface with the interface, you just need to direct your thoughts directly through the heels of your hands into the console as you are making contact with it. Eventually, as your power grows and as the Library becomes more synchronized with you, you'll just be able to send it a thought regardless of contact."

That sounded much more convenient to Quinn, but she obliged Lynx by waiting for him to finish his train of thought.

"Actually"—the manifestation paused—"let's double check the location of each book and lock them onto a mapping device you can take with you. It won't take long."

"Long enough for me to shower and eat before I head out?" Quinn asked. The timer in the corner of her vision refused to go away no matter how much she tried to dismiss it. And it was very loudly proclaiming she'd already lost a quarter of an hour.

"Sure, sure." He rummaged through several of the drawers, pulling out papers, strange devices that Quinn hoped he wasn't breaking, and a plethora of pens and quills, feathers, and ink pots. They were definitely going to have to reorganize a lot more than just the books.

This place was an administration nightmare.

"Aha!" he proclaimed, pulling out what looked a little bit like an e-reader or phone even. It was about three inches by four inches if Quinn had to hazard a guess, and fit snugly into Lynx's hand. Its screen lit up like it was backlit, and as she looked on, a map began to appear.

"That's strange," Lynx muttered, a frown appearing on his face along with a raising of his eyebrows. A slight power fluctuation ran through is body, giving it a rippling of purple effect. "Very odd."

Quinn didn't think she'd heard him sound surprised before, and she wasn't sure she wanted to know what could surprise a sentient Library manifestation. "What is it?" she asked, against her better judgment.

He paused a moment and then looked up, still frowning as he positioned himself in multiple places around the check-in area as if he was trying to get better reception. "Well, it seems that one of the books is approaching us."

And that's as far as Lynx got because the doors swung open on creaky hinges before bashing into the walls in a way that made Quinn cringe. She added general maintenance for everything to her list of things they needed to fix. After a second, through the blinding brightness that the doors let in, a solitary figure strode in.

They stood at least seven feet tall and were broad of shoulder, with long hair swaying in a light breeze, and beautifully sculpted pointy ears.

"It's about goddamn time," they said. "Where in the universe have you been? You better not even attempt to charge me overdue fees when I've been trying to summon the Library and return this damn tome for the last four hundred and fifty years!"

14

VISITOR

As the light from the open door receded, it left an extremely tall man with long blonde hair and pointy ears standing in its wake. It was all Quinn could do to suppress a gasp.

Instead, she gaped at him.

He was, for all intents and purposes, an elf.

A ridgy-didge, corporeal, in-the-flesh elf.

Up until that moment, she'd thought, maybe this was all an elaborate ruse, or an intricate prank, or something. Maybe there was just a small part of her that thought she could still be dreaming despite the resounding bruises that pinching herself resulted in.

But no, this man was indeed the mystical creature, the mystical species, an elf.

And he looked pretty irritated.

Lynx managed to get over himself first. "Oh, Milaro, I—how did you—" His eyes flickered for a moment before he glanced over at Quinn. She could practically feel the panic rolling off him. "You need to direct the Library to lockdown doors now."

Quinn thought at the console, keeping her heels centered on it. There was an audible click that echoed throughout the entire structure, and Milaro cocked an eyebrow. "You're locking me in with you. You know I could interpret that as an act of war, right?"

Lynx glanced around again, heaved a sigh of relief, and finally answered. "Stop being difficult. We're really not operational yet."

"What do you mean, not operational?" Milaro said, obviously annoyed. "I have been trying to return this book for the last four hundred fifty-two years. I've checked every single year on its due date since it became due just in case the book didn't tell me when you reopened. You just disappeared. No notice, no notifications, and no announcements. That wasn't part of the plan Lynx. You simply vanished. You weren't supposed to do that, you know."

Lynx took a deep breath, which was comical since Quinn knew that he didn't actually need to breathe, and let it out in a sign of exaggerated patience. "I know the Library was never supposed to close. But dire circumstances required immediate action to preserve what we could. We lost our Librarian and with her, a lot of magical power. I had to take drastic measures to maintain some form of equilibrium in the mana distribution until I could solve the problem."

Milaro cocked his head to one side and took a few steps closer to the checkout desk. His face had paled a shade, and he frowned. "So you shut the Library down, without a word to anyone, in order to preserve magic because you lost your anchor?"

"Pretty much. There was nothing left. We tried everything we could until we ran out of time. Every person, every Librarian, every assistant librarian, every potential librarian. Even the council. You know that. Everyone who had even a fifty-percent compatible magical signature with me was gone." It was the first time Quinn noticed just how vulnerable Lynx was. There was a transparency to his mood, not just to his visage, which had mostly solidified after the bookworms were defeated.

Milaro took the final few steps to the checkout counter and placed a massively huge tome down on the desk. He was tall enough that his elbows reached the desk quite comfortably, and he didn't have to stand on anything to do so. Leaning forward, he locked his gaze onto

Lynx. "Okay, well, I'm returning *Mantis Leaf's Advanced Combat Strategy* to you right now. Do I face a fine?"

Lynx shook his head. "No, no. I appreciate that you have been trying to return the book for so long. Quinn?"

She stopped gaping at the elf long enough to remove one of her hands and pick up the book.

Return Mantis Leaf's Advanced Combat Strategy to the Collection:
Yes. No. Extend Borrow.

With a simple thought of yes, the words flashed away.

The time reset to seventy-two hours remaining. Quinn let out a small sigh of relief even as she directed the thought a flood of power washed through her like an awakening, as if the sun shone on her and energized her with its rays.

"Whoa," she said, looking up at first at Milaro and then at Lynx.

They stared back at her. Lynx blankly, and the elf with wry amusement.

"You didn't tell me that was going to happen every time I picked up a book," she said somewhat defensively, suddenly feeling completely and utterly rejuvenated.

"The Library is hungry right now. I can't tell you everything at once. There's too much to know. That's why the guide was supposed to download for you," Lynx grumbled, without making eye contact.

Two could play the grumbling game. "You're not kidding. You've been telling me nothing. How's that guide coming?" Quinn shot back at him, raring for a fight she could pour all of her frustration into.

"It's getting…" But that's all he got to say.

Milaro cleared his throat, interrupting Lynx. "Is that everything you need from me?" There was a strange heaviness to that statement Quinn couldn't discern.

"That's more than enough right now," Lynx said.

And then the elf peered at Quinn and caressed his chin with his hand. "You are not from one of our usual worlds. How do you have magic?"

Quinn suddenly felt very self-conscious at his examination. Like he could look into her soul.

"Well," Lynx butted in. "I reached as far as I could go with as much energy as I could spare. No one with a compatible enough energy signature exists in our usual realms. I may have been rather desperate to find someone. I managed to pull her here with the last of my energy reserves."

"With the last energy reserves? It was that bad?" Milaro said, the horror plain on his face. "What if it had gone wrong?"

"Well, it didn't," Lynx snapped. "And it was the only choice I had left."

A brief look of confusion spread over Milaro's face. "I could have brought the book back. It would have given you—"

Lynx cut him off, patient no longer. "No, *you* don't understand how little was left. I didn't have the capacity to reabsorb book magic anyway. I searched for hundreds of years. There were no Librarians. How am I supposed to do everything without a Librarian?"

This time, Milaro turned and looked at Quinn with far more interest than he'd initially shown her. "So, then, you are the Librarian. The only one we could find," he said, pausing as if mulling over something of great importance, his gaze intense. "And it's just you, only you and Lynx?"

"And me," cried out Dottie, startling Quinn. She hadn't realized that Dottie was anywhere near them. She filed that away for future reference because apparently, all the furniture were ninjas. Which didn't bode well for being able to sneak around with anything.

"Yes, I'm the only corporeal person here. Except for you, who are a Library patron and has just returned a book," Quinn replied, rambling a bit. He was a damned elf!

He chuckled. "Yes, I'm very well aware of what I am. Thank you. Would you like some help?"

Lynx spluttered and then leaned closer. "I can't ask you specifically to come and help the Library when that help currently requires an inordinate amount of heavy lifting." In direct juxtaposition to his words, he seemed eager for aid.

"I wasn't thinking about myself," Milaro said, waving the idea away and studying Quinn again. "No, I was thinking my grandson would be an excellent fit to come and help you clean up the Library. He's in need of some responsibility."

Lynx's eyes narrowed. "Grandson? Since when do you have a grandson, Milaro?"

The old elf chuckled, although he didn't look old. He looked maybe forty, and a very healthy forty at that. From his skin to his hair and the straight way he stood, it was difficult for Quinn to even contemplate that he was even a few hundred years old. Which he had to be, if he'd been waiting to return a book for the last few centuries.

"You have missed a lot in almost five hundred years, my friend," Milaro said. "Much can happen in that space of time. Things aren't what they once were. When you cut the Library off, you cut yourself off; you cut most of the magic off."

Lynx actually grew paler, and not in a transparent sort of way, but in an actual paler skin way, like he was shocked, maybe surprised, maybe even a little guilty.

"Magic isn't completely lost without me, and you know what the alternative would have been," the Library manifestation said very defensively.

"No, you are correct." Milaro inclined his head. "I apologize for my hasty words, but the wild magic doesn't sit as well with any of us. It's barely contained."

"It's not my fault," Lynx said, but there was a hint of desperation in those words now. "You have to understand that I had to shut down. Everything froze when I lost her. Nothing worked. The magic... I had to keep what power I could for myself until I could find a replacement."

"Korradine truly retired then?" Milaro asked, his voice full of disbelief.

Lynx nodded slowly, his eyes fixed on the floor in front of him. "She began retirement before we realized the true state of things. It's the one thing I can't reverse. Remember? She'd spent millennia serving the Library. She was done. And we didn't notice, we didn't notice how few were left, how few were available to be trained, until it was too late to undo. Everything went to shit because I wasn't paying enough attention."

Milaro crossed his arms, a thoughtful crease in his brow. "Back then, it was surprising, but now? That timing seems awfully convenient, don't you think?"

"Guys, look, I'm so happy to let long-lost friends catch up," Quinn cut in on the conversation she couldn't see coming to an end if she didn't. "But I just need to point out that I've got, like, seventy-one hours and change to find two books, or the Library's screwed again. Which, from your conversation, I'm pretty certain we don't want to happen. That whole magic returning thing seems important. If you lose it again, it's going to be even worse than it was before. Can we just table this discussion and you guys can talk while I'm searching for the lost books and probably getting myself killed in the process?"

There were a couple of seconds of silence, and then Milaro laughed. It was one of those mystical, booming laughs that filled the entire library and made her feel good about herself.

"I like you," Milaro said. "Yes, I think Malakai will be in good hands with you."

"Hey, mate." Quinn stopped him, holding up her hands. "I am not, and I repeat, not babysitting your grandson. I don't have time for this. I have work to do. I'd like to not die. Okay?"

Milaro shook his head, amusement dancing in his gaze. "No, my grandson is... I guess you'd call him a teenager yourself, although elves age a little differently. But he does not require babysitting as such. You may need to keep him on track, give him instructions or direction. He is, however, excellent and proficient with multiple weapons and thus, should be able to aid you quite a lot."

"Oh." Quinn thought that over, considering how not good with weapons she was so far. "Okay. Um. Well, when can he get here, then, because I have to get going like five minutes ago?"

Milaro smiled. "Oh, humans. Such short lifespans. Always, always in such a rush."

"Did you miss the part where I mentioned that I have seventy-one hours and change to retrieve two apparently very important books.

Unless your hours are different than my Earth hours? That being sixty minutes long, then I still don't think we have much time because apparently I have to travel quite a ways for the prize." She realized something suddenly. "Oh that book you returned was one of them. I should thank you."

Milaro nodded.

Quinn suddenly felt just a little less pressure. Even though she'd known only two books remained to retrieve, she hadn't quite registered that at least one was already taken care of. It was quite a welcome feeling considering her track record of being in the Library since she got there.

Even Lynx smiled. "You're right. We've got one of the books back already. We only need to retrieve two more."

"Quickly," Quinn said, crossing her arms. "I seem to remember a certain Library manifestation telling me that until he had more power, he couldn't personally come and help me. I would like to remind you that it is, in fact, just me going to get these books and perhaps taking this nice gentleman's grandson with me isn't the worst thing I could do."

She declined to wait on Lynx's response and turned to Milaro instead. "Are you sure I won't actually need to babysit him? He's, like, a full adult size, being and good at weapons. He'll actually be useful?"

"Well, that's debatable," Milaro said, laughing again. "But yes, Malakai is very gifted when it comes to combat arts."

"Great, so I'll go get that shower and some food while we wait for him." The time limit was one thing, but she wasn't going to go solo on a mission when she could barely flail with a wooden sword. May as well make use of the time.

Lynx held up a hand, wordlessly asking her to wait for a moment.

Milaro nodded in the direction of the tome he'd just returned. "We were in possession of one of the master tomes for a very long time. Some might say it gave us an unfair advantage. He is at least as proficient as I am in combat arts now. Frankly, given a century or two, I'm thinking he'll surpass me."

"Yes, yes. The Seveshall Combat bloodline. I get it. Stop bragging."

Then Lynx pinched the bridge of his nose in a surprisingly human gesture. "Who is saying you have an unfair advantage?"

"The Degrash Empire has never liked magic, my friend. You know that as well as I do." Milaro's tone shifted ever so slightly and the conversation took a darker turn.

Quinn could feel the difference to the air in the room immediately.

A heavy scent of sandalwood suddenly flooded the area just before light flashed through Lynx for a moment before he calmed back down. "If you could fetch your grandson, it would be appreciated. It seems we have much to discuss."

"That we do, old friend. That we do. He's on his way as we speak." Milaro nodded gravely, and Quinn suddenly felt cold.

Anger appeared to have gripped a hold of Lynx. He flickered, and a sudden chill filled the air. Then, just as soon as it appeared, it was gone. She watched the manifestation with some concern, wondering if there was anything truly big he was keeping from her.

15

ELVES!

IT SEEMED THAT ELVES DIDN'T OPERATE UNDER THE SAME SENSE OF urgency as humans did. Quinn drummed her fingers against the counter while she waited for Milaro's grandson to arrive, her damn and free-from-bookworm-guts hair tossed up in a messy ponytail.

It appeared that even in a magical world, her curls refused to all stay in the damned thing.

Milaro had assured her that Malakai was already on his way. But as the counter ticked down, Quinn couldn't help but think that he hadn't realized the gravity of the situation. She was growing impatient.

Despite having the time to browse through information the Library offered to her, she did so without fully understanding what she was seeing. Pages and pages about overdue books and items, their locations and who had borrowed them. It was surprisingly in-depth and vast.

She couldn't wrap her head around the number of magical books that had been borrowed. Nor the fact that she could apparently create new tomes.

They were going to have to get the bookworms sorted.

Still, finding two books didn't sound like a difficult task, but they weren't *in* the Library. She had to travel through who knew what dimensions or universes or however this damned library worked, and find two people—two different people—who had borrowed one book each.

One of which, from Lynx's mumblings, it seemed might be reluctant to relinquish his.

These books were integral to the continuation of the Library and, apparently, magic as everyone here knew it. While she didn't understand the how of the situation, Quinn did think the sense of urgency should have been apparent to everyone.

Especially because of the counter.

The countdown timer sat in the bottom right corner of her vision, just so she could very conveniently watch the time limit she'd been given by the Library tick down by the second. There was no avoiding it; she couldn't even relax and forget about it for an hour or two. Not even closing her eyes made it disappear. Somehow, it just glowed brighter. There was apparently no way to dismiss it.

Because she'd tried.

"*DeKarlyle's Thesis of Spatial Distortion*, and *Tarlegish's Dichotomy of Herbal Evolution*. Shouldn't be too hard to find those, right? I don't really need an elven guide for it. I can just go myself armed with a rusty machete," she muttered to herself, trying to psych herself up for the inevitable.

She could see Dottie skulking around off in the distance, probably trying valiantly to overhear what the other two were talking about. With any luck, the bench's guilt from earlier would extend to telling Quinn all about their conversation later. But right then, Quinn had other things to think about. Relying on other people always got her into trouble. In group assignments. At part-time jobs. The only person she could count on was herself.

About to step down from the check-in desk and make her way to the doors, hoping they worked with mental directions, Quinn turned when a gust of wind suddenly appeared in front of it. Though it was more like a mini tornado hovering directly in front of the desk. There was a thud, a mildly irritated exclamation, and when the wind was gone, an elf crouched in the spot.

Malakai was definitely not what Quinn had been expecting.

She'd assumed, and wrongly it seemed, that he would be a carbon copy of his grandfather.

Well, technically, she guessed he was a carbon copy because he was the exact opposite. His skin held a mildly lavender-bluish tone, and he had long ears, pitch-black eyes that even extended through the sclera, and white and black hair, sort of like a salt-and-pepper shaker mixed together.

He was tall, but not quite as tall as his grandfather, maybe six foot five, and his hair pulled back into a sharp braid. He brushed himself down and glanced around the Library, his gaze falling on Quinn.

It only took a moment for him to calibrate what he was seeing. "You must be the Librarian," he said. His voice was gentle, with a strange lilt to it, yet at the same time, Quinn was sure he could probably command the pants off someone. His doppelganger appeared to model for romance novels back on Earth.

She nodded, eyeing him up and down again. How was it that another elf was standing in front of her and not just in a movie? She didn't know.

This one? Well, he appeared to be maybe a dark elf? Or at least a different type of elf. What if his grandfather had multiple wives over millennia? It made her wonder how one would go about being married to the same soul for five hundred years?

Still, idle thoughts were unnecessary when she was on a time crunch. She gathered herself together and nodded at him. "Look, you're about two hours later than I would have liked, and we have places to be. I hope you're ready. We have to go."

He raised an eyebrow in her direction. "I'm not used to being told what to do by anybody other than my grandfather. You'll have to let me check in with him first."

Quinn raised an eyebrow. "Well, I'm the Librarian and he told you that you needed to come and help me, is that correct?"

Malakai frowned. "Well, of course, it's correct. I wouldn't be here if he hadn't sent for me."

"Exactly, he sent for you to help me so that magic continues to work or something. So you do what I tell you so we can all continue to live long and magical lives, how does that sound?" A little of that was sheer bravado but most of it was pure impatience.

Malakai blinked and she wondered if he'd truly never been directed by anyone other than his grandfather in his life. She could see it as a distinct possibility with the way he held himself. She took a deep breath and decided it wasn't his fault that all this shit sandwich had landed in her lap and therefore she should probably be just a little bit nicer.

"Look, I'm sorry," she said. She didn't really feel sorry, she felt harried but if she was going to spend time with this person for the next two days she needed to make the best of it. "I got pulled into a new world from my own and I'm still a little disoriented. Sort of tossing up whether this is a bizarre dream or not. We have to go and retrieve these books and I appreciate you coming with me."

Malakai cocked his head to one side and studied her this time. She had to admit it wasn't the most pleasant feeling being scanned up and down like she was a piece of meat but she couldn't tell him not to. She'd literally done the same thing when he first flickered into her vision, and she was pretty sure she'd gawked at him a little bit more than he was observing her.

Mainly because he was an elf and this wasn't a fantasy novel. She really needed to get over that.

"That's okay." He inclined his head and his features relaxed. "Apology accepted. I will do my best to take orders and work together. Does that sound acceptable?"

"Yeah," Quinn said, suddenly relieved. "It does. Thanks."

"Malakai, my boy," Milaro cut in as he strode over. The man had a massive stride. He made it there in next to no time, with Lynx following behind, a trepidatious expression on his face. "I'm glad you could make it. It took you a while longer than I anticipated."

"Grandfather," Malakai said by way of greeting, "I was in the middle of something." He flushed a little bit and Milaro snorted.

"Enough of that. You can take part in your hobbies on time that is your own. You came to me for training. You will help Quinn. You will help the Library become whole. That is your task until I say otherwise. Do you understand?" Milaro's tone brooked no argument.

His grandson, however, apparently didn't get the no argument memo. "Wait, what? I'm not just going for a couple of days to help her get the stuff back that she needs?" Malakai crossed his arms, and his stance became rigid.

"No, no you're not. You are to stay here, at least for a while." The taller elf glanced over at Lynx, a brief crease appearing between his brows. "I have discussed it with Lynx. The Library will require more than one set of hands, and Quinn will have hers full."

"But that wasn't the deal. That's not what I'm supposed to be learning." Malakai appeared to be pouting.

Milaro, however, didn't appear to appreciate his grandson's mood. "You've been learning the art of combat for the past fifteen years. I believe it's time you put it to practical use."

Except Quinn could see that Malakai thought it was anything but fine. She only hoped it wasn't going to affect the tentative cooperation they'd been building since he floated into the Library.

Several seconds of complete and utter silence passed between the two elves. That's when Quinn realized they were probably using telepathy to speak to each other. After all, how else, other than magic or mind magic, had the grandfather contacted his grandson in the first place? That thought grabbed her brain and ran with it.

Magic abilities were paramount. Super important, even. She couldn't go out there like this.

"Hold on," she said suddenly, turning to Lynx as panic began to swell in her gut. "We can't go yet, Lynx. You can't send me out there with just basic knowledge of how to hold a wooden bloody sword. Why have I been sitting here waiting when I could have been learning? I need to know how to defend myself, how to protect myself. I might have Malakai with me, but there is no telling what we'll be up against. Right? You told me this was dangerous."

Lynx sparked for a second and took a step back. "I didn't... that's a good point. Okay, follow me. We'll leave these two to discuss whatever it is they need to discuss about this trip."

As they walked away, Quinn mumbled under her breath in Lynx's direction, "I think they're already talking about it, you know, like mind to mind."

Lynx had the grace to smile. "Well, you realize the more you learn, you'll be able to do that with me as well, right? The Library has a connection to you. You established it when you activated the core. We've already experienced some level of it when you think at me. We just need to get you and the Library a little bit more power."

"Isn't that what we've been trying to do all along?" Quinn asked.

Lynx laughed. "Yes, you're right. I don't know why I didn't think to have you absorb tomes before Malakai arrived. I apologize. I'm multitasking a lot right now."

"Well, we're doing it before I go out and get myself potentially killed, so I'll forgive you just this once."

"Great. How about we go get you some of the books you'll need? I'll get you..." He studied her for a moment, a thoughtful look on his face as his eyes switched back and forth through so many different colors. The irises closed over each other, whipping from side to side.

She could get lost in those; they were fascinating.

"All right, then," he said. "Okay, I think I have a good start. We're going to get you *Beginner Shielding, Machetes for Dummies...*"

"Seriously?" she interrupted him. "*Machetes for Dummies*? That's... there's literally a book called that?"

"Well, you seemed partial to the machete, so I figured we'd get you some more skills with it." He didn't seem to understand what she was asking.

"No, I meant the name of the book." Quinn was desperately fighting not to laugh. That was a particularly well-known type of help book for anything and everything back where she came from.

"Well, yes. It's hoping that you don't cut your fingers off like a dummy. Does that not make sense?" It seemed Lynx had no idea about the correlation.

"It's okay, don't worry, carry on. What else?"

"Poison or Just Disgusting."

"That's the name of a book?" Quinn bit out, trying not to laugh again.

"Well, yes. You know, you've got to get beginners to be interested in stuff. If you get them interested in it by starting with a book that is at least, you know, marginally entertaining in its name, then you can often get people interested enough to expand their knowledge base." Lynx paused for a moment, grabbing another book from a shelf. "It's all about the dynamics of knowledge and the magical power it contains."

"That tracks. That really tracks," Quinn said, mulling it over in her mind. "Okay, I'm sorry, keep going."

"Bright Light Starters is another one. It's going to let you produce light at differing levels when you might be caught in darkness or you may need a really quick fire starter. Let me think. Okay, *Blink and I'm Gone."*

That was a confusing title. Quinn double checked it. *"Blink and You're Gone?"*

"No. It's *I'm Gone,* not *You're Gone.* It's not quite right, though, is it?" He frowned, as if he'd only just got it. "Anyway, it's being able to camouflage yourself with your surroundings so that, in fact, the person blinks and then you appear to have disappeared." His explanation didn't make it any less confusing.

"Oh, I thought it was gonna teleport me away from where whoever I'm escaping from was." Quinn thought this book might have the worst title ever.

Lynx pondered that for a second. "That makes a certain amount of sense too. Like a blink step, you mean?"

"Sort of, I guess. I think I've played too many video games." Quinn shrugged.

"You're going to have to explain to me the appeal of those video games your world likes so much." Lynx continued to peruse the shelves in the next section.

Quinn couldn't help but notice how many of the shelves were empty, with not even dust in place thanks to the bookworms.

Lynx finally paused and pursed his lips before grabbing for another book. "Okay, and then I think we'll do one more. *Watch Out for That Tree.*"

Quinn actually laughed at that one. "*Watch Out for That Tree?* What is it, speedrunning through a jungle?"

"No, no, that would be the *Speedrunning 101* book," he answered without truly paying attention to her.

"There's a speedrunning book?" Quinn asked incredulously.

"Of course there is. There are books for everything." Lynx finally looked at her and winked. "Just you wait. Anyway, the *Watch Out for That Tree* is actually a minor teleportation one. Sort of a blink step like you were thinking earlier. It really wants to make really sure you don't teleport into solid objects because that's something you just don't come back from."

Quinn shuddered at the thought. "Yeah, I can see landing inside any object, including a tree, would be a life-ending decision."

What had she gotten herself into? Quinn could feel her body practically vibrating, and it wasn't excitement, it was nerves. She was a little bit scared. This world, this magic, it was all so... so much.

"Okay, give me some of those books," she said and took a few off Lynx, who was using his ability to solidify himself a lot more frequently right now. "Doesn't maintaining corporeal form take energy away from the Library?"

"I'm not holding it forever. It's fleeting in the grand scheme of things. Once we've restored the core to critical low power mode instead of emergency, things will run much smoother." He hadn't exactly answered her question, but it was enough. He gestured toward the middle seating area as he walked. "We're going to sit down over there, and you're going to absorb the books the same way you absorbed the *Beginner Sword Fighting* one."

"Okay," Quinn said. She walked over and patted the couch tentatively.

It's like Lynx knew what she was thinking. "It's okay, Quinn. It's not like Dottie."

"Oh, sorry. I just... I didn't... I didn't want to make it angry."

Lynx smiled. "Yeah, Dottie teaches everybody that."

"Well, okay, then," Quinn said, and positioned herself on the couch in a cross-legged position. She took *Beginners Shielding* into her hands and spread it on her lap, just like she'd been taught. Placing one palm on each side of the book, she let her fingers splay over the pages and took a deep breath.

Suddenly, an onslaught of power rang through her, threatening for just a second to tear her apart.

1 6

LEARNING CURVE

QUINN WAS CERTAIN SHE SCREAMED AS PAIN RIPPED THROUGH HER. AND not just in her head. But a full throated, audible scream. Much like the one she'd made when she'd first connected to the core.

Ironically, beginner's shielding didn't seem to be protecting her at all in that instant. The pain extended to every single nerve she was aware of, and many that she didn't know existed. It felt as though it bled through her body, her blood vessels, and into her very bones. There was a sharp jolt that ran through her system.

And, then, everything was gone.

She blinked her eyes open to find herself sitting on the same couch, cross-legged, with her hands still splayed on each side of the book. The only change to her posture was that her head was leaning back against the couch. As she moved her head forward, a tear dropped onto the page. She raised her hand, wiping it away.

"That *hurt*. Can you warn me next time?" she said to Lynx, her voice cracking ever so slightly.

"Damn it. I'm sorry. I thought you'd remember the reaction from the sword book and would realize that there was always going to be something. I apologize." He didn't sound contrite at all.

"It's okay," she said, even though it really wasn't. But it had to be, and frankly, she realized she was mostly fine. Her body wasn't sore at all. It didn't leave a lingering trace of anything. Right there, beneath the surface, she felt stronger, like perhaps it had reinforced her. Not a shield as such, but that her body had more durability now.

"What exactly did this book do for me?" she asked, as she tried to feel out the differences apparent inside her. They were so subtle.

"Maybe you should have read the, like, blurb on the back first." He seemed to joke, but realized she wasn't smiling and continued more seriously. "It enhances your skeletal structure. You'll be able to find it in your interface as a simple reinforcement switch so to speak. It'll let you know how to think to activate your outer shield. You just need to think 'activate shielding' when you want to initialize the protection."

She glanced at him like he was speaking a different language. Which, in a way, he was. She pulled up her interface but all it had on it was:

Body Shielding - On

And that wasn't helpful at all.

Lynx paused before continuing, as if reassessing how to explain things. "It won't drain much of your energy just to keep it active constantly actually. Doing that might build up your proficiency with it too. You can sort out any specific mental commands within yourself. It's very basic, beginner-level stuff. It'll make your bones tougher, and you'll take less damage as long as you activate the shield before the incoming damage hits you. Only when it fends off damage will it use energy. That's pretty much it," Lynx said, somewhat flustered by the end.

Maybe he hadn't expected her to scream so loudly.

The elves, it seemed, didn't care. They were still locked in some sort of silent mental battle of wits.

Anyway, she took a deep breath, closed the book, and picked up the next one, *Machetes for Dummies*.

"Is this one going to cut me?" she asked, eyeing it suspiciously.

"Oh, no. It's going to do the same thing the sword book did. It'll rush through you, make you feel a little, tweak your knowledge about how to utilize some different muscles, and imprint the theory behind wielding a machete in combat." He sounded like it was all just matter-of-fact.

"Great," she said, splayed the book open, put her hands on the pages, and *whoosh*, the information entered her brain. The sensations were slightly different from the sword book and far less painful than the shielding one. It felt like her brain was expanding, firing on all these different wavelengths with knowledge immediately accessible. Now she just *knew* things. If studying had been this easy in university, life would have been so much easier.

She sighed and cracked her neck from side to side, suddenly a little stiff. Closing the machete book, she opened the next with some hesitation.

"Hey, Lynx, *Poison or Just Disgusting*? Am I going to taste this book? Is it going to poison me to give me poison immunity? What's this one going to do?" Her gut was telling her this was definitely not a book she should take lightly. The pungent odor that wafted about the pages seemed to reinforce that fact.

"Oh, well, yes. This one is just the first step. It'll slowly help you start to build up an immunity to poisons." Lynx shrugged, like it was all self-explanatory.

"So it's going to train me to build up immunity over several years or books or whatever so that most poisons just don't work on me?" It sounded good, if she wasn't sure she'd also have to go through some measure of withdrawals while becoming accustomed to those poisons. Even if it was magically enabling or something.

Lynx narrowed his eyes and repeated himself slowly. "Like I said, that's pretty much what it's going to do. For the common and specific poisons it mentions, anyway."

"That's a little too much wiggle room for me. I'm going to keep this one for after I get back from the death-defying mission that I need to go on to retrieve books." She put it to the side and picked up the next one. "Building up immunity to poisons is something I don't want to risk right now in case of a bad side effect."

And, you know, poison, she thought, but kept to herself.

"*Bright Light Starter* it is," she said, ignoring Lynx's wide eyes as he realized she was probably right about the poison book.

She placed her hands in the correct positions again and closed her eyes. The information flooded her mind with warmth. It suffused her entire body, heating her up from the inside like a delicious chicken-soup did when she was sick. The feeling was bright and airy, like a spark in her soul.

She closed the book. "I liked that one a lot better." She clicked her fingers, and a tiny spark of flame emerged for just a moment before it went out. She'd need a lot more practice, but she could already see the benefits.

"Be careful of that around books" was all Lynx said, his voice sounding slightly strangled while he handed her the next one.

"Well, that's obvious. That's the fire starter. I liked that one. I can work with it." She had to push aside the part of her that was sincerely squealing with excitement at having done actual magic with a click of her fingers.

"Next up. *Blink and I'm Gone*." This one rushed into her like a cool whirl of wind, and then the sensation was gone. It felt far more subtle than the previous ones. It was just an ability to fade into the background.

There'd been a television show she used to love that always made a joke about this girl who nobody ever remembered, even though she was there and she tried her hardest all the time. And that's the sensation this lent to her when she called it up. Blending, fading into the background so that people don't remember you. They don't remember seeing you. That was going to come in handy.

"Are you feeling okay?" Lynx asked, his tone serious.

"Yeah. A little full, if that makes sense, and a bit fatigued, but I should be okay for one or two more."

He nodded and she picked up the last one. "Is there anything I should know about *Watch Out for That Tree?*"

He smiled. "No, just get ready to be flooded with information. You know how it works now."

Indeed, she did. She pulled all of the information into herself. This one didn't hurt. And it didn't feel like it had changed anything greatly. But she did realize this ability was intended as an escape tool, something to only ever activate if she was in a clear space where she wouldn't get sucked into a wall, a tree, or the ground.

It existed to allow her just enough time to get a running head start and escape. This one lingered in a melancholy way, dusting her thoughts with an odd sadness.

A sudden wave of exhaustion washed over her as she tried to get up from the couch. She stumbled, falling back into it.

"Quinn, be careful. You just absorbed five books of information. Your brain and your body are still calibrating. Your energy levels are low. You'll need to take some time to rest." Lynx placed a gentle hand against her shoulder, helping her steady herself.

But she pushed it away, exasperated. "Have you not noticed? We're down to sixty-eight hours now, almost sixty-seven. I should have been doing this while I was waiting, damn it."

"It wouldn't have made much difference." Lynx smiled softly. "It's not going to be as hard as you think."

"Are you sure? Are you me? Have you ever wielded anything ever before?" *Are you stuck in a fantasy world that shouldn't, by rights, exist at all?* She wanted to say the latter too, but was already too close to actual panic.

Lynx suddenly looked extremely sheepish. "I'm sorry. The information packet is still not synthesized for you, and I keep forgetting just how new this is to you. I do apologize that I'm also letting the few problems I'm having with the system's reboot distract me. One of the books is back and that's what's important. All you need to do now is get the other two. A day for each. It's not bad, with some change left over. You can do this."

"Sure, I can." She waved the comment away, even though she was secretly glad for his apology. "Is there anything else that I can take with me that's gonna help?"

All she wanted to do right then was topple over and fall asleep. It would be the best thing in the world to be able to just go to sleep right now. She took a deep breath, deciding to let things go, when a thought struck her. "How am I supposed to defend myself? I need some ability I can attack with."

"You have the machete skill. What else were you thinking?" Lynx tapped his chin thoughtfully.

"Something that can do damage and protect me. From afar. Where I don't have to flail around with a sharp object. I don't know. You're the catalog." She crossed her arms and glared at him.

"What about an ice skill?" Milaro inserted, having apparently finished with his conversation. Malakai was standing with his arms crossed behind his grandfather, quite obviously sulking. "Why don't you give her an ice spell? She smells sort of icy. Maybe you'll be able to use mind bullets or an ice blast. I think she'd like those."

"She's not advanced enough to use mind bullets yet," Lynx said, and his expression was in distant mode.

"I didn't say she was," Milaro said, "but you could start her off with a simple icicle punch or just an ice blast. That might be the best thing for her right now. Or you could give her the generic understanding of the region so she knows how to unmake what's there."

"Yes, but she has to understand how it's made before she can unmake it. We don't have time for that right now. Stop jumping the gun, Milaro." Lynx was quite obviously losing his rarely present patience.

"Temper, temper," Milaro said, chuckling slightly. His eyes twinkled very merrily. "Anyone would think you'd been locked away for five hundred years."

Lynx scowled. "You know I can do a lot more than just manipulate the magic in the Library, right?"

Milaro waved the borderline threat away. "Oh, pish posh, old friend. You know I'm just kidding. Besides, you've just given her a lot of tools. She'll have to get used to using them. Give her something she can defend herself with. Wielding a machete takes time and close quarters. And she doesn't appear to be very robust. Casting an ice blast into somebody's face, though, that'll be good for her. And thus, she'll still be around to help you put the Library back together again."

"You know I'm sitting right here," Quinn said. "Just get me the book."

Milaro raised an eyebrow. "That's a bit demanding now."

"I'm really bloody tired right now," Quinn said, using all of the energy that she had left to actually stay sitting upright. She was quite exhausted.

Milaro took a step closer to her, bent down, and actually looked. "I need to touch your head," he said. He didn't ask, but he did warn her, and touched her forehead very briefly. His fingers were cold, but not uncomfortably so.

"Hmm," Milaro said. "Have you even been feeding this poor girl? You can't send them out on an empty stomach. I shall go and use your kitchen. I have some stuff in storage. Get the book and bring it over. She doesn't have any energy left because she just sucked it out by absorbing all those books. Have you forgotten how organic life forms survive? Because you're not doing a very good job of taking care of her, Lynx. Do you need somebody to tune up your system? Are you sure nothing went wrong?"

Lynx seemed taken aback by that statement. "I... I don't *think* anything's wrong." His eyes began flickering again as if he was running through a plethora of programming alternatives, trying to figure out if something was missing. "I... I'll go get the book and then when they're gone, I will run a full diagnostic."

"See that you do," Milaro said as he ushered both Quinn and Malakai toward the kitchen.

"Here, chew on that," Milaro said as he plopped her down at a table. The bench wasn't Dottie, was her absent thought, as she took the jerky he handed her and bit into it. A burst of flavors exploded in her mouth. It was divine. She took it out, looked at it thinking it'd be sparkly or something, but no, it really just looked like a jerky stick.

"What is this?" she asked wanting to never stop eating it.

Malakai, who was standing between her and his grandfather who was now cooking, raised an eyebrow. "It's probably closest to what you would refer to as a deer haunch, cooked in our family's traditional herbs and spices. It's a delicacy."

"Well, it's delicious," she said. She could almost feel the protein seeping into her system, the herbs rejuvenating her. It was pretty amazing stuff. "So like, you don't call them deer?"

Her would be companion shook his head. "They don't quite fit what you think of as deer. But for now, that's probably the closest description you'd understand."

"All right, then," she said nodding. "Thank you for the food."

Milaro smiled. "It's okay. We've got to send you out there with enough power to function. You might only have sixty-five or so hours left by the time you've got enough spells and sustenance into you and a snack to take with you, but those hours will be more productive because you're not going to be falling apart when you leave."

"You make perfect sense," Quinn said around another mouthful of the beautifully spiced deer. It wasn't long before she was digging into a delicious, warm salad with more of the meat sprinkled through it. She had never felt so hungry in her life. Apparently, learning magical tomes made you legitimately ravenous.

It was difficult not to concentrate on the countdown timer. No one else seemed to have the same sense of urgency. Since Milaro had returned the first book and extended the timer back to the full seventy-two hours, even Lynx seemed more relaxed about it.

But Quinn—well, she couldn't shake that feeling of unease.

She was cleaning the bowl when Lynx arrived and placed a tome in front of her. "There you go. I got you *Icy Blast*. It's the simplest to use, and the easiest to modify as you progress. It uses the least mana, and directionally, you don't have to have perfect aim."

Once Quinn finished her last bite she thanked Milaro. "That was delicious. I could eat that food nonstop forever."

His eyes twinkled again as he inclined his head. "Anytime, young Librarian."

Quinn opened the tome on the table and placed both hands on either side, sucking all the knowledge into herself. This time, her body experienced the rush of cold air, like when snow fell for the first time in a season and the breeze brought that fresh scent along with it.

The sensation suffused her very body, down through her veins and her bones. It took away the mild headache she'd been getting with all of the skill adoptions, and then it was gone. Instinctually, she knew flinging out her right hand in an open palm while thinking of an ice blast was all she had to do to throw this ice attack.

She simply had to will the Icy Blast into existence. It would cost energy, sap her of some of her strength, and drain the mind power she was learning was magic.

When she got back after this little retrieval expedition, she was studying the Library. Once all this danger was out of the way and things were stabilized for the time being. She was going to devour every single book she could get her hands on.

Now, armed with more knowledge and power, she finally felt ready to get started. "Let's go!"

Lynx smiled and ushered them out of the kitchen and toward the door. "Milaro and I have things to discuss and arrange, while you two will travel to Hirish Highlands and retrieve *Tarlegish's Dichotomy of Herbal Evolution.* After that, you'll need to come back before you head out farther."

"Why? Can't we just go and get both of the books at once?" Quinn was genuinely curious about the answer.

"Two reasons. The first is that returning each tome allows the Library to regain different functions. And secondly, it's easier to use the Library to get to your destination."

Quinn frowned at him. "What do you mean?"

But it was Malakai who interrupted as he swung one of the doors open. "That's something you have to experience for yourself."

And Quinn felt herself falling backward as his push caught her unawares.

FALLING

THE SENSATION OF FALLING COULD BE OVERWHELMING, REGARDLESS OF how far one fell. Even when it was only about three feet. As Quinn plopped unceremoniously onto her backside, landing in what seemed like a grassy meadow, she glared upwards. Malakai was stepping through from the Library into what appeared to be a field with a copse of trees on the side. The doorway was embedded into one of those trees.

Yet another things she'd have to talk to Lynx about later.

"You have so much you better explain when I get back," she yelled as Lynx closed the door behind them. The next second, the entrance to the Library was gone.

"That's some screwed up shit there," Quinn said. "How does that even—I—"

Malakai sighed. "Look, the Library hasn't been active since before I was born, but I've heard the stories. It can appear anywhere and everywhere, all at once, as long as you have a need for it. And well, we're going to have a need for it, because we're retrieving one of its precious books that's going to power it, and you're tied to it. So you should be able to call it forth even when it's locked the rest of the universe out."

"Well, then." Quinn didn't dwell on what she didn't know right then. If she did, she'd have already given up, and she just wasn't that sort of person. Usually. Make a plan, execute said plan, get around any roadblocks that exist, and reach your goal. The same method would work in the wider universe as well as it did on Earth. Ignoring the other stuff until she couldn't had always been her motto. "I guess we need to head on our way, right?"

Malakai surveyed the area around them with a frown. "Did he give you a map or anything, or tell you where it would be?"

"No, but I have this little reader thing." She pulled out the palm-sized device that had a tiny blipping dot up in the right-hand corner, while there was another stationary dot down towards the middle left. "I'm guessing that's us, and this flashing one is probably where we need to get to." As if in response, the flashing light blinked even more rapidly.

Maybe her connection with the Library really was getting stronger.

"Sounds like a plan. Should we start walking?" Malakai looked around and they started to move.

It really was just a massive open field. There was very little shelter anywhere. Some mountainous rocks, a few other little copses of trees as far as the eye could see, but off to where they needed to walk, appeared to be a very large hill. Maybe even a mountain? She wasn't quite sure, since it was pretty distant and seemed more of a gradual slope from what she could see.

"I wonder why the Library didn't spit us out closer to our destination," Malakai mused, breaking the silence after twenty minutes of walking.

"Probably," Quinn mused, "because Lynx wants me to get time to practice or something—" But that was all she got out. Suddenly, there was a flock of birds simply dive-bombing the both of them. They'd only walked about a mile by this stage, and there were no trees and no shelter anywhere around them.

Quinn flailed around with the machete she'd managed to unsheathe, while Malakai pulled a massive bow out of she had no idea where and began firing at the flock of birds in the sky. He hit two of them dead on, and they plummeted to the ground with a resounding thud. She was fairly certain she managed to clip one of the birds as it attacked her head, but was a bit preoccupied by the thick stream of blood trying to get in her eyes.

As Malakai ended the one she'd injured, it seemed the rest of the birds decided this was probably not a good idea and flew away, leaving them in peace.

"That was really good shooting," Quinn said, still trying to wipe away the blood glugging down her forehead. She let herself crouch down as she examined the birds. They were like a large crow with flecks of silver and white interspersed through the black feathers. Almost the size of an eagle. She glanced up at Malakai from where she sat. "Have you seen this type of bird before?"

He raised an eyebrow. "You realize the universe is a very large place and I do not come from here, or we would have just gone and fetched the second book for you."

"No need to be rude about it." She pouted slightly.

"Sorry," he said, adjusting his bow in his grip and looking away. His cheeks flushed slightly as he continued. "I was not expecting to be attacked by birds, first thing. I misjudged the situation. I'll keep my bow out."

Then he leaned forward and briefly touched her head. For a second she felt slightly disoriented, and then she realized the pain was gone from her wound. "You healed me," she mumbled incredulously.

"Yeah, I'm surprised healing wasn't the first book Lynx gave you. But his current thought processing seems sporadic at best. He's more fragmented than I recall from the stories." Malakai had a tone of concern in his words.

"I guess that's another thing I have to add to my list for if I survive long enough," she half joked. "Make sure Lynx is functioning properly."

Malakai blinked and focused on her somewhat intensely. "You're going to survive."

No time like the present to change the subject. "Where did you pull that bow from?" she asked, eager to understand how it worked.

"Oh, my storage bag." He said like it was no big deal.

"That fits in a storage bag?" She eyed the bow. It had to be at least four feet tall. And it was supple wood, because it was very obviously bendy when he was using it, but it was large, with ornate carvings. There's no way that fit into this mysteriously invisible bag. Because he sure as hell didn't have a storage bag anywhere on his person that she could see.

"I keep forgetting you're new," he said. "Storage refers to the dimensional pocket storage most of us carry? It's how we function here. We keep everything in them. It's very easy. You're going to need Lynx to hook you up when you get back."

"Apparently, I'm going to need to talk to Lynx about a lot of things," Quinn muttered under her breath.

The farther they walked, the thirstier Quinn felt, even swigging water from the flask on the side of her hip didn't seem to allay the thirst she felt. Maybe it was the atmosphere. While it didn't feel much different than she was used to, it didn't necessarily mean that it wasn't.

She sighed. At least the silence while walking wasn't awkward. It gave her a chance to check on the map and really get a look at her surroundings.

"So, who is it we're looking for again?" Malakai asked his bow at the ready, no matter how far they moved.

"We're looking for somebody called Dinal. I didn't get any more of a name from Lynx. So maybe he just goes by one name, you know, like Beyonce or something."

Malakai raised an eyebrow. "I have no idea what you're talking about."

"Figures," Quinn said, juggling walking and navigating on her tiny map. She frowned as she highlighted his name. "Okay. From the limited information I got about this Dinal, he apparently lives in a small town that should be overlooking the ocean I assume is behind those hilly peaks. Lynx seemed to think he'd be pretty good about giving us the book back if he's still alive. Lynx wasn't entirely sure how long his species lived—he just said it varied. Dinal may even have already passed on."

Malakai nodded his understanding of the situation. "I would have thought he'd know all the species' lifespans."

"Yeah." Quinn frowned, because her companion brought up a good point. There were a lot of holes in the information she'd been given.

It was unnerving to spend time in silence as they walked along the vague path embedded into the grass. Not because it was awkward, but because it amplified the lack of noise around them. There were no crickets chirping in this grass nor any other types of insect sounds she could hear. Maybe they didn't have insects on this world. It would explain why the birds had been so hungry.

From the faint path through the fields, some people had walked this way before, but it definitely wasn't many.

She couldn't hear any birds flying overhead now either. There wasn't even rustling or digging or anything that might've given away that there were some forms of life living out here on the plains.

But they did start approaching the hillier area. Maybe a mountain *was* more accurate. The terrain was a lot steeper than Quinn had anticipated upon seeing it the first time. She trudged on with Malakai next to her, making her way slowly up the incline and wishing she could just jump into a vat of water and drain it all.

Still, at least she'd had food just before they left. She glanced in the corner of her vision and paled. Then she blinked just to make sure of what she was seeing. "How have five hours passed?" she said out loud, after looking. There were only sixty-one hours left and counting.

"We haven't been walking for three hours. It's been one, not quite two I'd say. What are you talking about?" Malakai shook his head. "That doesn't even make..." And he paused. "Oh, shit."

"What?" she asked.

"Harish Highlands, right? That's located in the Dharanin sector, which means time moves faster here. So yes, five hours have passed in the Library, and we've probably only been walking here for about an hour and a half or so? Can you run?"

Quinn tried to push down on the panic. Her nerves flared. Sixty odd hours left. Why hadn't Lynx told her about the time disparity? Probably because he was trying to avoid her panicking, or else because he completely forgot, or didn't believe it relevant. *Breathe. Okay, I'll make do. I can jog a little bit.* At least her one and only fitness skill might pay off.

"Looks like we're going to have to jog up an incline." She watched as Malakai took off in front of her, his long legs taking ground-eating strides as he raced up to the top. She plodded after him, frankly impressed by her ability to almost keep up with him.

Running had been her only source of exercise. She always thought it better to escape a situation where she'd likely otherwise be over-powered.

Maybe her beginner's shielding had helped a little bit of her stamina, too. More and more combinations and ideas for how to improve her chances in this new home came to her as she ran. She put as much effort into climbing that summit as she could. She was sweating. It dripped down her body, until they finally reached the top.

That's when she realized the hilltops were moss-covered crags, with only several trees scattered around.

Before her the ocean spread out and two suns, low in the sky, sent out white and golden fingers of light to interlock over the water.

It was one of the most breathtaking views she'd ever seen in her life, and it took six Library hours to get there—two in this world.

"It had better be worth it," she muttered under her breath.

"Hopefully, the Library will be able to open closer to this little village once we need to head back," Malakai said. Quinn took pride in the fact that he at least sounded winded.

"I mean, they've got to at least have doorways, right?" She glanced down the narrow path that wound down steeply. "Come on, I can see it down there. Do you see the smoke rising from the chimneys? They're set into like the cliff face?"

"This isn't a cliff, Quinn. This is a mountain region. They've set the houses into the face of the mountain. If you look farther down, you'll

notice evened-out plateaus here and there. It's for livestock and training. Sometimes even for trading markets."

"Wow!" Quinn couldn't help but be impressed. She could see that
the way the paths were laid out would require a lot of confidence and
sure-footedness to navigate. They appeared so precarious to her; she
wished she could climb like a goat.

They were going to have to walk a lot farther than she felt
comfortable doing on this terrain. But it had to be done. That blinking
icon on her map wasn't miraculously coming closer like it had with
Milaro. She took a deep breath and began marching forward, loving
the earthen scents that drifted around her and the clover-like fresh-
ness of the air, tinged with a hint of saltwater.

"This is really breathtaking," she whispered. Her voice carried on
the wind enough for Malakai to hear.

He simply nodded. "Yeah, the Harish Highlands are definitely one
of the more attractive ones."

She laughed. "You're speaking as if all highlands are different."

"Well, they are. Everything's different depending on where it's
located and how it was initially created. Stick around for a while,
travel to enough places, and you'll realize that and more." He smirked
at her. "You've got a lot of books to retrieve, so you'll be going on a lot
of trips."

Quinn always prided herself in being knowledgeable about everything she was interested in. It was difficult to hear someone, who
looked to be around her age, know so much more than herself.

Then she remembered something from a previous interaction
with his grandfather. Hadn't said that Malakai studied combat styles
for the last fifteen years? That had to make him a lot older than she
was, which was a little disconcerting in itself.

Elves and their anti-aging.

Still, his grandfather was likely thousands of years old or something , so she could easily suspend disbelief, having met the elf. There
were so many things she was going to have to get used to.

The bad thing about the path down to find Dinal was that they
couldn't go fast, despite the Library timer ticking down. It was like a

metronome with a fuse attached blinking in her vision. The ground they traversed was strewn with pebbles and steep, easy to lose footing on. And even though time kept bleeding away, Quinn thought it was better to come back alive with the book she needed to retrieve, instead of slipping and falling to her death over the side of the mountain.

Then the Library really would be doomed with that whole lack of magically compatible signatures out there.

Malakai's bow was now strung over his shoulder. She wondered if that was healthy for it, but assumed he knew what he was doing. She clutched her unsheathed machete in her left hand, hoping she wouldn't need it.

Or fall on it.

The smells and the sense of peace that drifted to her on this mountain path could easily lull her into a false sense of security. She made an effort not to be swept away by the tranquility of it all. Staying aware was vital to survival.

Just as they were getting closer to one of the smoke spires she'd seen from the very top of the mountain, she glanced back and realized they had probably descended three or four levels so far. It had to be a couple of miles at least. Just over another hour here made her dread looking at the timer in the bottom corner of her vision.

Fifty-six hours.

"Oh, that's just great." she muttered irritably.

All of a sudden, something jumped out in front of her. It stood about eight feet tall and was massive. It reminded her of a walrus with stocky and powerful legs and stood upright. Massive tusks extended from its mouth down to midway down its chest and it had two arms on each side, four arms in total. It was a dark brown and had tufted black hair spiking out from its head and flowing all the way down its back.

"Who goes there? Who trespasses on the Dinetian village?"

Spear tips dug into her back hard enough that she was pretty sure the tips had broken the skin through her clothes.

This was not the welcome she'd been expecting.

1 8

THE OLD SPEAR IN THE BACK TRICK

EVEN AS THE SPEAR TIP DUG INTO HER BACK, QUINN WONDERED ABOUT the strange, seaweed-like smell. She realized it came from the being in front of her. Perhaps that's why they lived out here on the crags, close to the water, ensuring they were near their natural habitat. She needed to know more about everything in these worlds.

"State your case," they said, a strange lilt to their voices.

Did that mean they were speaking English? Surely not everybody was speaking English. That was something else she was going to have to talk to Lynx about. The list just wouldn't stop growing. It didn't take a genius to realize that she should probably leave the talking to somebody who had been around in these worlds longer than her. And so, she deferred to Malakai.

"We seek Dinal, your leader," her companion intoned regally, as if he didn't have a spear tip grazing his back.

"Dinal? You are lying, like all Darigháhnish," their captor practically spat. His tusks were far longer than the other one in the party. Maybe six inches or so.

"No, we're not," Malakai said, his tone even and patient, ignoring whatever that insult had been. "We were sent to retrieve a book from him."

"Dinal has been gone for three score years. You want something from our deceased leader?" The derision in that tone was scathing.

"Oh." Malakai stopped short, shooting a glance at Quinn. She shook her head rapidly, having no idea that Dinal had passed away. "We come seeking a book on behalf of the Library."

The creature in front of them began laughing. It was a loud and guttural laugh with a hint of nastiness contained inside. "Library, what library? Do we look like readers to you, boy?"

Malakai's eye twitched ever so slightly, but it was the only outward sign of his annoyance. "The Library of Everywhere told us to retrieve an overdue book from here." He wisely didn't comment on their reader status.

Their captor scowled. "You claim to be from the Library. It doesn't even exist anymore. No one has been to the Library in almost two hundred of our years. It's gone along with every manageable magical aspect."

"You seem very knowledgeable," Quinn blurted out before she could stop herself. "Is there something you can tell us about the book?"

"Silence, human. You, you of all people, get no say in this." Again. Derision that cut like acid.

Quinn shut her mouth and wondered what humans had done to offend this species. Not that she was surprised. Humans could be pretty violent and selfish.

The spear tips prodded in her back, and she knew they were doing the same thing to Malakai as their captors urged them both down the path. They took a pace much faster than Quinn was used to and frankly, she half-slid several times, barely regaining her balance and thanking her four years of gymnastics as a very young child for not falling flat on her face.

It didn't, however, save her from badly tweaking one of her ankles.

It took forever for them to reach the first plateau. Opposite it was a room, or house cut into the cliff-face. Inside it had barred cubicles, sort of like cells, jail cells as she realized when they tossed her in one and Malakai in another.

"You will stay here until the Arbiter can see you. I do not like your chances," sneered their jailor.

Quinn waited until the guard left and moved over to stand as close to Malakai as she could. She noticed he seemed quite defeated.

"What was that all about?" she asked, in an urgent whisper.

"I didn't remember that the Walry lived here and that Dinal was one of them." His shoulders sagged.

"Is that their species name?"

Malakai grinned. "Oh, it's a long, really complicated word that your tongue probably could not pronounce. So Walry is their universal name, I guess you'd say."

"He didn't seem fond of you." She decided to just ask since they were stuck in these cells for a while. "He insulted you, didn't he?"

Malakai sighed and rolled his shoulders. It took him several seconds to speak. "The Walry are not fond of the Darigháhnish - my mother's people. Or"—and he grinned—"I guess it's more accurate to say the Darigháhnish are not on good terms with many species."

Quinn nodded and filed that away. "But you can all communicate? Right?"

He nodded, a bit of the tension leaking out of his stance as they changed the subject. "It's sort of... a magical side effect of the Library."

"Is that how I know what everyone is saying?" she asked, instinctually understanding that perhaps even Malakai was speaking to her in a different language and she hadn't realized it.

He eyed her for a moment. "Any person that can use an affinity should technically be able to speak to anyone else who can. Once you connected with the Core, you were able to understand all languages, both written and spoken. It's one of the biggest advantages of being bonded to the Library. Either as a Librarian or an assistant."

"Makes sense. Can't very well librarian if I can't understand who I'm talking to or what the books say." Quinn nodded while she mulled it all over, and then asked her next question. "He seemed to know about humans."

Malakai actually laughed. "Everybody knows about humans. Just when we think some of you are gone, you're back. Your species is like the cockroach of the universe."

"Oh," Quinn said. She wasn't sure if that was a compliment or not. She was pretty sure it was the latter. After all, even where she came from, nobody liked cockroaches, especially not the flying kind. And the fact that it seemed like cockroaches were universal didn't bode well. She couldn't even be sucked into another world and escape them.

"Okay, then, is there anything you can tell me about the Walry that could help us?" she asked, her hackles up a little. She was feeling extremely vulnerable right now, standing in the middle of a jail cell at the whim of these Walry people.

"Well," Malakai said, "let me do most of the talking. They like humans even less than they like my mother's people, and we need to come up with a plan, because we can't go back without that book anyway."

"Well, I know all of that. I was hoping you'd have something constructive." Quinn rolled her eyes.

Malakai raised a deftly manicured eyebrow at her. "Seriously, you need to relax and stop getting so snarky."

Quinn grimaced. "I'm frustrated. I'm not used to this world. Time is passing far too quickly for my liking in this new dimension or whatever we're in. I don't understand anything and it should all be a really nasty nightmare, but it's not. If turning my ankle and having it swell up like it is, is anything to go by, this is not just a random nasty dream."

Malakai chuckled dryly. "No, it's definitely not a random dream. Especially not if your pinching bruises are anything to go by."

Quinn felt herself blushing. She hadn't realized she'd been so obvious about trying to wake herself up.

Malakai continued, oblivious to her thoughts. "Anyway, the Walry are a seafaring species. They can survive in waters of freezing cold temperatures, but they do not do well in warmer water. Their livelihood is made through fishing and weaving. They're famous for their artistry in tapestries, and their storage baskets. Trust me, if you want one of their storage baskets, we better make nice. Apart from that, I didn't realize Dinal had passed. Granted, this was one of the first regions that we studied and Dinal was still in our histories. They're not a very open species, so they don't tend to share everything very often with anyone. We're probably maybe ten to a hundred or more years out of date."

Quinn blanched. "Ten to a hundred years. That much?"

"Well, if the Library hadn't basically gone missing, it would have been different. But without the Library to act as the information hub..." At Quinn's blank expression, Malakai continued. "You know, it hasn't been as easy as summoning a door, popping in and updating archives."

She mulled that over for a moment. "Then he could easily have been dead for these hundred years and nobody would have known. Well, they would have known here, which is why we have to wait and see who's in charge now. And the Library carries no weight anymore. Probably among the Walry, the Library's been relegated to nothing more than a myth. I mean, almost five centuries of absence in normal time is like what, a hundred fifty-odd years here? That's enough to make anything a legend or a fallacy or just fade in people's memories. How do we prove to them that we're from the Library?"

"Well." Malakai seemed to mull it over. "Don't you have like a tattoo or a marking or something you can show them?"

Quinn stared at him blankly, watching the time tick down in the right-hand corner of her vision. And for the life of her, she had no idea if she had a marking. She hadn't even had a chance to check for that yet.

Another, later, thing because their time limit was pretty much draining away. "I don't think so. What if we—what if we summon the Library to a door somewhere here? Isn't that possible?"

Malakai blinked. "That's a good idea, since you have access. It should also be able to draw from ambient mana around these parts so hopefully won't drain the minimal reserves it's managed to accrue. I wouldn't be able to summon it, but you can. That's the only way I can see that we could get out of this." As he finished speaking, Malakai actually sounded excited, like he thought it wasn't all hopeless, and Quinn felt good about it.

He crouched for a second and reached through the bars to brush a finger over her ankle. "I don't think it's going to heal it fully, but it should make it slightly better until we get back to the Library."

Quinn was genuinely touched that he'd thought to help her like that. "Thanks," she said and they settled into silence to wait while Quinn watched the timer click down ominously.

When their jailer returned, a few hours later in Walry time but way too long in Library time, Quinn was trying her best not to get super angry about the fact that she now had forty-eight hours remaining on her timer. It was running down so fast. Only two days left.

"Are you still claiming to be from the Library?" The guard was back in front of them, obviously derisive of the fact that they had said they were from the Magic Library of Everywhere.

"We are and we can prove it," Malakai said, his tone quite smug.

Their guard practically sneered. "Oh, and how are you going to prove that something legendary..."

"Oh, for crying out loud, Marron, you need to stop treating everybody as if they're criminals just because they've come to visit us in our village." A much smaller Walry pushed his way through to the forefront of the group and glanced down at the two of them in their separate cells. "Well, I'm terribly sorry that you've been treated this way, although you don't exactly look like the usual sort of visitors we get."

Quinn shrugged. "We might be unconventional, but we're making it work."

Their new visitor chuckled. "Allow me to introduce myself. I am Dinal's grandson, Tillip. I welcome you to our village and apologize for the overzealousness of my chief security officer. However, Marron did say that you claim to be from the Library, which I personally find extremely difficult to believe. My grandfather told me stories about this Library you speak of, and he was adamant that it had disappeared and been gone for hundreds of years in Library time, almost a hundred in hours. That is why we needed to safeguard this tome of herbology, just in case it was ever needed. But he seemed to think that there was no way he was ever going to be able to return it. He'd been trying for longer than he could remember."

"Yeah, that seems to have been a pretty widespread problem," Quinn said dryly, noticing that he didn't mention the actual name of the book, just the subject matter.

"Considering how long it's been," Tillip said, standing back expectantly, tapping his foot and leaving the doors barred. "You need to be able to prove in some way to me that you are indeed a part of the Library."

Quinn glanced over at Malakai, who shrugged. "It's going to be pretty difficult to prove that we're from the Library if you have us locked in an iron cage." They'd tried to summon the door to the Library in the cell door, but it hadn't worked.

Quinn guessed that the lock was probably providing magical interference of some sort.

Tillip blinked, and Quinn noticed, rather absentmindedly, that he had beautifully long eyelashes. The Walry were an extremely unique-looking species. She really wanted to know more about their history and their world, even as the timer ticked down to forty-seven hours.

Tillip narrowed his eyes as he watched them. He seemed to be weighing something. "Fine. Marron, let them out, but make sure they have guards on them. I can't be too careful. My grandfather told me to guard this tome with my life. And, well, I'm not about to do him a disservice."

Quinn stood back and waited for Marron to unlock the cells. She cast her gaze over Tillip, trying to figure out where he might have hidden the tome. He was speaking as if he had it on him. That's when she realized he probably had a storage item just like Malakai.

She really needed to get herself one of those.

Finally freed from the cells, Malakai brushed imagined dirt off his shoulders. He hadn't even sat on the ground, which meant he was still as impeccable as he had been when they arrived in the village at spearpoint. Quinn, on the other hand, had to dust dirt off her jeans.

She glanced around. Nobody else seemed to wear jeans here. Did they not know how comfortable they could be?

A spearpoint jabbed into her back as she half hobbled out of the cell again, wincing at the remaining pain in her ankle. "Seriously, I'm walking with you. Do I look that dangerous?" Which she wished a moment later she hadn't asked.

"Well, you did have this machete on you," Marron said. "I didn't think that looked like something someone who wasn't a threat would carry."

Malakai wisely kept his mouth shut because his bow was definitely a hunting bow and not some ornate replica that didn't work. Quinn wisely stayed silent as well and followed them out even if she was irritated. It wasn't wise to antagonize the obviously anti-human guard. She'd have to remember to thank Lynx for picking the machete as her damn starter weapon.

She hadn't realized how dark the cell room was until they stepped through the doorway into bright light.

Two suns certainly made a difference.

The plateau in front of them was rounded and held several little pens. Some of them had sheep and there were a few, maybe they were closer to boars than pigs, but they did resemble creatures on Earth, so she'd call them boars for now. Otherwise, there was a hut next to it and several people had gathered over in the corner between the pens and that hut. Apparently, new arrivals weren't a common thing in this village.

The guards, on Marron's orders, pushed their prisoners forward, jabbing them in the back with the spearheads again, so much that Quinn felt skin break. "Ow!" she yelled. "That hurt. I've done nothing to you."

"Apart from lie," Marron muttered.

But Tillip held up his hand. "Look, that hasn't been proven yet. Show our guests some courtesy until we know for certain that they are truly enemies."

Who hurt you in a past life? is what Quinn wanted to ask, but very wisely kept that to herself. The Walrys seemed to take this whole situation very seriously.

Finally, they came to stand in the clear area beyond the pens and in front of the hut. The hut was much like a yurt back on Earth. They were rounded and had sort of tent-like roofs. However, from what she could see there was deftly woven straw and mud used as the base instead of wood. At least if the doors were anything to go by. They looked quite comfortable.

Tillip cleared his throat. "Well, then, go on. Show us proof that you're the Librarian, that this Library my grandfather told me about in tales when I was young really and truly exists." He sounded like he wanted her to be telling the truth. Eager almost.

Quinn glanced at Malakai and shrugged. She had no idea how to summon the Library.

He cleared his throat. "I think you just have to will it to appear so you can enter it? Can't you use your interface?"

"Not yet," she grumbled to him under her breath. "Doesn't extend to here. Still reserve power only."

To the gathering, she spoke louder. "I'll need to approach the door," she said, pointing to the hut.

Tillip looked surprisingly unsettled like he knew she was truly lying now. "I knew you'd say that. Be warned, there's no other way out of that hut. It's the meeting room. You can only get into it by this door. You won't be able to escape through it."

Quinn sighed, put her hands on her hips and walked over, her spear jabber following closely behind. "You better have that book. The Library needs power and it needs its books back to do that," she said.

Then she took a deep breath before she placed her hands flat against the door and said, "Library, Lynx... I need you."

There was a shimmer to the air, a strange scent of old pages and knowledge, and a minor chiming that sounded sort of sad. Suddenly, the door in front of her rippled and the wood changed, becoming slightly translucent and yet resembling the petrified appearance of the actual core.

The door practically vibrated beneath her hands, still placed on its surface. She took a step back, shocked despite knowing something was supposed to happen.

Tillip blinked and rushed forward. "Can I?"

"I'm not sure. The Library is locked to outsiders right now and I'm the only one who can summon it," Quinn said, suddenly feeling very panicked. She probably shouldn't bring these Walry people to the Library. They were armed and had been very inhospitable to the whole concept of there being a Library. But now, with only forty-four hours left on the timer, she needed to get that book back where it belonged.

"Look, stand there and I'll open it." She reached forward and pushed the door open. It creaked ever so slightly, but there was a melodic undertone to the sound. Frankly, it made Quinn feel welcome, like she was coming home. The scent of worn leather covers and faded yellow pages reached out to her like a calming balm.

"Who's that?" Lynx walked up to the door, his purple hue glowing slightly outside of the barrier where his skin should be. He glanced out of the door. "You shouldn't... Quinn, what?" He looked beyond her, his eyes narrowing.

"You are not Dinal," he said, and Tillip paled. There was something about the timbre of Lynx's voice that made Quinn look up, seeing him for the first time in a sharper light.

The Library manifestation was angry, and she could feel it in the way the power rippled around her.

19

ANGRY LIBRARY

QUINN HADN'T SEEN LYNX ANGRY YET. SHE COULDN'T TELL WHY HE WAS upset. But there was no ignoring the wave of emotion that emanated from the Library.

Tillip felt it. Marron felt it, as did the rest of the guards. Even the people lined up near the pens backed away. The boars huddled and squealed. And for that moment, Quinn felt vindicated.

"I told you I was the Librarian," she said, just a little bit smugly. "You wouldn't believe me. Look what you made me do."

"Why didn't you just show them the mark of connection on your hip?" Lynx snapped, tossing her a glare.

"Because A, I didn't know I had one, and B, they think the Library is a myth." She shot straight back at him making a mental note to herself to check her hip later. "For all they know I drew the thing on myself."

"You think I'm a myth," Lynx said, a dangerous undercurrent to his tone as the runes woven into his hair began to churn. "Very well, you are permitted to enter. One guard and yourself, as I assume Dinal has passed and you are his successor?"

"Yes, Mr. Library, sir," said Tillip, flustered now for the first time.

"Library will do. We'll figure out how to deal with you inside."
Lynx turned on his heel. "Enter, now, and you better have my tome."

It was odd seeing how flustered their jailors got. Both Marron and
Tillip couldn't get through the door fast enough. The rest of the
guards remained outside and everybody looked pale and shocked.

Perhaps having a legend everybody thought had disappeared or
wasn't real to begin with, appear right in front of them like this wasn't
the easiest thing to digest. But Quinn didn't care, and she followed the
rest of them into the Library with Malakai bringing up the rear.

Tillip took very cautious steps through the Library and Quinn was
amused to see that the entrance appeared to be slightly different than
the one Milaro had walked through. But the desk was the same. She
was relieved to see that her timer was finally counting down in appropriate intervals, even if she only had forty-two hours left. At least they
were forty-two hours as far as the Library saw it and not the same as
it was in the Dharanin sector.

A whole day was gone now and a wave of unease wrapped itself
around Quinn.

The two Walrys crept forward, their heads swiveling about,
looking here and there. She had to admit the Library was pretty dim,
very musty, and still extremely untidy.

"What happened here?" Tillip asked, his voice full of awe with a
dash of fear.

Lynx flashed him a glare. "What happened here?" And he paused
like he didn't want to tell them or couldn't quite tell them, which
reminded Quinn all she knew was that the Librarian's magical signature had disappeared so it had been impossible to find replacements,
and thus required the Library to drop into emergency power mode in
order to survive until one could be located.

But why? She'd never found out the why.

Instead of a direct answer, Lynx side-stepped. "The Librarians died
out, and we needed to find a replacement. In order to complete our
search we had to prolong our power reserves. It took a little bit longer
than I anticipated."

Lynx flickered ever so briefly and Quinn noted that down again in her head in a mental note to check on him with later. There was so much she needed to do later.

"Well," Lynx said, his commanding voice resonating throughout the entire space around them, "Where is *my* book?"

This time Tillip looked a little sheepish and reached into what Quinn thought was a pocket and pulled out a massive book. Golden letters shone even in the dim light.

Tarlegish's Dichotomy of Herbal Evolution seemed alive and it looked like it had bark on the outside of it with tiny vines that moved. It had the exact sort of appearance she'd imagined magical tomes would. There was a scent of age emanating from it, like it had always been and always would be.

It was glorious.

Lynx took the book and placed it on the counter, his hands flaring brightly as he did so. "Quinn, stop standing there looking like you could catch flies and come over here."

Quinn shook herself and ran over, climbing into the returns desk. She lifted the tome, feeling the weight of it was beyond anything she'd imagined. It had to weigh twenty pounds, probably because its cover was indeed made out of a type of bark. She swore that if she pulled her hands away there'd be moss covering them.

"Stop gawking. You can look at it later, you need to check it in." An undercurrent of urgency wove around Lynx's words.

"Okay," Quinn said, feeling that urgency too.

"That took longer than I expected," Lynx muttered next to her.

"You forget that the Dharanin sector has a time shift or something?" she mumbled in response, perhaps a little snappy.

Lynx looked at her for a moment. "Damn it. Look, just check the book in."

Winging it, she placed one hand on the tome and the other on the console. There was a flash of light and it seemed as if the entire illumination of the Library went up a notch, just a couple of percentages, taking away some more of the Gloom.

An air of relief washed subtly through the Library. There was a thrumming through her feet from the Library itself, rejuvenating it, beginning to replenish what had been lost.

A strange voice sounded in her head. Not necessarily a voice, more like she was reading the words popping up in front of her in a different voice than her own.

Library calibration, three-quarters complete.

Dr. Carlyle's Thesis of Spatial Distortion *still required.*

Retrieval Timer extended by 4 hours

46 hours 27 minutes 32 seconds remaining

"It extended the timer again. I didn't think it'd be able to do that," Quinn said, trying not to let on just how relieved she was that she had regained a few hours. That meant she still had, well, almost two days.

"Take those additional hours and get some rest and eat," Lynx said, and then he looked up at Tillip and Marron, who had ventured a little further into the Library. "I didn't say you could stay. The Library is still closed. We have repairs to make and power to restore. We will send a universal message out when the Library is once again fully operational."

Tillip's eyes brightened and Quinn could tell he'd probably loved those stories his grandfather told him, all about a magical library that let you learn any power your brain had the capacity to take on.

"Really?" Tillip said a hint of childish wonder in his tone, "The Library's really going to open again?"

"That's the aim," Lynx said very dryly as he straightened his stance a little. He seemed an inch taller once he'd straightened his shoulders. Quinn could see he was happy with the question.

"Great. What form will the announcement be in?" Tillip asked, his words almost falling over one another.

"Anyone who has the ability to access the Library will receive a notification," Lynx said. Quinn could tell he was preoccupied with something and couldn't help wondering if it was wise to let everyone know. Wouldn't that include whoever had essentially organized for the Library to be taken offline?

Lynx looked at her sharply, like he'd heard her thoughts, and redirected his attention to shepherding their unwanted visitors toward the door. Finally, he managed to usher the two Walry back out of the Library and closed the doors. He turned to look at Quinn and Malakai in turn. "Your grandfather left you here. He has business to attend to. He'll be back when we've got the final tome. You both need to sleep. You have to recuperate. I'll give you five hours. You should be able to spare that."

"Do we really have the time for that?" Quinn asked, pretty sure they didn't.

Lynx shrugged. "It's either take a few hours now to go in rested, or make mistakes because you will be up for another forty or more hours once you leave."

Quinn nodded, understanding the logic even if she didn't like it.

"How did you forget about the time disparity?" Malakai crossed his arms and glared at Lynx.

"I have a lot going on. I'm performing many calculations. It just... it slipped my mind. I've been operating without all of my functions for a very long time, and not everything has finished recalibrating. I seem to be flying blind in a few areas." He seemed extremely concerned, which meant that Quinn in turn couldn't help but be concerned. She could feel how he felt. A little of it anyway. It was oddly disconcerting.

What was she supposed to do with a Library that was losing its memory?

"I am not losing my memory, Quinn. I am what you would call the definition of stressed." Lynx glared at her.

"Wow. No need to take my head off," Quinn said, trying to ignore the indication that he was now able to answer her thoughts. "Remember, you pulled me here. I'm allowed to have questions."

He watched her for a moment and nodded. "Speaking of which, I've almost got your packet ready. It'll be a little late in the coming, but it should fill you in on everything so much better. I don't know why it didn't transfer. I still can't understand that."

She paused and walked over to him, really looking at him this time. His human form was startlingly vivid. And his eyes were still so lizard-like in the way they shut differently. The sclera didn't quite work for his human guise. Wasn't he just a projection anyway? It gave her a lot of food for thought.

"It could have been when I hit my head," she said.

"Maybe..."

"Are you really okay?" she asked, softly.

He glanced down at her. "Well, I will be. I will be. There's a lot that I still need to do. There are still limited functions available, and not all the databases are accessible. It's frustrating not to have the power to do what is necessary."

"Isn't that why I'm here?" Quinn said. "Now just let me go get a power nap and we'll go get you that third tome. And after that you and I have a lot to talk about."

Not wanting to place any more of a burden on Lynx than was already on his shoulders, Quinn made her way up the spiral staircase, motioning for Malakai to follow her.

"Where are we going?" he whispered.

"What? I'm not taking you to my room. So get that thought out of your pretty elven head. There are quarters up here, and I'm assuming there is a spare chamber for you. It'll probably be dusty, and well, maybe not what your majesty is used to, but I'm pretty sure it'll be enough for you to crash on for the few hours rest we're going to get before we have to go and find, well, the difficult-to-find tome."

"What do you mean, 'the difficult-to-find tome'?" Malakai asked as they crested the staircase and came out on the landing.

"Difficult. This spatial distortion tome, apparently the person who borrowed it is somebody that Lynx has always had trouble getting books back from. Even before the Library took this hiatus." She shrugged, suddenly overwhelmed with fatigue.

"Oh, great," said Malakai, "and here I thought this babysitting job would be easy."

"You're not babysitting me." She scowled. "But thank you for looking out for me back there."

"No problem." Malakai peeled off into a smaller room than Quinn's.

She entered hers and even though she wanted to stay awake and figure things out, she was asleep as soon as her head hit the pillow. Her sleep was dreamless, and before she knew it, she woke to the smell of something delicious wafting up from the lower floor.

Quinn practically stumbled out of bed and almost slid down the stairs to find Dottie waiting at the bottom. Blocking the end of the staircase was probably more accurate.

She waved one of her little legs in a way that Quinn swore was supposed to be a shake of her head. "No you don't, young Librarian. You go back up, shower, change, and the food will be ready once you're done."

Blinking slowly, Quinn backed up the staircase and did as she was told. There were shirts laid out and pants, but still no jeans. Which wouldn't do. If the Library couldn't make her jeans, then she'd have to find a tailoring magic book or something.

Stubbornly, even after her shower, she pulled her trusty jeans back on, but did change everything else. Even if the dark red shirt she pulled over her head was a bit too flowy for her tastes. Her T-shirt was definitely rank.

Finally, she made her way back downstairs and to the kitchen. It seemed like it had taken her forever, but it hadn't been more than ten minutes and somehow the food smelled even better.

She was surprised to see Malakai dishing out something she couldn't identify onto a bed of what looked like wild rice again. She raised an eyebrow as he set it in front of her.

"Just eat it." He looked as tired as she still felt and she hoped he'd had some sleep.

Quinn poked it with her fork, but it didn't wiggle or anything, so she shrugged, took in the very mushroom-like aroma, and shoved a forkful into her mouth. It tasted vaguely of portobello mushroom with a dash of cream and some heavy salt and garlic. But the potato-tasting rice just added this undercurrent that brought out the flavors in an explosive way.

Her plate was empty before she realized it, and she sat back, smiling. "That was great."

"Good." Lynx walked in, his eyes giving away his current level of multitasking. "You're going to have to take rations with you. Kajaro is unlikely to give you the next book easily."

"Why?" Quinn asked, still basking in the glow of a good meal.

"Because he's... what would you Earthlings call it? A dick?" Lynx smiled. "Or, I believe maybe an insufferable jerk?"

Quinn laughed. "Okay, but does he have a reason?"

Lynx frowned. "None. He was already overdue before the Library had to resort to reserve power. Eight months overdue to be precise."

"That's a lot. Why hadn't your Librarian got it back then?"

A pained expression passed briefly over Lynx's face. "Because she'd already faded too much. We should have waited until her replacement was secured before I allowed her to uncouple from the connection." A wave of sadness breathed through the Library, expressing Lynx's memories.

Quinn wished he was solid enough to hug. It seemed like he could use one.

"Anyway!" Lynx looked up, the melancholy gone from his eyes. Banished forcibly. "Provisions have been gathered. It's time to send you two on your way."

"You let me sleep a lot longer than I thought you would." Quinn didn't like the current timer status.

40 hours 2 minutes 12 seconds

It seemed like far too little.

Lynx shrugged. "To be honest. An hour or two won't make much difference. There is no distortion on Kajaro's chosen homeworld. But it does possess a lighter oxygen level. You'll need to wear a breathing refresher when you begin to feel lightheaded. I only have a couple so don't waste them. They only have about two hours each. You should need ten minutes to reset. Malakai knows how they work."

It felt like she was being sent on an adventure with gear from the discount bargain adventuring co. And she cringed when Lynx shot her a look. She'd have to learn how to direct her thoughts away from him.

"Later." He answered that thought too. "After this, we'll have bought a lot of time, energy, and power. You just have to get this book. Understood?"

"And let's just play devil's advocate here," Quinn said nervously, "What happens if he won't give it to me?"

Lynx shrugged, but she could already see the defeat in his shoulders. "Then you either take it from him forcibly, or that was it, and we tried."

Quinn gulped audibly. She knew those were the stakes, but that didn't mean she had to like it. "Well, since I'm not partial to us disappearing. I'm going to get that damned book back."

The Library manifestation actually flashed her the closest she'd seen to a genuine smile. He nodded once.

Picking up the light jacket Dottie had somehow made appear next to her, Quinn nodded. "As good a time as any." She headed toward the doors.

"Remember. I don't have the ability to calibrate an exact location. But I think I have you within an hour or two of where Kajaro is currently located in Lapsaxum."

"You think?" Malakai snorted, but seemed resigned to the trip.

"That's why I need the book, young Darigháhnish," Lynx called after them. "Replenish my reserves."

"No time distortion, and for all you know, he shouldn't be dead this time?" Malakai asked as he sheathed a dagger.

Lynx snorted. "Of course not. It's not like old age will kill Kajaro. He's immortal."

Which wasn't the most comforting thing to hear as they stepped through the portal into a windswept wasteland. The sound of their exit blinking out of existence sounded oddly like the nail in a coffin.

20

HE'S NOT A GOD

"No pressure or anything," Quinn muttered under her breath as the portal Lynx shoved them through closed behind them.

"A bit passive-aggressive, aren't we?" said Malakai, although he sounded about as irritated as Quinn felt.

"It would be nice if, for once, he would give us, or at least me, the information in advance," Quinn said, feeling oddly disgruntled. She felt she had a right to be, considering she'd been pulled here against her will anyway. It felt like she was giving as much as she could in an amicable sort of way. It would be nice to be treated the same.

"He's got a lot on his mind," Malakai began.

But Quinn wasn't about to let him finish. "Isn't he like omnipotent or something?" she snapped.

"He's not a god; he's the Library."

"Same thing, he has like all this knowledge from everywhere, doesn't he?" In her mind, it was pretty much the same.

"Exactly, he doesn't have all the knowledge from everywhere because it's always evolving. And people took his books out and never returned them. And the bookworms ate some. Right now he's trying to consolidate his power base again." Malakai attempted to lay it out for her, but even he had a frown on his face as he spoke.

"Good point. The bookworms ate some. So the knowledge he had escaped?" She crossed her arms and stared at him.

Malakai ran a hand through his hair, obviously slightly flustered. "With low power, he doesn't have access to his full system. I think..." He shifted his weight, like he was trying to figure out another way to explain Lynx's behavior.

"Malakai," Quinn said, looking around him and stepping forward very carefully to reach out a hand, "don't step back."

"Why? What?"

She grabbed his arm and tugged him forward. He turned to look and saw that there was a gaping hole in the floor directly behind where his heels had been. He blanched a little bit, fading to a paler blue.

"He pushed us out of a well." He was blinking rapidly at the hole.

She shrugged. "Can you see any trees, like not in the extreme distance? Or areas to put a trapdoor? It's so rocky here, it's like there's nothing. I almost expect tumbleweeds to blow past and somebody to call me 'little lady' and step out with a gun and cowboy boots."

Malakai blinked at her, not understanding the reference in the slightest. Quinn sighed; her comedic talents gone to waste.

"This seems like a bit of a desolate wasteland," she explained as she looked around trying to get a feel for the rocky wasteland.

"Well, from what I know of Kajaro, that's not surprising." Malakai took a very deliberate step farther away from the well.

Quinn's curiosity got the better of her. "He's immortal, does that mean he's like a vampire or something?"

Malakai shrugged, "I have no idea of two things. First, what you mean by vampire because that's a mythological creature? And secondly, I don't have the map. You have to direct us to find where the book is."

"Oh right." She fumbled, tugging it out of her pants pocket and turning it in her hand. "Okay, let's figure out where we are and then we can take a moment to marvel at the fact that you're an elf calling a vampire a mythological creature."

Malakai scowled. "Hey. I'm standing right here."

"I'm very aware," she said pointedly. "And I'm also not from your universe-traversing world. To me, you're all not supposed to exist."

"How much time do we have left?" Malakai asked suddenly changing the subject as she was still trying to figure out the map.

"Thirty-nine hours and change," she said, trying to keep the worry from her voice. "It's okay, we've got this. We can do this, of course we can; we wouldn't be here if we couldn't."

She tried to sound reassuring, more for herself than for her adventure partner, but she didn't think she was very convincing.

"Okay." She turned around, frowned, and pointed in the northwest direction. "I think we have to go over there."

Malakai leaned over her shoulder and looked. "Given that we've no other points of navigation than the map, I would agree with you."

"Oh great, I'm so glad that you agree with me."

"That was unnecessary," Malakai muttered.

Quinn took a deep breath. She really felt on edge. "I know, I'm tired, and this place is freaking me out a little."

"Well, you had just shy of six hours of sleep."

"You think six hours sleep is a lot of sleep?"

"Well, it's more than a lot of people get." Malakai actually pouted. He took out one of the breathing apparatuses and handed it over, taking a breath from his own.

She didn't dignify his comment with an answer, but attached hers for some nice oxygen for a few minutes while they headed off in a northwesterly direction, hoping to find an immortal being who might or might not be a vampire. Things just kept getting better.

The more they walked, the uneasier Quinn felt. There was something off about this area. As far as the eye could see, there was just plain, black rock stretching out all around them, with some moss scattered through the cracks.

Every now and again a slithering sound reached her ears ever so briefly, and then it was gone. It seemed like the perfect terrain for all sorts of creepy crawlies. They didn't need to speak, they were each concentrating on keeping their footing.

They came across the occasional well, and after almost two hours of walking, they'd found nothing. There was no real change in land-scape, just perhaps a very slight rise and fall of the rocks. Some trees stuck out here and there from them, but nothing like what she'd been expecting. It almost felt like they were walking in a time loop.

She stopped and turned to her right. There seemed to be a darker spot of rock just over a very slight slope. She took several steps and fell. In the second it took for her to reach the ground she realized that this world had subterranean levels. The landing jarred her knee and made her wince with pain. Great, now that on top of her partially healed ankle.

Falling was getting to be a habit.

Why, on however many worlds there were, had Lynx failed to mention such pertinent information? Was the Library sick or something?

Malakai peered over the edge of the hole. "Oh good, you're not dead. That would have put a bit of a kink in the Library restoration plans."

"Gee, thanks." She stood up wincing as her knees ached a little and dusted herself off. Sure enough, there was a path leading down from the hole she'd fallen through. It was spacious around her too and a strange luminescent green moss clung to the walls of the cave.

"Huh," she said, "get down here."

"Fine." The next second Malakai stood next to her.

"Oh," he said, "it appears to be subterranean, then?"

"You think?" she snapped, immediately regretted snapping, took a deep breath, held up a hand, and said, "I'm sorry, I'm very tired and a little grumpy that Lynx didn't think to mention this to us."

"Well, he did mention the world name. He probably assumed that we knew." Malakai shrugged, and flipped his breathing apparatus around in his fingers.

"Why would he make that assumption? I'm not even from this, from whatever universe, galaxy, solar system thing is. I have no idea that Lapsaxum indicates this is a desolate rocky world." Quinn sighed as she began to walk down the singular path in front of them. The book still seemed so far away on the map.

Malakai chuckled as he fell into step with her. "Yes, but you're a Librarian and thus he's already forgotten that he still has to teach you so much. Especially since, as my grandfather mentioned, you didn't receive the information transfer."

"No, I hit my head when I was being transferred and something got scrambled. It was probably my brain. Who knows, maybe I actually fell down a rabbit hole and have been chasing a rabbit with a bloody pocket watch this whole time." She really couldn't seem to let go of the grumpy, so she raised her breather to get a few more minutes of air. Lack of oxygen made everyone moody.

Malakai raised an eyebrow. "I'm guessing that's a reference I don't understand."

"Yes, everything I say is a reference you don't understand." Nope. The oxygen wasn't helping her snappiness.

Malakai put his hands up. "Whoa, whoa, that's not my fault."

"No." She looked at him and felt somewhat contrite, "I suppose it's not. Anyway, this path leads mostly northwest and to the book. Plus, it's like the only way to go."

They did so for maybe an hour and Quinn was trying very hard not to focus on the timer in the bottom right corner of her vision. They had plenty of time, plenty of time.

Thirty-five hours and counting down. Nothing to panic about.

"Okay, this is okay. It's not a narrow tunnel, at least," she said, mumbling under her breath to stay calm.

He raised an eyebrow. "Why? Are you afraid of small, tight spaces?"

"Isn't everyone?" she said. But luckily, a little ways up ahead, it opened out into a massive cavern. They'd been steadily going slightly downhill while they'd been walking. And this thing had to have twenty-foot ceilings. There were stalagmites and stalactites and about six other wide tunnels leading off it headed in various directions.

"I guess we should pick the right path," Quinn said, angling herself around to find which tunnel was closest to the direction she needed. There, quite literally pointing exactly toward where the book was supposed to be, was a tunnel.

Malakai glanced at the map and up at the perfectly placed tunnel entrance. "I guess we're going down this one."

She looked around and was surprised that they hadn't encountered any people, any creatures, or anything living at all. Just a lot of sand and a lot of glowing moss and a hell of a lot of tunnels.

"Yeah," she said, "this seems suspiciously easy."

"Ugh," Malakai said, "I wish you hadn't said that."

Quinn cringed, belatedly realizing exactly what he meant. "Well, let's just keep going where we need to go." And so, they followed the tunnel. She could tell that this one also angled ever so slightly downwards.

She wished she had a motorized scooter, or a bike. All this walking was a lot.

As they walked, there was no sound but their own footsteps and the sound of sand as it fell away from their boots with each step. It gave her a rhythm to concentrate on because everything around them was so silent, like there was something waiting, as if something had scared away the type of creature that might actually live down here.

Her head focused on each footstep, on each movements, in a trancelike way. It made the sheer monotony of the whole trek bearable.

Then again, maybe the entire planet was devoid of habitation and Lynx had completely steered them wrong because the guidance system in the Library was currently crap.

It could be any of it, really.

"Did you hear that?" Malakai asked.

"No," she said, not wanting to admit that her thoughts had probably been far too loud for anything else to get past them.

"There, do you hear *that?*"

This time, however, she did. It was like a dripping sound. Perhaps there was an underground cavern stream. That would make sense since there was no water up on the surface but moss did appear to grow almost everywhere, and didn't it require moisture?

Malakai looked around and up. "Maybe that's why Lynx said that there wasn't much air. I mean, he did prepare us somewhat."

"Yeah, he did. It definitely feels like the air is heavier down here." She looked around, not seeing any other paths veering off from the one they were on, and shrugged. "Well, it looks like we just need to keep going." The path, luckily, didn't get any narrower. It simply continued on. But it did begin to get steeper and it became very obvious that their path was heading much farther down under the ground.

"Are we still on track?" Malakai asked, the hesitation in his tone obvious.

"Yeah, we're definitely getting closer," she said, looking at the map, following the dot right where the book was located. She didn't like that they were definitely on the right track, but couldn't deny that they were. As she looked around, the moss glowed even brighter. So much that she could see condensation on the walls.

"I'm not sure I like how wet this is getting," Malakai said.

"Can't swim?" Quinn asked, trying to lighten the mood somewhat.

"Oh no, I'm perfectly good at swimming. It's not wanting to swim in dark, unknown waters that gets to me."

Quinn shuddered. Yep, that was a thing of nightmares.

As they continued to move forward, the sand became damp. Which was better for grip, considering she'd already tweaked that ankle the last time she came to visit a different world. Speaking of which, that ankle didn't hurt anymore. Not even as much as the knee she'd tweaked falling down here. Maybe this area had some restorative properties, too.

There were apparently restorative properties in the Library, which bode well for future adventures if she ever made it out of the weirdly subterranean underground area that Lynx had sent them to without warning.

"Well," she said, "it's a good thing I can swim. Thanks for asking, Lynx."

Malakai chuckled. "It's not like Lynx really knew. Not on a personal level anyway. I mean, obviously, it isn't *just* underground water."

"Well, maybe Kajaro is a fish," Quinn said.

"I highly doubt that. I don't know of any immortal fish," he said, with an air of condescension.

"Do you know everything? On every world? In every dimension?" Quinn asked.

Malakai blushed. "No. No, I do not."

"Exactly. He could be an immortal fish vampire." There was a chuckle that echoed throughout the path as they rounded a piece of wall leading them into a large cavern.

There, right in front of them, spanning acres and acres, was a massive underground lake.

The bright side was that they could see three tunnels in the distance on the other side of it, if they squinted. And there was a raft-like boat anchored over with them, pulled up high onto the sandy path. Quinn gulped. Boating had never been her thing. Even Malakai looked pretty green around the gills. Although maybe that was just the strange fluorescent moss lighting down here reflecting off his blue skin.

A chuckle echoed throughout the cavern again. And that's when she spotted him, standing at the entrance to the middle tunnel, all the way across the lake. He had to be tall, and he definitely wasn't a fish. But that's about all she could make out, even squinting.

Kajaro laughed again, and it started to grate on Quinn's nerves.

But then he spoke. The sound carried all the way across the lake, booming and echoing off the stony ceiling. "I am here, and I am definitely not a fish. Should you be able to reach me, I will consider granting your wish."

"What's the catch?" Quinn raised her voice, knowing that there was going to be a catch. There was always a catch.

Also, she was oddly put off by the fact that he rhymed his statement.

"You have to make it from your side of the lake to mine. And let's just say, my friends *in* the lake here like visitors about as much as I do." As if to answer his words, or perhaps even punctuate them, there was a bubbling from the depths of the lake that shook the entire cavern.

Quinn was quite certain making it to the other side had just got a whole lot more difficult than sailing a dingy raft.

21

HE'S JUST A VERY NAUGHTY
LIBRARY

THE WATER IN THE LAKE WAS SO DARK IT WAS ALMOST BLACK, BUBBLING in such a way that it looked like boiling oil. Even though Quinn knew inherently that it wasn't, the sight was still unnerving.

"Show me your skills," Malakai said. There was urgency in his voice. She looked at him blankly.

"What do you mean, 'show you my skills'?" Quinn asked heatedly. "I don't think this is the time for me to pull out my machete and try to practice the skills the book apparently taught me."

He tsked underneath his breath. "I don't mean show me physically. I mean share them with me."

"Like list them off? I've got *Machete for Dummies, Beginner's Shield,*" Quinn began, having no clue why they needed to do this when something was emerging from the depths of that lake.

But he cut her off. "No! Did he not even show you how to share your abilities?"

"Obviously not, or I wouldn't be looking at you like a fish out of water." When she got back. Quinn was really going to have a word with that damned manifestation.

"That was a really bad pun, Quinn." He pinched the bridge of his nose and she could tell he was trying not to laugh.

She shrugged, pulling out her machete anyway. Just in case. "I'm a little stressed right now."

"So am I." Malakai took in a deep breath and said, "Look."

He focused in front of himself for just a moment, and all of a sudden, information popped up in front of her. Like it had when she first entered the Library. Back before she even connected to it. The information scrolled across her vision.

Recurve Compound Bow of the Lost Soul

Activation Capacity 225 pounds

Damage Capacity Multiplier of 37 dependent on Activation Capacity reached

She sucked in a breath as she read it. "Whoa, whoa, that looks really powerful."

"Yes. Yes, it is. Now show me what yours is." That was Malakai's impatient voice.

"Well, how did you do that?"

"You call up your abilities in order to recall them and you tell it to share with the person you're standing next to."

"Okay. Skills," she said and took a step back as they flashed up before her eyes with more information than she'd thought. "Oh, my god."

It was like the screen that popped up in front of her when she was in the Library in contact with its console. "But I'm not in contact with the Library."

"No, but you're literally the Librarian, which means it doesn't matter where you came from or what your species is. You have access to the interface at all times, just like anyone who has an affinity, even if you're not directly connecting to it. How do you think everybody knows where the Library is and when to return their books and what skills they have and how they process their knowledge? Everybody has access to the Library system because it's the best way to refine our magical system. Now show me your abilities."

"Share with Malakai," she muttered, with so many more questions popping up in her mind that it felt crowded. "Okay."

"Okay, we might be able to do this," he said, even as a tentacle shot out of the water and splashed down not ten feet before them, drenching them both with the aftermath.

Quinn swallowed a scream and steeled her nerves. "You think we can really fight that thing? That was only *one* tentacle."

"I realize this," Malakai said. "There is no need to get so worked up."

Quinn simply raised an eyebrow. "I'm sorry, I didn't have 'fight giant mythological creature' on my bingo card for today!"

Malakai took a deep breath. "Look, you're going to need to use *Watch Out for That Tree* for yourself and to boost me when I tell you. Keep your *Beginner Shielding* up and get ready to use *Bright Light Starters* when I tell you to distract it. That creature is used to darkness not to bright light. This is literally all we have to work with."

Quinn took a deep breath. "Okay, distract it like in a video game, right?"

Malakai didn't even bother glaring at her for that contribution. "Whatever it takes to make it clear in your head is fine. Just follow my directions and when we get back to the damn Library, I'm going to have to take over your training, because this is ridiculous."

"Hey, don't get angry at me."

"I'm not. Just a little frustrated." He stared at her, his expression serious as he drew out a sword, putting his bow back for the time being. "We need to get this done as soon as possible. You don't yet have the power to cast too many iterations of these spells. I'll do my best."

"How sweet," Kajaro called out, as he sat down on the opposite bank and pulled something out of what looked like a basket. He probably had either binoculars or popcorn. It was a pity that Quinn couldn't tell which from the distance. Another tentacle rose out and splashed them again, smashing where they'd have been standing if they hadn't jumped out of the way.

Quinn did not appreciate being sopping wet.

"Well, here goes nothing," Malakai said, and leaped into the air, and just as it looked like he was about to descend, he jumped again. Like he double-leaped on air and came crashing down as a tentacle rose up, severing it right next to the water before he jettisoned off the stub he'd created and performed a double flip through the air to land next to her again.

Quinn gaped at him while the thing in the middle writhed in the water as blood sluggishly pumped from the stump to mingle in the murky depths. More tentacles rose up, splashing water everywhere until they had their own rainstorm.

"That's about the response I was expecting," Malakai said, not even out of breath. And for the first time, since Kajaro had decided to spring this monster of the deep on them, Quinn finally thought they might have a chance to retrieve the book after all.

The creature wasn't stupid, however. It wasn't on a rotation; it didn't have stages like any monster in a computer game did. No, this creature learned from its mistakes. This time, when Malakai shot up into the air, the creature was ready for him.

Luckily, Malakai also wasn't an NPC in a computer game.

Instead of using the exact same move he did last time, he catapulted to the diagonal when he did the second step of his weirdly gravity-defying leap. "Light now!" he screamed. Quinn willed the light to appear exactly where he *should* have been, hoping she was A: aiming correctly, and B: using the spell correctly.

A brief blast of light lit up the cave like a Christmas tree. All she could see for several blinks was bright light in front of her eyes. She probably should have closed her eyes, but hindsight was always 20/20.

The squeal that emanated from the squid-octopus or whatever it was that was in the lake was high-pitched, quite ear-shattering. A couple of the stalactites on the ceiling rumbled. Pieces of them fell off and plopped into the water, even as Malakai angled down and forced his sword to lop off yet another limb of the creature. He barely alighted on the stub and flipped backward, landing a couple of feet into the water and wetting his boots even more than they'd already been.

This time, however, his exertion was obvious. He was panting a little bit.

"Nice shot," he panted out. "Next time close your eyes."

"Already figured that out, thanks." She was still seeing dark spots in her vision. "Could have warned me."

"Didn't think I had to," he said, his breathing almost back to normal.

She wondered what sort of life these people led that they were just used to battling octopuses in the middle of lakes, whereas she was used to doing all of her work with books in the school library. Apparently Library Sciences really had been her thing.

The creature continued to thrash around. It seemed, however, less occupied with them and more with perhaps finding a means of escape. It dove down and the water bubbled, it was tinged slightly reddish-green now.

Its blood, intermixed with the murky liquid, produced an odd color combination. It seemed scared more than angry and upset. Perhaps it hadn't thought that this would be such a big fight. Maybe it hadn't wanted to fight in the first place.

Maybe Kajaro was coercing it. Quinn suddenly felt sorry for the monster.

Malakai cracked his neck from side to side. "I'll go in once more."

"Are you sure?"

"Yep, once more should do. It should run away then."

"It'll grow its limbs back, right? It's a squid." Quinn asked. It really didn't seem that keen for the fight. It's remaining limbs were flailing more than aiming at anything.

"Well, it should, technically, but I don't know what that dude over there's done to it, so I can't answer any of that." Even Malakai seemed concerned about the creature he was fighting. He shook his head as our opponent began to calm back down in the water. "This time I need you to use Tree. I need to teleport a short distance and I don't know if you're able to aim me well enough, but we'll have to try it. It's going to know my attack patterns."

That's when Quinn decided it was a cephalopod. Sticking with the classification that included both was far easier. She understood that they were smart enough to be adaptively learning from every move her and the elf made.

Damn it, she was already feeling exhausted.

"Okay, are you ready?" Malakai asked, hefting his sword in his hand.

"Yep, about as ready as I'm ever gonna be."

The cephalopod had come to the conclusion that it couldn't escape yet. Maybe Kajaro had something blocking its escape route. She didn't know. Whatever it was, the surface bubbled again, and this time its bulbous head poked up just a little bit and Malakai flew in action, catapulting toward it.

"Now," he yelled.

She cast *Watch out for That Tree*, hoping to allow Malakai to land on its head, but he shot past that and glimmered over to the other shore landing calf deep in front of Kajaro. If she'd have realized that that was a possibility, she would have had him make the jump with her.

As its prey flew over to the other side where Kajaro was, the cephalopod stopped and looked back to where Quinn was standing on the shore with nothing to guard her. The little machete clutched at her side probably wouldn't even make a dent in one of its tentacles.

Quinn looked from it, back to the other side, and back to it again, and realized that this was not a good situation.

"Quinn, you have to move yourself over here!" Malakai yelled. Kajaro was standing now, leaning against the back wall, hunched over, watching them. He didn't make a move.

"It won't reach that far," she yelled, knowing instinctively that it wouldn't. It had been a stretch for him to make it over to the other side and he'd been halfway toward the middle with a sky high jump off. She frantically thought of all of her different spells. Surely there had to be one that she could use.

Wait, wasn't this whole thing water? Wouldn't water freeze if she cast that snowstorm thing on it? Wouldn't that work if she used *Ice Blast*?

She didn't have any more time to think because one of the tentacles bore down on her while another squirted sluggish blood in her direction, drenching part of her clothes as she tried to scramble out of the way. She felt tired and realized that she needed to keep a better eye on what powers she was using.

Quinn wasn't used to magic. It drained her energy or magic energy or mana or whatever it was probably faster than a person who'd been using it their entire life.

Malakai had sort of warned her.

She only really had one shot at this. Steeling herself, she summoned the icy blast spell in her head, raised her fist, and released the spell as she opened her palm, just as the tentacle was about to hit her. The end of the appendage crystallized rapidly. The transformation shot up the rest of that limb and passed quickly through the entire body of the octopus, freezing it in place. But it didn't stop there. Instead, it spread out to the water, to where even she stood, so fast that she had to scramble back and she fell, finally releasing the active spell.

The tentacle she'd originally been escaping still loomed over her. Gravity was working its wonder as it gave into its own weight plus the ice and fell toward where she'd been. It hit the ground in a spray of wet sand and ice shards.

Quinn realized she was absolutely exhausted—magically. But she couldn't stay where she was.

She got the distinct feeling that the beginner spell wasn't meant to do what she just did. It was likely she'd poured way too much power into it.

She knew, at any rate, that she'd kept it going far longer than she'd thought it could last. "Blast" implied short. That had taken several seconds. The water was frozen, even right up to the shore. Even the boat was frozen in place. She could almost feel the way Malakai kept half an eye on her from across the water, but that didn't matter.

He had to keep the other eye on Kajaro, who was lazily pacing, not taking his eyes off the elf. She had to get there before everything unfroze. With the amount of water and the size of it, there was no way it would stay frozen for long.

She jumped onto the ice, skidding and falling, slipping and sliding, until she finally made it to the other side. Her hands were raw and bleeding in places, her face flushed and cold. Malakai grabbed her by the arm and pulled her in close, once she got into the shore, trying to lend her warmth she didn't feel.

A trickle of healing from him helped her scrapes.

They turned to face Kajaro, who was clapping slowly from where he'd leaned back against the wall.

He was not what Quinn had expected. She thought he'd resemble a wise, white-haired wizard with flowing robes and a bushy beard or something, but he wasn't.

His skin was scaled like a serpent, and he stood and moved in such a way that she was fairly certain he was an actual type of snake or at least a reptile. He moved with a grace that belied having bones, and every single inch of her stood on end.

Complete and utter fear gripped her core. It was all she could do not to hide behind Malakai, considering he was a much larger target. The fact that she was freezing cold also played into the equation.

"Well, well, well," said Kajaro. His grin didn't reach his eyes. "I see we have a new Librarian." The S in his words was sibilant, definitely like a snake.

"What of it?" she said. *Probably not wise to antagonize the very nasty man standing in front of you*, she thought to herself belatedly.

"Well, it's good to see that we found a replacement, but I don't think I like you," Kajaro said.

"What does it matter if you like her or not?" Malakai interrupted. "She's the Librarian and she's here to retrieve a book that you've had for longer than the Library's been missing."

"Ah, yes, so close to five hundred years. I would have claimed it as mine by right of abandonment. Still, I don't like how you arrived on this side of the lake. You cheated," Kajaro spread his hands and electricity sprung up from each of them, arcing over his head, "and you're not going to like what I do to cheaters."

22

KAJARO

KAJARO'S LIGHTNING ONLY MISSED QUINN BECAUSE MALAKAI PULLED her out of the way in time.

To be fair, Quinn had never been the most coordinated person, but she had been fast. She'd always thought that being able to run away from incidents if she couldn't defend herself well enough, would be much more useful than trying to teach herself self-defense combinations.

She'd also never imagined herself having to run away from a lightning-wielding-snake-man.

"Sorry," she muttered, going into a crouch and getting ready to run.

Except that wasn't going to work, was it? Realizing her own mistake, she stood up and glared at the man who, well, to put none too fine a point on it, was being a dick.

"Just return the damn book and we'll leave you to play with your little octopus friends." She put a hand on her hip hoping to display more confidence in her words and her threat than she actually felt.

Kajaro's cackle rang through her ears like a high-pitched squeal. She winced. He didn't say anything, and there was no preamble, so she wasn't sure how she managed to dive out of the way to her left, just before a bolt of electricity hit where she'd been standing half a moment before. She blinked and rolled automatically again, dodging yet another hit.

Kajaro laughed again as the sand splashed up and around his target points. "This is fun. At least the Library found an amusing replacement this time," he said.

She wanted to ask what that meant more than anything, but this wasn't the time. She pulled her shielding around her, making sure it was tight and snug. It felt like a layer of invisible material that provided protection, which was good because it was the only thing she could use right then. She knew from the depths of her soul that the fatigue she felt right into her bones was because she'd already overused the magic she had. All she had left were physical manifestations, like the shielding spell.

She paused, glancing up at Malakai. She could have kicked herself for looking at him, because Kajaro had been occupied with watching where she was moving and aiming for her. In the meantime, Malakai was sneaking up behind Kajaro.

While Quinn thought the snake could probably tell where her adventure partner was, she didn't know for certain, but with her eyes gravitating toward Malakai's location, it gave away where the elf was standing. Kajaro turned, shoving an electricity-wrapped fist directly into Malakai's solar plexus as he was getting ready for an overhand hit with his sword.

She could hear the thudded impact as it contacted his chest and sent the elf flying back about thirty feet right into one of the rock walls. He hit it and slumped to the ground.

"Excellent," Kajaro said, wiping his hands against his robe. "One down, one to go."

"What do you have against the Library?" Surely she could at least try and stall him for time. Wasn't time what magic needed to regenerate in games?

Kajaro cracked his neck from side to side and jiggled around like he was about to have a boxing match, getting ready for a fight. "We don't hate the Library, as such. It really is a wonderful depository of knowledge. The Library has everything we want, all the knowledge, all the power. It just doesn't let me have it all to myself, or in its raw state. I don't like that."

He glanced down at his hands, with a frown, moving the fingers slowly. "Looks like my hands didn't like that ice spell of yours. How did you cast that? You shouldn't have been able to wield ice yet."

Quinn just shrugged and filed his ranting to the back of her mind. She had no idea what he was talking about or why she wouldn't be able to wield ice, or any of the other spells. She was the Librarian. Wasn't she supposed to be able to do it all or something?

She shook her head and said, "Well, I can and I did, and it wasn't cheating." She definitely sounded like she was confident. Much more so than she felt.

"Where *did* he get you from?" Kajaro began to move his hands again, this time coaxing much larger spheres of electricity.

The visual reminded her of those plasma globes that they'd had years ago, where his hands were the center of the globe and the electricity just drifted out from it in larger and larger spikes.

She backed up and her foot hit water this time. She wondered if that meant that the octopus was coming out of his stasis as well. It wasn't just ice anymore; it was like stepping into slush. She couldn't go back that way, so she began to sidle along the beach, for want of a better word, and move her way around toward the other tunnels.

She couldn't afford to look at Malakai, she just had to hope that he wasn't dead because that would definitely put a dampener on her plans. And this time, as long as she didn't look at him, maybe she wouldn't give away his position if he did manage to get up and execute a plan.

It was difficult to remain upbeat what with Lynx's statement before they left. Kajaro was immortal. But there was something about that tugging at her mind. Still, there were other things to occupy her thoughts right then.

This was starting to pose a very difficult scenario for Quinn. Running was all good, dodging was pretty fine, but the more she did that, the more potholes appeared in the sandy ground. Gouges really.

Tripping over them, stumbling through them, and crashing down because she didn't realize how deep one was.

It all culminated when she jumped to the side in a place that she'd been not five minutes earlier and tumbled unceremoniously to the ground, smashing her right elbow as she caught herself. Wincing in pain and getting her dark hair badly singed by the lightning that only just missed the rest of her, she cried out, "Shit!"

She jumped up again, scrambling to find a foothold as she leaped toward Kajaro this time. He stumbled back slightly, not as graceful as he usually moved, seemingly surprised by her frontal attack. She still didn't think he had feet, probably a snake body. She wasn't about to lift up the robes to try and find out. However, she did take advantage of his surprise as much as she was able.

Not using any powers for the last six or seven minutes, she hoped that it worked like it did in a computer game. Even though she wasn't out of combat as such, she should have regenerated some power.

Unless every game she'd ever played had completely and utterly lied to her.

A brief notification flashed in front of her eyes.

Mana: 78/642

Okay, maybe full regeneration only happened with sleeping here. At least she had something; she'd figure out the rest later, along with everything else that Lynx hadn't told her. But before she could second-guess herself, she flung her arm out and cast *Icy Blast* again.

The frost shot out of her hand and she remembered to close her fist again, lest she waste some of the precious energy that she'd regained. It stuck to the cowl that covered his face, reaching inwards and blistering his skin. Even as she dove back out of the way, as he tried to rip the hood from his head, the icicles spread farther and farther into the fabric, gaining traction as they shot down.

Mana 63/642

All it took was a thought, but that still cost more time than she liked right now. Training. She'd train like the dickens when—not if—she got back to the Library.

Maybe it wasn't that she had continuously let the power out.

Perhaps the spell was just this powerful. It spread all the way down his robe and when it touched his hands, it began to encase his fingers.

The sparks of electricity around them petered out, smoke wafting from the tips. Kajaro screamed, but it wasn't just in pain; it was more like frustration. A distinct smoky smell, oddly like roasting chicken, rose up from his arm where the icy burn caused friction with some of the electrical sparks running along his skin.

Now she knew what roast snake smelled like.

It was enough of a diversion for Malakai to get himself up and out of sight to do whatever he needed to. All she knew was that he wasn't against that wall anymore. That was fine. Quinn was absolutely okay with being a diversion, as long as Malakai was going to jump in and do something quickly because he hadn't been doing anything for the last ten minutes.

Everything in her body ached like she'd been thrown against the wall back when the engorged bookworm did just that to her. It was like she was pushing herself beyond the limits that she knew she had. And the other thing was that she didn't have any choice.

"Here," Malakai tossed her something, and not even Quinn was sure how she managed to catch it. It was a tiny vial filled with an oddly aquamarine liquid. She raised an eyebrow. "Are we kamikaze-ing out of this?"

"I don't know what that means," he said. "Just drink it while you can."

He was binding his leg, which she realized belatedly must have broken or been cut somehow because there was a lot of blood soaking the otherwise pale pants he'd been wearing. "Give me a few more minutes. We can do this."

She took a swig of the vial, draining it in an instant and felt immediately better. Not completely, but it helped. She felt replenished.

Meanwhile, Kajaro was still ripping at his face, but the ice had by now begun to stop spreading, and she knew they had very little time. As far as she knew, there was no way they weren't going to be able to kill this man. He was immortal, right? But she'd do her best to distract him. Maybe if they brought him to a stalemate, he'd give them the book.

"Kajaro, stop screwing around and just give me the damn book." She didn't even have to act that much frustration out.

She was getting really pissed off. All she wanted to do was collect a book from the guy, like it was that hard to return something that wasn't yours, even if you were a greedy bastard.

"Give it to me," she yelled.

"No," he screamed. "I refuse. You don't deserve it."

"I don't deserve it? I've been a Librarian for five days and I just burnt your skin with ice and you're telling me I don't deserve to take my book back?" Now, she was really pissed. Hauled out of her decent life to fight a snake man for a book?

He stopped and looked at her through ice obstruction. "Five days." And for just a few seconds, she thought maybe she'd won him over.

Except, she was *very* wrong.

With his hood thrown back, she realized that he really was mostly a snake man. His face was barely even humanoid. He looked like a snake standing upright, like a cobra did when it was warning before an attack. His eyes were completely black with no other color at all, and his tongue flickered out with a forked end.

She didn't want to get anywhere close to that.

"Five days is more than enough. You should be better than this." There was something about his tone that told her it was all bravado.

Quinn knew he was lying. She glared at him, and raised her hand to throw another ice blast. She had a few more in her if the mana cost had been correct. "I'll do that again. I'll use more power." To be frank, she had no idea why she'd hesitated in the first place.

"You'd have to hit me first," he snarled.

"Fine." She only hoped the bravado didn't extend to herself. She raised her fist and released the icy blast. A gust of very pointed icy wind jettisoned toward him, only to be swallowed by what appeared to be a vortex directly in front of him.

Quinn stumbled back, and Kajaro cackled yet again. He needed to stop doing that. He was starting to sound really evil and get on her nerves. Not to mention he'd just summoned something that simply sucked her spell away.

She managed to sidestep a large hole that had been gouged in the ground and moved to the side. His arms crackled as he broke more of the ice embedded in his scales, and sparks of electricity began to emerge again.

"See," he said, his S long, "it's not just a matter of having skills. You have to know *how* to use them."

"So I'm guessing the reason you won't give the spatial distortion book back is because you feel you should be able to use more than that little parlor trick you've got right there." She attempted to goad him. Something had to work. She had no idea how she was managing to speak like that because right now the very core of her soul was shaking so much she was surprised it wasn't reverberating through her feet and making the whole mountain or whatever this subterranean area was tumble down and bury all of them.

Kajaro grinned, and a snake grinning wasn't exactly the sort of thing that she wanted to see. It sent shivers down her spine.

"It's just one of the reasons," he said. As he spoke, he began slithering toward her, boxing her in toward the lake.

There was almost nowhere left for her to run. There were too many rocks around the right-hand side. She should have kept going to the left.

She had no idea what Malakai was doing, but Kajaro was bearing down on her. "Tell me. Do you know how the Library found you? Out of all the planets in all the universes, he shouldn't have been able to find anyone. How did he discover you? Perhaps the better question is where?" His snake eyes gleamed in their non-blinking way as he slithered closer to her.

"What do you mean?" she asked, not just to distract him but because she wanted to know. Why shouldn't he have been able to find her.

"Exactly what I said. There should be nobody left who can link with the Library, and once I kill you, well, then there won't be, will there?" Despite him being snake-like, she could tell he was smirking.

The cold sensation that spread down her spine this time wasn't just a shiver. It was a portent of her very own death. Kajaro was so close now, and the electricity was beginning to really sizzle around his skin, just like it had been before she'd attacked him with ice. And it was far too close to her for comfort.

She brought her fist up in front of her again. The icy blast was the only thing she knew how to attack with. It was all that she had. She had to try it. She opened her fist, directing it directly toward his face, and it spun forward even faster than it had the last time.

She saw his vortex, far too close to her, begin to spring to life, and suddenly an arrow protruded through Kajaro's eye socket. Followed closely by another in the second. The surprise on his face, just before the ice hit his skull as well, was almost comical if blood hadn't spurted all over her from the wounds.

23

RETURNS

"OH. MY. GOD," QUINN SAID, AS THE BLACK AND GREEN LIQUID DRIPPED through her hair, down her face, and all over the clothes she was wearing. "I'd better be able to get the bloodstains out of my damn jeans." Although, they had been able to get the bookworm goop out, so this might be possible.

It was a very odd first thought to have, followed by, "What the hell, Malakai? We needed to ask him questions, didn't you hear what he was saying? We should have interrogated him. What did he mean?"

Malakai was propping himself up on his bow, looking extremely pale and lacking what appeared to be a lot of blood. She rushed past the falling snake corpse that was toppling extremely slowly, probably due to the tail and the way it stood, and rushed to Malakai's side.

"Are you okay?" She rushed the words out, looking him over though not knowing what the hell she was doing.

He chuckled faintly. "Are you not mad at me, then?"

"No, no, I think I'll forgive you this once. Are you okay? Don't you have any more of those vial things?" Then she paused briefly. "Wait, is he really dead? How did you... isn't he immortal?"

"You're only immortal until someone uses the method needed to kill you to do so. Serpensiril are hard to sneak up on unless they're concentrating. Thank you for distracting him," Malakai gasped out as he inclined his head and Quinn felt her face flush slightly. "And I only had two potions on me."

"Not so immortal now, are you?" she muttered, glaring at the corpse, angry at herself for using the potion Malakai'd given her. It could have helped him now.

Kajaro was dead.

She blinked, suddenly feeling numb.

"Quinn! You need to summon a door after we get the book." Malakai's breath was coming in short gasps now.

Ripping his jacket off she wrapped it around his calf, hoping it would help slow the bleeding. She did her best not to get flustered. Dying elf right in front of her was the perfect distraction from the fact that she had just helped kill someone. "Right. And then you need to explain to me why the hell you just killed the only person who's ever mentioned anything about them supposedly not being able to find a Librarian or whatever that was."

"Yeah, that was really suspicious, wasn't it?" he breathed the words out.

"And your shooting was really well-timed with not getting the information out of him," she grumbled.

"No, my shot was really well-timed with his vortex being focused on you so that he didn't realize he was about to get arrows directly through the eyes. It's the only way to kill that species." Malakai attempted a shrug but it ended in a cringe of pain. "Otherwise they live forever. It was pure luck you'd made him take his hood down, or I couldn't have done it. Frankly, I wasn't entirely sure I hit the right points."

"That makes a lot of sense," Quinn said, and changed the subject. "What about the book? We don't have it. What are we going to do?"

"Settle. You need to go crouch over his corpse, place your hand over his robe, just above his chest, about an inch or two, and say the word 'storage.'"

"What?" she said, thinking she'd heard it wrong.

"Open your hand, place it palm down. Don't touch his chest, just above it about an inch or two. And say the word 'storage'."

"Fine." She crawled over, held her hand above his chest, trying not to look at the massive arrows that were still stuck through his skull, and said, "Storage."

This time, instead of words scrolling in front of her eyes, a translucent screen popped up instead. It was sort of like an overlay when you were using one of those graphics programs. There were so many squares holding items, items she wasn't even sure she wanted to look at. There were rows and rows of books. Probably not just the book that he'd borrowed from the Library. "There are a lot of books in here. A lot of things in here. How is this even possible?"

"It's dimensional storage. It has a lot of capacity depending on the item. I don't have the ability to answer you right now." Malakai had paled even more, and sweat beaded his brow. "If you see the book, we just take his storage container. He's dead; his rights are relinquished."

"Search for *DeKarlyle's Thesis of Spatial Distortion*." Quinn said, willing to try anything... and one of the squares highlighted. She let out a sigh of relief and then frowned. "How do I take a storage container?"

"Just say 'loot storage container'."

"Loot storage container." Suddenly, there was what she could only determine as a pop-up in front of her face that said:

Loot storage container belonging to KaajAriuusucjo
Yes or No

"Yes." The ring around one of Kajaro's fingers slipped off and hovered directly in front of her palm. She turned her hand around and it plopped into it.

"And there you go," Malakai said. "Now you have your very own storage container. Once you empty it and cleanse it. Please, before I pass out, get us into the Library."

Quinn clutched the ring in her hand and walked over to the rock walls, holding up her left hand against the door, she breathed in and out. The doorway into the path was very wide and only had half a rotting wooden door, but it was all she had to work with. At some stage, perhaps these corridors had boasted beautiful, ornate doors, but now they were dilapidated and old, bereft of life, much like the rest of the place.

She glanced quickly toward the lake and realized that the previously frozen octopus was no longer there. She only hoped that, with Kajaro's death, the poor creature had been able to escape. Maybe, just maybe, it would be okay now.

Holding her hand against what remained of the door, she spoke. "Library, I need you."

There was a shimmer, and it seemed to be fighting something. She glanced at the time while she waited for it to manifest. "Hey, twenty-six hours left, not too bad."

They'd wasted a bit more time than she would have liked walking through all the tunnels but, ultimately, managed to come in under the wire. Suddenly, the door was there. She pushed it open and went back to help Malakai hobble up on one leg. He was pale and sweating, and she could tell that he wasn't doing well. But that was just going to have to hold on.

They hobbled towards the entrance and suddenly Lynx was there, peering out. "This isn't a commonly used entrance. What happened?" He glanced outside, saw the corpse of Kajaro, and looked with panic at Quinn. "Come inside, come inside. Milaro, get over here." There was panic in Lynx's voice, something she'd previously not thought he was capable of, but he definitely wasn't himself right now, or, at least, not the controlled self that she'd grown used to over the last few days.

They managed to usher Malakai inside before Milaro made it to them. He took one look at his grandson and grew pale. Dottie trotted over. "Put him on me. It's okay. We can do this." It was odd seeing a bench take more charge than a grown man and a manifestation of the Library.

"What did you do?" Lynx said. "You weren't supposed to kill him."

"Well, he was pretty intent on killing us," Quinn snapped. "So we kind of had no choice. I don't know if you've noticed, but I'm not exactly uninjured either. And Malakai is almost dead. So can we just focus on the important stuff? You still have a day before you need the book. Deal with this first." Quinn stopped and stepped back. "I'm sorry. It's been a really shitty fourteen hours."

"I can see that," Lynx said. "I promise. Once we've got the book back, we'll talk. First, we need to get Malakai healed."

Quinn nodded and made sure to clutch the ring tightly in her hand. She didn't really know how she felt about putting it on, and didn't want to put it in her pocket. She needed to feel it tangibly. Even though it was so tiny, she needed to know that what she took was the right thing.

Lynx looked at her, one hand on the door, hesitant. "Are you sure you have the book?"

Quinn opened her hand to show him the ring. He gasped slightly, which was odd considering he didn't really need air to breathe, but whatever. She needed to get used to his eccentricities.

"Ah, I see. It's in there." He sounded almost reverent like he couldn't wait to get his hands on its contents.

"There are a lot of books in there, and I think it showed me that it was in there when I checked." She shrugged, feeling a little defeated, truth be told.

Lynx blinked out of whatever information pit he'd been in and finally gave his full attention. "Let's go help Malakai first."

Being in a different wing of the Library was disconcerting. She hadn't been down this side hall before, and there were cobwebs on top of books littering the floor. So many cobwebs actually. Running into massive book-eating spiders wasn't on her bucket list. This area was so badly taken care of. Her heart ached at the fact that the Library was just pretty much dilapidated at this point.

"It's okay. We will fix it," Lynx said out loud.

"Yeah, I know. I just... it's sad."

"You have no idea," he said.

Finally, they came out into the main hall, except they didn't go the way Quinn was used to going. Not toward the kitchen, and not toward the stairs, nor the front of it where the check-in desk was. No, this time they moved to the left beyond the kitchen in the back, and when they walked into the room, Quinn couldn't help the gasp that escaped her.

It was the only well-lit area in the entire library. Perhaps Lynx had turned the lights up, but whatever had happened, the room was brightly lit, with pale blue walls, and a very soothing tone to it. There were cots around the room, sort of like a sick bay, and that's when she knew what it was. This *was* a sick bay, or a nurse's station or something, because Milaro already had his grandson propped up in one of the beds.

He was working fast, ripping the material of the jacket wrapped around the leg, and then the pants away from his grandson, and that's when she saw it. The massive gash from midway down his thigh to just below his knee. No wonder he was bleeding so much. How had he held out?

"What can I do?" she asked softly.

Milaro glanced at her. "Can you just talk to him?"

"Sure," she said, moving over. "Hey, Malakai, no dying."

"I don't think that's what my grandfather meant," he deadpanned.

"Well, I'm telling you not to die, because you just went through that hell with me, and we need to have this bond because I need some sort of friendship that isn't a hologram." She focused on his face, hoping for color to enter his features again.

Malakai actually smiled. "Okay, deal. I don't think I'm gonna die. I'm just very tired."

"Stay awake, son," Milaro said to his grandson. He was more serious than usual, and very focused. A strange green-blue glow emanated out of his hands as he ran them over his grandson's leg. Malakai grimaced.

"Oh, that does not feel good." He bit out the words through clenched teeth.

"Of course it doesn't feel good. I'm knitting your tendons and muscles back together." Milaro's words held no warmth, just clinical common sense.

Malakai however, had no problem putting zest in his words. "You could have given me a painkiller, a sedative, anything."

Not really sure what possessed her to, Quinn leaned over and pinched his arm.

"Ow," Malakai said, looking up at her in shock.

"There, see? Now you're not even thinking about your leg."

He looked at her for a moment and blinked, and then he started laughing.

"Ah, good, you're laughing." She turned to Milaro. "Does that mean he's gonna be okay?"

"He'll be fine."

"So your magic is healing magic?" she asked. It was a lot stronger than the little spell Malakai used on her.

"Some of it, yes." Then he continued, "My grandson just needs to sleep for a day or two now."

"Really?"

"Well, maybe not that long, but yeah, he needs to recuperate his strength naturally. This is no longer a battle, so just go with Lynx and get done what needs to be done, so that I didn't just tap into and drain ten hours of the Library's power for nothing." Milaro flashed her an understanding smile.

"Oh." She looked at her counter, and it was, in fact, down to sixteen hours. She felt beads of sweat start to form on her forehead, behind the nape of her neck. What if the storage ring had lied to her and the book wasn't in there? She gulped and hurried out of the room to find Lynx waiting there for her.

"Are you ready?" the Library manifestation said.

"About as ready as I'm gonna be, aren't I?" Quinn couldn't help the nerves nipping at the back of her mind.

After several moments of silence where Lynx seemed disconnected again, he turned to her. "Okay, give me the ring."

And she did. She handed it over, and it opened up in front of both of them. All of those little cubbyholes were visible to both of them.

"This is insane. You need to explain this to me as soon as you have time." Quinn really wanted to understand how this dimensional storage worked.

"I know and we'll get you your very own soon," he said, while scanning the contents. "Okay, now reach in and take the book."

"Which one is it?" she asked, peering at the six odd rows of books.

"Third from the left, four rows down." Lynx said pointing at the slightly glowing square.

She reached forward, and the book actually materialized in her hand. But it wasn't until it was fully out of the dimensional space that she could feel the mass of weight to it.

"Whoa," Quinn said, having to use two hands to hold it before it smashed down on the counter. She placed it there with some considerable impact and dust clouds.

"Check it in," he said.

She looked at it. It was very nondescript. A plain black leather cover with *DeKarlyle's Thesis of Spatial Distortion* written in plain silver script over the front of it. That was it. It was, however, about four inches thick.

"Okay," she said, "here goes."

Right hand on the tome, left hand on the console. She accessed the system before her and willed the book back into the Library system.

Return De Karlyle's Thesis of Spatial Distortion to the Collection:
Yes. No. Extend Borrow.

She activated *Yes* with her mind.

The console beeped softly and low for about five seconds. Lights flickered all around her. Suddenly, lines of script began to appear before her eyes. This time, however, it was more akin to the screen she'd brought up when she needed to access her abilities. They spread before her eyes as if she truly had a heads-up display in front of her.

All this strange code, in pictures, words, runes, and a myriad of languages, some of which went past so fast she couldn't even identify, scrolled before her.

Library system reboot Finalized
Library system reset Initiating
In Five. Four. Three. Two. One.

A loud click resounded through her ears and the entire building, then everything went dark.

24

ACCLIMATION

IT WASN'T MERELY DARKNESS THAT SURROUNDED HER; IT FELT LIKE AN inky blackness. Suddenly, a stream of words flashed before her eyes. All she could think of was that it was the code she'd seen earlier. Except this time, she could understand most of the words she saw. Abruptly, lights began to flicker back on until the library was much brighter than it had been. A soft, low whirring sound echoed throughout the large hall.

Library system Reboot - Success

Library system Reset - Minimum

Calibrating... Calibrating...

Guidance system available.

Return trolley available.

Golem creation beginning stages available.

Assistant seeker calibrating available.

Terrarium warmers recalibrating available.

Night owl habitat reestablished.

Librarian status upgraded. Reactivating administrative permissions. Reactivating administrative access.

Links F-4-5-2 reestablished. Reestablishing levels. Reestablishing links. Access granted.

Library status reestablished.

Power levels low - critical

Power usage optimized

Reestablishment almost reached

Quinn stood there, staring as most of the words faded from her eyes. All of these options sat in front of her. Guidance system. Return trolley. Golem creation. She didn't really understand it all, but there was no time like the present to dive in and start learning.

Lynx stood next to her, and she looked at him. He wasn't as translucent as he'd been. In fact, he seemed almost corporeal. She reached over and touched his finger, and sure enough, still smoky in essence, but more solid than he had been several minutes ago. His eyes lit up, their strange double eyelids working overtime. He must have been calibrating a lot of things himself. After all, wasn't he the Library?

He finally focused on her. "You did it. It's... we're not going to wink out of existence. You actually did it. Thank you." The relief in his tone was palpable, almost human itself. It gave Quinn second thoughts about what she'd expected from him in the first place. Maybe she'd been unrealistic, and that wasn't fair to him.

"No, Quinn, I owe you an apology. The guide you should have had upon entrance to this world is ready now that we've restored more functions and can be downloaded as soon as you're prepared to do so." He didn't even seem to notice that she hadn't voiced her thoughts out loud.

She scowled at him. "So I guess this is the part where you outright admit you can read my mind instead of just subtly answering questions I pose in it?"

"Oh, I'm sorry." He didn't sound sorry at all. Every word was punctuated with excitement. "I will set my parameters so that I do not read your mind without direction. Our connection has grown. It's about where a new Librarian should be now. You're finally a real Librarian."

"Wait, I wasn't a real Librarian before?" She had to digest that fact for a moment. "So, I was risking my life and not actually a Librarian."

"No, you were, but it was more low-key and interim because it didn't have enough power to connect you properly. Now you are. Now everything's going to work again."

Quinn wasn't sure how she should feel. It was a little bit anticlimactic. The Library hadn't magically transformed back into an amazing architectural wonder. It was still musty, a little dim for her liking, but much brighter. And now, with the Gloom fully dispersed, she could see the extent of the damage. Still, Lynx's excitement was a bit contagious.

"What happened here? Did like a whirlwind blow through?" she asked.

"No, that was rampaging bookworms about a hundred years ago," he answered, focused on something only he could see. "Oh, yeah, I managed to sequester them in the wing that they were, and that's about as good as I could until you got here to massacre them."

"Wow, okay." He was much more talkative, much more expressive now the Library had more power. She liked this Lynx even more. "You keep saying that you'll explain stuff to me. What the hell is a golem?"

Lynx paused for a moment and pulled a screen up in front of her face. On it, an outline of a large figure rotated. Lines pointed to different parts of it, and a lot of description filled the right-hand side. The words "Library Golem Supervisor Required" were displayed prominently.

"Okay," she said, looking at the diagram. "Explain this."

Lynx blinked at her. "Oh, that's right. Here, first of all, I need you to swallow this." He held out what looked like a chip, like a plain old crinkled chip she could get at any supermarket in a massive bag full of them.

"You want me to eat a potato chip?" She raised an eyebrow at him and crossed her arms. "A chip is not going to make a dent in that gnawing hunger I'm feeling."

"Yes and no. It's not meant to fill you up. It's not a chip as you are thinking, but as you chew into it and it breaks down, it will flood you with the information packet that you should have gotten a few days ago." His tone was filled with patience.

She took the chip and eyed it suspiciously. "You can't just tell me the contents?"

"Remember the information that flooded your memory and mind when you initially connected with the Library core?"

"Of course I do," Quinn said, vividly recalling the scream and the pain that spread through her at the time. It hadn't been pleasant.

"Well, this will be very much like that, so you might want to sit down before you take that." Lynx sounded like it was just an easy stroll in the park.

"Thanks for the warning," she said, not at all grateful. But she thought it was about time she had all the initial information and everything in one place.

Lynx pulled out a rolling chair that she hadn't noticed before. As she looked around the check-in desk, she realized that while the rest of the Library still looked pretty much dilapidated and torn apart, the desk itself appeared to be in much better repair. The wood was more polished and a deeper mahogany. Even the carvings weren't flaking anymore.

And the beautiful chair that Lynx offered her looked like it was going to be amazingly comfortable. It was the perfect place to sit and eat a chip that was probably going to rip right through her brain and inflict a lot of pain on her.

She couldn't believe this was her reality. If she'd had a choice in the matter, she might be completely and utterly rethinking her life choices right now. She plopped down on the chair and put the chip in her mouth before crunching down and feeling it break into thousands of tiny little pieces on impact. And then, like fading into dust, they disappeared on her tongue.

A second passed.

And then another.

Just as she was about to tell him she didn't think this was working, an onslaught of knowledge poured into her head. It was agony, pain, and just this fundamental rush of things she couldn't understand yet. So much about the way the world worked, about the way the Library worked, about how people were going to be able to interact with it.

Different worlds, different species, gravitational pulls, dimensional rifts, dimensional frequency, which she didn't even realize was a thing.

So much raw information. It wasn't that she immediately understood any of it, but it was there, like a database for her to pull from when she needed to.

Theoretically, anyway.

This time, she was pretty sure she didn't scream, but it was a very touch-and-go thing. Finally, after what seemed like an eternity, she blinked her eyes open, marveling at the bright light in front of her, and looked up expectantly at Lynx, who was watching her very closely.

Did it work?

But he didn't speak to her, his mouth didn't move. Instead, the words flowed into her mind. She started for a second, and then grinned up at him, nodding.

"Yeah, it worked, but I still prefer to speak out loud when possible. Thanks."

He chuckled. "Yeah, I thought you might. Okay, well, we have a lot of work to do."

Her head was pounding, not quite into bad headache territory, but it felt swollen with clinical knowledge, about to burst. "I'm aware of this."

"No, no, you're not. We need golems who can clean up the Library. We have to make sure the guidance system is working correctly before we allow people to return to the Library. We need to activate the return trolleys so that they can go about their business helping the golems do what they need to do. And then we also need to see if we can activate an assistant application, not to mention we're going to have to deal with the filtration system at some point in time." Lynx listed of a plethora of things, and Quinn knew, deep down, that wasn't even half of it.

"Okay, I'm going to skip over everything you want to say for now and go straight to the assistant application stuff." She tried to access information on it, but none of it was helpful. All she got was a listing of copious amounts of species listings and abilities and words she didn't yet comprehend. "What exactly does that mean? I thought you said nobody other than me had the Library signature."

"Assistants should have the Library signature because there's always a chance that they may need to step up and become a Librarian, but not all of them have it. There are people who just want to work in the Library. Those don't need a signature, but they do need a Librarian to answer to." He paused, making sure she was keeping up. "But there is a certain criteria that they must meet and there are magical signatures, or affinities if you will, that are much more suited to becoming a Library assistant."

"How many magical signatures are we talking about here? Like, just give me a ballpark number." Quinn couldn't seem to figure out how to track that down in her head by herself yet.

Lynx raised an eyebrow. "You could technically research that yourself."

"Just tell me."

"Well, you're probably looking in the ballpark of about seventeen hundred different magical signatures. One thousand seven hundred twenty-two currently, actually." Lynx's eyes did that weird color shifting again.

"Okay, so why did Kajaro seem so surprised that I could use ice magic?"

"Well, first up, you're a human." He paused, frowned, and then continued. "Anyway your body's molecular structure shouldn't really be conducive to using ice because you're made up of like, what, seventy, eighty percent water or something like that. On the other hand, most Librarians have a Library-matching signature. Yours matches a lot more than the Library. It kind of matches, like, everything..."

Lynx hesitated again, then shook his head and continued. "Kajaro just wasn't expecting you to be able to wield magic that wasn't based on pure knowledge." Lynx smiled like he was giving her good news.

Quinn shook her head. "Wait, wait, wait. Rewind. I have what magical affinities?"

Lynx grimaced. "Yeah, I was hoping you'd let me kind of scoot over that. Look, I searched far and wide for any type of signature that matched the Library. There isn't just one specific type. It's not the rarest signature; there are a lot more that are rarer. It's just that your signature matches every single type of magic that I have, that exists, that we know to exist. Maybe a few more that we haven't discovered yet, but that's neither here nor there. That just means that it's easier for you to quite literally learn every single thing the library has to offer."

Quinn stared at him. She didn't know how much time passed, but all she could think of was, how could she absorb every single book in the Library. Wasn't that, like, impossible? She mulled questions about in her mind and finally settled on one. "Okay, but I am compatible with the Library. What is a Librarian usually able to absorb?"

"Usually they can absorb any book that is bound on knowledge. So let's say you encounter a minotaur, okay? Let's just use that as an example. You have read a book on minotaurs, you understand everything about minotaurs, how they come to be, what their skeletal structure is, how the nervous system works. That would enable you, the Librarian, to literally unmake that creature, if you encountered them and they were a threat to you." He watched her expectantly.

Quinn blinked at him. "Yeah, that's—that's not much power at all, makes total sense."

He looked at her. "I don't like that tone."

"Of course, you don't like that tone, because this is just ridiculous. How can that even exist? Unmaking things sounds ludicrous." And it was threatening, ever so slightly, to unravel her.

"You're asking that now?" Lynx raised an eyebrow.

"That's beside the point," Quinn said. "Look, okay, so let's just not focus on the big elephant in the room. We can get to that at a later stage."

Lynx actually chuckled. "You know, that's the first time you said that and not me."

"Great, I am so glad I'm amusing you," Quinn said. Taking a deep breath, she calmed her nerves and carried on. "Okay, where were we?

Activating return trolleys? Do you expect people to just come and return the books once the Library opens?" She conveniently glossed over everything else, because right now she could only deal with so much new information.

"Yes, they hopefully should, once the message goes out that the Library is back in business. I'm hoping several thousand of those books will just return themselves." Lynx was so much calmer now than he had been before they restored the Library. It was grating.

"We need assistants, but before that, we need to activate the return trolleys. And how the hell do we build a golem?" All of her to-do list was flooding her mind and Quinn just needed to take a minute. The information from the chip was still dissipating and her head felt heavy.

"Ah, excellent, excellent question. So we're going to need to build the golems. We'll need a kitchen golem, a supervisor golem, we'll need a golem that tends to the creation of magical tomes, and we'll need maybe three or four shelving golems who can, you know, help shelve the books and tidy the Library and keep everything in order." He listed them off like it was the most natural thing in the world.

"Okay, that sounds great. What do we need to do to activate all of these?" Quinn asked, looking at Lynx expectantly.

He avoided her gaze and moved a couple of steps to the left.

"Lynx." She followed him, boxing him in so he couldn't run away even though she technically knew that he could blink in and out at any given time.

He sighed. "We should have most of the ingredients, I think. For most of them anyway."

"Should have?" she asked, not liking where it looked like that was leading.

"You may need to go out and fetch some." He paused. "Maybe."

"Okay, what do we have to do now then?" Quinn sighed this time. What she wouldn't give for a full belly and a good night's sleep right now.

At least the timer in the bottom corner of her screen was gone.

2 5

HELPERS

THERE WERE A LOT OF THINGS QUINN WANTED TO DO RIGHT THEN. Getting stronger was the highest priority on her list. Then maybe understanding exactly how the Library worked and how to utilize her connection better. Far down that list, at the very bottom to be precise, was her wish to venture out and find bits and bobs needed to replenish other aspects of the Library.

As she waited for Lynx to answer her question of what they needed to do, something dawned on her.

"Wait, have you checked out that storage container we got from Kajaro?" she asked.

Lynx's visage brightened. "That's a good idea. But I also want to be cautious. A ring full of non-Library books seems too good to be true. I'll need to make sure he didn't sneak something in there just in case," he said.

She frowned, not having thought of it that way. He was very preoccupied, as far as Libraries went. She'd realized that he often got preoccupied with everything. He had a bit of a scattered mind, really.

"Okay, anyway, what can we activate with the stuff already on hand?" she asked.

"Yes. Best to concentrate on that first," he said, and she got the impression he'd been running other computations or whatever he did when he was multitasking. "We can create a few golems, I believe. Summon a couple of return trolleys and we can definitely do the guidance system—at least at the basic level, anyway. That's why you needed to get the dimensional book in the first place. Our ability to locate potential Library seekers is hampered without guidance accuracy."

Quinn allowed herself a moment to absorb that. "Okay, so explain to me, is the return trolley like our little friend who scooped me up after the bookworm fiasco?"

"Oh, you mean Carty?" he asked, and proceeded to speak without waiting for an answer. "Yes, the return trolleys are really similar. So you already know how that's going to operate.

"Carty?" Quinn asked, despite her best efforts not to.

Lynx raised an eyebrow. "We've already established I'm not the best at naming things."

She laughed softly.

"But you're a Library, how can you not word well?" He simply shot her a glare and she backed off, changing the subject. "How much sentient furniture does this place have?"

"Apart from Dottie, there's a couch, a wardrobe, a bed, and a couple of lounge chairs." He listed them off easily.

She mulled that over, fairly sure the bed she'd used hadn't been one of them. "Okay, am I ever going to meet them?"

When Lynx answered, he sounded distracted. "Probably, but they're just in a different wing of the castle right now."

"The castle?" She crossed her arms and glared at him some more, but he didn't even turn to look at her as he answered.

"The Library. Stop being pedantic." Then he shook himself and turned toward her. "What do you think we should do first?"

She glanced around the Library in its state of disarray. "We should probably do the golems first."

"That's very decisive of you," Lynx said.

"Well, one of us has to be," Quinn snapped out and took a deep breath to steady herself. "Okay, golem creation. Library, what's the first step to creating a golem?"

"You could have just thought that at me."

"Yes, but you're standing right next to me, so why don't I just ask you?"

"I won't always be standing next to you, so you need to get more used to your interface. And eventually you'll need to get used to just talking to the Library itself." Lynx pursed his lips and the screen flickered across Quinn's sight.

Golem Creation:

Requires: Golem Supervisor.

Quinn got distracted from the question she was about to ask, because of the words in front of her face. She paused a moment and shook her head. She'd think of the question later if it was important. "Okay, then, create golem supervisor."

A screen, much like that in the storage ring from Kajaro, popped up in front of her. There were thousands of squares in this storage area though. All tiny so they were in her vision.

"That's ridiculous," she said.

Lynx looked over at her. "You really like that word, don't you?"

"What word?"

"Ridiculous. You use it a lot."

"Well, it's really descriptive and extremely apt for what we've got going on here." When he had a point, he had a point. Then she directed her question to the Library console. "Can I narrow down the storage display to items I need for golem creation?"

Instantly before her eyes, there were about twenty-four squares left. Twenty-three with contents. The bottom right one was blacked out.

"Oh, that's much better. Show me what I need to create a golem supervisor."

There were hundreds of blocks of clay in this inventory and many parts she wasn't even sure she wanted to recognize. A prompt flashed in front of her face.

Golem Supervisor Creation Access Granted

Warning: Golem Supervisors are Limited - Each Branch can have a maximum of one.

How many Golem Supervisors do you wish to create?

"One," she thought at it. The screen flickered. The words changed.

Golem Supervisor Capacity Criteria

She paused and looked at Lynx. "What does that mean? Capacity?"

He glanced up at the message and shrugged. "What do you want it to be able to do?"

"I don't know, Lynx. What do I want it to be able to do? Can't you just create these?" She felt a little flustered.

"Technically, no. There are fail-safes in place, just in case."

"Just in case what?"

"Let's just say 'just in case.' We'll leave it at that." He sounded sullen about it.

Well, two could play at that game. Quinn was disgruntled as well. "This need-to-know basis is really starting to piss me off."

Lynx shrugged. "You just want one, and you want it to be able to do all pertinent functions to maintaining the Library."

She looked at him. Directed her thoughts toward the screen again. "Capacity. All pertinent functions involved in the upkeep of the library."

Golem creation initiated.

Duration 1 hour 59 minutes 56 seconds

Warning: Avoid Incubation Area

"Okay. What does that mean?"

"Yeah, just don't go downstairs. The incubation chamber will be reactivated—it's not very nice to watch."

"Incubation chamber? Is this like birthing a golem?" Quinn was genuinely curious.

"No," he said, but didn't sound like he meant it.

"Why does it sound like it's actually a yes?" Quinn asked.

"Golems are created in a chamber. They're molded and infused— it's not a pleasant sight to experience. I'm not trying to be secretive, I just think it would make you nauseated like all the worm guts did. So just leave it be. Your supervisor is being processed." Lynx already sounded weary.

"Fine." Quinn moved on, even if she was even more curious now. "Return trolleys. Will we have the ingredients for that?"

"Take a look," he said, watching her closely.

Quinn realized she should have figured that out on her own. "Access inventory for return trolley parts."

The inventory screen popped up again. There were so many more than twenty-four windows for this one.

"Wow, that's a lot of parts. Why are some of them redded out so I can't really see them?" she asked, turning to Lynx.

"That means you can't access them right now. There's not enough power to use those items yet. They're generally for more advanced options that we don't need yet anyway." He paused for a moment, and then amended himself. "We have to be cautious and make sure we leave the Library with functional reserves."

"What sort of power would you need for a return trolley? Doesn't it just take books here and there?" She just envisioned little trolleys running here and there.

"You'd think that," Lynx said. "But, you know, think first."

She asked the Library to show her its blueprints. The scale that appeared before her was more than she'd ever imagined. It was massive. So many avenues were blocked off right now, but she could easily tell how much work they had to do.

Quinn did. "Oh my gosh. The Library is huge. A school?"

"We are nowhere near that level yet. First of all, you need to activate all of the different wings. You need to make sure the branches are all completed first. The alchemical and medicinal, horticultural, culinary, bardic and musical, weaponry, combat et cetera."

"Okay, I get it. I get it." But she felt a renewed energy surge in her. This was actually amazing. "Then we'll activate two return trolleys, I think. Two basic return trolleys. Not rudimentary. Basic. Level up. Does that sound like a good idea?"

"Yes, it sounds like a great idea. You can always upgrade them later when it's busier." He flashed her a grin.

Quinn turned back to the console. "Activate construction of two basic return trolleys."

Trolley Construction activating now.

Return trolley construction complete in 1 hour, 36 minutes and 25 seconds.

"Excellent." For the first time since she got there, Quinn actually felt a modicum of control. "Guidance system requirements. Basic guidance system."

Basic guidance system requirements met.

Energy levels: 423 out of 75.

"Okay, I don't know what that means, but it looks like we've got enough." She glanced at Lynx who just nodded, so she continued. "Activate guidance system. Basic level."

Guidance System Activated

Insufficient status for opening.

Advise against.

Open Library to all Library Cardholders?

Yes or No

There was a thrum and a pulse that shot through the entire Library.

"Not yet," she said. "Let's just keep it locked for now."

Library Locked.

And a checkmark appeared next to it.

"Okay, is that what we need for now?" she asked, still excited by the progress.

"Yes, that's about it," Lynx said. He sounded tired.

She took a long hard look at him. "Are you okay?"

"Yeah, just, I need more books checked back in. More items collected. The reboot means I have a lot of functions to go over, and I'm trying to multitask but it's more draining than I remember." He smiled. "But I think everything might even be okay."

Quinn sighed, "I really wish you hadn't said that."

"Why? Why shouldn't I have said that?" Lynx asked, genuinely curious.

"It's one of those things where when somebody says that, anything that could have gone wrong is probably going to go wrong."

Lynx grimaced. "Great. Like enough hasn't gone wrong already."

Quinn clapped her hands together, "Now that we've started setting all that up, we have a couple of hours to kill. How about we go and check on Malakai and get some damn food back in my stomach?"

"You really eat a lot," Lynx commented.

She shot him a side-eye. "No, really, I don't. Generally, we're used to three meals a day and I've been lucky to get one right now. You need to feed me decent food."

Just as they were about to reach the sick bay, Milaro walked out. "We're not in there anymore. Malakai is fine. He just needs to sit and eat food and rest a little bit. Come on, I'm whipping something up to eat."

"You're cooking again? This is fantastic," Lynx exclaimed.

Milaro raised an eyebrow in Lynx's direction. "Well, for now, I'll cook. I don't generally do so. I usually have people to do it for me. However, our new Librarian requires sustenance."

"Yeah, I get it, I get it," Lynx said, sounding like he was the most long-suffering Library manifestation ever. "She's already activated a supervisor golem. Everything will start to fall back into place in the next day or so."

"My, my," Milaro said, "I'm glad to see you're moving along nicely. Malakai tells me he wishes to overtake your combat training since I'm going to lend him to the Library as an assistant anyway. Seems like that's a pretty good fit, don't you think?"

Quinn nodded and sat down next to Dottie as Milaro walked towards the stove and began cooking.

"How did it go? You got everything? I'm so proud of you," Dottie said, her words practically running into each other.

Quinn raised an eyebrow at the bench. "You really *have* changed your tune since I first got here."

Dottie preened. "Sort of, maybe, sometimes."

Quinn wasn't exactly sure how to read the bench.

"Well, I apologized for being presumptuous. I didn't realize that you didn't have all the information that you should have, and that you'd been dragged here by Lynx. I sincerely do apologize for my behavior. I have your back. Let me know how I can help."

A lot of things passed through Quinn's mind right then. For one, Dottie was a bench. She really had no idea what benches could do. "Are you able to morph your shape as well?"

"No, I'm a bench. A superellex futora, to be more precise," Dottie replied.

Quinn blinked and stared at the bench blankly, bringing up the info even as the bench kept talking. "I don't understand what that is."

Dottie

Status: Sentient

Species: Superellex Futora

Power Level: Intermediate (Stationary) - non-progressive

"I'm a creature; I haven't been brought to life by magic. There are lots of us scattered throughout the universe." She leaned closer like she was sharing a secret. "We're not furniture, we just look a little bit like furniture."

But that just made Quinn even curiouser. "And why are you here?"

"Knowledge, of course, like the rest of you. I have a fire affinity," Dottie explained.

Quinn squinted at the bench. "Isn't that like really dangerous when your limbs are wooden?"

"Well, yes, I guess, sort of." The bench seemed a little taken aback.

"Well, Dottie, I am glad to formally make your acquaintance, and that you are here, and that you have my back. Thank you." Quinn tried to sound as formal as possible.

Dottie definitely had a smug expression on her very wooden carvings. Quinn then turned her attention to Milaro who was lounging in the corner.

Malakai simply stared at her. "You like Dottie a bit, eh?"

"Well, she's pretty nice. We've grown on each other," Quinn replied.

Malakai chuckled. "Yeah, I can see that. Anyway, once I'm healed up tomorrow, we're going to start your training."

"Great," Quinn muttered. She'd really just like a nice long relaxing sleep.

Malakai kept going as if she hadn't said anything at all. "And now that I'm an assistant, we need to go over my permissions in the Library."

"Isn't that jumping the gun a bit?" Quinn said, at the same time that Lynx raised an eyebrow and said, "Really, are we? How about we put you on a probationary period?"

Malakai grinned at them both. "Fine by me. Less responsibility all the way."

Milaro interrupted him. "Less responsibility is bad, Lynx. Make him earn his keep."

Lynx shrugged. "He's going to train Quinn. That way, I don't have to make myself solid. It drains less energy. While we're out of immediate danger and pretty good for a good chunk of time, I still don't want to use unnecessary energy until more books have been returned and allowed us to filter more mana. Luckily, I think we'll be fine."

A few moments later Milaro was done cooking and placed a wonderful plate of steaming wild-rice-potato-vegetable mash stuff in front of Quinn with a delightful aroma that she couldn't quite place but really wanted to devour. Not everything about this new world was bad. Magic existed. She had good food. She gobbled it up, loving it, and was really tempted to lick the bowl.

Milaro chuckled at her actions. "I've cooked before, but I've never really had anybody enjoy it quite as much as you do. It's very simple fare, you realize that, right?"

"When you're starving, it sometimes tastes like a feast," she said, meaning every word, then held out her bowl again, shaking it hopefully. "And it really was good. I could do with more."

Milaro laughed again. "Fine, but this will be enough. You don't want to overeat when you haven't been eating frequently." He shot a glare at Lynx.

"What?" said the Library. "I keep track enough. She hasn't lost weight, I don't think."

"You should take better care of your Librarian. You used to take amazing care of Korradine." Milaro admonished, his tone serious.

Lynx's scowl could have scorched earth for a moment. Something had changed in his tone when he spoke. "I'm rusty, okay?"

He obviously didn't like being reminded of his last Librarian. Or perhaps he didn't like being reminded that she was gone. That was definitely more the undercurrent coming from the connection she had with the Library.

Wait, stop, rewind.

It was definitely there, like an attached string. Or maybe like a magnet that radiated this sense of self from the Library. Wow, that was complex. Quinn couldn't wait to see what else she could do, what they could do. That was dangerous. Had she just sensed some of Lynx's thoughts? Maybe... but that was about as far as her train of thought got.

An alarm blared out, not like it had when the core was in restricted power mode. No, this, this was a different alarm. A very vocal one.

Warning.

Warning.

Golem Supervisor Incubation Period Shortened.

Golem Supervisor Completed.

Golem Supervisor Not Within Normal Parameters.

"Damn it," Quinn said, taking a deep breath and pushing herself up out of her chair to rush with the rest of them to the check-in area.

"No way!" Lynx said his eyes myriad of colors, blinking furiously. "I didn't mean anything by it, I didn't want this to happen."

Quinn glared at him and tried not to be too angry about missing her second bowl of food. She'd told him not to say everything would be fine.

Instead she stood up, flexed her arms, and glared at the Library Manifestation even as smoke began billowing up out of the spiral staircase to the basement. "I told you so."

26

SUPERVISORY GOLEM

The smoke was coming from within the stairwell, spilling out like low-hanging clouds visible in the light breeze. It didn't rise above the floor as the wind blew through. Quinn studied the smoke skeptically. It looked like it was being blown from dry ice at a rock concert.

Then, footsteps resounded through the Library. They didn't vibrate as much as she'd anticipated a golem's footsteps would, but they definitely rang out. A clear and distinctive sort of clang. Three more steps and the smoke around the golem cleared. There, right in front of them, stood, what had to be the supervisory golem.

Quinn wasn't quite sure how to describe it? Her? Them? It was entirely not what she was expecting.

As the smoke cleared, it revealed a being almost as tall as Quinn. So, very short. And they were metallic, with gleaming skin. Much slenderer than she'd anticipated.

They appeared sort of silver but with a black undercurrent. Their hair was like wisps of liquid silver, spun finely and delicately draped all around their face, and their eyes shone like the moon, sort of like Mother of Pearl crossed with an opal.

Petite. Tiny. And yet somehow completely and utterly robust.

"Hello. You did summon me, correct?" The voice rang out clearly in a melody that was neither high, nor low pitched, but just right and in the middle.

Quinn blinked. She didn't know what to say. Well, she knew words, but she hadn't been expecting the supervisory golem to be so… human in appearance. Not even Lynx seemed to know what to say. His eyes were still fluctuating, blinking, doing that strange reptilian sort of flabbergasted look. She guessed he was checking something internally.

And she didn't have time to balance something on his head right then. What a missed opportunity.

Quinn cleared her throat. "Hi, I'm Quinn. I'm the Librarian."

The golem looked Quinn up and down and nodded curtly. "Yes. Yes, you are."

Feeling slightly emboldened, Quinn continued. "You know, you didn't take as long as we thought you'd take."

The golem blinked rapidly, and angled their head toward her. "I do apologize. But the Library has been storing me for a very long time. The mold was mostly finished."

"Mold?" Quinn asked.

Again, the eyes flickered quickly, like the golem was now accessing files. "I was created. I am needed. I'm very necessary." The little golem sounded very self-important and proud. But from the way they walked, and the weight that fell with them as they did, Quinn wouldn't ever want to make them an enemy.

"Okay, let's start from the beginning. What do I call you?" she asked.

The golem blinked at her, their moon-like eyes strangely intense. "Technically, my designation is G-Alpha-724. You are the Librarian. You can choose what to call me."

"Yes, they're right." Lynx had finally come around after doing the gods know how many tasks. There were so many computer-like aspects to him, Quinn wondered why he wasn't as fast as one. Then again, she didn't know what sort of computations he was making. So she had to assume that he wasn't a computer. But he wasn't just a repository of knowledge either.

All things she could learn about later, after all the more important stuff was taken care of.

"Yes, a name," he was muttering. "Well, it's your job to give her a name, I guess."

He seemed flustered.

"Are you okay?" Quinn asked him, lowering her voice.

"Yeah, just that was unexpected, and it shouldn't have been unexpected. I need to fine tune some things." He shot her a perplexed glance. "I'll explain it later."

"Along with everything else," she deadpanned, and turned straight back to the golem and smoothly said, "How about Misha? I think Misha is a fine name for you. It suits you."

The golem brightened up and a gleam ran through their skin.

Supervisory Golem naming protocol initiated.

Misha allocation completed.

"I like Misha. I will be Misha, your supervisory golem. What is my first task?"

Quinn just stepped back so that she didn't block Misha's line of sight and just gestured at the Library as a whole. Misha leaned over, looked around, and a small whimper escaped their throat.

"Oh, I see" was all Misha said. Just as Lynx appeared about to say something, Misha piped back up. "Okay, it looks like we will need two shelving-cleaners, and perhaps, well, your bookworm repository seems to have barely anything useable in it. The night owls have been thoroughly neglected. I think we can combine that role for now; I may need to split it up later. Are you okay with allowing the king of what you would call elves to cook?"

Quinn blinked. "The King of Elves? Milaro is the King of Elves?"

"Well," Misha corrected, "he is the king of a faction and planet of Areiltháhnish. Which you call elves. So yes, that would be accurate."

Milaro sauntered out from the kitchen, an apron tied around his otherwise regal robes, and his long hair tied back in what she thought was a scrunchie. He looked thoroughly domesticated, and other than his ears and willowy height, he really didn't look like an ethereal fantasy creature or a King of Elves.

"Does that make Malakai a prince?" Quinn couldn't get that visual out of her mind.

Milaro guffawed, literally. His laugh was explosive and loud, and when he finally got control of himself, he wiped away fake tears. "Yes, but in the grand scheme of our lifespans, that means relatively little. Anyway, I am happy to cook occasionally, but I do not wish this to become what I do when I have offered my assistance. You would benefit from a lot more than my cooking."

"Duly noted, your majesty." Misha nodded curtly again and turned their attention to Lynx. "I would like permission to also create a domestic gauntlet, please."

"Permission granted, just don't waste resources. Make sure we have what we need, and only what we need—we can upgrade later." He paused for a moment. "Well, the cleaning wands are necessary."

Misha nodded. "Yes, because somebody appears to have forgotten to clean up worm guts correctly. I can smell it from here." Somehow even their nose wrinkled.

Quinn sniffed the air. She'd noticed that strange musty smell. It wasn't just books. She'd known how books smelled for a very long time. This was something else, and she could see, now, that it was rotting worm guts. Not the ambiance a library of any caliber needed.

Misha turned to Quinn. "I need access, please. Restricted supervisory access is enough. I will take care of the golems, and begin the Library's rehabilitation. Internal rehabilitation," they added, flashing a glare toward Lynx, but the manifestation didn't appear to notice.

He was obviously taking care of something, frozen in place, eyes flickering with eerie colors and even images. Runes flashed across his eyes, and the runes that made the stripes up in his hair glowed briefly, intermittently, and not all at once as they swirled around his head.

Fascinating, really.

Quinn took as much charge of the situation as she could, and climbed into the check-in desk. She placed her hands on the console. "Permissions, supervisory golem."

The heads-up display flashed in front of her, with so many options she needed to narrow them down. She scanned the long list of options and picked what she hoped was the correct one. "Golem creation and control access." That list was a lot shorter, and she sighed with relief.

There were a few options available.

Supervisory Golem Special Access

Supervisory Golem Rudimentary Access

Multiple Supervisory Golem Conference Access

Supervisory Golem Access Upgrades in Times of Emergency

Quinn frowned and asked it to expand the first option. While Misha was obviously just asking for rudimentary access, Quinn felt slightly lazy and didn't want to have to upgrade it again any time soon. The list of abilities was long, but there were several things that jumped out at her.

Allowance:

Determination of golem requirements for entire Library

Access to activate and create golems as needed by the Library

Ability to command, discipline, and maintain all golems created

Answers only to the Library and Librarian

"I'll grant you Supervisory Golem Special Access, so we don't need to do this again later," she said, and glanced at Misha. "Just make sure you don't exhaust all the materials we have on hand. Lynx won't like that."

Misha nodded. "This is appreciated. Access to two cleaning, sorting, shelving golems." They fiddled with the settings and allowed housekeeping options, and what seemed to be called nursery options, because it was the only option she could find that included bookworms and night owls, and while Quinn still didn't understand the connection there, she realized that they were related, and that that's what Misha meant.

Quinn loved that she could watch how the golem worked, too. She even learned a few ways to push the Library system a bit farther in divulging information. She'd definitely be trying that out in her spare time. A couple of prompts came up for Quinn to attend to.

Supervisory Golem requesting access to limited materials.

Deny Request. Approve Request. Limit Request.

Quinn scanned it over and decided to approve access to half of what they had in stock. While she had no clue what other things those items could be used for, she erred on the side of always-hoard-your-items-in-your-bags-in-a-game-just-in-case-you-need-them.

Finally, she sat back and looked at her results and nodded to Misha. "Okay, you're all set up. You can do what you need to do to create the golems. But I have limited your resource access, as we don't have too many resources right now."

"Thank you, uh, Quinn, is it?" Misha was cocking their head to one side again in that weird way they seemed to do.

Quinn blinked. She *had* introduced herself. The golem should have known. It was logical that they'd know her name. They probably had access the information via their own connection to the Library anyway.

"Yes, do you have access to the Library database?"

"Limited, yes, limited to the scope of my services that are required." They had paused over the word.

"I have to say, I thought you'd be a bit bigger," Quinn said.

Misha raised an eyebrow, a very delicate eyebrow, "Well, size can be deceptive. I am very strong, and I will do very well at my job. I am not a recreation of the previous steward; however, I do retain all of the knowledge and some of the traits and personality."

"What happened to the previous steward?" Quinn rushed the question out before she could second guess herself.

Misha's eyes blinked. "Reversion."

"To the Library?"

"We return to the source of power from which we were created." Misha's eyes shone brighter for a second. "Everything has its place."

Quinn was fascinated by this in both the golem and the manifestation. "So you're going to evolve and become your own person? I really love that you're not an automaton."

Misha preened a little bit, quite pleased with themself. "I have to admit, I quite like that as well. I will grow. I will grow with the Library and with you as its Librarian. Thank you. I will go about my work now."

Quinn watched them disappear down the stairs and turned to look at Lynx and wait for him to come out of whatever trance he was currently in.

She started twiddling her fingers while it took him longer than she'd expected. Eventually, she got tired of waiting and picked up one of the smaller books sitting on the counter and balanced it on his head.

Good. He was solid enough. She'd been worried it would fall through his body. Now she just had to wait and see how long it took for him to notice.

When another minute or so had passed, she added another book.

All in all, it was at least more amusing this way.

In the meantime, Quinn studied him and the Library around them. She noticed that Lynx had a very faint glow to him. His lilac skin was almost luminescent, even though he wasn't translucent anymore. She followed that glow to the rest of the Library.

Now she could clearly see how there was more light, more life in it. The books on the shelves actually looked fairly well taken care of. It was the ones that had been knocked to the ground by whatever it was —rampant bookworms, stray whirlwinds—she really had no idea. Maybe a murder of crows had flown through here and ripped everything off the shelves. She didn't know.

But it was a beautiful Library. And it was massive.

She picked up what looked like a solid circular paperweight and balanced it on top of the books on Lynx's head.

Now that the Gloom had cleared, it was easier to look around and get her bearings. The details she'd overlooked initially because of the dim lighting had come to the fore. There was no doubt in her mind that at the peak of its power this Library had been a wondrous sight to behold.

It made her want to return it to its former glory, to restore all the missing books, all the missing magic. Not to mention the branches. But she had to get to know the Library first. How it worked, why it was here, and what it needed a Librarian for.

Above all, she wanted to find out who has set the wheels in motion to devastate the Library to this extent. They needed to pay. No matter what their reasoning, how dare someone try to deprive anyone of books!

Taking a deep breath, she took in the sheer beauty around her, finally accepting where she was and who and what she needed to become—as long as she got an actual explanation before she had to do anything.

At least within her limited scope of understanding.

Lynx really was taking his time this time. Maybe she could balance another book on top of the paperweight. She searched around for one that hadn't been checked in yet. But she'd used up the objects on the counter already.

She distracted herself with surveying the Library some more.

Bookcases rose from floor to ceiling, even boasting those rolling ladders, on both levels. She'd always dreamed of a library just like this. Above the first level of books was another level. She'd seen it when she first came in, but not really processed it. Each level of the Library was about twenty feet tall. So the landing up there, with a beautifully carved wooden railing, was just as filled with books as this one down here would be.

From what she could see, which wasn't much because it was far away and the light still wasn't perfect yet, those shelves up there had a lot more books still in them. Maybe the ground level had had most of the destructive traffic.

So much knowledge.

She turned around slowly, taking in the whole Library, the vaulted ceilings forty or fifty feet up, where the columns on either side that went down sort of leaned over like branches of trees twining together up the top. It was breathtaking in better light.

"I take it you like what you see," Lynx said, finally snapping out of it. He moved slightly and the books and heavy paper weight fell down with a smack on the desk.

He stepped back, alarm clear on his face.

Quinn burst out laughing. "You should see yourself." She pointed at him.

He scowled. "That wasn't funny."

"No, it was hilarious." Quinn was still grinning.

He glared at her for a moment. "Terribly sorry for my absence. There were some settings and protocols and procedures I needed to tweak within my matrix. I haven't had access to the full scope of my power for a very long time. A lot of my powers are still restricted, and I'm having to flush out new pathways due to the passage of time. Anyway, I see that you granted Misha a name and their job access. That's fantastic."

Quinn glanced past him. Milaro was gone. Maybe he'd gone back into the kitchen to spend time with Malakai. She couldn't tell. He did flit in and out a lot. Then Lynx moved from where he stood and pulled out a second chair she hadn't noticed the last time. Did things just appear in here? She guessed magic could do anything. He sat there watching her for a few moments.

"So, Quinn, my Librarian, tell me, how is the integration of the information packet I gave you going?"

"Well, it was a lot of information to absorb. I don't understand a lot of it. I don't quite get how the manifestation system works, nor do I quite get why or how the Library is the hub for that. I understand my duties as a Librarian but none of the history behind it, and now that I've met Misha, golems make a lot more sense. The guidance system, I gather, is what allows us to let the Library open wherever and whenever we need it to?"

"Not whenever. Time is still technically linear in a wishy-washy sense. It just goes faster in some places."

"Okay. I'll get back to that. You sort of sound like a science fiction show I remember from my Earth days." For a moment she felt a little nostalgic.

He chuckled. "Your Earth days, because they're so far behind you."

"Yep. They seem like a lot more than what, five, six days behind me?"

"Seven, actually."

"I've been here a week already?"

"Well, yes, the dimensional speed-up that we had in that one world didn't help. It probably seemed like eight hours to you, and it was a day."

"True. Damn it. I need to explore this place and know the ins and outs. No more gallivanting for me until I've made the Library my new home." She half scowled even though she wasn't really annoyed.

Lynx nodded slowly. "We can do that... I think. For a short while at least."

Quinn rushed straight ahead with her train of thought. "Anyway, anyway, the return trolleys make sense. I get a lot of it, but I don't get exactly how I get my powers and how the magic works. I mean, it's here in my head... but for some reason it seems to keep sliding around. Like it doesn't want to stick." She paused, trying to access the information. But this whole manifesting knowledge as power thing still felt out of her realm of understanding. "Is that something you can better explain to me?"

He looked at his expression serious. No hint of mirth in his eyes. "I know you have a lot of questions. So how about we start at the beginning?"

"That," Quinn said, "sounds like a very good place to start."

27

FROM THE BEGINNING

"THE BEGINNING, HUH?" SHE MUMBLED, THINKING. QUINN HAD SO MANY questions. There was so much Lynx had simply told her tidbits of.

"Okay, but first..." She looked up expectantly. "Why couldn't you find any Librarians? How did that even happen? I don't understand."

Lynx blinked at her slowly, and for one odd moment, she wondered if he even knew. Just when he was about to say something, Dottie butted in, tossing the manifestation a grumpy look. "That's not where you should start! You know better than that. How about you give her an overview of how the Library works. What it does and why it requires a Librarian."

Quinn was really growing to like Dottie, and she nodded emphatically as if reinforcing what the bench said.

Lynx looked like he wished Misha would come back and put him to task cleaning up the Library instead of making golems to do it. But finally he took a deep breath, floated himself up so he was sitting on top of the check in counter, and crossed his legs.

Quinn tossed herself into the big comfy chair and wished she had some popcorn to chew on.

"I can hear you if you don't keep it to yourself, you know." Lynx scowled at her. "It's not that entertaining."

"Please. You've had me locked in this world with no access to social media for like a week now. Anything is entertaining." She flashed him a grin.

"Social..." Lynx appeared to be counting to five before he spoke. "Whatever. I guess you're in for the long haul, then.

"I, as the manifestation, do not remember a time before I existed. It's not uncommon; I simply was. But I do have access to information from such a time, and there is relatively little. In order to interact better with the Librarian and Library patrons, the Library created me —or a version of me—to work in concert with it and those it took on as assistants or Librarians."

"The difference between an assistant and the Librarian is that a Librarian *must* be compatible with the neural network magic that the Library accesses. There are specific affinities that would clash if they aren't tempered by one that matches. Librarians must have this signature. The more of them, the better."

"And an assistant doesn't have to," Dottie butted in. "It's why I've always been a bit of an honorary assistant myself."

Quinn reached out and gave the bench a soft pet, hoping Lynx would continue.

"For this reason," Lynx began again, "the Library usually has dozens of assistants, sometimes even hundreds. A percentage of these have compatible signatures. Just in case."

"Just in case?" Quinn asked, not sure she wanted the answer.

He fixed her with an appraising gaze. "I told you Kajaro was immortal. And he was. He would have lived forever, but for the fact that you and Malakai killed him. Everyone has a weak point, even a Librarian."

Quinn didn't like the whispered thought she heard in her mind.

Even the Library.

No shit, she thought. *Considering what had almost happened. They'd almost succeeded in wiping out everyone.* She shook her head, clearing those thoughts. "Okay, but what I don't get is why do you need a Librarian. I mean, you seem pretty capable and getting more so the more of the power returns to you. Why does the Library require a Librarian to run it?"

This time Lynx's eyes shadowed over, the purple-black in the sclera bled clear briefly before returning. His multiple eyelids flickered. "The interface requires a lifeform to interface with it in order to reach its full potential. Without the natural ambient magic that the Librarian inputs into the system, many of the Library's functions won't reach maturation."

And Quinn knew, without a shadow of a doubt, that his answer was at least a partial lie. Still, there had to be a reason that he wasn't telling the full truth right now. She'd take it up with him after she got all the other information she needed.

"So, basically, the Library needs to leech off the ambient mana of the Librarian?" She knew she was pushing it a little, but sometimes Lynx needed her to goad him.

"That's a very simplistic view point to take. But the link allows both the giving and receiving of magical energy. Your mana and magical energy are also separate, even though related. Once linked, the Librarian becomes an integral part of the core and benefits just as much as the Library gains." There might have been a hint of melancholy in Lynx's voice with that last statement.

Even Dottie didn't appear to know how to react.

An awkward sort of silence fell over them and Quinn glanced around valiantly trying to find a way to break it.

Which is when Milaro cleared his throat, startling all of them, and grinned like he'd enjoyed surprising them. "Have you explained magic flow to her yet? Might want to make sure you're really getting all the beginnings."

"Hey, I'm the Library, she was asking me the questions," Lynx said hotly, somewhat defensive.

"No, you are the Links of the Library. Which is very different and yet entirely the same." Milaro laughed at his own joke. "Anyway, you have to understand the chaos that is magic in order to fully appreciate both magical flow and the relationship the Library and thus, the Librarian, has to it."

Quinn was confused. She held up hand. "Wait, I thought without the Library, there was no magic."

"Ah, you see, that's where you're wrong, but also partially right," Milaro continued in that infuriating way that made Quinn want to punch him. "Without the magical partitioning and filtration that the Library provides, the pure chaos of magic will infect those who attempt to wield it. It becomes more dangerous than you can imagine."

"If the Library ceases to exist, magic runs wild?" Quinn asked, testing the words for herself.

"Yes, yes, it does. And wild magic tends to destroy things, passes chaos onto people and things because harnessing it in its raw state is dangerous. It devours people from the inside out, making them husks of magical direction." Milaro raised his hands allowing a bolt of power to spring up between them.

He lowered his hands, maintaining one on each side of the power he held. It wasn't quite electricity, but it crackled and was a shade of blue. More liquid and yet, even Quinn could feel the danger emanating from it.

"See. Magic is a chaotic force, pure chaos, really." There was an urgency to Milaro's words that hit Quinn right in the gut. Milaro released his left hand and the bolt no longer contained, jumped out and shot across the Library, directly impacting one of the pillars.

A brief scent of sulfur reached Quinn. Like the magic had burned the stone it hit.

"Magic alone is dangerous. Magic unchecked is bad. Right?" She thought she got it now, even if it felt like there was still something missing.

"More than that." Milaro lowered his voice. "Magic running rampant will destroy everyone. Even those who think it won't. Without the Library to insert itself and to act as a filtration system for the power in the universe, well, we're all pretty screwed."

Quinn did a double take though. "Did you just say screwed?"

Milaro chuckled, "Yes, yes, I did. I looked up a little bit of Earth's history while you and my grandson were gallivanting around, and I decided that I liked some of your colloquialisms."

"Okay." Quinn smiled. She decided, once again, that she liked Milaro. "Okay, so it's like an air filtration system where it sucks in the bad and churns out the good?"

"More like a water filtration system on your planet. It brings in the mana, runs it through a filter, purifies it, and then sends it out to refill wells of power so that they are calm waters, more like a lake or a dam like you have in your worlds. Somewhere the power can sit until it needs to be drained, until the people who use magic need to access it and funnel it through their own magical systems."

"So beings have magical systems within themselves, too?"

"Yes. And they require filtration to harness the most powerful properties of magic without being lost to a chaotic mess." Milaro hesitated a second before continuing. "Which leads back to why a Librarian is needed in the first place."

Lynx groaned.

Milaro ignored him. "The first manifestation was not a fan of sharing the power the Library had access to. Thus, a Librarian tempers the system."

"Okay, I think I get it," Quinn said. She really did. The fact that a Librarian was a necessary corruption counter also made complete sense. Magic was powerful and dangerous if the encounter with Kajaro was anything to go by. And if that was the filtered version... "What happened while the Library closed itself off?"

"The Library has been minimally filtering, but didn't have enough power to do it properly," Lynx finally cut back in, pouting like a champion.

"Couldn't it have just pulled ambient mana from the little bit it was able to filter?" She didn't understand the problem here. None of the information in her head gave her clarity.

"A small amount, yes. But a little from a small well was barely enough to keep us from completely running out." Lynx seemed proud he'd inserted himself back into the conversation. "Ambient mana is only meant as a complement; it's not supposed to fully fuel the Library."

Milaro nodded. "There have been a lot of accidents out in the universe during the absence of the Library's maximum output, and there's been a lot of trouble since not all of the magic was filterable, for want of a better word."

Quinn tried to absorb all the information. "So all of your worlds have had pretty much five hundred years of chaos. If the Library were to disappear. It would be thrown into a tumultuous mess."

Both Lynx and Milaro nodded vehemently.

"Okay, then," Quinn said, "Got it. Library good, no Library bad. Let's move on."

This time, Lynx chuckled. "Okay, are we done?"

"No!" Quinn cut him off. "Are you serious? You haven't been answering anything. You've just been like, 'I'll explain that later. I'll explain that later.' This is later? This is as later as we're getting. And I'm putting my foot down?"

He raised an eyebrow and glanced at her foot. "Okay. What else?"

"You said everyone has an affinity."

"Yes, everyone has at least one affinity."

"Well, how do affinities work?" She paused and then added, "Explain it to me like I'm from a world where there's no magic."

Milaro laughed and Lynx flashed a mild glare, but gave in anyway. "Well, people will generally have an affinity to a type of magic, often elemental."

Quinn stopped him and tapped her head. "Got that much. Every single person, being, creature, species, has a magical affinity."

"Yes," Lynx said. "Most will have at least one, often around ten, a dozen to maybe twenty, is pretty average. On the upper level, you're probably looking at thirty, then forty to fifty for the more powerful mages. Librarian-specific affinities number in at forty-two. Having them all is very rare and not necessary to connect to the core. Now, Korradine actually had thirty-nine of the Library's necessary affinities, which was amazing. Yours however, is very unique."

Milaro scoffed. "That's a good way to put it."

"Before we get to my uniqueness..." The word sounded odd on Quinn's tongue. It sounded too much like one of those anime tropes. "Explain to me how affinities work."

"Okay, each element or each type of affinity has multiple branches of affinity. So a water affinity, you can have four water affinities. You can have the manipulation of water, the creation of water, resistance to water, or the deconstruction of water. The same with fire. Everything has a manipulation, creation, resistance, and deconstruction." Lynx waited to make sure she was digesting the information.

"Some things, like weapons, will have combat applications. If you get to the mastery level, there might be even more branches that veer off," Lynx began again, but Milaro placed his hand on the manifestation's shoulder and took over.

"Not everyone can manipulate power in all the available ways. Some may only have the ability to manipulate water. So if a body of water is sitting there, they can make it move around. But they can't create water out of thin air, nor can they dissipate the water once it's there. They can just use it. Some people might just have resistance-based affinities. Maybe they have an elemental group of resistances. That makes them strong as a common fighter. It's vast, and there are books you can absorb just on the information about affinities." Milaro seemed able to put it in layman's terms a little better.

Quinn raised an eyebrow and said, "You could have told me that earlier. I'm going to have to absorb some of those knowledge books, you know."

"Yes, but I didn't, and I apologize," Lynx muttered.

She raised an eyebrow. "Fine. Okay. Now I think I get it a little bit more. So how many total affinities are there?"

"Right now?" Lynx's eyes flickered slightly. "One thousand seven hundred twenty-two."

Quinn blinked. "Did you say there are *currently* one thousand seven hundred twenty-two magical affinities?"

Milaro and Lynx shared a look.

Quinn glanced back and forth between them, then put her hands on her hips and glared at them. "This is not the time to be, 'Oh, well, she won't understand,' or, 'Oh, well, maybe don't overload her with information.' I refuse to go in blind."

"New magic is being discovered all the time. It doesn't matter what you think you know about something. There is always more to learn. Magic is the same. Just because nobody's ever combined a water and fire spell together, for example, which they have, but they hadn't at the time, whatever. " Lynx paused for a moment, as if he was resetting his train of thought. "And the moment somebody does that, then that particular magic exists. There are fusions of magic that exist because people have pushed boundaries and because people have studied and learned and wanted to create more."

"I get it," Quinn said, "You're saying that the magic in the Library will never stop growing."

"Yes, which is why the Library exists outside of a solid state. It's like its own little dimensional pocket." Milaro sounded quite pleased about that fact.

It made the information in her mind click together. Thousands upon thousands of possibilities flashed across her vision in the blink of an eye. "Okay, I've got this."

Milaro smiled. "I knew she was pretty smart."

Lynx rolled his eyes. "Of course she is."

"But that doesn't get you off the hook." She looked Lynx square in the eyes. "Tell me about your previous Librarian."

"Ah." He breathed out, and this time she could tell he'd been trying to avoid precisely that topic. "That's what got us started on this."

Dottie nudged her way underneath his feet, providing a comfy footstool for him. Lynx's expression softened slightly. Quinn made a note to thank the bench later.

"When a Librarian has been a part of the system for a long time, they often choose to retire. A thousand years, a couple of millennia, a few millennia, whatever. Kor decided that she wanted to retire. She was done and satisfied with everything that we'd accomplished together. And I didn't see a reason not to let her retire."

He sighed and a wave of sadness washed over Quinn.

Finally, he continued. "It's not unusual for a Librarian to retire. It's just not a frequent occurrence. To that end, there are always at least assistants with library affinities. We had so many. There was no reason whatsoever to be suspicious or cautious. Once the retirement clause is activated, it cannot be reversed. It takes maybe fifty years for the whole thing to complete so that the new Librarian can be trained, acclimated, and synchronized. However, soon as she initiated the sequence, we began losing our assistants."

His hair lit up, spirals of runes sparking at once. "At first it seemed like accidents. A few died very nasty deaths when they went to retrieve books. When it became obvious the deaths weren't entirely coincidental, we searched for replacements for new trainees, new assistants, but found none. Nowhere. Anywhere. Everywhere."

Lynx spread his hands out in a futile encompassing gesture. "They were just gone. I hadn't actively recruited for about half a century before she activated the clause. It'd never been a problem before. The years ticked down, and Kor just didn't have any time left. She faded and withered and passed."

"You sound really sad, Lynx." Quinn reached out to gently place her hand on his shoulder for a moment. "Almost human."

"I'm not human." And as if to prove a point, he promptly changed into his Lynx form for about five seconds. Then into some strange sort of bird that looked oddly like an ostrich crossed with a flamingo. Its feathers glowed pink with trails of golden runes that cascaded to the floor. Song burst into Quinn's head in a calming, soulful sound that almost brought her to tears.

Just when the emotion began to overwhelm her, he changed into a beautiful, ethereal, eight-foot-tall, slender woman with wispy silver hair falling down her back and one eye on her forehead. He twirled around and then presented himself with a bow. "This. This is what Kor looked like. She was gorgeous, inside and out."

Quinn couldn't help but stare. If she was as lovely inside as she was out, she must have been amazing. "She was a cyclops?"

"No, cyclops are a little bit more thick." Lynx's voice sounded strange coming out of Kor's body. He turned and swapped promptly back into himself, falling into the chair. "Kor was the heart of this

Library for so long. I never thought she'd leave me, but I think she just got tired."

Quinn wasn't sure what she should say, so she changed the subject. "Okay, so do you have -enemies? Other than Mister-Tried-to-Kill-Me-with-a-Cephalopod, is there any reason, any natural reason, why the Library's magical signature could have disappeared?"

"Nope, no magical reason, no natural reason. It was deliberate," Lynx said. There was a hard edge to his voice.

"I guess you've been too busy the last few centuries trying to keep the Library from fully falling apart?" She mulled that over in her head. What would have happened if he hadn't found her?

Lynx scowled. "No time to dwell. Now that the Library is partially restored, I can divert some of my resources to researching just that."

It was the first time Quinn heard Lynx sound vengeful. "Well, let me know what I can do to help," she said. "You should make a list of potential enemies, of factions. I mean—I, personally, think the Serpensiril are a pretty good starting point. But there's got to be factions in, like, the multiverse, right?"

He chuckled. "It's not a multiverse, it's just a universe. Anyway. Enough of that. More detail won't help us any. What's your next question?"

"Bookworms," Quinn said promptly. "The ones I don't have to kill."

"Oh, you're going to love them once you see how cute they can be," Dottie piped up, like she was trying to chase away the lingering sadness from the previous topic.

Milaro continued smoothly, not letting Lynx get a word in. Frankly, the manifestation didn't seem to mind much. "When the bookworms are small, they are used to absorb the dust from their specific affinity tomes. With me so far?"

Quinn nodded. "Yes."

Milaro dove in deeper. "Those worms are fed to the night owls, which are currently hibernating up in the rafters and have only just begun to rouse."

"Okay, owls in the rafters. Why have we not been crapped on?" It was the first thought she had. Birds in an enclosed space were just bound to crap on them. Despite squinting up, she just couldn't see any owls above them.

"Magic!" Milaro wiggled his fingers at her and Quinn laughed despite herself.

"The cycle works thus: bookworms get fed to their matching magically affinity night owls. The birds shed feathers, but only one special one or two per year. Usually anyway. Hoping we can get around that for a while. That feather produces a quill. That quill is capable of creating the tomes or codices of that affinity."

"So we need the worms to make the tomes." This was getting very complex in Quinn's mind.

"Yes. Or reproduce fading tomes or really popular ones," Dottie threw in, glee in her voice.

Lynx held up his hands. "You're forgetting the silverfish. We have to locate those and grind them down for the appropriate ink."

Quinn's head was pounding by now. "Okay. So we have magical worms that get fed to magical birds that get dipped in magical ink to write magical books."

"Yes, exactly." Lynx sat back, beaming with pride.

Quinn rolled her eyes. "Oh, that's so simple. I don't know why I didn't think of it before."

28

GOLEMS

BEFORE SHE COULD ASK ANOTHER QUESTION SHE GOT A NOTIFICATION.

Notification

Return Trolley's completed

Status: Active and awaiting orders.

She dismissed the notification's interruption in her train of thought, slotting it in the back of her mind to deal with later. She still had Lynx, Milaro, and Dottie with her, and she wasn't letting a chance like this go.

"What are you doing?" Misha was suddenly standing next to her, and Quinn almost peed herself with fright.

She cleared her throat as she composed herself, trying to ignore the badly suppressed giggles from the others. "I didn't hear you arrive."

"I did not announce myself until now," Misha said, very matter-of-factly.

Quinn realized the golem just didn't react. "That's good to know. What can I help you with, Misha?"

"The initial golem contingent is finished."

"It is?" Quinn was surprised, but she guessed they'd all got caught up in chatting for a bit there. She'd found out a lot of information. "Wait, so the return trolleys and the golems are now functional?"

Misha nodded. "Yes. I would like to introduce you to them. Is that acceptable?"

"Yes, of course." Quinn couldn't help a sliver of excitement. But these golems took a fraction of the time to create that she'd thought they would.

The supervisor continued. "They will take commands from you, myself, and from Lynx. From my memories, Lynx has changed. Perhaps it was the time alone."

"Lynx is different? How do you mean?" She was curious now, despite how eagerly she wanted to meet the new golems.

"To repeat something new I heard recently," Lynx piped up. "I'm standing right here."

Misha's moon-like eyes blinked slowly as they turned to face him. "It would seem so. Did the Library's emergency mode injure you?"

Lynx scowled. "No. I'm fully capable of all my functions. Certain aspects just require a process of reactivation."

"Excellent." Misha, apparently satisfied by the answer, turned their attention back to Quinn. "Shall we meet the golems then, ma'am?"

"Please don't call me ma'am. Quinn. Call me Quinn or Librarian." She certainly didn't feel old enough to be a ma'am to anyone.

"Okay, then. Quinn. Registered." The golem's moonlike eyes flashed through a flurry of colors before Misha continued. "Misha does seem very fitting. I thank you again for my name."

"When are the shelving golems getting here?" Milaro looked around them, his arms crossed, an expectant expression on his face.

Misha swiveled slightly to look at the elf. "They are incoming." They raised their hand and clicked their fingers. Except, because they appeared to be made out of a type of liquid-ish metal, there was a clang to the way they clicked.

Like a resounding gong.

Quinn, Milaro, and even Dottie strained themselves to look over the desk in the direction of the sound. All them waited with bated breath.

Lynx, on the other hand, appeared entirely disinterested.

Fog like that from dry ice once again billowed around them. It appeared Misha had a flare for the dramatic. An idle thought occurred to Quinn: perhaps it would be a good idea to go and visit the core again now she'd somewhat acclimated to the connection. But the clearing of the fog stole her train of thought, and she gasped softly as the golems stepped into full view.

Now two of them looked exactly like the clay type of golems she had been expecting all along. They were orange-brownish and stood about seven feet tall.

"Oh, fantastic." She breathed out the words, quite fascinated. She meant it, too. They moved smoothly, and even though Quinn knew they must weigh a lot, they didn't make the ground reverberate or anything. Their steps were stealthy.

"These are the cleaning and shelving golems." Misha gestured to the golems as they came to stand in front of the check-in desk.

Both Quinn and Milaro leaned over the desk, trying to get a better look at them.

Quinn blurted out a question: "Do they have names?

"One and two?" Misha asked, like they hadn't given it any consideration.

"One and two..." Quinn frowned, while she was sure she heard a snicker from Milaro. She didn't like quantifying things like that. Especially not things that were sort of like people.

"More accurately: Shelving One and Shelving Two." Misha's tone this time sounded certain. Like they'd just come up with an appropriate system designation.

"Okay, Shelving One and Shelving Two." It still didn't feel right though. "Are we not *supposed* to name them, Misha?"

Misha turned their head and blinked at Quinn several times before answering. "We do not generally name them, no."

"Well, maybe we should think of a name for them. You liked your name," Quinn tried reasoning.

Milaro piped up. "If you name all of your helpers, Quinn, you're going to have a lot to remember." His tone was gentle.

"I'm sure the Library will help me remember them. I'd feel weird going around and telling thing one and thing two what to do. Names help me." She shrugged, not backing down from the idea.

Milaro shrugged right back at her. "Suit yourself."

"I will." She resisted the urge to poke her tongue out at him and turned back to Misha. "They look pretty heavy. Will the ladders be able to hold them?"

"Oh, they don't need ladders." Misha's eyes flashed and they gestured toward the golem on the left. "I will show you later in action, but for now: Shelving One, please show the Librarian how you will reach the top shelves."

Right in front of her eyes, he literally grew to twenty feet tall. Quinn gaped. "Okay, I guess he can reach the top shelf."

Misha actually laughed, although it sounded more like a tinny chuckle. "Yes, he can definitely reach the top of those shelves. Okay, next. This is the cook."

"We have a cook?" Quinn asked, surprised. "Oh wow, so does he take care of plants as well?"

"He can grow and maintain rudimentary ingredients and cook them all to a very palatable level of taste," Misha explained.

The cook was stocky, shorter, and more powerful in appearance, about maybe five foot eight. A little bit taller than Lynx, or perhaps about the same size since the manifestation wasn't always the same. Cook bowed, and didn't say anything. It made Quinn wonder what he'd be cooking to need his apparent strength.

"Can they not speak?" Quinn asked.

"Well, they can, but they don't generally speak unless absolutely necessary," Misha replied. Quinn wasn't sure how she felt about that. They seemed very robotic and like they didn't have personalities.

Cook's eyes, however, followed Quinn's every move.

They definitely needed names.

"Okay, so that's the cook, and next we have our caretaker," Misha continued.

The caretaker was willowy and around the same height as the cook, but not made out of clay or metal. It almost appeared to be wooden, like a carved doll that moved. It was really quite beautiful.

Quinn piped in, "So this guy will take care of the bookworms and the night owls and maybe the silverfish, depending on how recovery goes?"

"I am glad to see Lynx briefed you on this," Misha said. "Anyway, I just wanted to introduce you to the new workers in the Library." They clicked their fingers twice and the new golems fell in line. It seemed as if Misha was about to leave. Quinn put out a hand to stop them.

"Wait, I'm going to name them. I'll have names for you by the end of the day. I don't want to have 'caretaker one' and 'shelving one'. I don't operate that way. It makes them seem like they're not part of the Library," Quinn said.

For a moment, Misha watched her unblinkingly, unflinchingly with those moon-like eyes. It was like she was calibrating, maybe computing something, understanding whatever it was that she was trying to understand. "I understand. I think that is a very good idea, but keep in mind that eventually there will be hundreds of working golems in these halls. We will await your designations."

Quinn watched as Misha began to lead them away. She was trying to think of something simple, but Tom, Dick, and Harry seemed as though she wasn't putting any thought into it. She did like Tom, though. Tim and Tom, maybe, for the shelvers. Frankly, Cook really fit cook. She was sure Lynx, in all his rudimentary naming conventions, would approve.

"Wait. Misha!"

The supervisory golem paused with her little procession and glanced back, waiting.

Quinn steeled herself and caught up to the group. "I want to see the Library. I'd like to see it as it comes back to life." She paused, waiting for a reaction, even though she knew Misha wasn't overly reactionary.

The golem seemed to consider the statement and then nodded. "It would be a learning experience for you to see how the Library attendants function. Very well. But we will move fast."

With that, Misha began walking again, and Quinn kept stride with them all. She glanced around, quite fascinated. "Tim and Tom." She gestured to the two shelving golems.

"Very apt." Misha agreed.

A notification popped up in Quinn's vision.

Shelving One renamed to Tim

Shelving Two renamed to Tom

Accept these changes?

Yes. No.

Quinn didn't think she'd thought Yes at anything so fast since she got there.

As soon as the Yes went into effect, Tim and Tom changed. Not hugely. More in a subtle way. Tim remained at seven feet tall, but his head became smoother, almost as if he were bald. Tom, on the other hand, grew several inches, almost a foot maybe, and his head, while still clay, looked like it had hair carved into it.

They both directed their gaze on Quinn and bowed their heads briefly in what appeared to be acknowledgement. Quinn blinked, and Misha made a sound that resembled a metallic clicking of the tongue.

"It seems they appreciate their new designations," the supervisor said.

It took several moments of walking for Quinn to really take in what such a simple thing had done. By naming them, she'd perhaps given them some sort of agency, or identity? She had no clue how magical creatures worked, but these ones already felt special to her.

The little procession made its way to the kitchen. As they walked, Quinn could feel a soft breeze following them. Or perhaps it was more accurate to say *flowing* from them to the rest of the Library.

As if a cool breeze were washing away the dust of eons, waking it up from its centuries long slumber.

It felt alive, and empowering.

As they stopped at the kitchen, Cook stepped forward, their eyes surveying the area.

"Hey," Quinn blurted out, unsure of how else to bring it up. "Would Cook be an okay name for you. It looks like it suits you."

The cooking golem turned slowly and fixed her with its stare again, before slowly nodding. "Cook." It pronounced the word with difficulty, a strange foreign aspect to the syllable.

A ripple of power cascaded down from the tip of its head to its toes. Cook grew perhaps an inch, and the muscles refined. The top of their head turned into a chef's cap, and their face took on slight human definition.

"Cook is acceptable," Cook said again, and that thin line that was their mouth spread into the semblance of a slight smile.

Quinn grinned. "Awesome." She had a feeling she was going to like Cook.

Misha stood watching, an impassive expression on their face. "Is there anything else you need here to make this area function?" they asked Cook.

Cook shook their head. "No. I will manage. I will request as I make assessments." And with that they made a wave of their hands and Quinn gasped in surprise.

What she could only call magic—because *hello*, she'd been kidnapped by a magical Library—circled into the air. It appeared almost like smoke as it wound its way around the food terrariums, and the cooking area. Everything it touched either rejuvenated, or began to clean itself.

Quinn knew that the next time she saw the kitchen, it would be like brand new.

"We must move. I must install all of our new helpers into their relevant divisions within a certain time period," Misha explained, as they ushered Quinn and the other three golems out of the kitchen and toward an area Quinn yet to visit.

This was another section to the side of the main Library thoroughfare, just like the kitchen and the sick room. It made Quinn wonder how Malakai was doing in there.

Malakai is sleeping to heal.

Quinn started at the words scrolling across her vision even as they echoed somehow in her head. It appeared that her connection to the Library was indeed getting stronger. She wasn't entirely sure she felt comfortable with it knowing everything she thought of.

They'd have to address that soon.

Misha stopped in a very dimly lit room that smelled oddly of both fresh and rotting vegetation. It was warm, almost muggy inside. "This is the bookworm habitat."

The long and willowy golem stepped forward. Quinn got the sudden impulse to name them Farrow. "Hey!" she called out. "Is Farrow acceptable?"

The golem resembled a living tree, and slowly turned toward her. They inclined their head and another pulse of power washed over them. Their limbs became more defined and their appearance altered to look like they were wearing a long wispy dress. "Farrow is suitable."

And Quinn knew without a shadow of a doubt that Farrow would take care of everything in this area. She was so dryad-like in appearance that Quinn was taken aback.

Raising an eyebrow at Misha, Quinn smiled. "Awesome. I can't wait to see what you do with the actual bookworms."

"I shall endeavor to reignite the magical tome creation process." Farrow bowed, and immediately began working on one of the worm farms.

That just left Misha, Quinn, Tim, and Tom.

"Now where to?" Quinn asked, as they made their way back through to the Library proper.

Tim raised an arm and pointed. His gesture encompassed most of the Library. Quinn flashed him a smile and got a nod in response.

So the shelving guys weren't talkative, but they did seem to want to communicate. That was a plus. It took a couple of minutes, but they finally stood back in the main Library chamber.

Quinn could see so much dust filtering through the light that got in. Specks of it floating in the air, illuminated by golden beams of sunlight. Just how the shelves were too bare. And far too many books remained on the floors with their pages torn, their spines cracked. Some of them were ragged, others had bookworm bites...

It was quite pitiful and sad.

Misha stood in the center of the hall and snapped their fingers again.

This time, however, the clang took on a deeper, longer tone. And all of a sudden, three carts began rolling out of the front of the Library area toward them.

One of which was Carty. The other two, the new return trolleys.

Quinn grinned at the former. She'd had a soft spot for Carty since he'd schlepped her to her quarters somehow while she was injured. His strange accent made her like him even more.

"Ready and reporting for duty," he said.

She could imagine him grinning, if he, like… had a face.

Come to think of it, how could she always tell Dottie's mood without an actual mouth and expression? Maybe that was through the core too. It looked like visiting the core was something she had to do sooner than later.

"Excellent." Misha made a sweeping gesture, unleashing a ripple magic toward the bookshelves. It was odd. Quinn wasn't sure if the magic was visible to everyone, or if she could just see the traces of it because she was connected to the system in a more personal way.

But as she watched the effect in front of her eyes, all other trains of thought fell by the wayside.

Power wafted off those strands of magic that wove their way around. The trolleys shot out to gather the books strewn on the ground. Magic lifted them, placing them lovingly in the carts' care.

Tim and Tom made their way to the bookshelves, moving quietly and smoothly, hypervigilant about not stepping on pages or books on their way to the shelves. They practically floated.

After a few moments, Quinn realized that the magically zipping-back-and-forth books were being sorted into different piles on the return trolleys and Carty. One of the carts was for books that could be reshelved, which were then ferried to Tim and Tom immediately.

Then another for those that required repair. And another… for those that were so badly damaged, they'd likely have to be recycled, or put to rest.

The latter gave Quinn an overwhelming sense of melancholy. Some of these books were ancient, and she didn't need magic to tell her that. Any damage to books saddened her.

But even so, she couldn't take her eyes off the scene in front of her. It was like all the childhood magical stories she'd read rolled into one.

It made her happy and sad at the same time, and fiercely protective. She needed to become strong enough so that this never happened again.

A long droning tone filled the Library. Soft, and underlying, but commanding at the same time.

Core system: refiltered.

Refined calibration: necessary

Librarian summoned: Core Room

Quinn smiled softly at the very convenient summons. She guessed that was as far as she was going right now. Apparently now was sooner.

29

POWERED BY THE CORE

"OH, WHAT DOES THAT MEAN NOW?" QUINN GROANED AS SHE TURNED on her heel and made her way back to the front of the Library.

Even as she did so, she noticed a lot of doors she hadn't seen before. Or at least that she hadn't previously taken notice of. Door-ways. Some small, some large, some stretched. Some were in obvious, door-like places leading into hallways or other sections, but some were wedged between bookcases, one even on a pillar.

And some of them almost appeared to be illusions, like they weren't there when she did a double take.

She frowned, finally cresting the check-in desk and realizing Lynx was the only one still there.

"Are you going to tell me what that notification means or is that another thing you'll tell me later?" she teased him lightly.

Lynx sighed. "It just means that the Library wants to see you directly. The core has finished calibrating to some of the new wave-lengths and power levels that have entered it and it requires you to go and align with it."

"Like I have to place my palms on it again?" She wiggled her fingers, like Milaro liked to do. "Tap into its fathomless powers?"

"Yeah, pretty much. The Library's alive; you realize that, right?

It's nothing like one of your Earthling computers. It's sentient. I learn, I feel, I'm learning to feel. I create, I travel, I take care of. I am a being, and there are parts of the Library that require physical contact with its Librarian in order to fully access its maximum capacity." He paused, giving her time to take that in. "And in order to do that, you will have to technically realign yourself with it every now and again. That enables the Library, and you, to function at peak capacity."

"I guess I'm going to go visit the core, then." Quinn wasn't entirely certain why, but she could feel this tiny amount of worry leaking around her, she thought it was coming from Lynx. She hoped that didn't mean this was dangerous.

"It's not dangerous," Lynx called after her, as she made her way to the staircase. "It's just a power boost, like before."

At least that explained some things. He was warning her to be ready for the pain she'd previously experienced. And he was sticking his nose into her thoughts, again.

They were truly going to have words soon.

Taking a breath, she walked cautiously down the several flights of winding stairs. Nobody wanted to slip on wrought iron stairs and go thudding to the bottom of it. Especially not Quinn, considering how fragile tailbones were.

When she reached the bottom and set her foot on the floor, a cascade of dim white lights spread out in front of her. She sucked in her breath at the sight before her.

While she'd been here before, red lights and alarms going off had done the room no justice. It looked like an underground cavern filled with a massive tree. Now that the soft glow suffused everything around her, she could see the branches as they extended high up into the ceiling. Those branches drooped down and their leaves were beautifully crafted, absolutely gorgeous, with glowing purple and bright luminescent blue leaves. Like an incorporation of Lynx into the whole scheme. Their veins stood out when they lit up.

Though many of the leaves were still dark, some of the branches and some of the leaves weren't.

And that's what lit the entire cavernous area up with a soft and soothing glow.

The whole room was welcoming and encompassing, like it was the heart of something. It beat ever so softly in her ears, through her veins, right into her very own chest. But it wasn't *her* heart. It was in sync with her own, beating in time, eternally, always, as a constant underlying trust.

Wow.

She stepped forward and toward the core that now looked more like a glowing petrified tree than she'd ever realized. All of the intricate veins running up through the bark, right into the tree itself, it all made so much more sense now. And with some actual power restored to it, it wasn't scary. It was relaxing and beautiful. All she wanted to do was sit, cradled by the roots, and just breathe.

Then a message flashed in front of her eyes, but it wasn't on a screen. It was more just in front of her, like the lights were playing around her to give her the message. So she sat at the base of the tree with her back against it and felt a soothing calmness wash over her.

Refined calibration necessary. Do you consent?

Now that was an odd way to put it. She was used to being asked if she would do something, yes or no, but this... this was specifically asking if she consented to calibrating again with the core. It reminded her of the copious amount of images and information and the abundant pain that shot through her the first time they connected. And then, well, it really sort of made sense after that.

This time however, it was different. It *felt* different. It felt right.

Yes.

There was a thrumming in the back of her head that ran down her spine all the way through to her tailbone as if making a point. She sank into her seat and let herself relax. Being in closer contact with the core definitely made the reception of the information much easier, even if she understood a bare fraction of what was being thrown at her. There was so much. All of the different branches, all of the different books. Eventually she'd know them all, but right now it was something she'd be able to search for.

There was history there too, but it was so fleetingly imparted in such a way that she couldn't take it all in right then. She'd need to have another nap just to absorb it and understand some of it. The beauty of the Library and its relationships with multiple different solar systems and planets.

It serviced and spanned galaxies, everywhere, yet nowhere and anywhere all at the same time. How it could do this, she had no idea.

The ramifications were too vast for her to comprehend above the simplistic view she could understand of it. Time would allow for her to grasp the facts more deftly, but for now she needed to accept the information as fact.

The Library was a marvel, and, in a way, it was a little scary and powerful to have that much magic in the palm of her hand.

But even as soon as she'd had the thought, the Library sort of thwapped it out of her.

No, it's not in the palm of your hand. It is a part of us. Magic belongs to the universe.

Quinn understood. That's what the Library was. It was a hoarder of knowledge. It was the keeper of magic. To make it safe, not to limit it. To stop it from wrecking people who didn't understand and who couldn't control the wild surges of magic that otherwise littered the galaxies.

Melancholy waves drifted to her, thoughts from the Library, its previous Librarians... even some echoes of Lynx. So many people didn't understand that the Library was there as a measure of protection against that which many couldn't withstand.

There were so many species, so many planets, who just wanted power for themselves. To those people—the Library stood in their way. The Library was a keeper, a gatekeeper, despite the fact that it was open to everyone, regardless of their intentions, regardless of their background, all in an effort to make magic more accessible and safer for everyone.

Elements of it sounded like utopia, but the Library's aim was never going to align with everyone else.

Quinn couldn't see it happening. Not everyone always wanted the best for everyone else. All she knew was that in its effort to help everyone, a select few had disagreed. Those few were vocal, powerful, and they had had horrific consequences for everyone in undermining the Library like they did.

Kajaro's entire speech to her and Malakai needed to be dissected, once the latter fully recovered. Lynx had been pushing off a direct answer about why the Library had to shut down for too long.

The stream of information cut out, and for a moment, Quinn was plunged into a deep, serene darkness.

Just like she had been upon first being transported here.

And then silver words flickered up in front of her, in a beautiful cursive script.

The Library of Everywhere is almost ready for patrons.

Please complete the following procedures to finish preparations and unlock the doors.

- *Complete the Library reshelving*
- *Complete the bookworm habitat rejuvenation*
- *Activate the book restoration workshop*
- *Assign combat instructor to Librarian*
- *Increase Librarian defensive and combat power by 5*
- *Recruit a minimum of five (5) assistants through a universal call out with requisite minimum qualifications as specified in the manual*

A surge of excitement ran through Quinn at the words. Across her face, a look of pure joy spread. She jumped up, energy suddenly surging through her as the lights came back on, suffusing the area once again in that blue-silvery glow.

Quinn turned and hugged the trunk. As she did so, a rush of energy entered her, like a surge of affection. Then, she dashed over to the staircase and ran up the stairs, two at a time, before landing on the main level, three stories higher, barely out of breath.

Sure, there was still a lot to do, but they'd already begun some of it!

"We can open soon!" she said to no one in particular, as she ran out into the main area.

Lynx and Malakai both stood at the check-in desk, going over something that she couldn't see.

"Guys, did you hear me? We can open the Library soon!"

Lynx looked up at her and blinked. "Yes, I'm aware. Did you forget who I am?"

"No. You won't let me forget who you are, even for a minute," she mumbled, her good mood suddenly gone. "I was just excited."

The manifestation paused for a moment. "It's good that you're excited. We just have several things to set into motion before we can open. But we are that much closer."

Malakai chuckled. "You realize we have to complete a list first, right?"

"Well, yes, but that shouldn't amount to too much," Quinn said. "I'm guessing Misha can take care of the first three things? The shelving, the bookworms, and the restoration of the workroom?"

Lynx nodded. "Easily. The book hospital is one of our most important components. The Library will shift to create whatever else is required as needed. For now the supervisory golem will be in charge of said restoration, until we gain more power and supplies that allow us to create the requisite specific golem for that task."

Misha suddenly stood next to them, apparently looking at the list displayed in the check in area too. "Excellent. I will aim to have this finished as soon as possible."

Malakai paused, his eyes lingering on the message. "We have a book hospital?"

Lynx raised an eyebrow. "Of course we have a book hospital. Why wouldn't we? We're a Library, they get hurt."

"Because it's a book and it's an inanimate object? How are we supposed to make a book better?" Malakai sounded genuinely confused.

Misha stepped in with an answer. "By refining its pages, seeing if we can just simply replace the pages, see if it is salvageable, or if we have to create a whole new tome. Which, right now, is troublesome because as we do not have any magical quills and we do not have any bookworms prepared. And we still have not replenished the silverfish sufficiently."

"Well, that's sort of one of the things on the list, right?" Quinn pointed at it.

Lynx glared at Misha. "I know where the silverfish are, we just need to corral them and find more."

Quinn paused, pursing her lips in thought. "Would Farrow be the best one to reclaim them?"

Misha nodded. "Farrow is already in the process of doing this."

And, suddenly, Farrow was there.

One of these hours, Quinn was going to ask how all the Library's connections were able to appear with a thought, but she couldn't.

Farrow was just an amazing creation. The wood-like appendages she brought to the role just made Quinn think of her like a woodland nymph. She was definitely suited to raising the worms and keeping the magical aspects of the Library going.

"What's the silverfish status?" Quinn asked her directly.

Farrow cocked her head to the side and then spoke in a very whispery voice, rustling like fallen tree leaves. "Silverfish status: twenty-seven retrieved. Copulation cycle beginning."

"Bookworms?" prodded Lynx.

"Seventy-nine of them are still being reduced. Forty are preparing for copulation. Half a dozen are ready for feeding." At Farrow's words the bookworm item was miraculously crossed out of the list. Blacked out of the list was probably more accurate.

"Oh, wow." Quinn couldn't help the excitement in her voice. "We can actually get this done. Misha? How is the cleaning going? How are Tim and Tom doing?"

"They are doing very well. They are currently working their way through the Library with the trolleys."

Quinn pressed a bit harder. "What do you think, then? How long?"

Misha's eyes glistened for a moment. "I would give them approximately forty-three more Library hours. This is my worst-case scenario."

Quinn slammed her hands down on the counter with glee and turned to Lynx. "That means the Library can open in a couple of days at most!"

"Technically." He seemed less excited than Quinn would have thought, because hadn't he been aiming for this for five hundred years? Maybe it suddenly felt anticlimactic. She stepped closer to him, peering up into his purply-black eyes. With no pupil, it was hard to tell where exactly he was looking, but she couldn't see his eyelids doing their crisscrossing thing. So he wasn't looking far away, he simply appeared to be thoughtful.

"Hey, Lynx, are you okay? You're looking a little, well, you're kind of worrying me," she said softly.

He blinked at her. "What do you mean?"

"I mean, you don't seem happy about the Library potentially opening again."

"Oh, I'm definitely happy, but you're missing three glaringly huge items on the list." Frankly, Lynx sounded grumpy.

"What do you mean?" she asked, crossing her arms and glaring at him.

Lynx pulled the last three items on the list up and enlarged them over the tops of their heads. It was pretty hard to miss them that way. He gestured wildly at them.

- *Assign combat instructor to Librarian*
- *Increase Librarian defensive and combat power by 5*
- *Recruit a minimum of five (5) assistants through a universal call out with requisite minimum qualifications as specified in the manual*

"Yes. I can see those. What's the problem?" Quinn asked, genuinely curious.

"First up we need a combat instructor for you..."

She cut him off. "That's Malakai. He already volunteered, and I'm holding him to it. Now he just needs to live up to his promise."

The elf half scowled at her, but she could tell he was definitely feeling better after resting.

With her statement though, the combat instructor line had also been blacked out. Good to know.

Lynx appeared to be slightly mollified. "But we also need to recruit a minimum of five assistants, which is difficult with the Library currently closed."

Quinn squinted at him. "Aren't you the Library?"

He seemed a bit flustered. "Well, yes, but..."

"No buts. You won't let me forget how you're the Library... so make it so we can find assistants. Plus, we only need three. We already have Malakai, on loan to us by Milaro." She glanced around with a frown, wondering where the elder elf had gone to while she calibrated with the core. "And we do have Dottie."

"That's barely two," Lynx began begrudgingly.

"But it is two. Two that we can use for now and worry about later. So all we need is three, right? We can find those in a couple of days, I'm sure of it." Quinn stood her ground, not about to let him talk her out of it.

All she could think of was seeing the magical Library in action. She was so excited she couldn't think straight.

The line crossed out the five and replaced it with a three.

"See. Even your subconsciousness agrees with me," Quinn said, feeling a little bit smug.

Lynx let out a sigh. "Fine. I'll go and fine tune a broadcast to send out. We'll hook an entry pass into the applications so people who are earnestly applying can gain entry. We'll look for species that have a long running history as solid Library assistants and take it from there, so we don't unlock for just anyone, until we are up and running."

"Do we discriminate..." Quinn began, suddenly feeling off.

Lynx shook his head. "No. Anyone can be an assistant if they qualify affinities-wise. But, for the sake that we're not actually open, I want to direct the recruitment call to a few select places that we can be certain weren't a part of the plan to shut the Library down, and hope we can get our initial three so we can open."

Quinn shrugged. "Okay, but then we can open up applications like usual, right?"

"Once the doors are open again, Quinn..." Lynx flashed her a grin. "We can do almost anything you can imagine."

And then he flashed away, leaving Quinn there with her combat trainer and a lot of questions.

Again.

30

PICKING BOOKS

"He does that an awful lot," Quinn grumbled underneath her breath. There was no time to dwell on the Library manifestation and his habit of disappearing, however.

She needed to get stronger.

Now.

Honestly, she needed to get stronger five days ago. There was no way she was going to wait for a bow-wielding elf to rescue her, when she needed it, ever again. But there was so much still to learn. Still to do.

"He really does do that a lot, doesn't he?" Malakai spoke softly, gesturing at the spot Lynx disappeared from.

"Yeah. I know." She knuckled down, trying to wrack her brain to figure out directional thoughts she could give the console... the core.

"Have you even figured out how you work within the system, as the Librarian?" Malakai asked gently.

She flashed him a scowl. "Literally what I'm trying to do right now." But then she sighed. She'd lashed out again.

He gave her one light pat on the shoulder. "I get it. It's all good. I can't imagine being pulled into a magical world from somewhere with no magic. I can see how coming here and suddenly having magic would be jarring."

Quinn flashed him a grateful smile. "It is, a bit. Very different, and yet..." She took a look around the brighter entrance area. It was beginning to look like a majestic library. "This... this seems like one of my wildest dreams."

Malakai chuckled. "Good. Good. Let's figure your stuff out, then. Shall we?"

Quinn nodded.

Summoned by her thoughts, the HUD popped up in front of her with her statistics.

Energy levels 438 of 438.

She looked at it and said, "Okay, is that what I use to cast with?" She aimed the question directly at the Library. Instead of giving her a direct answer, a description showed up underneath the bar and numbers that had previously appeared for her. She ignored Malakai, who was clearly trying not to answer the questions for her.

Mana capacity.

Trying not to get frustrated with the apparent lack of intuition, she took a breath and phrased another question. "So that's the capacity I have for mana? Does that mean that's my mana count?"

No.

Mana Pool

728/728

Quinn was getting very confused.

Malakai cleared his throat, unable to help himself. "The first is your energy. That's the ambient mana your body produces. It's very unique to the Librarian from what I understand. It allows you to absorb much more information, connect with the system when it might need an extra energy boost, and enables your connection with the core."

"How did you know..." But she tapered off when she realized exactly that was now flashing up on the console. She laughed. "And here I thought you'd suddenly become all Library knowing. Okay. So it's like excessive mana that exists close to yet outside of my own core."

... Yes.

Quinn nodded.

Something else flashed up on the screen.

Mana capability is separate from capacity and pool.

Do you wish to calibrate for assessment?

She glanced over at the elf, who shrugged, and basically decided *What the hell?* "Sure."

Calibrating culmination of mana-based specialization: allocation: Librarian

Calibrating...

Aligning...

101%

error miscalculation

error miscalculation

The error messages kept spamming beneath each other. She directed it to stop, just as Lynx flashed into place right beside her.

"That's not supposed to happen," he said. And his form flickered briefly, momentarily massively cat-like, and back to his human form. The runes in his hair ran wild and wound all the way down his body.

He frowned again, and Quinn could feel him pushing enquiries through the system so fast she couldn't understand them. Which made sense, right? He was the Library, wasn't he?

The scowl on Lynx's face deepened, and an aura began to radiate from him. A softly glowing, almost black-like purple. It bled around him, suffused with anger and confusion.

Quinn was pretty sure it was a bad thing that the Library manifestation of the Library of Everywhere... was confused.

The light that played through the Library windows, shifted through the aura, dappling the interior with both shadow and light.

"Lynx?" she asked gently, worried for him.

He blinked at her, double blinked with the way his eyelids flickered. "Sorry. It's just..." He gestured at the console read outs. "This isn't right. I know we're nowhere near full power right now, but this shouldn't be... doing this."

There was a mildly frantic undertone to his words that sincerely concerned Quinn. "Is it... glitching?"

"That's precisely what it's doing. But there's no way it *should* be able to do that." Lynx flickered again. This time the forms practically superimposed over each other. From the lynx to the phoenix-type creature he'd once demonstrated, through to a scaly creature that passed back out of view so fast she almost thought it was an alligator, and then back into himself.

"Settle." Malakai did that calming pat thing on the manifestation's shoulder. Lynx's flickering subsided.

Quinn determined then and there that Malakai had some sneaky magic shit he hadn't told her about. There'd be words about that later.

"It's not sneaky magical shit," Lynx breathed the words out, like he'd had trouble finding breath. "He's part Darigháhnish... you'd probably call them dark elves. It lends a sense of emotional manipulation ability. He can, essentially, soothe you."

Quinn blinked. "Like I thought. Sneaky magic shit." She cleared her throat and changed the subject. "So why isn't the system supposed to glitch. Like I get that it's not ideal, but... why wouldn't a system not glitch sometimes? Especially after a few centuries of inactivity."

Lynx stared at her. "You realize the Library isn't some super computer, right?"

"Well, of course." She had known that... but probably not truly understood it. "But it is a system, right?"

"Yes. But it's not powering up properly out of its hibernation." Lynx seemed perplexed. "Certain information and calibration tools should just be available and functional. It's not like they can rot over time or anything."

Quinn got the distinct impression that there was a lot about the system she didn't know. But neither Lynx, nor the system itself, seemed inclined to tell her what it was just yet. There had to be a reason for that. Right? "Okay, so what is it missing?"

"It's connected to you, through you. Able to use your energy, even.

It's even going to pull from your energy when it needs some until its functions are all solidified. There should be no problem with assessing you, or calibrating with you." He frowned again, trying to activate something else that made him flicker and then tsk with annoyance. "Something isn't sitting quite right. I'll have to spend time in the core to sort it out."

Then he paused, the frown deepening. "Wait, that makes no sense at all. You need to check your affinities."

As soon as he spoke, the console scrolled letters and runes across its screen so fast it was hard to identify any of them. Several question marks flashed through with them, though; they were easy to see.

What is my strongest affinity? She willed the thought at the system.

1722...

Calibrating.

Calibrating.

Insufficient data.

Quinn blinked at it. Lynx looked like he wanted to kick something again, and Malakai frowned. "How can it have insufficient data? I'm standing right here."

Lynx shrugged uncomfortably. "You are. But you're also a bit of an anomaly. When I pulled you through the door, it was the first time the Library had ever been to your solar system. There isn't anyone around Earth who has magical access to us. And we both know it didn't go exactly as planned…"

Several other whispers lingered in Quinn's head, just out of her reach of understanding, as Lynx queried more avenues. He was practically growling under his breath.

"So, I'm guessing you're not liking what you're telling yourself?" Wait. That sounded wrong. Quinn tried again. "Not finding solutions, then?"

"None. No answers. No reasoning why it won't calibrate your affinities. It's okay with access. You have the access…" He sighed and rubbed his temples in yet another very human gesture. "At least that's something."

"I should at least be able to have some books pulled for her to use right away, right?" Malakai asked. "I mean, we've got to train her. Even if the Library is having a few... issues right now."

"Yeah." Lynx seemed highly preoccupied again. "Sure. Of course."

He snapped his fingers, which gave an entirely different sound than when Misha did it, and suddenly Carty was just outside the check in desk. "Carty will fetch you whatever you need."

Quinn raised an eyebrow. "Hey, Carty."

"Hello," the strange delivery cart responded, in his wonderful accent. "I will bring you books."

Both Malakai and Lynx had their heads bent over the console, so Quinn shrugged and pulled up information herself so Lynx didn't have to personally add her questions to the mix.

So do I have all of the affinities, she mused to herself, not actually expecting the reply she got.

All of the current affinities, yes.

As little as she still knew about affinities, she knew that was unusual. She'd come back to that later. *Well, how much mana do I require in order to absorb a book?* she asked.

Dependent on type, level, affinity of book targeted.

"That's not helpful," she muttered at the Library, and in response to her thought, it elaborated up underneath the initial statement.

Each book has its own mana and/or energy requirement for learning the spells within. Should you have insufficient mana or energy, you cannot absorb the book unless you have exceeded the capacity for that affinity.

She glanced at the 101 with the error and thought, *I don't think I'm gonna be not compatible with any affinity.*

Apparently, that didn't give enough for the Library to respond to her. *Okay, so what would I use if I were an all-powerful magician and I wanted to be able to protect myself and my books and my Library?*

Insufficient data.

...

Damn it.

"Will you stop making me do that, Quinn?" Lynx snapped at her.

"Sorry." She hadn't really thought that through.

"Don't worry. We've almost got it nailed down. I have four books so far." Malakai frowned and Lynx pointed at something Quinn couldn't quite see from the angle where she stood.

The elf frowned and then shrugged.

"I think we're good," Lynx said. He glanced around. "I have to get back to the core. There's got to be some reason this won't align properly."

And then he was gone.

Malakai raised an eyebrow, but turned to speak to Carty anyway. "Okay, we need *Dodging All the Things*, then we need *Counterattacks 101, Destruction is My Middle Name, Ice Blast Basics for Dual Combat Ideals*." He turned to Quinn and gave her a wink. "My ancestor wrote that one. You'll probably get a kick out of it."

Quinn rolled her eyes, and Malakai cleared his throat, continuing. "The last one we'll need is *Earth Manipulation: Branching Out*. Those should be enough for some good, steady defensive and offensive abilities. If you could get them to us, we're going to be in the training room."

Carty simply nodded by moving his handle ever so slightly, and vanished. How did a cart simply vanish? Yet another thing to add to her list of questions.

"I wish I knew how they did that," she muttered under her breath.

"Why don't you just ask the Library?" Malakai asked quietly.

For some reason the question irritated Quinn. "Because there are enough rabbit holes for me to go down information-wise as it is. What I need to know, right now, is how to fight."

"That's solid logical thinking." There was a hint of approval in Malakai's tone. "Let's get you to the training room."

"Where's the training room? Is it the little room I used when I learned how to sword fight?" she asked, hurrying to catch up as he left the check-in area. She had seen a lot of the Library when Misha took the golems to their divisions, but she'd not seen a training room.

"You think you learned how to sword fight?" he asked, with some amusement. "Even your machete skills are more akin to flailing."

She ignored that. "Well, I got to practice bashing things for a little bit before I had to go and kill some damn engorged bookworms and then fight an absolute maniac down in a cavern in a subterranean world who appeared to really want to kill me, not to mention destroy the Library as a whole." Quinn scowled and took a breath before continuing. "Speaking of which. Why aren't we talking about that?"

Malakai shrugged. "Pretty sure some of that is what Lynx is doing right now."

"I hope so," she muttered, oddly conscious of the target on her back.

Malakai was quiet as they made their way through the Library. "You're not what I expected when my grandfather told me about Librarians."

"Well, you're not what I expected when I read about elves, so we're both even," she shot back at him.

Malakai grimaced. "Okay, you got me there. Expectations are a misleading. Fine. Where is Lynx?"

"I don't need Lynx. I can pull up a map myself." And Quinn did exactly that. The map flashed in front of her face. It was a very simple drawing of the Library. It reached through to where the worms had been killed and off a right-handed corridor. She shared the vision with her teacher, just like he'd taught her to do with skills, while they fought Kajaro. "Hmm. Can you read this? Because I'm thinking we're gonna have to go past a bajillion worm corpses to get to where we're going."

"The worm corpses shouldn't be there anymore. They were probably your golems' first task, so I'd say they've already cleaned them up," Malakai reassured her. Somewhat. "Let's just get you through to the combat room and we can take it from there."

Malakai hadn't taken them far when Lynx flashed in front of them and dropped into an amicable stroll with them. "What are you two doing?" he asked. There was an odd edge of suspicion, perhaps even mild jealousy, in his tone, which didn't make sense. After all, the Library could track her every move, couldn't it?

Quinn nodded toward Malakai. "He's taking me to the combat room. Training, remember?" she explained.

"I'm well aware of that. I just didn't think you'd use the training room." Lynx was in an odd mood. Quinn cocked her head to one side and squinted at him.

"What's your problem?" she asked, stopping in her tracks and glaring at him. "I thought you had things to check with the core."

The Library manifestation shrugged. "I wanted to double check he was giving you the right instruction."

There was a lot Quinn wanted to say, but thought better of it. She'd already gotten her way, after all. "Well, you picked the books with him, so there's not that much else, right? I need books to absorb, and I need fighting skills to use against the next crazy-ass magician that you send me up against who doesn't want a Librarian to exist. This is important."

He looked taken aback. "You've only been here a week."

"Yes, and in that week, I've almost died to an engorged massive wormzilla, bookworms, and Kajaro, who was a snake-like freaking magician who wanted to blast me away. And that was if the cephalo-pod, or whatever that thing he had summoned from the depths of an underground lake, didn't kill me first." She realized just how much it had been, and for a brief second, it really felt like a weight.

At least Lynx had the grace to look sheepish. "Well, when you put it that way," he said.

"Yes, when I put it that way," Quinn retorted. She was getting worked up about this, but that wouldn't help anyone right then. "I know you have your reasons for not talking about the massive elephant in the room called 'Kajaro admitted to not wanting the Library around,' but I'm only going to wait so long."

"Got it," Lynx said, and fell back, following them silently.

They made their way up the couple of steps and into the area she'd fought all of the worms in. She noticed that there was still some goopy guts lying on the ground, but the gag-worthy smell had mostly dissi-pated. And apart from some books that were stuck in the goop, well, most things seemed cleaner.

They made their way through and then took a right into, what looked like, a massive gymnasium. It reminded her of where she had PE lessons while she'd been in elementary school. It wasn't quite as big as a high school gymnasium, but it was still very large. There were mats scattered everywhere and everything had a coat of dirt and grime. Some windows had broken and there was glass lying on the ground, but otherwise, it looked mostly usable. Especially the few training dummies that sat at the far end. They looked in much better condition than the one she'd practiced her sword work on.

Malakai glanced around, frowning slightly. "Well, it's not perfect, but I suppose it'll do for now." He snapped his fingers. "See? Nothing happens when I click my fingers. How do we summon a golem so they can clean it up for us?"

Lynx actually turned and smiled at Quinn for the first time since he'd appeared. "You know you have the power to command them, right?"

"Oh," Quinn said, directing her thoughts directly at the Library, directly at Misha. *I need one of the cleaning golems to come and just give a really quick tidy to my location.* It was much easier than telling her that they were in the training annex because she wasn't even sure if that was what it was called.

The golem was there before she'd finished that last thought.

"Wow," Quinn breathed out. She was really starting to like this telepathic link thing.

3 1

ENERGY EXPENDITURE

IT WAS TOM, THE CLEANING AND SHELVING GOLEM, WHO ARRIVED. HIS slightly taller body and sculpted hair gave his identity away immediately.

In a whirlwind of movement, Tom righted everything, cleared up the glass, and repaired the damaged windows above them. In no time flat, it looked like a well-organized gymnasium, even if some of the mats and the training dummies were a little worse for wear.

Quinn stood there looking around at the room and then she smiled up at Malakai and Lynx. "Looks like a perfect place to learn some magic, right?"

Lynx groaned. "You'd better teach her theory, too. Or at least make her understand what she can look up on her own." He began to fade, but Quinn put a stop to that.

"Where are you going now?"

He solidified enough to blink at her. "To set up the recruitment process for our new assistants."

"Oh." She paused. "Yeah. Sorry. Just thought you'd help train," she finished lamely. She'd forgotten about the rest of the damned list.

"Malakai has agreed to train you, and if what Milaro says is true, he should be fully capable of at least teaching you the basics of combat and magic." Lynx nodded in the elf's direction.

Malakai chuckled. "Learning magic isn't necessarily the first and only thing we're doing. Once you've absorbed the knowledge, we need to get you into the habit of using the actions. Muscle and mind memory."

Lynx faded out, just as Tom appeared next to Malakai, with five books stacked neatly in his hands.

Quinn took the books from the golem and thanked him. Tom inclined his head and was gone before she could say anything else. She shook her head, marveling at magic. Where had it been her entire life? Besides in a galaxy far, far away, that is. "Now, how about we sit down and learn these?"

"Wait," Malakai said. "First things first. You understand nothing about how to interface and integrate with the system."

She pouted. "Spoilsport."

"Maybe, but I'll be the spoilsport who keeps you alive," Malakai continued, without batting an eyelid. "Pull up your energy reading and let me explain how this works."

Quinn knew how to bring up information about creating items for the Library, and she knew how to ask the Library to inspect stuff for her and give her a readout on it. She assumed bringing up her own information should be as easy as a thought.

Lo and behold, it was, except she didn't understand everything in front of her.

Energy usage, tome knowledge, affinity levels. It was all so very intricate.

Energy Usage
472/583
Tome Knowledge: 5
Affinity Level: 3
Determination: Wasting
She raised an eyebrow at the last listing. That wasn't very nice.

"Why the look?" her teacher asked.

"I think the Library has some of Lynx's attitude, or perhaps vice versa."

Malakai laughed. "Likely. Share with me."

He frowned when she did so. "Okay... wasn't your Energy lower earlier?"

Quinn shrugged. "Yep. But I assume the Library knows what it's doing."

The elf eyed her for a moment and then cleared his throat. "Well, energy replenishes itself and it usually expands depending on the books you've absorbed—up to a certain extent anyway."

Quinn didn't say anything, but nodded, allowing him to go on.

"Okay, so you've gained energy levels, although it really seems to be increasing faster than I'm used to seeing, but like I said, you increase energy by knowing and being able to use more magic. It's like leveling yourself up, increasing your abilities." Malakai suddenly seemed less confused and more focused. "The Library, right now, needs you and your energy as well, so you're going to have a consistent drain on it. You'll continue to regenerate energy and mana you've used, and sleeping pretty much allows you to recover everything."

"Got it. Will it always pull energy from me?" she asked curiously.

"Right now you're part of the Library's main power source. It's been so low on energy that it needs to pull from you. So you should always keep some of your energy in reserve just in case." Malakai looked through the tomes Quinn was holding and nodded. "Yeah. Make sure to always leave some left over."

"So no matter where I am, the Library can pull on my power right now because it has to?" she asked, a little worried.

"Yes, as I understand it," Malakai said. "No matter where you are, you always need to make sure that you pay attention to your energy levels because we can't afford to drain you."

She didn't even want to ask the question, but it spilled out before she could top it. "What happens if it accidentally drains me?"

"If you're in the Library, you'll be fine. But if you're outside of the Library, then you're outside of the protective zone, and we can't guarantee that we'll get you to a safe enough place to wait out your energy regeneration." Malakai shrugged like that was no big deal.

"Does draining me potentially kill me?" she asked, her voice small.

"Only if you're out alone in a wilderness. I don't think you should go anywhere alone for a long time." Malakai watched as her expression grew even more somber and added, "The Library won't need to tap into you forever. Later, when it has its own power generation levels back to normal, this won't even matter."

Quinn nodded and realized she should probably feel mortified at the prospect of death. But since coming to the Library, she'd almost been eaten by bookworms, nearly killed by a giant cephalopod, and then by a snake-man wizard. She couldn't even pretend that she was shocked at the possibility of dying.

"Look, the best way for me not to die is for me to understand how to defend myself." She plopped herself down in the middle of the floor with her books and opened her interface with a thought. Frankly, she didn't understand why Malakai was taking so long. The sooner she learned to defend herself, the sooner she could also technically defend the Library.

And open it.

But who was counting?

"First things first." She finished her glare at him and hefted the books in her hands. "Time to learn me some skills. Show me the energy cost to consume or learn each book in my hands please."

Dodging all the Things

Energy Requirement: 84

Counterattacks 101

Energy Requirement: 102

Destruction is My Middle Name

Energy Requirement: 72

Ice Blast Basics for Dual Combat Ideals

Energy Requirement: 89

Earth Manipulation: Branching Out

Energy Requirement: 112

Quinn mulled it over in her head.

Energy Status: 491/583

All right, then. Her regeneration appeared to be pretty fast when she wasn't using her energy.

Which meant she could technically absorb all of these skills and still have thirty-two energy left over. Then she frowned and looked up at her mentor. "What happens if I use so much of my energy that I only have thirty-two points left?"

Malakai shrugged. "It'll fatigue you. Once your energy levels hit zero, you become sluggish, and depending on further expenditure attempts, you could just pass out. It's perhaps best not to learn all five of them at once if that's all it's going to leave you with. I'm not sure if we have any energy replenishers on hand yet."

Quinn nodded thoughtfully. So it wasn't like hit points in a game. If this energy was meant as her way to support the Library, either through absorbing knowledge herself or using it for the Library's good, then she needed ways to expand her energy and replenish it faster.

She frowned at the information in front of her. If she was going to be the Librarian, then she'd just have to be the best Librarian. And, like everything else she'd encountered in life, that meant she had to study. "Okay, how do I expand both my energy cap, and my energy replenishment?"

But instead of Malakai answering, the Library popped up its very own answer right in front of her eyes.

The more information you absorb, the larger your ability to absorb it grows. Regeneration is broken down into multiple categories, but should you wish to increase your own energy and mana replenishments, then the following are the Library's suggestions:

Mana through the Ages: A Definitive Look at Magical Essence
Energy Requirement: 275 - 35 continuous for the duration of absorption
Magical Energy Absorption and How It Can Save You
Energy Requirement: 312 - 42 continuous for the duration of absorption
Energy Absorption Pitfalls to Avoid
Energy Requirement: 218 - 27 continuous for the duration of absorption
Mana Oversaturation is Poisonous

Energy Requirement: 287 - 36 continuous for the duration of absorption

It is recommended that you take time between absorption of these inter-mediate tomes in order to fully process their information. Each book varies in duration, but should not exceed half a day. Be aware of your energy levels.

Quinn blinked at the titles and narrowed her eyes. They sounded so very on the nose. But then, she'd witnessed Lynx's ability to name things firsthand. She supposed this wasn't too much of a surprise.

Okay. She could do this.

A plan began to form in her mind as she realized how much work there was to do. Knowing that he wasn't going to teach her offensive magic yet anyway, Quinn left the *Destruction is my Middle Name* text out of her absorption cycle.

It was ridiculously fast to simply open a book onto one's lap, place palms face down on the opened pages, and suck in all the knowledge it had to offer.

Fast, however, didn't always mean simple.

There was more to it than that. The words, the images that they conjured—the meaning and the understanding of them—all bled through her soul. There was a literal suffusion of understanding the subject matter with the person she was. And each piece of information expanded her worldview and knowledge base just that much.

It tingled as it ran through her, and then using her as a veritable conduit, it moved farther along to her connection to the Library and the core. In short, it came full circle, bringing its cycle of information through all the avenues it needed to light up and be functional.

Technically, anyway.

Practically? That was a whole different ball game.

First up, some of the information overloaded her briefly and made it painful. Quinn wasn't sure if it was just the type of information determined the amount of pain, or else, that she'd just gotten used to it.

And, with all four of the defensive or counterattack books Malakai had got for her under her belt, she felt like she might just be able to put some of them into action. She pushed herself back to standing, leaving the tomes on the floor.

At first, there was a wave of dizziness, but then it was gone. Just a weak vertigo spell.

Maybe absorbing the information got easier the more she did it.

Incorrect assumption. The type of knowledge and level of current concentration value dictates the difficulty of absorption.

She ignored the Library, and looked up at Malakai, grinning. "I'm ready now. Come on, teach me, show me how not to die."

"Sounds like a great plan," he said, cracking his knuckles while returning the grin. He rubbed his hands together and looked at Quinn. "First up, I think we need to make sure all of your defenses are well in place, okay? We have to activate that knowledge and beat it into your muscles as muscle memory."

"Got it. Just tell me what I need to do." She braced herself, having no idea what would come at her.

Malakai spoke in a soothing tone filled with patience. "You've absorbed the knowledge. Your brain knows what it needs to do. It's your body we have to train. Then we need to make sure that you can reinforce the shielding you *already* have with earth magic and or ice magic. Then we're gonna move on to counterattacks and then we'll move on to destructive attacks, okay?"

She counted to five running all the new information in her head and nodded. "So, counterattacks use the opponents energy against them... in a way?"

"Sort of," Malakai said, "but also not really. Not when it comes to magic."

"I'm ready." She was almost surprised at how much conviction she felt. Because she really was ready.

He threw a full-on spear at her.

Okay, so the tip was dulled and it was made of a rubber-like substance, but it still smarted when it hit her.

"Avoiding being hit is the whole reasoning behind dodging." Malakai stood with his hands on his hips waiting for her to stand up. "Come on. Up and at 'em again. If you can't dodge something this big and slow... you can never go out in the field, and that's not an option for a Librarian.

Quinn groaned, scowled at him, but pushed herself upright again. This time she concentrated harder. And she was rewarded. This time, when he threw a spear, she barely danced out of the way of the tip.

However, he didn't wait for her to be settled again, and another flew at her. She twisted to the side in such a sudden movement that she tweaked her side. The point of the rubber spear hit her foot, and she crumpled to the ground.

"Damn it, that hurt." She scowled back up at him. Fiercely this time.

Malakai shrugged. "Access the information. Allow it to flow through you. Let it move your muscles in the way it knows they can be moved."

That was more difficult than he let on, of course. Quinn had always been a bit of a control freak. How was she supposed to just let magic do what it wanted to?

She sighed. "Fine."

This time. This time she wasn't going to let it get to her.

Over the next couple of hours, Quinn thought she was going to die, for real. Not to an icy blast, not to drowning, not to attack by an octopus, or even a black hole.

No. Dodging, it seemed, required a lot of stamina, a lot of energy, and a lot of perseverance, none of which she really possessed. Sure, she'd been able to run a couple of miles. *Run* being the generous term. Jog was much closer. But that took like twenty minutes. Her endurance needed to increase badly.

Yet.

With each and every attack Malakai threw at her, she could feel herself amalgamating just a little bit more of the knowledge. Her muscles screamed at her, but they began to know what to do.

She felt powerful, proud, and like she was starting to really get the hand of it... until she fell flat on her face, tripping over the tail end of one of Malakai's magical attacks.

"Oof!" she yelled, as she fell on the mat, for the—she'd lost count of how many times. "I really thought I was getting better at this."

"You are," Malakai said. "Despite a severe lack of natural ability, it seems."

Quinn grimaced up at him. She wasn't even going to try to put enough effort in to stand up. "Fancy that."

She liked the mat. It was oddly comfortable, and she'd rolled over to look at the ceiling far, far above her. Maybe a nap was in order.

"Quinn, now is not the time to be lying down on the job."

"I'm not lying down on the job. I'm contemplating what is apparently going to be my very short future." She was still gasping for breath, so her words came out punctuated.

"It doesn't matter if this is your forte or not," Malakai said in an extremely controlled tone. "If you can't even manage the basic books' skills, we're all dead."

"You're being a little dramatic, wouldn't you think, Malakai?" she muttered sullenly.

But the elf was pissed off. "No, I'm not. You remember Kajaro. He's the first of many people who want the Library gone—if what he said is true."

"Hey, I smashed his face with an icicle." Quinn felt the need to defend her pride.

"Because you caught him unawares. Fantastic instincts, but you can't survive all the time on instinct." He sounded tired too.

She pushed herself back up, and studied him. He was right. Taking a deep breath, she nodded. "Ready."

Malakai sighed and apologized. "I'm sorry, I just... it's imperative we keep you alive."

"Yeah, yeah," Quinn said. "I know."

There was a tiny part of her that was excited about how her life had turned out, but there was another part, even if it was smaller, that was extremely loud, screaming at her that this wasn't normal. It wasn't the life she'd been planning on, and frankly, it was damn downright scary. But if she needed to do this, then she *would* do this. She was going to be the best damn Librarian the Library had ever seen.

Or, at the very least, she was going to try.

She hunkered down in a squat and put her hands out to the side like she'd seen wrestlers do on television. "Okay, I'm ready."

Malakai stepped back, looked her up and down, and sounded very bewildered when he spoke. "What are you ready for?"

"To get really serious about this?" she said, even as her thighs began to burn holding the position.

"Serious about squats?" He seemed genuinely perturbed. "Wait... hand to hand? You're too short and too small, and you don't have the muscles right now, nor any natural ability whatsoever. I'm head and shoulders taller than you, so logistically that's not even going to work at your current level. So for now, with the amount of work we still have to do, I think we're going to concentrate on your magical abilities."

"Hey," she said. "I don't suppose you've got a training chamber that extends the time inside it but not out here in the real world? So, you know, I can do a training montage in there and get really strong over a period of like four months that's actually only an hour outside."

Malakai scoffed. "You are kidding, right? That's just like a total fantasy story."

She remembered back to all the anime that had obviously betrayed her in this isekai moment, and let out a big sigh. "Yeah, I know. I was just hoping it was real in some part of the universe."

Lynx popped into view, looking thoughtful. "You know, if we were to harness the time dilation from—"

"No, stop it," Malakai said. "We're not going to wait for however many years this experiment you're considering is going to take. She needs to be trained now."

"Of course," Lynx said. "I wasn't considering not training her. I just thought it posed an interesting scientifically magical question."

"Is that speaking as the Library?" Malakai asked.

Lynx nodded. "I always speak as the Library."

"Except when you're not, right?" Quinn asked.

"Exactly."

"Aren't you busy?" she asked him.

Lynx smiled. "Oh, I've completed the advertisement for an

assistant. Just running it through a few more processes to double-check the current inhabitants of the worlds I picked to run it in. And then I can launch it."

"When?" Malakai and Quinn blurted out together, the mood in the room considerably lightened.

"A few hours at most." Lynx didn't appear to sense their excitement. "Show me how far the training has come."

Quinn sighed and smiled. It might not be the worst place in the universe to be here, training alongside these people, being connected to a magical universal Library at its core. For just a moment, Quinn felt like things might actually be okay, that everything was going to come together.

And then Malakai threw a fireball at her face.

32

FOOD AND FACTS

Every part of Quinn's body hurt.

Dodging and rolling from fireballs strategically placed to trip her up was definitely not her favorite pastime. But at least now her muscles moved in accordance with the information in her head.

Speaking of information in her head.

The chip she ate had been rather anticlimactic. She felt like she'd gained more information about the Library from the books she'd absorbed, and the fighting Malakai was teaching her than from the chip.

As she walked slowly back into the main section of the Library it was easy to breathe in and inhale that amazing aroma of books and dust and knowledge. The light shone down, no flickering or glitching at this exact moment.

It really was wondrous.

The Library finally looked like a library.

All of the benches, couches, and armchairs in the middle pathing area had been righted, as well as the tables. Those that were broken were back in action. It made for a comfortable seating and research area for anyone who might visit.

There was room for a lot of people in here.

There were times when Quinn was skeptical of just how busy the Library might get, but... that was something to think about once they officially opened.

Thanks to the information that was slowly soaking into her brain, she could see a copious number of doors littered through the entire place. Where there was a space on a wall, she could see a door.

Sometimes just a potential door. Like it was somewhere a person could come through if they summoned the Library. But with this brain boost, she understood the entire concept more than ever.

Maybe the training had done more than develop some combat muscle memory. It seemed to have jolted her entire nervous system to be more synchronized with the Library.

Dottie, with her beautifully plush royal-blue-velvet cushion, walked around a corner with a couple of sofas trotting behind her. Quinn didn't quite have the guts to walk up and introduce herself, but she couldn't help thinking she'd like to get to know more talking furniture.

She stood at her vantage point, able to see back the way she came, and through the odd hundred feet to the massive check-in desk. The Library was gorgeous.

"What are you doing?" Malakai asked, stepping out from the corridor that led to Farrow's worms.

"I'm observing." She didn't even move to look at him.

"Observing what?"

"My Library. Have you seen how beautiful it looks now it's not all Gloom-ridden and musty?" She took another look, just for good measure. The pillars were clean and shone brightly. The books were in the bookcases. Return trollies bustled about, obviously bringing books to Tim and Tom, or else they shuffled the damaged books off wherever they were storing those for now.

The damaged books always made Quinn angry.

Books shouldn't have been harmed.

The Library was almost ready for patrons again. She could feel it in her bones.

"Okay, so what do you think?" She looked across at Malakai. She couldn't help her eagerness at feeling like they were at a precipice, standing on the verge of opening the library back up to the public.

She also couldn't help but be extremely nervous about the fact.

Malakai paused, scanning the library himself. "It's not bad, perhaps still a little more dilapidated than I'd have expected. But I'm no expert. I'd have to ask my grandfather, because I never saw this in its heyday. I am pretty young. I'm only thirty."

"In elf years?"

"Yes, in elf years. What other years would there... oh." He paused. "Sorry, I forgot that human Earth years are, well, much more limited, shall we say."

"That's a good way of saying short-lived," Quinn noted.

"Yes, I was quite proud of that." Malakai bowed deeply. "But you don't have to worry about that. You realize that, right, Quinn?"

She blinked at him. "What do you mean? What wouldn't I worry about? Longevity?"

"Exactly. You're not fully human anymore. You're a Librarian. You are now part of the Library. The core lives within you, and you're technically a part of it too. Or you will be. You're only going to die if somebody kills you." He sounded like he thought that would make anything that wasn't great, better.

Maybe it would have felt better if there hadn't been all those pesky near-death incidents already.

Quinn mulled that over in her head, unsure how she really felt about it. She'd heard Lynx speaking about Korradine. Maybe that meant Quinn was going to live for centuries. Whoa, that was one daunting thought that she pushed out of her mind and decided to completely ignore for now.

Malakai snapped his fingers, drawing her attention. "Anyway, let's not talk about that. Do you really need a break from training?"

Quinn groaned. "Look. I have to absorb those energy books and let them, like, percolate overnight, and I need to eat. Like—do you not eat?"

Malakai shrugged. "I do. I'm just a bit of a snacker."

She squinted at him. "I've seen you snack like once."

"Rogue snacker. You'll never see me eating." He wiggled his eyebrows, oddly independent of one another. Must be an elf skill.

Quinn laughed. "Okay. Fine. But... how are my levels? Have we done what we needed?"

Energy Usage

98/592

Tome Knowledge: 5

Affinity Level: 5

Determination: TBD

She raised an eyebrow at that last one and sighed. Bring up the task listing.

The Library of Everywhere is ready for patrons.

Please complete the following procedures to unlock the doors.

- *Complete the Library reshelving - Complete*
- *Complete the bookworm habitat rejuvenation - Complete*
- *Activate the book restoration workshop - Complete*
- *Assign combat instructor to Librarian - Complete*
- *Increase Librarian defensive and combat power by 5*
- *Recruit a minimum of three (3) additional assistants through a universal call out with requisite minimum qualifications as specified in the manual*

"Hmm" She flashed the list to Malakai.

"I know. I can see it too. Any of us who are marked as an assistant can." His tone was a little smug.

She shrugged. "Why isn't mine crossed off? My Affinity is 5."

In response, the Library popped another message up in front of her.

Previous Affinity Level: 2

Current Affinity Level: 5:

Previous Defensive capabilities 2 - Combat power 1

Current Defensive capabilities 5 - Combat power 4.

Please raise your defensive and combat power BY 5, not to 5.

She turned and glared at the elf.

"Fine. Learn the other tome. But replenish some of your energy first." Malakai gave in.

Quinn grinned and moved toward the kitchen. "That's precisely what I was doing when you so rudely interrupted." She could sense his footsteps following. While it might be something she should question, she was beginning to learn that the Library would eventually be an extension of herself.

Right now it was just little things, but soon...

When they had more power, when they were fully operational again. She simply knew everything would be so amazing.

Best way to regenerate energy and mana? She pushed the question inward.

Energy and regeneration are regained through:
Sleep
Rest
Meditation
Sustenance
Potions and Alchemy

Gee, thanks, she thought directly at the Library. If she didn't know better, she almost felt like the massive repository of knowledge shrugged at her.

Cook was already at the stove when she walked in. But that's all she noticed before she turned around to get a really good look at the place.

It had a massive—what appeared to be—eight-burner gas stove. The range above it shone like it was newly minted. The silver walls shone so brightly they could almost be used as mirrors, and all of the terrariums were freshly trimmed. The ones without contents had freshly turned earth in them.

The dining tables, plural, stretched out where there had once only been one. Each had ten seats spread around it. Light filtered in through here, too, given it an almost sunny disposition.

And whatever Cook was cooking smelled oddly like cinnamon.

"Come in, do not dilly-dally." The voice of Cook was somewhat robotic, hollow, like the sound a bell might make that wasn't quite right. Yet, in some way, it was still soothing. Like Grandma when she used to bake cookies as far back as Quinn could remember.

She smiled and stepped farther into the kitchen, making way for Malakai to do the same.

"What is troubling you?" Cook asked, whisking something in an implement that looked like a wok, but rounder. Quinn still didn't understand the kitchen. All Quinn understood was how drastically it had changed in a day.

"Oh, nothing's wrong," she said, but her stomach growled and gave away her lie.

"Would you like a doughnut?" Cook asked, their syllables clanging oddly over the middle sound.

Quinn blinked. "A doughnut? Like a sugar doughnut?"

"Yes, I believe cinnamon sugar."

"How do you know about cinnamon sugar doughnuts? I only ever had them once on a vacation." She was genuinely shocked. Those were some amazing treats.

Cook winked. A legitimate straight-up wink. Quinn laughed.

"Okay, so let me guess. You've been researching Earth?"

"Earth and what the Library senses from you. I believed that was the best way to understand the new Librarian." Cook's words were stilted, not quite as flowing as a human's, but it didn't matter. There was sentiment behind them, and Cook... Quinn definitely liked Cook.

"Sit. I will make you food. You will eat. Then you will go find more assistants so the Library can open."

"I like that plan," Quinn said.

In no time, there was a bowl of what looked like oatmeal, porridge, whatever you wanted to call it, sitting in front of her with a delicious cinnamon and apple aroma that Quinn didn't even want to know how Cook managed to replicate. The point was, it was there, and it smelled delicious.

And right next to it was what looked like a freshly made cinnamon sugar donut. When she broke it open, it had that beautiful fluffiness. Combined with the cinnamon sugar on the outside—it was perfect.

It was nice to have these aromas floating around what had once been an extremely musty library.

Cook even plopped a serving down in front of Malakai, who eyed it with suspicion.

"Eat it. Trust me, you're in for a treat." She gently took a spoonful of the food and blew on it because she could see steam billowing up from it, and put it in her mouth. It just exploded on her tongue like apple pie on acid. It was amazing. She may have let a very small moan escape her.

"Is everything okay?" Cook asked, probably alarmed, or at least about as alarmed as a golem cook could get.

Quinn nodded and shoved another, hotter spoonful into her mouth. She didn't care. This was amazing and delicious, and everything she needed right then. "Thank you, thank you so much."

"Excellent. I will use this recipe again."

"Please do, for everyone. Every single person needs to taste this." Then she corrected herself. "Every single organic person needs to taste this because nobody else can."

Cook flashed what might have been a smile in her direction. At least the line that made up Cook's mouth sort of moved more than just up and down. Quinn was going to take that as a win.

She glanced at Malakai, who was still digging into the food, a small look of wonderment on his face. "I take it you like it?"

He nodded as he scraped another spoonful. "This is amazing."

"I know." Then, satisfied that Malakai was hooked on her home world cuisine, she turned back to Cook. "Have you seen Lynx?"

Cook shook their head. "Not recently, but the Library has not gone anywhere, thus Lynx is here."

Of course, it would take a golem cook to speak the bleeding obvious to Quinn.

She scraped the bottom of the bowl, shoveled the last of the food into her mouth, and pushed herself back from the table before checking her regeneration progress.

Energy Usage
498/592

Excellent. That meant she'd be able to slurp down the remaining tome and have another offensive capability—and voila, they'd be able to open the Library.

After they got some assistants, anyway.

Everything seemed right with the world. The Library was coming along. Quinn had good food that she could eat to sustain her while she trained and absorbed magic and became basically a wizard. Which was kind of cool, to be honest. Then soon, they'd be able to open the Library and get all of those eighteen thousand books back.

She knew she didn't have to go out and fetch them all. Probably, hopefully not, but then they'd be done and the Library would be operational and everything was going to be wonderful.

Quinn could see herself loving life as the Librarian.

"Why are you not listening to me?" Lynx's voice pulled her out of her reverie.

"What, now you turn up?" she said, turning to blink in his direction, annoyed that he'd interrupted her perfect visualization. She wasn't in a bad mood, but she had been having a rather nice daydream and he'd interrupted quite rudely.

"Are you not seeing the flashing in the corner of your vision? Did you minimize your notifications? I've been trying to talk to you through your extremely obscene train of thought for the last five minutes." Lynx's mood seemed a tad volatile. He'd been in a much better mood earlier.

Quinn blinked at him and thought at her notifications and they popped up. There were a lot of them, and most of them were correcting almost every thought she just had.

Leafing through them, she realized he'd been asking her to come to the console at the check-in counter so they could navigate getting the word out and recruiting the final three assistants that would allow them to reopen the Library.

But then she saw listings of books that she didn't understand with branch divisions and collection timers, not to mention orders of importance.

So. Many. Numbers.

"Wait, what?" She couldn't quite make sense of it.

Lynx sighed, like he was just drained. And perhaps he was. She couldn't imagine how much effort it took to restart an entire Library.

Especially one, she realized, that seemed to have a very distinct personality of its own that had nothing to do with any of them.

"I didn't explain myself properly did I?" he asked, pinching the bridge of his nose in an odd mimicry of her own bad habit.

"Well..." she started, but Malakai cut in.

"You've been doing a bang-up job of not explaining yourself like... ever lately. But do go on." The elf grinned, finally putting his spoon in his empty bowl.

"Well, would you like the good news explanation or the bad news explanation first?" Lynx asked.

Quinn wondered if he'd settle for neither of those but realized quickly that wasn't about to happen. He'd probably speak directly into her mind next.

Well, I've been trying to respect your privacy.

"Stop that," she snapped out loud.

Lynx actually grinned at her, before sobering at her expression. "Well?"

"Good. Give me the good, so it takes the edge off the bad." That was the best way, right?

"Great." He genuinely seemed pleased. "We need to activate the search for our assistants. I need your help with that at the console, because this advertisement will basically scan them for the relevant skillset, and then, and only then if they choose to apply, will they have access to enter the Library for their interview."

Quinn felt a real wave of relief rush through her. "That is fantastic! Do you have any idea how long that will take? What sort of worlds are we sending this to?"

Lynx held up a hand to stop the obvious tirade of questions. "There are several worlds which have a history of providing the Library with great assistants and occasionally Librarians. I've chosen those places to send the first round of applications to." He frowned at the end.

"Still having problems?" Malakai stood, his brow crinkling like he was thinking overtime.

"Some. Not that we've ever had to reboot and reset before... so I don't have a precedent. But things are not working the way I assumed they would." Lynx was being transparent for once.

Quinn wished this was the one thing he'd tried to couch in better terms. "Assumptions are the mother of all fuck-ups."

"What was that?" Lynx asked, frowning.

"Never mind." Quinn shook her head, not wanting to get stuck on the saying. "So what does that mean exactly?"

The manifestation shrugged. "Not the thing we're worrying about right now. The Library needs to open and reactivate all its branches so it can regain the energy it needs to rebuild itself properly. So let's concentrate on that."

"I will assist with the culinary branch, once we reach that stage," Cook piped up.

"Much appreciated." Lynx flashed the golem a smile and then turned back to Quinn. "Speaking of branches. That's the problem. Once the eighteen-thousand-odd books have been returned or retrieved, enabling us to open the branches... well, then we have to retrieve those books that *belong* in those branches, too."

Quinn blinked. "So, to not put too fine a point on it, the eighteen thousand books are just the beginning?"

Lynx smiled, apparently happy he'd got his point across. "Exactly!"

Quinn needed to sit down.

33

THE MORE YOU KNOW

Q UINN STARED AT L YNX. H E LOOKED THE SAME AS ALWAYS. H E WAS still about five feet eight, glowing purple with black runes striping his hair, and he had an insufferable look of expectation on his face. He wasn't being facetious; he simply assumed she'd realize the initial books were just the start of everything.

If she was going to stay here as the Librarian, she was going to have to get used to his idiosyncrasies. And if magic was always evolving, it only stood to reason that there would be hundreds of thousands, if not millions, of books about magic. She didn't even want to think about that.

"I'm sorry," she said. "I didn't understand. I thought we just had to restore the power to the Library by restoring the books."

Lynx studied her for a moment, his eyes flickering. Something sparked briefly in them, and he nodded his head, as if agreeing with his own train of thought. "Okay, the reserves are at their lowest point right now. We aren't running anything major, so we're receiving enough ambient to maintain them for now. For a while, at least."

"And returning books means the Library regains more of its mana income?" She frowned, getting used to sorting the information in her head now. "The ambient mana... wait, that's wrong. The ambient magical energy emanating from both the books and the person returning it, as well as each usage of the book and its exposure to the worlds outside, feed back into the magical system and replenish the Library." She blinked. "That's it, right?"

Lynx laughed. Cook didn't. Quinn didn't. And then Dottie walked in.

"Why are you laughing, Lynx?" she asked, in that very prim and proper way that Dottie had about her. "You better not be picking on Quinn again."

Lynx threw his hands up in the air. "I'm not picking on her. I'm just impressed that the chip I gave her finally conveyed something."

"Oh," Dottie said, and shuffled her little wooden legs to turn and look at Quinn. "And how are you feeling with the knowledge, dear?"

Quinn shrugged. "Not gonna lie. It's pretty daunting. But I get it."

"Excellent." The bench actually sounded excited. "This portion of the Library holds only beginner texts on every single branch of magic that exists, but it does or should hold the deeper magical scrolls for things unrelated specifically to branches. You get that, right?"

"This larger main portion of the Library is responsible for magic— like affinity magic and telekinetic for example that don't belong somewhere like combat or culinary." She smiled tentatively.

"Exactly!"

Quinn nodded. "I understand it much better now. There's a lot of give and take in the borrowing system, but all of it adds up to allowing the Library to bring in the magic, cycle and filter it through its system and return a form that won't poison people? Right?"

Dottie butted up against Quinn like a cat. She could practically hear the bench purring. "That's about it," Dottie said. "We remove the chaotic elements from the magic."

"Great. Now that we've cleared that up." Lynx's grin spread, almost too wide for his face again as he clapped his hands together.

Quinn wasn't sure she liked that statement. It sounded very much like the precursor to something bad. She grabbed at her ponytail and twisted the tip around her fingers. It was a habit she'd been trying to break for years, but right now it felt more like a security blanket.

Lynx cleared his throat. "Come on. Console. Don't you want to open the Library?"

She perked up. "Oh! You want to send out the advertisement!" All of a sudden, a well of excitement bubbled in her. Opening the Library, the Library that could be anywhere and everywhere all at once.

Whose doors could open into any world.

Yeah… that's what she wanted, all right.

Quinn waved at Cook as they exited and noticed both Dottie and Malakai trailing after them.

Once they got to the check-in desk, Quinn practically bounced into it. "Okay. Tell me what to do."

Lynx frowned at her. "You know your penchant for wanting to verbally ask and do everything is severely limiting, right?"

Quinn digested that, refusing to react. While reacting to things was often the easiest course of action, and had been much of her to go to for the last few days while dealing with complete and utter over-whelm, she had learned long ago that taking a moment and analyzing what was said before responding often helped head off silly misun-derstandings.

Often.

Not always.

"I'm not used to internally directing what I think. Give me more than a few days with this newfangled magic stuff." She fixed her gaze on him until he nodded, and then continued. "How do I push this notification—advertisement?—out into the worlds?"

Lynx smiled, his entire body lighting up with a brief flash of purple happiness. "Fine. I'll speak out loud too." He didn't sound grumpy about it at all.

He reached across, pulling up information onto the HUD in front of her.

Library Assistants Needed for the Library of Everywhere

Positions Available: Three (3)

Limited Access. Applicant must fulfill at least three of the following criteria:

Affinities (3) required but not limited to:

Language - absorption, retention, expression, pronunciation
Knowledge - capture, processing, teaching, notation
Scribe - assessing, deciphering, reparation, notation
Tome Creation - deciphering, reparation, binding, scribing

If you meet at least three (3) of these affinities and are interested in becoming an assistant at the Library of Everywhere, activate your interface and request a transfer for an interview.

Warning: Do not do so until you are ready to apply.

Once the positions have been filled, this notification will be deactivated and an announcement will be sent out.

Application acceptance countdown in 48 hours unless special conditions are met.

Special Conditions: All relevant affinities are present in the applicant.

Quinn scrunched her brow. "So... you're sending this out to everyone?"

Lynx shook his head. "No. Only announcing it to worlds where we have previously had great luck acquiring assistants."

"How many?" she asked, genuinely curious.

"About thirty-seven."

"Thirty what now..." Quinn gaped at him.

"I know, it's a very small percentage. But I'm sure we should find at least three applicants." Lynx stared at her until he realized, through however their connection worked, that she hadn't thought of it as not many at all. "Oh, you think that's a lot. There are a lot of worlds out there."

"Yeah. Sure. Of course." She'd seen some of it firsthand, but the realization that the universe was so big, was a bit daunting. "How do I send it?"

"Oh, sorry." Lynx grimaced. "Forgot. Palms down, activate recruitment sequence, and then will it to go out."

"Don't need a passcode or anything?" Quinn placed her palms down carefully into the grooves.

"It's not a computer, remember?" he said again. "You are the passcode. Sort of."

"Will it is, then," she mumbled, and tried to channel her will into the console at the same time as thinking: *activate recruitment sequence.*

A tingling rushed through her like a gust of wind, pushing right through to the tip of her ponytail.

Recruitment sequence activated.

"That's it?" she asked, somewhat disappointed. "Did you really need me to come do that?"

Lynx watched her for a second. "You're the Librarian. The only thing I can recruit personally is you."

Quinn took that in, strategically ignored being called a thing, and nodded. "Okay. How long will this take?"

Lynx shrugged. "I can't really say. Frankly, out of those thirty-seven worlds, it could be that twenty of them no longer remember the Library. But I did at least double check that they all still exist. That ruled our other worlds out. They're relatively short-lived species, even if they're not as bad as humans. The others... could be days. Weeks, even."

"No!" Quinn gasped out. "That's way too long. Can we speed it up?"

"Not likely." He shrugged. "That's why I put a countdown on when applications can be accepted. I want people to really give it some thought first.

Her shoulders sagged. She'd been really looking forward to opening in a few hours if they found some assistants. With an almost five-hundred-year absence, though, that was probably too much to ask.

She sighed. "Fine, then I may as well learn something while we wait. What exactly are the different branches?"

The information, obligingly, popped up.

There are seven different branches to the main Library:
Horticulture
Bardic and Music
Culinary
Crafting
Alchemy & Medicinal

Combat

Schooling

Keep in mind all branches have their own divisions such as food crops, feed crops, crafting crops for the horticulture. Or leatherworking, blacksmithing, and so on for the crafting one.

"Oh," Quinn said. "How do we enable these?"

After merely a split second, a whole list appeared before her, speaking into her head.

All of the following book amounts are included in the missing 18,039 books. They are required in order to fill the main branch with the correct magic and knowledge levels needed to reactivate the branch. Once the branch is opened, more work is required.

Horticulture requires 720 books to be located to open the branch.

Bardic and Music requires the return of 897 volumes and 282 instruments to open its branch.

Culinary Arts requires the return of 282 volumes to open its branch and 287 herbs, plants, and other ingredients.

The Crafting branch requires the reclamation of 730 instructional tomes.

Add to that 315 tools, and supplies that are required to execute the contents of those tomes.

The Alchemical and Medicinal Branch requires the retrieval of 384 Scrolls.

Not included in those scrolls are the 1,257 varieties of plant life, herb life, trees, flowers, and weeds.

Caution: Alchemical and Medicinal Branch staff must be specifically chosen for their medicinal aptitude.

Note: Some of the required plant life may overlap with the Culinary Arts

The Combat Division splits needs the retrieval of 837 different books, instructional crystals, and weapons. Weapons (of which there are 423) are not counted against the book total.

Quinn simply stared at the numbers in front of her at least relieved that these books were a part of the massive initial undertaking. "What about the Academy?"

Computing.

Calculating.

Calibrating.

Yes, these are part of the 18,039 books that remain absent from the collection today.

These books will allow the branches to become operational.

The tools (herbs, weapons, supplies, etc.) are not tomes and therefore additional requirements.

The approximate 785 learning tomes required for the academy are not included.

Quinn pinched her brow. One step at a time.

Malakai cleared his throat. "You realize a lot of them will just walk back to the Library with someone, like my grandfather did, right?"

"How do the people know to bring the books back?" It was so much information to take in, her brain was tired. Quinn wanted a nap.

"Well, that's easy," Lynx said, back from what appeared to have been another one of his multitasking moments. "There's a magical alarm built into the books. We can send out a pulse to let them know that they have a certain amount of time to return the books before a fine is leveraged. Sounds fair, right?"

"People will come and return the books eagerly once they know we're open again for business?"

"Yes and no," Lynx said. "Some people will probably be like Kajaro and not want to return the books."

Quinn shook her head and held up her hand to stop him. "Let's stop right there for now, because we need to talk about Kajaro."

Panic tried to work its way into a tight little ball at the base of Quinn's stomach. Despite her relatively short life, which seemed ridiculously long in a futuristic sense, she had experienced a lot of hardship.

Her parents died when she was twelve, and she'd been thrown into the foster system as a relatively well-adjusted child with no surviving relatives. She'd been lucky, but her luck depended heavily on her staying small, being quiet, and getting her work done as she was told.

That was the easiest way to survive, and she'd been focused on it her entire teenage life. Now, she was supposed to throw herself into even more danger, to retrieve some books?

Okay, she thought, *I can do this. Panic is manageable. Once you understand why you're panicking, it's easy to pull it back, examine it, and find an alternative way to not freak out.*

Finally feeling more solid in her own mind, she asked, "So once the Library's ready, we reactivate it and wait for the books to come back?"

"Yes," came Lynx's reply. "And once the books begin trickling back in, the Library will regain more power. There'll be a lot to do and assess and probably repair, like the filtration system, but that's the start."

"Have you figured out the glitch?" Quinn asked.

"No." Lynx's brow furrowed in irritation. "That's another thing I should work on now."

"Not yet. You should work on the Kajaro talk you've been avoiding, for what... almost two days." Quinn stopped. "When did I last sleep?"

"Before we went to get the last book," Malakai added unhelpfully.

"After this, I'm napping."

"You could nap first," Lynx began.

"No. Stop it. Talk to me. Why haven't you said anything about the glaring fact that Kajaro quite obviously said, in no uncertain terms, that he was one of a group of people who wanted to destroy the Library?" She put her hands on her hips and glared.

The Library manifestation was quiet for so long, she thought he was doing that multitasking thing badly again.

Malakai cleared his throat, and tried to get Lynx's attention. "I mean, he was having a pretty happy time monologuing there. I think he was telling the truth."

Lynx sighed. "I know. I didn't want to think it, but the more energy we gain, the more I realize none of this could have occurred naturally. Frankly, the Library's entire existence should be inevitable. But... everything has a weakness, right?"

He sounded genuinely sad.

Quinn frowned. "How can you get more information about what

happened? I mean, I kind of get how the Library works now. Mostly. It just all seems so implausible to me. But I've seen the doors, or the prospective doors. Is there a limit to how many people can enter the Library at once?"

Lynx shook his head. "Technically no. Several criteria have to be met. Magic user, specific book or task in mind. Or else just a genuine thirst for knowledge. The doorways give a cursory scan of everyone as they come through to make sure their motives are knowledge related. But anyone with ill intent toward the Library itself will be barred from entry. The Library can also continue to monitor fluctuations as the people traverse it."

"What about intentions toward other people?" she asked.

"That's not the Library's concern. But if they harm a book in the process of their actions, they will be dealt with accordingly."

That statement sent a shiver up Quinn's spine.

"Yeah, my grandfather regaled me with stories about that." Malakai shook his head. "I would not want to be on the receiving end of a pissed off Librarian's fines if you dare to damage a book."

"That sounds like fun," Quinn said, rubbing her hands together. "But that wasn't my point. What if people entered the Library, not to get books, but with the specific goal of trying to remove someone from it? Couldn't they have made your assistants disappear?"

"No." Lynx shook his head for extra emphasis. "I would have sensed that. Or at least I think I would have. The Library is a neutral zone. No one with ill intent toward another person in it should be able to get through. But then..." He shrugged helplessly.

"Hmm." Quinn chose her next words very carefully. "But didn't you also say the Library doesn't glitch?"

"Well, yes." Lynx seemed flustered.

"And it did, just a while ago. So... all I'm saying is: look at every possibility, no matter how improbable you might think or calculate it to be," Quinn finished, proud of herself for getting to her point in such a succinct way.

Lynx nodded. "I understand. To be honest, the Library has never once been shut down to emergency power until this time. This whole rebooting and resetting process, and reactivating... it's a lot more than I ever realized. I've had to do an occasional reset and alignment with the core before, but never the whole Library. There are parts of me... missing. Or lingering but not reachable. Thank you for all your help."

And in the next heartbeat, Lynx was gone.

She sighed. "Damn it. I wish he'd stop doing that. I hadn't even got around to asking him how the borrowing system works."

Malakai shrugged. "The Library will feed you information. You know this."

"Fine," she grumbled and asked the system to show her borrowing details.

But before it could flash up, something else crossed her screen.

Main door in Main entrance activated.

Salosier entrant - one - permitted.

Applicant arrived

Quinn did a double take and turned to grin at Malakai. They both rushed down from the check-in desk as the massive main doors began to swing open.

She wasn't sure what she was expecting, but it certainly hadn't been the willowy and delicate being that pushed their way into the room.

Half overshadowed by the door, their first applicant was about six feet tall. Their form was reminded Quinn of a willow tree, similar to Farrow, but much more tree-like. Their hair was dark green but upon closer inspection made of leaves that cascaded on thin vines down their back all the way to the floor. Their skin was a pale green, with obvious yet faint bark lines, and their eyes glowed silver like a lake of mercury.

"Hello." Even the voice sounded like the rush of wind in the leaves during fall. "I... have come to apply to be an assistant?"

34

FIRST APPLICANT

BEFORE QUINN COULD SAY ANYTHING, LYNX MATERIALIZED RIGHT IN front of her. "Ah, a Salosier, I should have expected you'd be the first to answer the advertisement." He smiled. "Come forward, come forward. What's your name?"

"Narilin," she said.

Quinn couldn't take her eyes away from the way Narilin moved. She was languid, like a tree, sort of like a weeping willow. When the wind bent the boughs and blew the leaves ever so gently. Narilin moved forward and placed what looked to be a piece of paper, and yet somehow it had a fabric quality to it, on the counter. Lynx glanced at it.

"Quinn," he said, "come over here."

"Hi, Narilin," Quinn said, feeling the word a little alien on her tongue. It sounded like Narilin, but it lingered there, like maybe it had its very own power.

Narilin bowed in front of her. "I received notification of the Library's imminent reopening and its need of assistants."

Quinn raised an eyebrow at the archaic speech pattern. "Yeah, we hope to be opening soon. We need some assistance first, though."

Narilin smiled. It was beautiful, like a summer's day, like fresh new leaves. It sent sensations running through Quinn. It was a very whole-some experience, even just speaking to their guest.

"Quinn, place one hand on the application," Lynx said, in a low tone, half under his breath.

She placed her left hand on it, and all of a sudden an input of information flooded her mind. Narilin was 297. She was top of her graduating class, and she *was* female. She also had every single one of the sixteen requirements they had outlined in the application.

The Library had flagged it as exemplary and allowed her special permission to enter earlier than any other applicant could.

"Wow. What's next?" She turned to Lynx expectantly.

He shrugged. "That's up to you? Do you like her?"

Quinn glanced between the two of them, as if she wanted to ask him, *Why would you say that in front of her?* but Lynx didn't always have the best ability to read people.

"Well, I think maybe we should sit down for a minute and talk." Quinn gestured beyond the check-in desk to the newly tidied seating areas.

"I would love that," Narilin said in that clear, beautiful voice.

For a second, Quinn felt a little overwhelmed by Narilin's pres-ence, and then she realized that perhaps there was some sort of charismatic element to this species. She'd remember to ask Lynx.

You know you can ask me in your head and then nobody hears us, right?

Yeah. She'd forgotten about that. *Okay then, is she using charisma?*

She's not not *using it, but you're right, the Salosier are very influential. I wouldn't call it manipulation, but their very presence soothes and gives you sort of a new lease on life.*

Wow, regenerative?

In a manner of speaking, Lynx replied.

"Okay, then," Quinn clapped her hands together softly, eager to get to know her new assistant. "Let's go talk."

Each step Narilin took sounded like the whooshing of leaves in autumn just after they'd freshly fallen to the ground. Very soft, even with that sort of lingering leafy smell. Not the rotting vegetation type.

They'd had enough of that in the Library with the engorged bookworms.

They made their way, about twenty feet, into one of the couch sectionals, with separate armchairs on each side of a coffee table. Quinn sat in one of the armchairs, while Narilin took the couch. Lynx practically hovered around them. Quinn shot him a sideways glance.

She wanted to... oh wait, she could.

Why are you here?

Because I'm the Library. You're a new Librarian interviewing a new assistant and I thought you could use some help.

Supervision, you mean. Quinn hoped speaking in her mind didn't change her facial expressions.

You know, potato, potahto. Lynx flashed a grin.

Quinn had to suppress a laugh. She hadn't expected to hear that expression here. Taking a mildly deep breath, she remembered the two interviews she'd been on the other side of in her life. It was all the experience she had to pull from.

She got herself in hand and did her best to speak in an even tone. "Okay, Narilin. What reasons do you have for wanting to be an assistant?"

The very tree-like being paused. And Quinn was pretty sure she cocked her head to one side.

"I have heard stories of the Library since I was very young. My entire family has been guarding the books we borrowed before the Library closed temporarily. We did not expect it to take this long for the Library to reopen. I did bring all of the books with me that my family borrowed." She paused and removed a massive stack of books from her holding ring followed by a second stack of books and a third.

Quinn's mouth dropped open. There had to be about maybe sixty-odd books.

"You have a big family, I take it?" Quinn asked, already feeling some relief that a lot of the books might come back to them on their own.

Narilin inclined her head. "Yes, our family is very large. These are just the beginning. I am having the rest rounded up while I speak to you."

Quinn simply loved the fact that they already had these books. Surely they could check them in and begin filling the system past its low spot? She glanced over at Lynx. *Can we just give this girl the assistant job?*

Lynx seemed to be fighting a smile as he shot back another thought at her. *Well, technically, yes. She fulfills all the criteria that we sent out, but are you sure you don't wish to get to know her better? You will be spending a lot of time together.*

Quinn felt she could get a pretty good read on a person, or being. Even with these species she'd never encountered before. Narilin didn't make her gut twinge, so Quinn would go with her gut. She cleared her throat.

"Okay." Quinn pulled up the information in her HUD with a though, pleased to see the application appear before her. "You have the language abilities of absorption, retention, expression, pronunciation. Well, you seem to be completely and utterly qualified with all sixteen affinities we listed when we only needed three. What other qualifications do you have?"

Narilin smiled again and Quinn could have sworn she felt a breath of fresh air rush past her.

"I love books. I am exceptionally adept at handling papers and repairing books and trees and plants. I can definitely help in the tome creation or the tome reparation sections, if that is something that would assist the Library."

Quinn paused. That wasn't just going to assist reopening the Library; that was going to be a big bloody asset to the ongoing maintenance of the Library considering the state of some of the books. She nodded. "Okay, I think we should be good."

She looked at Lynx, who gave her a very slight nod of acceptance. "Well, then, Narilin, I'd like to welcome you to the Library as our first assistant."

There was a clearing of a throat, followed by a very theatrical cough. "Excuse me," Dottie said. "She's not the first."

"Ah, yes, my mistake." Quinn couldn't help the grin that spread across her face. "Meet Dottie, Narilin."

Narilin looked at Dottie, frowning ever so slightly. "Oh, you are a superellex futora," she said, and there was a glimmer of interest in her eyes. "I have only ever read about your species in books or heard in stories. I believe we are distantly related. Cousins, if you will." Then she paused, leaned forward and studied Dottie unashamedly. "You are not what I was expecting."

Dottie, despite having literally no facial features, frowned. "Well, I am definitely here and definitely real," the bench said, very proudly and perhaps somewhat offended.

Narilin sat back. "I do apologize. I did not mean to offend you. I meant that you are positively delightful."

Before Dottie could utter a retort, Malakai strode in. "And I am Malakai, a partially willing assistant to the Librarian."

Narilin raised an eyebrow very delicately. "Why would you only be partially willing?"

Malakai stopped as if he really had to think about that. "Well, I guess I am actually willing. I just... my grandfather made me volunteer."

Narilin chuckled. "The Library has a way of getting under your bark, or so I'm told. My people have revered the Library for a very, very long time. We were often a part of its larger purpose." She then turned, dismissing Malakai, to Quinn and Lynx. "My family would like it if you could consider more of us as assistants as the opportunity arises. Several of my cousins are almost at a stage where they will qualify, not quite as abundantly as myself, but very convincingly."

Lynx nodded, and Quinn wondered why she had to ask that. *Is there a familial restriction on how many people work in the Library, Lynx?*

Lynx shook his head ever so slightly, and then apparently thought to elaborate. *No, no we don't have that, but the Salosier are very particular about politeness and decorum and etiquette. They do not wish to appear indecorous, I guess you would say. They are fully aware of the effect their presence has on people and know not everyone is appreciative of it.*

Quinn shrugged internally. *Well, I can't think of a better feeling to have in a library than a sense of peace and tranquility that makes you want to sit down and absorb every bit of knowledge you can get your hands on.*

I knew there was a reason I liked you.

Quinn couldn't quite hide her smile even as she asked him another question. *Are assistants for life or if I find them suspect later, can we let them go?*

We can always let them go. It's not that difficult to uncouple an assistant, only the Librarian. Then he turned to Narilin and spoke out loud. "I think we could definitely accommodate your family in the future. We're still waiting on at least another two qualified applicants. You are almost overqualified as an assistant. But considering your extensive experience with restoration, we'd love it if you'd join us here."

Something like a beam of sunlight seemed to swish through Narilin's hair. The leaves rustled and she radiated happiness. "This is a dream come true. We believed the Library still existed. I think we would have felt its absence more than most. Thank you for this. As my family gathers more of the books, I will make sure that you receive them."

Quinn was curious now. "Can I ask how many books your family borrowed?"

"Oh, we were very frequent visitors to the Library. My entire family is approximately four hundred twenty-seven people large now. Though it was much smaller then. It has definitely grown since the Library was last open. I believe we have another two hundred sixty-seven books we will be returning."

"On top of this stack here?" Quinn blurted out incredulously.

"Yes. You see, my grandmother was very set on opening her own Salosien delicacy establishment and we do still have more than a hundred very specific and advanced culinary books that I hope you have a place for. Even if"—she glanced around—"even if the branches have not yet reappeared?"

She seemed slightly unsure, and Quinn, for one, wanted to know how the hell she knew that.

But Lynx beat her to the punch with a huge grin on his face. "Yet.

It's not reactivated yet. I've always loved the Salosier connection to the tomes and the Library itself."

He turned to Quinn. "Their species can essentially feel and sense anything that's come from trees or plants. They have a very tender and dedicated relationship with books and their upkeep. And thus, it trickles over to the Library itself."

"Okay," Quinn said. She'd never interviewed anybody for a position in her life and had no idea what she was supposed to be doing. Her only experience was her high school fast-food position, and the library reshelving gig she'd got once she went to university. Which was nothing like it was here.

Books seemed to do what they were told here.

However, she assumed that she would need to have Misha show Narilin around so that Narilin would know the layout of the Library and where everything belonged. Getting used to being in charge of other people was foreign to her, but she'd handle it.

She directed the Library that she wished to add a new assistant.

Library Assistant addition requested.

Do you wish to proceed?

Yes or No?

She picked yes. Just as she was about to speak, a notification popped up.

Library Assistant accepted: Narilin Jenishu'Salosier

Proceed to console to complete the registration process.

Quinn shrugged. *That was perfect timing.* "Let's take you to the check-in desk and get you, I guess, attuned with the system," she added.

Lynx snorted, probably amused by her self-satisfied expression. *Don't think these applicants are all going to be this easy. I must admit I was sincerely hoping we would find a Salosier who was qualified. This blew away my expectations. Narilin is the epitome of what you want in an assistant without having actual Librarian potential. Damn it. I wish she had one of the Library affinities.*

Still can't figure out why that's happening? Quinn asked.

No. Lynx's answer was curt and he changed the subject. *I assume there might be some more Salosiers, but she is probably going to be your most qualified candidate. Now we just have to wait and see who else comes. This was extremely fast.*

Okay, so it wasn't just me. This happened within, what, a couple of hours? Quinn asked.

Yeah, I was not expecting it to be so speedy. But Salosiers are very attuned to the Library's wavelength, not just in a magical way, but into what the Library holds, Lynx replied.

Yeah, I gathered that. Okay, let's return these books to the Library, Quinn said amazed at how much faster it was to speak mind to mind. Time barely even passed.

At the speed of thought! She chuckled internally.

Tim and Tom were suddenly there, picking up the massive stacks of books and bringing them over to the counter area. Just as quickly, they were gone. Quinn, Lynx, and Narilin clambered into the check-in desk, and Quinn glanced at Lynx questioningly.

"Okay, Quinn, left hand on this indent. And Narilin, your left palm on this indent," Lynx instructed, taking his cue.

It was the first time Quinn noticed the Salosier's fingers. There were many more than five, and they were like beautifully manicured little branches. Nine. Nine long and delicate fingers, probably better for handling all the books with. As their palms hit the indents, the HUD flashed up in front of their faces.

New library assistant candidate: Narilin Jenishu'Salosier

Protocol seven initiated.

Scanning.

Scanning.

Scanning.

Not only did the words appear in front of Quinn's face, but a voice echoed throughout the Library. A slight trill and several chimes rang out.

Scan completed.

Candidate accepted.

Awaiting approval of the Librarian.

Quinn gave her assent.

Librarian assistant, Narilin Jenishu'Salosier, activated.

A whoosh of air ran around all of them that stood in the check-in desk area.

"That's it," Lynx said out loud.

Narilin pulled her hand back, looking at it as she spread her fingers out thoughtfully. "I expected there would be a far more magnanimous procession to becoming a library assistant," she said, shrugging with a rustling of leaves. "But it is good. For now, there is more time to spend with the books. Do you have a book hospital wing? I imagine, after such a vast amount of time has passed, that some of your books are in dire need of care."

Quinn nodded, wondering why she hadn't had to register Dottie and Malakai. "Yeah, they're..." and Misha was suddenly there standing at attention and ready to take over.

Quinn was really going to have to get used to people just popping up in the Library.

35

RETURNS

QUINN WATCHED AS MISHA SCURRIED AWAY WITH NARILIN, BOTH OF them chatting amicably about books. A part of her wanted to follow them and see just how many books were piled high in the book hospital. What would Narilin think of how many books had been damaged?

Quinn frowned. "That was a very fortuitous recruitment," she said slowly.

Lynx shrugged. "Sometimes the Library works in mysterious ways."

Quinn scowled at him. "I feel like I'm missing something in this information you had me absorb. There's more you're not telling me, isn't there?"

Lynx shook his head. "What you received is the bare minimum to help you understand how the Library works. And I'm still unsure as to whether or not the transfer fully took this time as well. You're not missing anything integral to the way the Library operates. It's more of a..." He paused, his eyes flickering for a moment. So long in fact that Quinn was tempted to balance some books on his head again.

But his eyes flickered back again, and he flashed her a small grin, like maybe he'd heard what she was thinking.

"Some species," he continued, "have a direct correlation to knowledge and the way knowledge is created, the way it's stored, preserved, and spread. Many of those species have always felt drawn to offer the Library assistance. They have voluntarily come to us and served us in whatever capacity we needed at the time. What I did, when putting out the call for assistants, was make sure those species were still in existence. Five hundred years can change a lot of things. Once I knew they were still around, I made sure to open the communication channel only to those species. It's nothing I'm keeping from you. It's simply a thing that the Library can access. Now let's get these books checked in so we get a little bit more juice in the tanks?"

Quinn couldn't help the smile that came over her face. She glanced to the side where Malakai was leaning against the check-in desk, a thoughtful look on his face.

"What's on your mind?" she asked, somehow a little sad that she couldn't just read everybody's minds because that would just make life so much easier. Still, there were bright sides.

Malakai sighed. "I don't know. The Salosier felt a little bit too prepared."

Lynx shrugged, as if he'd already thought of that and dismissed it. "Well, there was that initial pulse your grandfather felt when we were searching for his book. I'm quite sure that the Salosier have a bunch of the culinary books that we require to open the culinary wing. Actually, I know they do. That first pulse might have already alerted them to some activity in the Library and thus they were already preparing because they sensed that the Library had returned. Which would explain why they were already gathering books. That and their natural affinity for all things books. It could have been that."

Quinn watched Lynx, pretty sure there was something else he wasn't telling her. And she knew that he knew that she was thinking that because she wasn't thinking it softly or surreptitiously. She was very pointedly directing it at him. He ignored it, which meant he chose not to talk to her about it. He must have his reasoning, but she'd only give him so much time to let her in on it.

He was going to have to let her in on everything eventually. And if he didn't realize it yet, she'd make him see that soon.

"Anyway," she said, "let's check some returned books in."

Quinn hefted the first book. It was thick and heavy, the leather binding scuffed. She read the title and balked at it: *Culinary Delights: How to Find the Correct Spices for Cannibalism.* She paused and turned to Lynx, her tone flat when she spoke. "Cannibalism?"

"Not what you think," Lynx replied. "I get it's anathema to you. There are some species who honor their dead by consuming their flesh. It's just an imperfect, shall we say, title of that book."

Quinn raised an eyebrow but checked the book in. "Can't we, like, name change it to *Burial Rituals that Sound Disgusting?*"

Lynx flashed her an unexpected glare. "That's very short-sighted of you. How would you feel if that were your ritual? If it were your heritage? That's an offensive suggestion."

Quinn blinked. "Oh."

"The current title, at least, spells out what the content is without diminishing the meaning the species that practices those rituals puts into such events."

She took Lynx's words and mulled them over. He was right. "I get it now."

"I know," he said simply.

Quinn went back to checking in the rest of the books, her head swimming once again with the fact that this wasn't Earth. With the fact that she was literally able to travel to different worlds to retrieve books. Excitement welled in her as she quickly sorted through all of the books in the piles. Out of the sixty-seven books, there were already twenty-nine culinary-based ones. That was a lot of culinary books. She worked through each one of them, acknowledging the "return book" on every single one. Then she paused.

"Hey, aren't I supposed to levy fines to people whose books are overdue? Why isn't that option popping up?" She frowned at the notifications.

Lynx stared at her long and hard, as if he couldn't decide whether she was truly asking that question or not.

Then it dawned on Quinn. "Oh, sorry. Brain like a sieve. Because the Library's been closed for so long, the fees are all waived, right?"

"Precisely," Lynx said. "Only makes sense. It's not people's fault that they couldn't return the books. We give them a show of grace and a little bit of leeway. And if the people don't return all of our books, we will go and get them."

"Like we did with the other ones, right?" She gulped down the feelings of dread and anticipation that clashed. Traveling worlds was the fun part, but forcing the return of a book...

"Exactly like that," he responded. "They shouldn't all be as difficult as your previous retrievals. Plus... if you think about it. The library isn't actually open yet. So those books, don't technically get fines."

Quinn liked the sound of that, especially for their first haul of books. Plus, retrieving more books sounded right up her alley, although she didn't want there to be any more Kajaros. "Okay, so how long were we thinking?"

Lynx actually paused his own communication with the Library systems. "Well, I mean, I was gone for a very long time, almost five hundred years. I say we give them like thirty days?"

Quinn raised an eyebrow. "Isn't that a bit generous?" She really just wanted to get the Library back up to full power.

"Of course it is. The Library is accessible anywhere, everywhere, all at once. I've lost count of how many times I've told you that." He sounded slightly haughty as he spoke.

She ignored his mood and tone. "So basically, they're just being lazy or they can't find the book if they're not returning it within the thirty-day window, correct?"

"Or they're dead," Lynx said. "And the book is floating in obscurity."

"In which case, as long as we can locate it, that's an easy retrieval, right?"

Lynx nodded. "Or they've decided they're going to keep the book regardless and see if they can escape the Librarian coming to get them."

"Can they do that?" she asked, curious.

This time Lynx's stripes whirled faster in his hair, briefly descending in a fascinating runic pattern all down his body before flickering back up. "Oh. They can try."

Quinn got the distinct impression that trying to avoid returning the books wasn't going to end well for anyone. Kajaro was only the start. She shivered. Killing others wasn't something she relished, but he'd been particularly hellbent on meting out the same fate to her. She took in all the culinary books, piling them high.

The Culinary Delights of the Fushpa People.

Culinary Intricacies and Etiquette.

Presence of the Royal House of Culinary Expertise.

"You would think the Library could use some magic to make this happen faster," she muttered under her breath as she separated the books into their categories.

Malakai laughed from his position in the corner where he was doing absolutely nothing as his assistant job. "You realize we're trying to replenish the Library, Quinn? We're not trying to use extra magic that we don't need to use right now."

She scowled at him. "Yes, I do."

Before she could say anything, a notification popped up.

Remaining culinary arts books required to open the culinary branch:

253 Books/Tomes/Codex

225 Herbs/Spices/Plants

She frowned at the screen. "Do you think Cook is already working on the food portion of the restoration?"

Malakai shrugged. "Probably. They do seem oddly devoted to food."

"Comes with their territory," Lynx inserted and then directed his words to Quinn. "You can access what your assistants and golems are all currently undertaking if you utilize the Library properties information you have available to you."

Quinn blinked at him and willed the Library to show her that information. A sheer wall of data flickered past. So much it was impossible to retain it all, but it did let her know she needed to be more specific next time.

Sometimes, it seemed, the Library was all too literal.

She turned to Malakai and crossed her arms. "You owe me a training session."

It was Malakai's turn to scowl at her, but before he could speak, Tim was there and the book stack was suddenly gone.

"Wow, our shelving golems are super efficient." She blinked in the wake of the whirlwind that was Tim.

"They're tuned into the Library, they know when the books have been returned, and they understand when to come and get them," Lynx explained patiently. "You'd know that if you slowed down for an hour and properly perused the information you absorbed."

Quinn shrugged. She didn't really like to admit that after a week in this place, she just wanted to chat sometimes. "It's easier for you to just tell me. If I can't reach you, I know how to find out what I want to know. But wouldn't the trolleys usually come and get the books? I mean, they are return trolleys."

"The trolleys can do that too, but Tim was apparently between jobs."

What do we do now? Quinn thought to herself.

A graph flashed up in front of her.

67 books returned.

Flourish of magic accepted.

Magic confined to the filtration system.

Levels 0.37% higher than previous.

Addition of Salosier to the assistant tract.

Increase of 2% Energy Total.

Emergency power mode previously dissipated.

Critical power mode: low power mode still active.

Progression toward unsustainable – mid-level observation power level - negligible

Quinn blinked. "Wait, I thought we were out of emergency power mode and in low power mode."

Lynx winced a little. "We are in low power mode, but that is also known as critical power mode because we need to get out of the low power mode in order to reach one that is more stable."

She squinted at him. "But that says it's unsustainable."

"It would be if we somehow reached that level with the current intake of power. That's what it bases that off," Lynx explained patiently.

"What you're saying is we still have a long way to go," Quinn said.

"I thought that was pretty obvious with the fact that we have to get tens of thousands of books back."

Quinn glared at Lynx. "I know, just... it's a lot, Lynx."

"Yeah, I get that." He actually reached forward with his solid smokey-like hand and petted her shoulder. As she glanced down, she noticed, for the first time, that his fingers resembled claws. Quinn filed that tidbit away.

She felt it was a little anticlimactic to get such a chunk of books back and have barely any energy register on the scale of the Library. Everything felt insurmountable right now. But at least the numbers were going down, which made it quantifiable. It helped to keep it all together if she had something tangible she could reference.

Lynx squeezed her shoulder once more and then spoke softly. "Hey, you need to practice your skills and, well, we need to start thinking about what other skills you need to absorb. Also, and I think this is the most important, maybe it's time you went and had a nap," Lynx suggested.

Quinn looked up at him. "Why, do I look tired?"

Lynx scowled at her and continued, "Look at your energy levels?"

Quinn looked down. She had two hundred of five hundred and eighty-three. "Oh, does checking the books currently pull energy from me?"

Lynx frowned. "It's not technically supposed to. At least when the Library is up and running fully. But, like I said, I haven't been in quite this position before. The Library has never been this bereft of books being rechecked for so long, nor has it ever been this empty of power, so I guess every previous experience I have doesn't count."

"It's okay, Lynx, you don't have to be perfect. You're not a god," she quipped, even if it fell a little flat.

He scowled at her. "No, I'm not a god. Would be nice. But we don't need to get into how I feel about gods."

Quinn watched him and his reaction to that statement. Little pieces of the Lynx puzzle were falling into place. She had a feeling there was something there that she didn't quite understand yet. About who the Library was, and by extension, who Lynx was. Neither of those things had anything to do with how the Library operated.

But with enough time she'd get there, she knew it.

"You know, I think you're right. I'm gonna go upstairs and have a sleep."

Lynx cut her off before she could finish. "It's well earned, Quinn. I know I pulled you here without any information. The download failed, the worms went crazy. You had to go retrieve books from extremely unfriendly places, almost got killed by a raging psychopath, and have had to clean up the Library, learn how to defend yourself, and adapt to an entirely new world. I get it. It's tough." He sounded so genuine, like he really meant it, and she had to believe that he did. "Thank you."

"Hey, it's okay. I mean, it is. It really is." And Quinn was surprised at how perfectly fine it actually felt. "Don't get me wrong, if I didn't know here, I wouldn't miss it. But I didn't have that much to look forward to back in my world. Could I have built a life for myself? Sure. But this? I think this is going to be a lot more interesting."

She paused. "Which is why I'm going to go and check out the book hospital before I sleep!"

And with that, she patted Lynx on his mostly solid shoulder, ignored Malakai completely, and sprinted off toward where the blueprints said the hospital was.

3 6

BOOK INFIRMARY

QUINN HADN'T BEEN ENTIRELY SURE WHAT TO EXPECT FROM A BOOK hospital. She'd imagined a large room filled with broken books and perhaps a huge table for repairs. However, as she stepped through to the space nestled between the infirmary and the kitchen, she realized she'd been vastly mistaken.

The very first thing she noticed was Narilin standing behind a massive table. But it wasn't just a table; it had sections cut into it where paper was draped over bars in huge sheets. Reams of paper were attached to one end, ready to be pulled across the table. Cutting implements hung over the same section, attached to the ceiling. She assumed were used to cut the paper into tome-sized pages in an automated sort of way. It was a very Industrial Revolution-esque setup.

It reminded her of the days of the huge Heidelberg printing presses.

Over to the lefthand side were piles and piles of books. So many that it made her feel a little queasy. There had to be hundreds, if not thousands, of books piled up there, and she could see just how damaged some of them were. Would it even be possible to repair those?

Narilin looked up. "Oh, hello. Have you not been to the workshop before?" she asked, in her lilting, breezy, beautifully naturalistic way.

"No, I've been a little bit busy," Quinn said and gestured vaguely with her hands, "getting used to everything else around here."

Narilin laughed, a sound like leaves fluttering on a breeze. It filled the room with a beautiful, calm sensation. Quinn could see herself seeking out Narilin's company on a fairly regular basis, especially as she kept getting worked up about some of the stuff in the Library.

"Would you like me to show you around?" Narilin asked.

Quinn shook her head. "I didn't want to come and interrupt you or anything."

Narilin glanced around and spread her many-fingered hands out, gesturing to the room in general. "As you can see, I have a lot of work ahead of me. I don't think a small interruption from the Librarian is going to make that any different."

Quinn would have chuckled, but it didn't seem the right sort of place to do that. The room felt sad to her like the Library was hemorrhaging knowledge, like it was traumatized by how many books had been damaged.

Like maybe, if she closed her eyes and listened really hard, she could hear it weeping.

"Do you think you can really fix all of these?" Quinn asked hopefully.

Narilin looked around again and gave a half-shrug, which rippled her leafy hair. "I cannot say with precision. I should be able to help the majority of these books, but it may be that some must be repaired in such a way that they are recreated instead of pieced together."

Quinn sorted that out in her head. "Okay, and do we have the things for that?"

Narilin shook her head. "I doubt we have all of them, or even enough at this point, but by the time I know what books will need to be recreated or restored, I will definitely have some, if not all, of the equipment I require."

"Okay," Quinn said, glancing around again at the massive room. "There's room for people to help you, yes?"

Narilin nodded emphatically. "Yes, indeed. I would welcome help from qualified individuals," she said.

Quinn got the direct impression that she meant others of the Salosier species, people that Narilin could trust to take the correct care of the books that were injured.

"Well, we'll see what we can do about that." It only increased Quinn's burning need to make sure that the books were taken care of.

Narilin's face lit up, and she inclined her head in acknowledgement. Then she pulled a book from the pile to the table in front of her. Quinn walked around the room, looking at the books that were damaged, watching as Narilin lovingly touched the tome in her hands. The book doctor had transparent, skin-... or bark-tight gloves on. Like she was cautious about harming the pages.

The Librarian took her time navigating the room and taking in all of the various apparatus that went into the repair. She could also see all of the stitching apparatuses that were obviously used to bind the books.

There were shelves and shelves of leather over on the right-hand side, stacks and stacks of different colors of the material. Next to those were embossing powders from what she could tell. Quinn didn't want to touch them. They were in tiny clear containers made out of glass. And the lettering stamps were exactly what she remembered from an assignment she'd done on printing presses back in the day.

Maybe her whole life had been subtly steering her toward being here right now.

The room was a strange mix of magic, Industrial Revolution technology, and old-world charm. She hoped that it was the sort of place where books could truly be fully restored. She didn't relish the Library losing magic because of books that had been so badly damaged they were no longer salvageable. Expending the energy it'd take to recreate them also seemed like something they couldn't afford right now.

Quinn stood and watched Narilin work for a little while. Her long fingers were deft, managing to reach even the largest edges of the tome. The Salosier was an enthralling species. Quinn could watch her for days.

Suddenly, there was a chirp of some sort. It sounded more like a hoot. Quinn looked around and finally noticed the stand in the far right front corner, closest to the door she'd walked through. It wasn't so much a stand as a perch. Made of extremely sturdy-looking wood, it went straight up into the vaulted ceiling with massive logs stretched out from the midpoint on either side. It was like a ladder with one pole running up the middle.

Perched on some of those branches were the most beautiful owls Quinn had ever seen. A rainbow of dark colors, with the occasional smattering of white, as if moons nestled between them all, their eyes were watching the people in their room with interest.

The closest owl was only a few feet up, and it was watching Quinn intently.

She could see that its flanks and belly were pitch black, so dark that it almost seemed like a void around its throat, mantle, and back. There were purpley-black sheens to it with gorgeous purple undertones that winked in and out as the light hit them through the window. When it moved, its tail had a rainbow of black plumage with different iridescent colors streaking through it—purples, blues, deep greens—like an oil spill on dark water. Maybe there was a red in there too.

They were simply breathtaking, and the bright purple eyes almost glowed, sort of like the way Lynx's eyes glowed sometimes. Their claws, though, were deep red. Quinn decided then and there that she did not wish to be scratched by one of these owls.

They had to be the night owls she'd heard mentioned on numerous occasions now.

The owl she'd been studying turned to look at her and blinked very slowly. There was so much intelligence in those eyes. It was beautiful.

Thank you, it seemed to say.

Wait, what? Did you just speak to me? she thought at it.

Yes, it said, and then it hooted in this beautiful, melancholy way that rang throughout the whole room.

Narilin looked up. "Oh, she likes you," she said.

Quinn turned to her. "How can you tell?"

"It was an approving hoot. They're not usually very fond of humans." She said the word distastefully. Quinn really wanted to dig into some of the history about humans on worlds other than Earth.

Just as she was about to ask another question of the Salosier, the owl in question swooped down and landed on her shoulder. Quinn fought the urge to scream, until she realized that it had landed ever so gently, and the claws weren't digging into her but only finding balance with the slightest of pressure.

Will stay, the owl said. In her head, the words echoed colorfully inside with all of the rainbow iridescence that the creature's tail had in it. Images of happy places like fields of flowers flashed through Quinn's mind.

"Okay," Quinn said, not really knowing what else to say to the night owl that had decided to attach itself to her.

Protect, the night owl spoke again. And Quinn wondered just what its name was.

Aradie. Aradie protect Quinn.

Quinn had to admit it was quite a nice feeling. Now she had a guard night owl thing.

Is this supposed to happen? she asked it.

Sometimes. No. But now. Now is right.

Aradie leaned forward, grabbed a small piece of Quinn's hair, and hooted softly into her ear. Quinn shook her head slightly, shocked at the breath of air that hit her. The owl sat back, making an odd cooing noise that sounded very similar to a laugh.

Narilin chuckled from over at the repair table. "Yes, that one really seems to have taken a liking to you," she said.

Quinn paused, marveling slightly at the owl on her shoulder. "Is that a good thing?"

Narilin shrugged. "I have never heard of it, but that does not mean that it has not happened before. It also does not mean that it is a bad thing. You should enjoy it. Night owls are very particular."

Quinn glanced at her shoulder. That sharp black beak looked like it could kill her on the spot, or at least peck an eye out. The owl flashed images in front of her and words. *Will not harm Quinn. Protect Quinn.*

She looked at the owl, wondering for a moment. What had the Library thought or encountered in the past few days that made it think she required a guard?

Not Library, Aradie said. *Not Library. Just Aradie.*

"Okay." Quinn could deal with that. She continued to examine the room, the bird sitting very calmly on her shoulder. Only sometimes, when Quinn turned a little too quickly without considering the balance of weight on her shoulder, did the owl dig its claws in a little more, but never enough to break the skin or to truly hurt her. It was fascinating. She was really enjoying having this bird near her—for all the five minutes it'd been there.

It made her feel less alone in this entire place.

As Quinn was examining the embossing inks again, Narilin called out to her. "You should take some of the leather and create padding so that your partner there, your new companion, does not accidentally tear your shoulder flesh."

Quinn paled a little at the thought of that because she could definitely see how those extremely sharp claws would be able to rend flesh quite graphically. While she understood that the owl had no ill intentions toward her, it didn't hurt to take precautions just in case.

In that second, the fatigue and weariness that Quinn had been somehow holding at bay washed over her like a deluge released from above. She stumbled slightly and leaned against the massive bookcase that held all the intricate parts required to complete the covers of the tomes.

The bird pushed against her head very gently and softly in an almost reassuring manner. That's when Quinn realized that it also had a soothing scent—woodsy, owly, like down in a pillow, and soft. She half smiled.

Sleep, the night owl intoned in her mind.

"Not yet." She chuckled out loud. "I need to make it to my quarters first."

She got the distinct impression from Aradie that the owl was impatient for Quinn to do so.

Narilin spoke up again. "You should really listen to the night owl. They are intuitive creatures. It is why their feathers, and their feathers alone, can be used to construct the Library's magical tomes. If it's attached to you, there is a reason. You will find it out in time. Not even the Library will know it. It does not know everything."

Quinn glanced at Narilin, rather taken aback by that comment. She knew the Library wasn't a god, definitely wasn't omnipotent. But the way Narilin said it made Quinn want to question her further. But her thoughts were too jumbled to follow it up in the way she felt necessary. They were going to sit down and have a chat one day when Quinn had all her thoughts on the matter sorted, and wasn't marred by lack of sleep. "We should talk later when I'm not asleep on my feet."

"That would be a very good time to speak," Narilin said, an amused tone to her voice. "I do have a lot to do right now, and while I appreciate the visit, I would like to get back to completely concentrating on the task at hand. While you, it seems, are about to fall down. Use the rest of your energy to rest, to make it to your sleeping quarters."

"Okay, Mom," Quinn said, laughing.

Narilin cocked her head to one side. "Mom, a maternal figure, correct? I see how that could be humorous."

Quinn blinked at the Salosier. "Uh, yeah, it was pretty sarcastic."

Another wave of exhaustion hit Quinn, and she realized that she'd only slept a few times, one of which she'd been knocked out for since coming to the Library. It was truly catching up to her now, magic or no magic.

Sleep now, the night owl spoke in her head again, and Quinn decided she would take its word for it. She plucked some extra padded leather and waved it at Narilin. When the Salosier nodded, Quinn took it with her and decided that she would figure out how to make a padded shoulder piece once she woke up from her nap.

She trudged through the Library, up the stairs, not seeing anybody else. Not Lynx or Malakai, none of the golems, no one at all. Her energy had risen more while she'd been in the book infirmary, and since it obviously wasn't the sort of energy she needed right now, one of her books was waiting for her. She barely paused to absorb the next energy efficiency book on her list so it could marinate in her overnight.

Her footsteps echoed through the Library, even though the soles of her shoes made her footsteps soft. She got to the staircase and walked up the winding frame.

When she made it to her bed, she remembered that she'd wanted to take a good look around her quarters, but all she could think of was the soft mattress, the sweet scent of the bird that suddenly took off and perched at the head of her bed, and just how soft that pillow would be when her head hit it.

37

SLEEP TO DREAM

QUINN BLINKED HER EYES OPEN, BUT IT WAS STILL PITCH BLACK AROUND her. She pushed herself up and looked around for Aradie, but the bird was nowhere to be seen. In fact, this didn't even feel like her own room. Not that she'd been in it enough to really have it feel like her own room, but the principle was still there.

She listened and heard a dripping in the distance, as if drops of water were coming out of a tap and into an already partially full sink.

Very slow, very deliberate.

Almost hypnotic.

Concentrating so hard on that noise, the slither she heard felt like somebody was banging on a bass drum. It was that loud. She gasped slightly and jumped a little in her bed. She pulled the blankets up to her chin, feeling a sudden chill cross over her flesh, giving rise to goosebumps.

She forced herself to take a deep breath and calm herself down. She looked around, logically, suddenly becoming accustomed to the darkness, and she could make out vague shapes. The bed she was in was not the bed she fell asleep in. It was nondescript, plain and dark. The blankets felt oddly similar, and yet there was something about it that felt decidedly off.

They scratched her skin where before it had been soft and safe. This was decidedly not.

There was no smell permeating the entire space. It smelled like nothing at all. And that was entirely abnormal. Everything had a smell.

Quinn looked up and realized that, instead of the large door that led to her chambers atop the Library, there was a massive arch in front of her. The darkness from beyond it encroached into her space. She glared at it for a moment, before pulling the blankets even tighter and listening for the sounds of the dripping and the slithering, like a snake careening across the floor.

And then she heard a voice that she'd never thought to hear again. Not since two days ago, not since they killed Kajaro and took the book back from him to refuel the Library. There was a sibilant hiss, the echo on the S sounds that made her unequivocally understand who it was.

Despite the fact that it was impossible.

The timbre and tone exactly the same as it had been when he spoke to her, full of venom, full of hatred, and a strange sense of being better than everybody else around him.

Ego incarnate.

"You don't know what you've done." The words echoed through the completely black space, all the way to her ears. There was no Aradie to go and attack him, so obviously this wasn't real. Although, she wasn't sure why the owl would be an attack bird anyway.

Right? Wasn't that telling?

"Everything is real. You have yet to comprehend that," the voice said, echoing inside her head this time, and not just the space around her.

She'd been through so much in the last week, had to accept a lot of stuff that she never would have accepted before, because she was thrust into it. This was no different. She just needed to calm down and think.

"You took what was mine," began the Kajaro voice, again.

"The book didn't belong to you," she spoke very clearly, confident in her conviction. "That book belongs to everyone as a part of the Library. It's a part of its integral systems; you know that, and I know that." She marveled at how confident she managed to sound in what apparently was her subconsciousness.

In a dream that didn't feel like a dream.

The snake-man chuckled. The serpent's surreal flares around his head bled bright for just a moment, and then it was gone again, sinking her in inky darkness, leaving only the shape directly in front of her eyes as she blinked.

Quinn heard more slithering approaching the first figure, more than just one serpensiril. It wasn't just Kajaro in this space, this was some bloody vivid dream, or projection, or whatever this was.

"This isn't a dream." Another sibilant whisper hit her ears, one that she'd never heard before, one that was not Kajaro. "This, this is a vision, a warning. Perhaps one we should have sent sooner. The Library cannot exist anymore, and we will find ways to make sure it's destroyed."

Laughter mixed with hissing played along Quinn's spine like a piece of barbed wire.

"You want to plunge the world into chaotic magic, all of the worlds. You want to destroy people with magic that will burn them from the inside out," Quinn said, her statement flat, and her dislike for whatever this was growing by the second. And still, she refused to examine this strange calm that had come over her.

"Magic is meant to be wild," another of the voices said, this one higher pitched, with venom tinting every single syllable. "Magic is meant to be wild, and those that cannot harness it deserve to be swallowed up by it, deserve to fuel the chaos farther. The Library stands in magic's way. Everything that cannot handle the chaos should be consumed, devoured, destroyed."

Kajaro's next whisper punctuated the former. "Only those powerful enough should wield magic, the rest are merely fodder to increase the chaos."

The hairs on Quinn's arms stood on end as each word absorbed into her skin. Still, there was no scent, no smell and she knew, without a doubt, that Kajaro'd had one when she previously encountered him.

This had to all be in her head. Perhaps a remnant from when his magic made contact with her? Was that even a thing? Had he somehow left a piece of consciousness behind? That sounded like something out of a fantasy book, which was precisely where she found herself. So, surely, surely that was possible.

"Everything is possible with magic." Kajaro's voice leaked in through her ears. "Everything is possible, but only if you're willing to sacrifice everything to achieve it."

"And by 'sacrifice everything,' I take it you mean to say you will sacrifice everybody else and not make any sacrifices yourself?" She couldn't keep the derision out of her tone. These voices, the content of their words... it made her feel sick to her stomach.

Kajaro laughed at her comment, and it was a cruel sound. It bit down her spine, making her shudder all over. He practically spat out the next words. "You think I haven't sacrificed? What do you call what you did to me in that cave?"

"Just desserts," Quinn said, suddenly confident at a level she didn't think she should be able to reach, but found herself there regardless. This was maybe not a dream, but it wasn't real because there was no scent. Scent permeated everything, and that meant that whatever this was should be able to keep her safe.

"You can't touch me here, can you? Not in the Library, and not in whatever this thing that you've conjured is." The blankets still felt real. Grounding.

There was a harrowing, bitter laugh that echoed around the chamber, multiple from Kajaro and whomever else had somehow infiltrated this mind space of hers. She couldn't help thinking that maybe this was a portion of the Library or perhaps there was a booby trap built into the book they took from his corpse.

Nothing made complete sense, but there were so many different theories she could come up with. In magical worlds, wasn't anything possible?

Hand-wavy stuff and all...

But she didn't have time to figure it out quite yet. Something told her that at least.

"You'd like to think we can't touch you, and I might not be able to in a physical sense... ," Kajaro said, his voice that sibilant, slimy sound. "But there are others who work with me. Not only of my species, but of others too. You'd be surprised if you knew just how many people want chaos to reign."

And with that, a thunderous crash echoed throughout her head and she sat bolt upright in her bed, for real.

It took her several seconds to realize that the sound was actually a very loud and panicked hooting coming from Aradie, who still clung to the top of the bed, her claws shredding the ancient wood.

Finally, words and images projected to her through her connection to the bird reached her mind, of freeing her, of getting her out of that dark area, squawking and warning of the danger and that she needed to come back.

Quinn reached up and scritched the bird behind its head. "Thanks, girl," she said out loud.

Safe now, promised safe, were the images and words that echoed through her mind. And suddenly, Lynx was in the room too, a panicked expression on his face.

"What happened?" he asked. "There were so many fluctuations just now. I couldn't reach you. None of the notifications went through. And why do you have a night owl on your bed stand?"

Lynx was actually flickering in and out. It meant his concentration was spread thin, as far as Quinn had been able to gather so far.

"It was nothing. It was just a dream remnant or something." Now that she was legitimately back in her room, the previous interaction seemed distant and smokey.

"Who of? Who contacted you? How did they contact you?" Lynx was still grasping at straws and it seemed desperately trying to sort through images and files and words, whatever he could.

Quinn could tell that now. When had she gotten that portion of the connection to integrate into her mind? Maybe she really had needed the sleep on all different levels.

She glanced at Aradie, who gave a tiny hoot, looking very pointedly at her. As if telling her to go ahead and inform Lynx of what went
down.

"It was Kajaro," Quinn said, hesitant to say so because hadn't they
killed him? Wasn't he dead? How the hell had he infiltrated her
dreams? "I could have just been having a really overactive imagination, you know, because the encounter with him was pretty bloody
traumatic. And I haven't really slept since then. It's been playing on
my mind a lot."

But Lynx walked up to her and looked her dead in the eyes,
leaning over. If it had been anybody else, that might have been intimi-
dating or scary even. But Lynx was full of concern, a concern that
radiated out toward her.

"Kajaro? Was it just him?" he asked, his voice gentle while his eyes
flickered in their multitasking.

"No, there were others there. The serpensirils?"

"Yes, serpensirils. How many others were with him?" Lynx asked,
and there was an air of desperation in his voice.

"I think two or maybe even three others. I think there were three
different voices, other than his." While Lynx's tone was off-putting,
with all its worry, Quinn wanted to recall as much as she could while
it was still vivid.

"Did you see them?"

"No," Quinn said. "I only heard them, all of them, since I couldn't
see them. It was so dark, at most there were silhouettes. And I
couldn't smell them. He had a very distinct smell when I met him. I
would have thought that if he was really there, I would have
smelled him. Or even remembered the smell, but that didn't come
to me."

She pushed on, figuring she should tell him about what they had to
say. "They really don't like the Library. They said that chaos should
reign and that the weak should perish before it or something equally
as fanatical. Basically, they want magic to run unchecked." Quinn
watched Lynx for any sign of surprise, and surmised that he knew
what their faction thought.

"I'm aware. I just didn't realize it had spread this far. I've been gone too long." Lynx had a hint of melancholy in his tone.

"Should I be worried?" she asked.

Lynx's eyes began working overtime, as if he was calculating a million different things at once. When he spoke, he had barely enough attention to direct it her way. "You were in a projection, probably a failsafe, from when he attacked you originally. I'm unsure why. He couldn't have known that we had a new Librarian, or perhaps... damn it. The alarm would have gone out to him too."

"But Tillip had no idea we were coming." Quinn pointed out.

Lynx shook his head. "Tillip isn't a mage." The manifestation paused for a moment. Finally he began speaking again. "Kajaro would have known the Library was back in a functioning capacity, and that it required that specific book. He knew and he had time to make a plan for if something happened to him. Although I am surprised he wasn't so arrogant that he didn't. Quinn, I'll make sure that someone is here to guard you," he started.

But Aradie interrupted him with a loud squawk. Lynx finally turned his attention to the owl.

"Well, that's odd," he said thoughtfully. "Aradie hasn't bonded with anyone for millennia. Like, *hundreds* of thousands of years. I guess I don't need someone else to watch over your sleep. You have yourself a companion."

"A companion?" Quinn glanced up at the bird. "Like attached to me?"

"Sort of. It's a willing thing. Like a familiar. Except she's related to the Library," Lynx tried to explain. It was obvious that the thought of this gave the manifestation some sort of ease of mind.

"So it's a good thing that I now have an owl-familiar." Quinn wondered what the connection meant.

Yes, echoed Aradie's voice in her head, as well as Lynx's words outside of it.

"Very well, I guess I have an owl-familiar. Speaking of which, I need some padding made to protect my shoulder from vicious claws."

She loved how silky Aradie's feathers were, but those claws were lethal.

"Yes. I'll see to that." Lynx paused. "You'll be able to access Aradie's information through the interface. Check up on it when you have time. Keep the bond strong. Follow the advice."

"Okay." Quinn adjusted herself in the bed and then threw herself back against the pillows. "How long did I sleep for?" she asked, staring up at the intricately carved ceiling. She only just realized that there was actually a scene carved into it, of books flying to shelves, of golems making their merry way around.

She squinted and gasped. It wasn't a carving, it was moving, like the golems were literally doing the actions down in the Library.

Wow, that was almost as good as television. Probably better once they started having Library patrons. Oh, that could get fun.

"Quinn!"

She blinked back at Lynx. "Sorry, I got distracted by the ceiling."

He smirked right back at her. "You only just noticed what it does?"

"Yeah, that's really cool."

"It is, and that's great, but we need to discuss you absorbing some books about mental fortitude." His tone had turned stern.

Quinn blinked at him. "What do you mean, mental fortitude?"

"Look, the serpensiril are a reptilian race. They have the ability to worm into your mind, to get under your skin, as it were. I don't want you to risk believing anything they say, or perhaps not understanding what it is they're trying to get you to do at certain stages, if they have any plans like that." He sighed.

Quinn blinked at him. "You mean you think they could, I don't know, hypnotize me or influence me?"

Lynx shrugged. "Maybe. Probably. I haven't had this problem with a Librarian before. I also have never had an Earth human Librarian or assistant, and am thus not up to date on how good your innate mental protections are. Considering how often you broadcast your inner thoughts to the Library, I'm betting on not very good."

"You've never had a human Librarian?" Quinn asked, curious, and chalking the rest of what he said up to observation and not to an insult.

He shook his head. "Nope, never. Not a one. Not ever in millions of years."

"You're telling me the Library is millions of years old?"

Lynx sort of half shook his head, but then nodded. "The library is older than you can imagine. In this specific format, it's almost a million years old. There have been other types of appearance, making it easier to move with the times. It morphs to what is needed, to what best serves its patrons. But magic and knowledge have always existed. And thus, the Library has always been here."

"Okay," Quinn said squinting her eyes at him as if it would wring more of an explanation out, "I can get that. Anyway, back to protecting my mind, you need me to get some mental fortification, is that right?"

"Yeah, mental fortification. You need to make sure that your mind is your own and cannot be infiltrated by anybody else. And doing that, I will come up with a list of books that you will need to absorb. And in the meantime, I'm going to entrust you to Aradie's care."

"Okay," Quinn said. "Is this something I should be worried about?"

Lynx cocked his head to one side. "Not necessarily, as long as you realize that it was a dream and not real, that they were trying to worm into your mind, separating reality and I guess dream or thought walking is very, very important. Even once you've absorbed the abilities."

Quinn nodded. "It's dangerous, right?"

"Let's just say having you as the Librarian is fantastic. But having you with your mind under the control of a serpensiril is something we cannot afford."

38

MENTOR

As much as Quinn enjoyed that her chambers were larger than almost every house she'd lived in, she took only a quick shower, pulled on fresh jeans and a T-shirt, tugged on her combat boots, and headed downstairs with Aradie in close proximity. She stood and surveyed the Library from the top of the spiral staircase.

It was only just hitting her that Lynx had somehow managed to get her favorite jeans, and T-shirts. She'd have to thank him later, and then look into just how he'd even managed that feat. As the Library spread out beneath her, she realized it had truly come together in such a short time. It was such a vast difference to the dilapidated wreck of a place she'd first encountered.

The news Lynx had imparted to her still played over in her mind.

Quinn had to get stronger. They couldn't risk her being compromised by a faction who wanted the Library gone. She still had one more book to help her increase her energy regeneration that she needed to absorb next time she slept. But right now, she had a task.

Getting stronger meant more combat lessons from Malakai, and grabbing whatever volumes Lynx suggested to strengthen her mind. While she was getting used to communicating with the Library with only her thoughts, she was going to have to make sure that she had complete and utter control over them. This would probably keep her innermost thoughts safe from the Library, too. Her own thoughts gave her privacy and while she was getting used to the idea of being part of the vast knowledge entity, a bit of "me time" didn't hurt.

Thus, making sure she knew how to compartmentalize her thoughts was paramount.

It was a win-win situation, really.

So many thoughts ran through her head. From how they could use the serpensirils' contact with her to perhaps find out more about this conglomerate, alliance, or league of supervillains, or whatever they were. These people who had decided chaotic magic needed to rule the universe and that the Library was outdated and was no longer required made her stomach churn. Those thoughts plagued her.

She didn't understand why anybody would want chaotic magic to reign if the destruction she'd heard described was even slightly true. It would seem they wanted chaotic magic to perform a natural selection type of deal. One they seemed absolutely certain they'd survive through.

How ironic.

Which made her wonder just how the serpensiril could be so sure they were strong enough to withstand the onslaught of the raw magic to begin with. What else did they have up their sleeves?

"You're deep in thought," Milaro said, suddenly standing in front of her at the bottom of the staircase.

The taller elf, or perhaps she should inspect him and figure out what they called high elves here.

Milaro Seveshall

Species: Areilthâhnish

Yeah. She was sticking with high elf, in her head at least. He'd always struck Quinn as kindly. His robes flowed in a way that she'd always imagined a wizard's would. He reminded her of the magic users she'd read about in books, from wizened wizards, to teachers, to the old ones who hid in the woods and didn't really want to share their abilities with anybody, but begrudgingly would then teach some new little whippersnapper.

Milaro was everything she thought a high elf would be, appearance-wise, at least. His personality was much more approachable. Although, perhaps basing her knowledge of a species on the elves she'd seen on television wasn't exactly the way to go about it. Especially considering Earth had no idea that they actually existed.

"Is everything all right?" Milaro asked, leaning down slightly. "You look like you're having a lot of thoughts in that head."

Quinn grinned up at him. "Sometimes I think my thoughts are my own worst enemy."

Milaro chuckled. "I think that's true for everyone. Speaking of which, Lynx has inquired of me that I teach you some mental fortitude skills. Would you be amenable to that?"

Quinn grinned again. "Yeah. Yeah, I think I'd be amenable to that."

She scanned the Library, like she knew what she was doing. "Okay, so, which books would be best for me?"

Milaro pursed his lips and walked farther into the Library. "Okay, we're going to want *Stop Your Mindless Rambling.*"

"Is that seriously what it's called?" Quinn asked. Although she thought she'd gotten used to the odd naming conventions... they still blindsided her sometimes.

Milaro winked at her. "You'd be surprised. The best way to get people interested in books is having a catchy title."

"So I've been told," Quinn said, finding it odd that Lynx said precisely the same thing. Then a thought occurred to her. "What about covers?"

Milaro waved that concern away. "These aren't fiction books. These are factual books. And thus, you need a catchy title, not necessarily a catchy cover, because, let's just face it, leather-bound covers are always going to win out when you have a lot of wear and tear." He paused, obviously looking through a refined catalog index. "Next, *The Mind You Forgot.* That's a really good one. It's great for beginners, and it's going to give you a basis of how your mind works and what powers your species has probably forgotten, which, considering *your* species, is probably a lot."

"Well, I guess they always say that we only use ten percent of our brains," Quinn joked, but it fell flat because Milaro just raised an eyebrow and moved on.

"Okay, so you should hopefully have *Segmenting of Thoughts* here. And if it's not in stock right now, then you might have *Mind Compartmentalization for Beginners*. Yes, we could probably use both of those. But one will suffice if this mark next to the listing means *Segmenting* isn't here..." He pursed his lips for a moment as if considering other options.

"Tom," Quinn spoke the name out loud, and immediately the golem was there. It took maybe three seconds. She looked at him, and she swore he was smiling. "Thank you, Tom. Could you get the following books for us? *The Mind You Forgot, Segmentation of Thoughts, Mind Compartmentalization for Beginners,* and *Stop Your Mindless Rambling.*"

Tom cocked his head to one side, gave her a nod, and then he was gone.

"That will never not be unnerving," Milaro said. "Even after all these years, their ability to understand without speaking has been quite remarkable. Shall we find a place to sit?" And he gestured in front of them where Quinn was happy to see that all of the seating areas were beautifully relegated now. Comfortable chairs, little tables, even small trolleys that weren't the return trolleys they had crafted, but were just little rolly shelves to put your books on when you were finished.

It was wonderful.

"Is that a water dispenser?" she said, pointing off to the side.

"Oh, yes, people do get thirsty. There's a lot of dust in here," Milaro said. "They're just put out of the way so they don't accidentally get spilled on books."

"Wise choice." Quinn thought fire and water were probably two good things to keep away from books.

Tom was back with their stack already and he placed them on the closest little table to the seating they'd chosen.

"Time to sit on the couch and absorb a few books." Quinn sat down and went through the energy requirements for each book while

Aradie perched herself on the back of the couch looking over her shoulder. It almost seemed as if the Night Owl wanted to read too.

Segmentation of Thoughts
Energy Requirement: 192
Stop Your Mindless Rambling
Energy Requirement: 167
The Mind You Forgot
Energy Requirement: 120
Mind Compartmentalization for Beginners
Energy Requirement: 85

"Is that a lot of energy expenditure for beginner books, right?" she asked.

"What do you mean? Haven't you been eating?" Milaro shot the question at her rapid fire.

Quinn blinked at him. "Of course I've been eating."

"No. Not just meals. What did you think magical culinary books were about, Quinn? Magical cooking replenishes your energy, mana, so many different statuses depending on what recipe you're using. There are thousands of them. Different species react in specific ways to a whole range of foods. But there are cooking volumes for every single type of energy expenditure. And especially if it's you, you should be eating regular snacks from..." He paused, looking slightly irate, and shook his head. "Give me a minute. I will go and talk to Cook."

Quinn reclined back into the couch, not opening any of the books. She didn't want to accidentally absorb a book when she was already full of energy. 597 out of 597. That was interesting; it had increased ever so slightly with the absorption of that other energy book the previous evening.

Her stomach rumbled, reminding her of her hunger. She might have said she was eating, but the fact was she often forgot. The Library had a way of distorting time around her. Even though time definitively passed, she could tell that she wasn't as attuned to the passage of it as she usually would have been.

The wonders and constant stream of things to do probably didn't help her concentration. This meant that her mealtimes were out of sync, and she was starting to get a little lightheaded when she forgot to eat.

Like now.

Lynx had never answered her and told her how long she'd been asleep. She glanced around, but the semi-permanent light still beamed through the windows so much that she couldn't what time of day it was. Did they even have clocks in here?

There was a slight buzz in her head, and she glanced down at the bottom corner of her screen where the timer for the book retrieval used to sit. There was a tiny clock.

Anundrum 15th 12:37.

She wondered if that was the time, and the 12:37 flashed in big numbers in front of her eyes for several seconds this time.

"Okay, okay, I guess that's your way of telling me that that's the time," she muttered to herself. The fact that it had taken her a week to even care about it told her a lot. She liked being here. It made her feel at home, useful, needed, and a little bit adventurous. Damn hungry. A little empty.

So time, in a way, felt almost irrelevant to her.

Maybe it was time to just take a breath and analyze things. Find out what she knew and what she didn't. The Library was vast —huge, in fact—but it wasn't complete. The levels were at a critical mass. They needed to retrieve a lot of books, and specific books if they wanted to open the branches before collecting all of them.

She understood all of that.

Quinn now knew that food could replenish energy, specifically magical energy, and could target what she needed to replenish. She knew that dream experiences, or whatever it was that had happened, was a thing. That the Library could open onto any world it was so directed to, at any time, anywhere.

Heck, she'd even taken the same door to two completely different places.

And that people, once the Library was open to patrons again, would be able to summon one of the doors to open where they were as well. She really wanted to know how that worked.

But maybe dimensional theory was a little bit beyond her. At least for now.

She glanced around, none of the golems in sight, and wondered what it would be like when more people visited the Library. Wouldn't they need more golems then? Wouldn't they have to go out and find more ingredients so that they could make more golems, make more carts? It was going to be so busy.

This was like a lull before the storm, and she should really enjoy it.

Quinn leaned her head back and looked up at the ceiling. It was so far away, maybe forty, fifty feet. But she could see the carvings of books and the sprays of light that spread across it. It was so beautiful, magical. She let out a deep sigh. Aradie pushed her softly feathered head close and hooted out a soft inquiry.

"Are you okay?" Dottie's voice was soft, not startling, even though Quinn hadn't noticed that the bench was sitting near her.

"Hey, Dottie."

"Hello, Quinn. Did you have a good sleep?" The bench inquired, her tone still soft.

"Do you know how long I was asleep for?" Quinn asked instead of answering.

"Approximately twelve hours and twenty-three minutes," Dottie said. "And that includes the horrible nightmare you seemed to have."

"It wasn't horrible. It was just a little informative and slightly confusing," Quinn said.

Dottie shuffled herself under Quinn's feet, and Quinn rested them on the bench.

"Are you sure that's okay? Last time I tried to put weight on you, you almost bit my leg off." Quinn teased.

"Well, that's water under the bridge, under the legs, whatever," Dottie said. "Do you have any questions? I know it's been a little fast, and Lynx seems to be off."

Quinn perked up at that. "What do you mean, off?"

Dottie seemed confused for a moment, but her demeanor brightened again almost immediately. "Oh, you wouldn't know of course, having only just met him. You have nothing to compare him to."

"Compare him to what?" Quinn was pretty sure the confusion had been passed on to her.

"He's not functioning the way I'm used to seeing him," Dottie answered, very slowly, as if she was trying to taste the words in her mind before she spoke them. "You have to understand, I've never known the Library to be this low on power, ever. Frankly, for a while there, we thought we were all goners because we were trapped in the Library. It didn't have power to get us out and still search for a way to continue existing, and we just sort of were withering away."

"What do you mean?" Quinn leaned forward, her curiosity spiking.

"The Library has always been at full power, until no Librarians could be found, and right now, getting it to reset and reboot itself through its systems, well, it almost seems like a part of Lynx is missing," the bench said, in a conspiratorial tone.

Except what she said sure as hell made a lot of sense to Quinn. If she thought about the way he multitasked and didn't appear to be present. How his countenance flickered and became staticky. "What do you mean, a part of him?"

"It could just be the power levels," Dottie said. "But Lynx isn't himself."

Quinn frowned. "Like he's not acting like the Lynx you know—or the Library you know?" Because realistically, Lynx was an individual, as well as an entity. If she'd understood it all properly.

"Well, I believe it's a little bit of both," Milaro cut in, as he returned with a full tray of various types of food, including a sugar doughnut. Quinn's mouth practically drooled on the spot. Milaro turned to the bench, and said, "Thanks, Dottie."

Quinn made to reach for the doughnut but Milaro pulled the tray away. "Now wait a second. That is a treat from Cook. The rest is very specifically targeted food. This here is your meal." He placed down a bowl of something that suspiciously resembled ramen.

"You need this to replenish your energy and mana." He paused. "Even though you've been asleep. This will ensure that your energy regeneration increases for the duration the food allows. I guess that's the best way to put it."

He then gestured to the other items on their plates. "These are for you to eat after every book that you absorb, so that your energy levels do not fall below two hundred. I don't want your energy levels below two hundred ever. Or the Library could, inadvertently in its current state, drain you. This bread roll has a timed-release mechanism that will trigger the moment you start to dip under two hundred, and the effect will last a whole day. The Library currently has no power, and it's still pulling from your direct energy pool to enable some of its functions. You cannot afford for it to empty your energy pool. Do you understand, Quinn?"

"I understand. I understand," she said. She wanted to say more, but Milaro cut her off, gesturing to the next plate.

"These are boiled lollies, hard candies, whatever you want to call them. They are low-grade, but will offer your regeneration a bit of a boost, without having to rest or refuel. Take some and keep them on you. This was what I could get on short notice. Cook will now be preparing more for you." Milaro really seemed to be put out, annoyed even.

"Thanks," Quinn said, and meant it. Taking a massive bite out of the doughnut, she chewed a bit and then continued, "But Dottie was just telling me some interesting stuff."

Milaro turned to the bench. "And what was that, Dottie?"

The bench cleared her throat, even though Quinn still couldn't tell where her throat was located. "Well, it's just I was explaining to her that Lynx is not quite himself."

"That's a good thing to explain to her," Milaro said, with a deep sigh. "I'm uncertain what's happened, but I have a feeling that he will tell us what's happening when he knows what's happening and when he can tell us."

Quinn swallowed another bite of doughnut and mulled that over in her head. "Are you telling me that he may not know himself or he may literally not be able to tell us?"

Milaro nodded sadly. "Yep. Both of those are exactly what I'm telling you."

39

CONFESSIONS

QUINN SAT ON THE COUCH, THE BOOKS NEXT TO HER, ARADIE STILL close to her shoulder. She wasn't entirely sure how to interpret what Dottie and Milaro just told her—to digest it, even.

What she did know was that she needed these books. She placed her hands, spread out and face down, on the open pages of *Segmentation of Thoughts* and absorbed it into her being. It was fragmented information that, surprisingly, made her thoughts more clearly aligned and less unevenly jumbled in her head. It was a way to pinpoint focus on small details with so many nuances. It was fascinating.

She opened her eyes and didn't experience the immediate rush of dizziness. Without hesitation, Milaro handed her one of those candies to begin regenerating her energy again.

And frankly, it made her start connecting some of the dots between what they were telling her and her own observations. Maybe Lynx wasn't just trying to be infuriating all this time.

Maybe something was wrong.

"And then you can have one of these." Milaro interrupted her analysis, pulling out what looked decidedly like a cake pop from behind his back. "These will give you instant boosts of eighty energy each. You cannot consume more than ten of them a day. These are supposed to be for emergencies only. Cook is working on a better option."

He said the last as Quinn took a huge bite out of the one he'd handed to her. She grinned up at him innocently.

"And, if you check now that you have absorbed another book, your energy capacity is greater again." Milaro continued like she hadn't attacked the cake pop with gusto. "That's just how it works until it hits the cap."

Quinn glanced at the energy level and realized she'd crested six hundred. Look at that. He was right.

Milaro hadn't stopped his information spiel. "Eventually, your energy level will outpace all possibilities of instant regeneration. So you cannot rely on this. Instead, you must eat more fulfilling meals. Cook is also preparing something that I believe the closest thing you would know it to is maple-candied bacon. It's something you can carry with you always and will give you an immediate emergency boost as well. They are, however, more finicky and when Cook has made them, I will explain more to you about them. Anyway, here."

Then he reached and pulled something out of the pocket of his robe. "And take this so your night owl can sit on your shoulder without goring you to death, until you can get the leather one properly crafted."

Quinn grabbed the strange piece of padded fabric with ties that Milaro briefly helped her tie into place. Aradie stepped onto the perch, sort of biscuiting it like a cat while she got used to the footing, and then settled into a comfortable weight on Quinn's shoulder.

Then Quinn dug into the bread rolls and the lollies. And set about absorbing all of the books in front of her. It took a good hour, and her head was definitely running full of so much information by the time she finished absorbing 564 energy points worth of knowledge.

But with the help of three cake pops and her regeneration lolly at the end of it, she managed to still finish with 280 remaining, and now her cap was 629.

"Is there a rational reason as to how my energy capacity is going to increase every time I absorb a book?" Quinn asked, because there literally didn't appear to be any specific reason for the numbers to increase like they did. "Or is it just arbitrary?"

Milaro shook his head. "Not really a specific reasoning behind the amounts. It's very individual. You are a slightly different case, with your ridiculous amount of affinities, anyway. It's highly fortuitous to have a Librarian with all of the affinities."

"See, Lynx," she said, looking up at the ceiling as if to summon him. "I'm not the only person who uses the word ridiculous, thank you very much."

But there was no quip, nor an answer flashing up in front of her face. She paused, a little worried. Usually he seemed to hover around just out of sight and pop in whenever someone wanted him, or, more often, didn't want him to appear.

"How do we find out what my max capacity is?" she asked, trying to push the worry out of her mind. It wasn't working.

"Well, usually it would peak around two thousand after slowing considerably to maybe like one or two points a book. Pretty negligible, really. We'll see where yours constricts itself and go from there." Milaro paused and then added hurriedly, "You have to understand your energy is more about how you regenerate your mana, and how fast, and how much magical capacity you have."

"Yeah, I've gathered that much. I really love how the rest is a non-answer," Quinn said, slightly disgruntled. She glanced over at Dottie and then up at Milaro. "Where's Malakai?" she asked.

"I sent him back home to retrieve his things, so that he might stay here in a little bit more comfort, and perhaps less begrudgingly." Milaro grinned. "He'll be back very shortly."

Quinn paused, looked around a bit more, and decided she was just going to grab the bull by the horns. "Okay, so what are we going to do to help Lynx?"

"Well, I'm sure he'll come to us when he realizes what sort of help he needs," Milaro said, obviously uncomfortable.

Quinn shook her head. "No. Because despite everything, I think right now he really needs all of us. And I think he might be a bit stubborn."

Milaro chuckled but it sounded somewhat forced. "The Library, and Lynx with it, are an extremely complex organism."

"I get that," she said gently, because in truth she did. "Trust me. I've been right there up in that link with the core, and the glimpses of a history I still find too complex to piece together."

"Ah." The elf watched her for a moment, and Quinn saw Dottie, very decidedly, raise one of her wooden legs and smack him directly on the top of the foot with it. Milaro winced and glared down at her.

"Fine," he grumbled. "You realize what Links stands for, right? Library Interface Neural Knowledge System. That's why he's called Links. I realize you think of him as the cat he sometimes presents himself as, but that's what he is."

A lightbulb practically went on in Quinn's mind. She'd seen it come up of course when information referred to him as Links whatever his designation was. But she still liked the Cheshire-like cat she'd first encountered and insisted on calling him Lynx. The acronym made a lot of sense. Sort of. She'd have thought it would be a lot longer. "Well I guess he sort of is the interface, right?"

"Not entirely. Lynx enables the full interface to activate. If the manifestation is not able to be projected, then the bare minimum the Library needs to function is not present. Lynx is literally what links everyone to the Library. He is an integral part of it, and yet also partially his own entity."

Quinn mulled that over while she munched on another piece of that candied bacon stuff. "So... is the Library also its own entity."

Milaro nodded emphatically. "Yes. Entirely. But it is also a part of Lynx and the latter cannot survive without the former."

Quinn shook her head. "That's enough of that. What we should be talking about is just how we're going to help the stubborn cat out."

Dottie pushed gently against Quinn's leg, before speaking softly. "That's just it, I don't know that we can help him. I think calling him stubborn is an understatement. For him as well as the Library."

A whoosh of air breathed over them all, and Quinn paused her next bite, a smile crossing her face even as the pages of the still open tome on her lap fluttered.

"I'm really not that stubborn, you know." Lynx was there. In all his softly glowing purple and black rune-ringed self. "I do appreciate the concern, though. There's really nothing you need to be concerned about."

Which was the precise time his form decided to flicker. Ever so slightly, but to Quinn it appeared like a glitch.

Not like when the television got a bit of static or anything. But more when she thought of some of the anime or even movies that she'd watched. That type of glitching. Like a hologram having issues remaining solid. She frowned up at him and decided that maybe it wasn't the best idea to just take what he said at face value.

Everyone's survival depended on this, not the least her own. His. Dottie's... anyone who'd get gobbled up by chaotic magic if she'd understood that whole spiel correctly.

"I don't think you're being entirely honest. And well, while we're talking about honesty. I actually think I can feel the lie." She tried to lock gazes with him, but he avoided looking directly at her. "Lynx... you need to talk to us. I can't read your mind when you're not letting me communicate with you. We're all in on this. We're here to help reopen the Library, to recruit assistants, to return books, and make sure we filter the chaos out of the magic. But we can't do any of that if you're withholding what seems to be pretty heavy stuff from us."

"Heavy?" Lynx cocked his head to one side, but then he sighed. Because he knew full well what she meant. "You *are* right. This is just a lot for me, and it's very difficult to admit to others."

Malakai stepped into view, obviously returned from his trip, and plopped down on the armchair to the left of Quinn. Folding his arms he cleared his throat and got straight to the point. "It might feel difficult to tell us, but you could also just export it to every single one of us through the system that reacts to your every thought, and then you wouldn't even have to speak. So you can't use that as an excuse."

Quinn wanted to hug Malakai right then and there, but she was too comfy in her perch on the couch. "There. No excuses, spit it out."

Aradie hooted for punctuation.

Lynx sighed and a ripple of runes wound around his body. They seemed to do that when he was accessing information, or in a mood about information, or sometimes even just irritated. Quinn frowned, because this time even the runic line appeared to be somewhat glitchy.

"Very well. But you asked for it."

There was silence for several moments, but Quinn ignored the prophecy of doom in his words and concentrated on going over how her mind felt now that the information she'd absorbed was making the rounds.

She felt like a computer, with a heap of space had been emptied into her mind so that she might categorize and arrange her thoughts more efficiently. Like there was a lock on the door of her mind. It wasn't very sturdy. So after some analysis, she realized that there was information she had to attune to and understand in greater depth that would then allow her to protect herself in a way that maximized her energy output.

Hours of fun, instead of television. All the building blocks and tools, with basic blueprints. She couldn't wait to get started. Once Lynx had finally told them everything, anyway.

Finally, Lynx squared his shoulders, and she gave over her full attention. She'd figure out how to compartmentalize later when Milaro could help her practice the basics.

"You have to understand, when we first lost Kor and had no one to replace her, there were very few options open to me. Continuing the Library's function as they were was not one of them. We would have run out of power in a matter of months. I did what I had to in order to preserve the primary function of the Library." Lynx spoke softly, and there was pain hidden behind his words.

"To control the chaos, right? To prevent the magic from blowing up in everyone's faces?" Quinn asked.

"Yes. That's a decent enough summation." Lynx began pacing ever so slowly, back and forth in front of where they were all sitting. "You see... I knew we couldn't let anymore magic out, because until we found a replacement we'd need every single drop to maintain our cycle as best we could."

"But wouldn't all that magic you were filtering have ambient mana you could pull from?" Quinn asked, the idea occurring to her suddenly.

Lynx and Milaro winced, and the elf spoke up to explain. "Wild magic is unrefined. While you can get some energy through ambient magic, it wouldn't be enough. Wild or chaotic magic requires energy to refine it. Any energy the Library pulled from that process would have gone back into refining it. Leaving it pretty much zero sum with no excess energy. Frankly, I'm surprised it lasted so long."

The manifestation shot the elf an unreadable look before continuing. "Anyway, to cut a long, almost five-hundred-year boring story short, I conserved magic where I could, while constantly scanning for any sign of the correct magical signature in any of our usually traversed worlds, and only managed to sustain the bare minimum of filtration of the chaotic magic at all."

He took a deep breath before continuing. "It was rough. Bumpy, even. I had to conserve all of the energy to such an extent that some of the bookworm containment areas broke, silverfish escaped, night owls hibernated. And still I had no sign of a signature, nor a reason for why it had suddenly disappeared. There were so many of my abilities, my functions that I couldn't utilize. I had chalked it all up to lack of power. Even while chaos started to leak into the filtration chamber."

He sighed and focused on Quinn. "I discovered Quinn in a last-ditch effort scan. Basically it was the final chance I had to do a long-range sweep that might find someone, anyone that was compatible. Just on the off chance. Nothing else yielded results."

Quinn stayed silent, and Aradie pressed in close to her head offering soft, feathered comfort. The Librarian could tell that this was something Lynx had mega difficulties with, so she pushed the questions back and listened. Apparently, everyone else felt the same way.

"Quinn's energy was wispy at first, as if the system wasn't entirely sure she was real. But it was the only lead I'd had in so long, it was my literal last chance." He sighed.

Silence engulfed the room for several seconds and Quinn wasn't sure how to break it. But she needn't have worried.

Lynx flashed a very forced smile. "Anyway, Quinn is here now and her energy alone allowed the Library to wake up some of its functions. Add to that the return of three integral books to the system and while our power levels are still critical, we've moved ever so slightly out of the danger zone... but even though we've rebooted, there seems to be so much missing from my usual box of tools." He flickered again as he continued to pace back and forth, making eye contact with none of them.

"I haven't been able to access segments of information, or whereabouts of some specific books or exact locations, or even just some of the things within the Library. I just thought it was all a matter of the system not having enough power, or still rebooting, or else just being rusty after almost five hundred years' lack of use."

"But that's not it, is it?" Quinn asked, as trepidation tried to choke her.

"No. That's not it at all." Finally Lynx looked up, and his double eyelids open and closed in rapid succession. "It has nothing to do with the current Library power levels, or what magic is available. Right now... I'm quite literally glitching. The system isn't working as it should, and I have no idea why, nor how to rectify it."

40

BREAKDOWN

QUINN WASN'T SURE WHAT SHE WAS EXPECTING UPON THE REVELATION that Lynx had no idea what was wrong, how it had happened, or how it could be rectified, but it wasn't complete and utter silence. She glanced around at Dottie, Malakai, who'd just wandered in, and his grandfather. All of them were simply staring slack-jawed, as far as Quinn could tell.

Once she mastered her most recent texts, she was going to find ones on mind reading.

Quinn, on the other hand, felt like her mind was completely and utterly open to the possibility that something had gone inherently wrong, but that it could be sorted out. While she knew the Library wasn't a computer, it acted in much the same way, and the system was inherently like an operating system.

Her connection with the Library was oddly calm, she sensed no panic, just an idle curiosity. It seemed that the Library itself wasn't too concerned, at least not yet, whereas Lynx seemed to be taking the news a little harder.

Granted, he was the one who had to interface with everyone, for want of a better word.

She didn't want to repeat what he'd said. She didn't want to ask him to repeat what he'd said. But at the same time, there were a few points that Quinn wasn't clear on. "Okay, so it's not working in the way you're used to, which means you're not functioning at peak capacity. So the things that you've forgotten to tell me or forgotten about, like the time disparity when we went to the Highlands, those sorts of things, those are because the system isn't working correctly. Is that right?"

"Yes and no. It's more than that. I cannot access elements of the system that I've always had access to. It's like they're corrupted, or how can I put it? It's like there's something in the system, like sludge, causing it to stick together. I can't pry my way into it." He nodded, as if he was reaffirming that description for himself. He looked up expectantly, right at Quinn, like she should suddenly have some amazing solution for him.

She didn't, but she wasn't about to sarcastically dismiss him. He didn't need that right now. None of them did. "Look, I don't know how things were supposed to work before, but I think we could start by maybe making a list of exactly what it is that you can no longer do or gain access to."

"That's perfect," Milaro piped up. "Do that. Do you have exact knowledge of what it is that you're missing access to?"

Lynx perked up a little bit. "Well, for the most part, yes. The functions and the system allocations that I'm missing. Just give me a moment." His double eyelids flickered in and out of each other, blinking in that odd way.

Quinn glanced around and wondered how much time she had, and if she could balance a plate of food on his head this time without him noticing. But his focus was already coming back.

Damn it, she thought. *I'll have to do that another time.*

This time, Lynx seemed to take a slightly different path to process the information he was trying to access. His form wavered, and for a few seconds, he diminished down to what almost looked like a crocodile, before morphing back into human form, through that of the lynx. Quinn occasionally wished he'd just revert back to being a talking cat. It had been adorable.

Besides, who didn't want a talking cat?

Finally, he solidified enough and began listing out.

Links A542 Edition Category F manifestation has processed the following information.

Manifestation lacks access to the following areas:

Recollection - holes in past data. Including events, locations, and items.

Further defined: Type of texts required are not all clear, occurrences jumbled, locations hazy.

Dimensional Locators not fully functional. Precise drop-off points unattainable. Visitation locations will require specific buildings. No wilderness drop-offs for the immediate future.

Calibration and reconfiguration of files and history must be established. Errors in memory amalgamation.

Retention of specifics is fragmented. Memory and functional assessments require attunement.

Connection to Links A542 is tentative, lacks cohesivity, and is obscured.

Connection to Librarian Quinn, designation LA342, not fully functional, mind meld not complete.

Communication system is currently in critical mode, closed to outsiders, preventative measures sought.

The words came out of him, slightly robotic, and less human than she was used to. It was as if he was just rattling off something he'd read, almost like an automaton.

Not to mention the words hung in front of her eyes like a visible bad smell.

Quinn didn't like how long the list was. But the good thing about lists was that they always gave you somewhere to start. A launching point.

Both Milaro and Malakai looked slightly shellshocked, and Dottie was actually shaking. Quinn pushed herself up from the couch and walked over, approaching Lynx. She waved her hand in front of his face, and he blinked rapidly before focusing on her.

"Sorry, that was a lot of information to organize into a cohesive list," he said, cocking his head to one side. "There's something in the system that wasn't there before, or at least, I couldn't sense it. And

I've got to figure out a way to clean it out. It just feels extremely elusive. Every time I think I've found the problem, it slips through my grasp."

She pondered exactly how to phrase her next words. "Which means somebody, besides you, managed to insert something into the collective stream of the Library, right?"

Lynx started to shake his head, as if it was an automatic response, but he paused. "Well. While I think that's unlikely, I have to confess it's the only thing that makes sense."

Quinn pushed on. "And how is that even possible?"

Milaro looked very shaken up, somehow even paler than usual. "That can't be possible. You don't operate like that."

Lynx sighed. "I know this, and you know this. And sadly, the more I discover, the more obvious it is becoming to me that this was done by somebody, perhaps even someone I trusted." There was a hitch to his voice as he said the last bit.

Quinn did a double-take. Somebody Lynx trusted? Did he mean it could have been a member of the Library or even a Librarian? Surely not. That would devastate the manifestation. And besides, who would kill themselves just to pull one over on the Library?

Then again, there were people on Earth willing to die for a cause, she had to assume they existed everywhere in the universe.

She kept a close eye on Lynx as he continued his conversation with Milaro.

"Do you really think she..." Milaro let the question hang in the air.

Lynx shook his head. "If you'd asked me two weeks ago I would have adamantly said no. I would have banned you from the Library for suggesting it." He paused, his eyes rapidly blinking as he processed.

"Now? I don't know. All of those memories from that period, they're distorted and fragmented. They're not cohesive enough for me to get a read on anymore. Yet, I know they were clear while the Library was disconnected from the Universe. I'm sure there's a way to restore it. I just have to... I need more energy, and I need several of the more advanced books back." There was a deflated quality about the way Lynx spoke now.

"Okay," Milaro said, his voice heavy with determination. "I will aid you. I will fetch you help."

Lynx actually flashed a half-hearted smile. "Thank you, my friend."

Quinn thought maybe Lynx'd hit a low point. He seemed so bewildered, and not the same Lynx she'd met when she first arrived. Gone was the expectant and mostly cocky cat who'd greeted her, and in his place was a slightly lost library manifestation.

It was as if everything he'd been aiming for had somehow completely and utterly fallen apart.

She clapped her hands, disliking the sight of the downtrodden library. "Listen, let's just focus on one thing at a time. Just one item in the list at a time. We take it, item by item, and we will figure out ways to circumvent it. Surely there are magical books that can do that, or magical people. Are there any species that would be, like, well-versed in any of these sorts of things?"

Quinn was really trying to be proactive, but the truth was, she knew nothing about this universe. Almost surreptitiously, Malakai handed her a book. She glanced down. *The Universe Not as You Know It.* She looked up at him. "Let me guess, a brief rundown on the universe, its species, inhabitants, and the different worlds?"

He flashed her a grin, and she sighed. This should have been the first thing that she'd absorbed. Lynx truly was off his game. But even with the information that she got from the chip he'd created for her, it was all just very basic Library stuff. It didn't take into consideration that she had come from an entirely different sector, galaxy, whatever it was. She didn't understand how the scope of all that worked.

Lynx shot her a glance, and a half-hopeful smile. "Well, if I can trust the someone we get to help." He let it linger. She knew that he knew just how dangerous Kajaro had been. And it made her understand his reticence to trust anybody.

He trusted Milaro because he had known Milaro before the shutdown, and thus Malakai as his grandson was also trustworthy. Lynx pulled Quinn through to the Library himself, so she was also trustworthy. He probably trusted the golems because the Library had created them.

But she was fairly sure that Narilin was not somebody Lynx was about to trust. She could understand and respect that, though. Which meant that he probably wouldn't trust any of the other assistants, not fully even once they'd checked them all out.

They'd need to figure out a way they could vet them, they could test them. Because right now, this malfunction, or however the library worked, wasn't natural, and it wasn't good.

"I've got it," Milaro said, suddenly breaking the awkward silence with a snap of his fingers. "I do have several highly competent dimensional magic theorists and engineers in my entourage. I can bring a couple of them to the Library. You know them. They've been here before."

Lynx's eyebrows shot up, as if he'd been surprised at himself for not having thought of that. "Oh, do you mean Harish and Siliqua?"

"Yes, and they have sons now." Milaro smiled softly.

"Oh wow, a whole family?" Lynx actually laughed, and for just a moment it sounded like maybe he thought there was a bit of hope. Like maybe he hadn't lost centuries and friends. It struck Quinn that Lynx's whole existence must be so lonely. To exist for eons... eventually, everyone he knew would pass.

Maybe that's why he appeared to have been so attached to his previous Librarian.

Milaro appeared to have caught onto that note of hope in Lynx's voice. "I will call on Harish and Siliqua and get them here. Is there a way I can allow them entry through me?"

Lynx paused for a moment, and suddenly the display in front of Quinn activated.

Allow Milaro assistant access to the library, including all privileges as well as guest invites?

Yes. No. Refine parameters further.

Quinn just chose yes.

"There you go." Milaro laughed. "I'm a library assistant now. That's just perfect."

He sounded oddly smugly satisfied about the whole thing. Quinn chalked that up to it perhaps having always been a secret wish of the king's to do exactly that. She didn't expect him to pull his weight, but at least his number would count toward the opening.

"Anyway," he said, "I will be back." He turned on his heel and teleported out of the area.

"He obviously has access to exits and waypoints. What does it mean the location device in the Library isn't working properly?" Quinn half mumbled the question as she watched Milaro exit.

"It's not like that. Usually we can open a door almost anywhere with pinpoint accuracy. As long as there is something that a door can be set into. Like the floor, because it can be a trap door. Into a tree, it can be a door to a building. A car door, or vehicle door, or a cart back. There are ways for the Library to appear everywhere. Right now, the locator isn't working properly. I barely managed to get you guys close to where you needed to be in order to retrieve the last two books. And if you recall, you had quite a way to travel to go to the location you needed to." Lynx ran his hand through his hair in a gesture that jostled all of his runes.

"Yes, I will not soon forget those treks we had to make," Malakai grumbled, from his armchair.

Lynx looked over at him, a harried expression on his face. "Exactly! So that makes this difficult. The Library must be able to find locations with pinpoint accuracy. It's going to hamper any borrowers, and frankly, returns as well. While I can probably get people close to their original locations, for all I know some could be days travel out. The Library isn't supposed to be inconvenient. It's here to share magic and knowledge and make it easily accessible."

"Well, let's see if these engineers Milaro is getting can help," Quinn said, keeping her tone soothing. She remembered all too well one of her older foster sisters a few years ago. Panic attacks were the things of nightmares. They didn't need a panicking Library manifestation. His worry was almost palpable. "It's worth a shot, right?"

Lynx nodded, his eyes perhaps a little calmer than they'd been before. "It's more than worth a shot. We can give them access, and they can help me sort through what I can't. I should be able to do this myself, Quinn," he said in an extremely low voice, directed solely at her. "This isn't how I function. I'm not meant to need help like this."

She paused, looking at him. "You keep saying the Library's not a computer. What are you?"

He looked up at her, his eyes blinking back and forth. "It's not easy to explain."

"Well, how about you try me?" she said. "Doesn't it have an impact on how I do my job? Doesn't being your Librarian mean that I need to help you in these circumstances?"

Lynx actually laughed, and it was a freeing sound like music to the ears. "Actually, what I am has nothing to do with how well or badly you can do your Librarian duties. What it has to do with, however, is me trying to understand how somebody managed to corrupt my internal operations. That's more what it has to do with."

"You're not going to tell me, are you?" Quinn crossed her arms and glared at him.

But he shook his head gently. "Not right now. Your understanding and grasp of the universe as it is, is still rudimentary."

"Whose fault is that?" she grumbled.

"And besides, I think it would be more fun if you found it out yourself." Lynx gave her a wink, and his eyes started twinkling.

Quinn was ready to punch him in the face... figuratively, at least. But as she was about to start berating him further, an alarm went off in the Library. Not loud and glaring and danger, danger, library is in trouble, but more of a gentle alert.

Multiple doors have been accessed.

Multiple authorized entrants in the library proper.

Library has applicants.

They are being channeled toward the lobby

Quinn looked around, and all of a sudden, there were probably a dozen, a dozen and a half people walking into the Library, looking up at the ceiling. They were all different species, species she couldn't even define visually. Things she'd seen in television shows, things she'd never even read about in books. They were amazing, and there were so many of them. They were chattering amongst themselves, to each other, some of them huddled alone, some of them in small groups, and all of them bearing a library assistant application.

41

ASSISTANCE

It took several seconds for Quinn to comprehend what appeared in front of her. The sheer magnitude of this gathering of beings was almost beyond her comprehension. Of course she'd been expecting applicants, but this variety of species were all so fantastical. She utilized the Library's system to identify some of them.

First, she looked over a group of three huddled spider people. They appeared to have the body of a spider and four legs that touched the ground. Their torsos, however, had four arms. Their upper bodies were segmented slightly like ants, and their heads appeared to be a mixture of ant and human.

Aracnios - Arachnid-based species
Located in the: Illukai Region
Library Allies for: 24,382 years

Quinn blinked at the information. That was a long time to be allied with the Library. She knew Lynx said it was infinite, but she hadn't really understood the ramifications of that.

She shook her head and switched her focus, trying to get through this as fast as possible.

They were four centaurs. She recognized those. They had horse bottoms and a human-appearing top. They looked a lot more built and stocky in their human portion than she would have thought. Very powerful. Their hooves didn't even make a sound as they jiggled slightly in place.

Centaur – Equine-based species
Located in the: Malino Sector
Library Allies for: Since Library Creation

Quinn realized she needed to grab a map or a guide to take her through the sectors so she could understand what the locations meant.

Next were the tiny ones. There were four of them, standing about three to four feet high. They looked like mini humans. All she wanted to do was lift them up and hug them, but she was pretty sure that would end up with her being punched in the face.

Ilgonomur - humanoid species
Located in the Dalyid Region
Allies of the Library for: 235,001 years

Her next inspection simply read:

Imp
Gates of Halschius
Number 7
Time immeasurable

She did a double take. This read out was nothing like the others. *Why the discrepancy?*

Imps are a separate classification. Their ilk stems from old-world gods and mythology given form. They are creatures in and of magic.

She took that at face value and mulled it over. Okay, magical creatures that were likely a product of the Library or...

Imps are the direct result of unrestrained chaotic magic gone wrong. The Library helped them become a viable species.

Guess that answered her question. Imps were also tiny, a little bit shorter than the Ilgonomur, but they had wings, fiery red eyes, and skin that was tinted red and black. Like a mixture of embers and ash. They had little horns that grew out of their head and sharp, pointy ears. Their fangs resembled vampires, and she was very certain that she would never like to be bitten by one of them. They darted to and fro and then back into a huddle together. They were oddly, dangerously, adorable in appearance.

In a melt-your-face-off sort of way.

Then there was a group of what had to be fae, fairies. They were colorful and simply breathtaking. Their little wings fluttered so fast they almost appeared to stand still.

Fae Firionas - Firionas elf-type species
Travelled from: Dimensional Portal L25
Ally status: 2,483,000 years

Quinn blinked at the information. What the hell did Dimensional Portal L25 mean? She waited for a few seconds, but when nothing popped up in front of her from the Library, she simply moved on. She'd figure out location nuances later.

At this rate, map wouldn't even be the right word for what she'd need.

What did matter was that these fantastical creatures were hovering right in front of her, applying to be library assistants. She glanced over and noticed that Lynx had a smile spread over his face at the sight of all of the applicants standing in the hall. She felt far more equipped to deal with the influx of applicants now she'd taken a few minutes to familiarize herself with all the different species.

"Welcome," Lynx said, his voice booming through the hall. All of the fidgeting and talking amongst themselves stopped, and everybody looked up at where Lynx stood on top of the check-in desk.

"I am Lynx, the Library's manifestation. This"—he pulled Quinn up by the hand to stand next to him, with strength that she didn't know he could access—"is Quinn. She is your Librarian, and technically your boss, if you become an assistant to the Library."

There was a low murmuring, and she swore she could hear the word "human" thrown around a couple of times.

Quinn did her best to smile and appear welcoming, even though she was nervous as hell. She glanced over at Lynx, unsure of what she should say. Unsure as to why these people had all grouped themselves up together and decided to visit the Library at once.

"Just do what you would at a normal job interview," he suggested, his tone soft and encouraging.

"I've never given job interviews before, except the one I gave to Narilin," she retorted. It was a speech she was getting quite used to over the last couple of days. There was so much she'd never done before and here she was in charge of a universal Library...

She couldn't help thinking someone, somewhere along the way had screwed up.

Still, Lynx was right.

With a very soft hoot, Aradie came and sat on her shoulder. Quinn immediately felt just that little bit less lonely. She kept her smile up and clapped her hands to gather the attention of the still-murmuring crowd beneath her.

"Everyone, if you could please come forward. Malakai and I will take your applications and get you sorted as soon as possible."

There, she thought, *that sounded pretty grown up.* Even if the entire group was eyeing her and then eyeing the elf who begrudgingly stood up out of his sofa seat and began to saunter over to the check-in desk. He looked up at Lynx as if he was the one in charge of everything. Which, technically he kind of was, but for some obscure reason, the whole set up meant she was actually in charge of most of the stuff.

Quinn snapped her fingers at the group. "Hey, Lynx has a lot of work to do, so I'm in charge of you right now, and you'll be working with me if your application is accepted, so frankly, you just need to deal with that."

This time, there was some murmuring, but a lot of nods, and even some resigned sighs. Lynx had mentioned they'd never had a human Librarian before.

The very first person to come up to her was one of the fae. She was maybe two and a half feet tall and hovered in the air like a humming-bird. Her coloring was beautiful. She had long, literally golden hair and skin that was faintly golden-tinged as well. Her tiny feet ended in points with little shoes on, and her wings had iridescent rainbow colors running through them. She wore a striking deep red dress that offset the whole thing.

"Hello," she said, and her voice sounded soprano. It was high-pitched but very polite. "I am Geneva and I would like to apply. Here is my paper."

She spoke very haltingly and Quinn wondered if that had to do with the way words translated to her from other species.

"Thank you." Quinn took the application from her tiny hands and glanced through it. The letters jumbled for a second before they settled in front of her eyes and she realized that the Library enabled her to even read the writing or the text of other species. It was definitely handy being connected to the core. *Note to self to explore the connection more when I actually get a moment to myself.*

Quinn placed her hand on the application and absorbed the information like she had for Narilin. It flooded her mind. Geneva was a little older than the other assistant at 321. She was in the top five percent of her graduating class, female, and had twelve of the outlined sixteen requirements, so nine more than they absolutely had to have.

That was a pretty good catch.

"What reason do you have for wanting to be a Library assistant?" Quinn asked, after wracking her brain to think of questions she'd been asked when she went for her part-time job at the university Library. She heard Malakai echoing that question over in the other corner. She was fairly confident he could filter through some of the other applicants.

Geneva cocked her head to one side, her pretty wings fluttering rapidly. "Books and magic, it's why we exist. We are a part of magic and only function through magic. If I help filter the chaos, then I will help my species and the rest of the universe to thrive."

Her voice was so lilting, very hesitant, but she seemed just lovely, tiny, and very slight, and Quinn wasn't sure at all if she'd even be able to lift up one of the tomes. Information flashed across her screen for just a second, enough to tell her that this species was one hundred percent capable of carrying three or four massive tomes. Quinn felt like she'd been a little bit judgy, which made her feel guilty.

There was an underlying nervousness to this small fae creature and Quinn probed that nervousness as much as she could with her mind and sent an inquiry to the Library about it. After several seconds, the Library flashed information up.

Nerves, heart rate elevated. Excitement spread. Applicant earnest. No deception detected.

Didn't know it could do that, she thought to herself.

Lynx shot back, *You didn't ask.*

Will you get out of my head? She flashed him a brief glare.

When you've learned your mental exercises from Milaro, you will be able to keep me out of your head when you want, he retorted.

Quinn sighed and thought of ten thousand things to say.

I'm not trying to listen, Quinn, you just think very loudly, Lynx said, his tone gentler, which made Quinn almost laugh out loud.

"Is there anything else you'd like to add?" Quinn asked her fluttering little applicant. It was amazing how much could be exchanged in the blink of an eye when communicating mind to mind.

Geneva hesitated for a moment before nodding her head. "Yes, knowledge, magic, it's all very important. I would like to have access to it and help preserve it all."

Quinn smiled. "I understand. Go take a seat over there." And she pointed over to where Quinn had been sitting earlier with the others.

Dottie raised herself on her back legs and jumped around, waving her little arms in ways that shouldn't have been possible if she really was made out of wood. There was a flicker of surprise that passed over Geneva's face before she shut it down. Quinn flashed her a grin.

"Go sit with Dottie for a bit, okay?" And Quinn turned to the next applicant, as a sudden sharp pain hit her between the temples. Headaches were horrible, and right now she didn't have time. She'd have to see if this place had anything like ibuprofen. But first, she had some applicants to get through.

After Geneva, Quinn interviewed a centaur, an aracnio, and then, finally, it was an imp's turn.

So far, she'd found one possibility in Geneva and definitely the aracnio even though she was terribly confused by the way the other species moved. He'd seemed highly motivated and she hadn't even attempted to pronounce his name. And yet the Library had managed to twist her tongue effortlessly into it. But he'd smiled, or she thought he had, and said to call him Steve.

The first imp she interviewed was, quite simply put, fascinating. With blackened skin and what looked like fiery embers at the end of the fingertips and toes. The imp had sharp teeth and red flaming eyes. Even the long black hair was tinged with what looked like a never-ending flame-fall. Quinn was beguiled.

"Your name?" she asked.

At first, there was a guttural response, and Quinn couldn't quite grasp the words.

Then the imp coughed and spoke. "My name is Ekirusca Marabiza, but most people just call me Eric."

Quinn did a double-take, blinked a couple of times, and said, "Excellent. Eric it is."

"I am he," he clarified. Which was good because Quinn could not tell. It was always good to know how to refer to somebody.

"Okay, then, Eric." She placed her left palm on his application and realized that the imp was several thousand years old. 7,682 years, to be precise. She could feel the color drain from her face. He was a powerful being if his resume was anything to go by. He was in the top percentage of his power class and could rain down brimstone and fire on any *future* attacks on the Library. He'd literally put that as a perk of accepting him.

Oh, how she wanted to ask him how they knew the Library had been sabotaged. Then again, maybe it was obvious to those from outside.

"Why would you like to work in the Library?" she asked.

"I was sent here by our Lord, who commanded us to come and lend aid to the Library as is written in our accords that are as old as time," Eric replied, his facial features not even budging a fraction.

Quinn blinked. "Your Lord sent you here to work?"

"Yes. I am fully aware that I will be compensated in my species' currency and that I will have somewhere to stay within the library so that I might render assistance as needed." Again, his face was stoic.

"Excellent. And do you have any personal reasons for wanting to be here?" She pushed the question a bit. Her gut instinct told her that whoever worked here needed to want to work here for their own reasons. For their own attachment.

"The Library has been a part of my life for millennia. While it was gone, I did not get to visit or absorb magic or knowledge in the same way as I had become accustomed to, and I would like to rectify that and prevent such an occurrence from ever happening again." This time the little imp cocked his head to one side, like he was truly analyzing the question.

Quinn nodded completely and utterly happy with the answer. "Great! Go sit over there with that fae." He glanced over to where Dottie was chatting animatedly with the fairy, and a grimace crossed his face.

"She won't bite, I promise," Quinn hurried to reassure him.

Eric flashed her a grin. "She won't, but maybe I will." He darted off before Quinn could say another word.

She looked around for Lynx, but he wasn't there, and yet his voice echoed in her head. *Yeah, you've got to watch the imps. They can be a little more mischievous than I think you're ready for.*

Gee, thanks for the warning. Could have used that five minutes ago, she responded.

No need to snap at me. Maybe if you pulled up more information through your interface, you'd understand more before you spoke to them.

Quinn didn't retort because she knew he was right, and she didn't want to admit that right then. She glanced around and heard a clearing of a throat beneath her. She looked down.

"Oh, I'm so sorry," she said. Most of the others had been tall enough to talk with her still standing on the desk, or at least had wings with which they could fly up to her on the desk. The Ilgonomur, however, was not.

Quinn jumped down. "Hi, I'm Quinn." She decided that the Ilgonomur definitely looked like the gnomes she'd met in computer games. Small, petite, and with huge eyes that just seemed to see everything. She took the application that was offered without a word and placed her hand on it. This Ilgonomur was known as Finn, short for

Findalay. So Finn it was. It rhymed with her name, so Quinn was already partial to it.

Finn graduated in the top five percent of their class as well. Quinn was seeing a pattern here. All these high-level graduate numbers seemed a little sus for a Library assistant position. For all she knew their class consisted of twenty people, and they were the top student. Making them the five percent.

Quinn frowned, pushing those thoughts back. The Library was probably considered prestigious, even after the almost five-hundred-year break.

Finn was a little over two hundred years old. That made them one of the youngest applicants that she'd seen so far, and had specific experience in working in the Ilgonomur main branch library.

Quinn looked at Finn. "What makes you want to be here?"

Finn cocked their head to one side. "I love knowledge, and I love books, and those are the only reasons why I want to be here."

Quinn decided that was the best reason she'd heard yet.

Lynx rematerialized next to her as she watched the applicants they'd chosen settle in. Eight in all.

That's more than we needed, he spoke into her head in a satisfied tone.

She nodded. Frankly considering Malakai and Dottie were assistants and would frequently be busy, it was better that more applied. The list popped up in front of her:

The following have been completed. Please see the adjusted requirement.

- *Complete the Library reshelving - Complete*
- *Complete the Bookworm habitat rejuvenation - Complete*
- *Activate the book restoration workshop - Complete*
- *Assign combat instructor to Librarian - Complete*
- *Increase Librarian defensive and combat power by 5*
- *Recruit a minimum of five (5) assistants through a universal call out with requisite - minimum qualifications as specified in the manual - Complete*

Assistant training and quarters allocation must be completed prior to opening.

Lynx flickered in a concerning manner, his form winking in and out, his mouth moved but no words came out.

Error

Lynx A352 - Error detected

Core connection required to avoid imminent meltdown.

42

THE UNIVERSE AND EVERYTHING

QUINN BLINKED AT THE EMPTY SPOT WHERE LYNX HAD JUST BEEN.

That he disappeared wasn't even the most perplexing part. It was the announcement before his departure that made it that much more worrisome. Logically, she knew he was currently in the core. Or at the core...

Frankly, she usually would have been freaking out, but there was this calmness suffusing her. Like she knew, despite how desperate the system message had appeared, it wasn't as dire as it sounded.

Probably.

Maybe it was the mental fortitude given to her by those books. Perhaps she understood everything on a more visceral level now. And she'd assessed the whole situation in a fraction of the time she would usually have spent thinking on it. Not to mention her connection to Lynx and the Library allowed her to know that he was currently okay and that the Library would take care of him.

Right?

"Quinn," Malakai spoke softly to her, pulling her out of the several seconds of shock she'd just been standing in. "You should go and check on him."

"Yeah..." But she glanced over at the group of new assistants, worried about how to get the last step finished. She could sense that Lynx wasn't in any imminent danger, but there was still something tugging at her.

"You're the only one who can go down there." His voice smooth like velvet, and she wondered if he had some of that soothing magic too. "We can take care of the rest; the system allows us to at least give them rudimentary permissions. It's enough to get them started. Go."

Quinn realized he was right. She couldn't recall anyone other than Misha entering the lower level. And once the golems were created, they didn't venture back down as far as she knew. A wave of urgency entered her mind, rushing through her like a gasp of air after almost drowning.

Resolve in place, she turned without a second thought and sprinted for the stairs.

Darting down the spiral staircase two steps at a time, she gripped the railing tightly as she moved. While she might be able to communicate with the core and access information, she needed to see it, to touch it. There was still something about her connection that felt missing. It wasn't whole.

And hell, even Lynx's announcement said her connection wasn't complete.

Running to see him was her only choice. Being down there was so much more of a suffusion of the Library. It was all around her, encasing her.

The clarity in her mind made it much easier to think, without attaching particular emotions to it. There were feelings, of course, but she could sense them, understand them, and relegate them to the side while she allowed the rest of her mind to address the problem at hand. This would have been a really handy tool to have while she was studying on Earth. That way, she could have just put the stress of the exams aside and done the studying easily.

As it was right now, she had to get to Lynx. Her feet planted on the soft floor of the Tree Level, as she liked to think of it. It was no longer that beautiful blue hue; instead, there was this orange underlay to the lighting, like a warning light.

Sort of like the amber streetlights, where you should stop, but not everybody did. Caution. She could sense in the thrumming that went through to her feet and up into her entire body that this wasn't something that should have occurred.

It definitely wasn't something the Library had foreseen or expected.

She walked with purpose toward the center where the trunk was. Even now, some of its veins were suffused by the same orange glow as if an infection slowly crept up toward its heart. She didn't like the look of that. And infected Library sounded even worse than a locked down one.

Placing her left palm on the tree so she didn't have a complete circuit of a connection, she closed her eyes.

A pulse entered through her hand and suddenly images flashed through her mind. She could see Lynx and the trunk, but where their usual connection would be, the pathway was fragmented.

It wasn't obvious at first, but as the Library got more power, and especially when all of the new applicants entered the library, something within the core shifted. The ambient mana couldn't flow the way it needed to in order to give the Library the energy it wanted.

While Lynx wasn't exactly impeding it, he definitely wasn't helping it. At first it appeared like a blockage, but that wasn't the correct way to describe it. Not even the fragmentation that she'd first thought it was was accurate.

It was like some of the pathways had deteriorated so much they were broken. They were misaligned.

Fresh blue pathways looked like they were growing into place. Like blood vessels needing a workaround to make the blood flow functional again.

Quinn couldn't figure out why, and the worst thing was, it appeared neither could the Library. Instead, it was simply trying to fix things the only way it could figure out how. *We need to find the root cause,* she thought.

Lynx is currently unavailable. For his own protection and to prevent the damage from spreading further, he has been placed in hibernation mode for now. The Library almost sounded worried, which was something Quinn hadn't witnessed before. The Library was always in control of its emotions.

It was, as far as Quinn knew, an entity, so it suddenly having emotional reactions worried Quinn a bit. It also made her wonder.

After all of the creatures she'd just met, she wouldn't put it past the Library to be some sort of massive spatial entity.

That's nothing to concern you right now, the Library said, the words flowing into Quinn's mind. *Lynx requires incubation for approximately 68 hours. During that time, you will need to do the following: You will need to start your own training, and make sure the assistant training meets the following guidelines.*

A list of fifty things shot up in front of her eyes and were gone as suddenly as they'd appeared, leaving only a flashing access exclamation mark in the top corner of her vision for later recall.

The Library must open. We require the sustenance that newly returned books can provide. We also need to research the serpensiril, their allies, and their actions over the time period we have been indisposed. We must discover the truth behind Kajaro's words.

Is Lynx gonna be okay? Even though Quinn got the gut feeling he'd be fine as long as they could recalibrate him, she still needed to make certain. And for her, at least, it took precedence over other things.

Lynx is always okay in the end, but he's currently fragmented, and thus must be defragmented. His alignment is off, his pathways are infected with a sickness.

Like a virus? Quinn asked. *I thought you weren't a computer.*

We aren't a computer, but virus is an apt analogy.

Quinn mulled that over. *Okay, what about our connection? Mine and the Library's? It said something about it not being solid.*

The petrified bark beneath her hand rumbled and became warm briefly, pushing something out into her palm which she took with the other hand. It was like a small rounded precious stone, about an inch and a half in diameter. It was polished and the same color as the trunk.

This will help deepen our connection and bond until matters are resolved.

Quinn blinked at the strange grey, pulsing, smooth stone in her hand. A better connection to the core was a great thing. *Thanks.*

There are multiple books you must pull. These books must be absorbed as quickly as possible.

The list popped up in front of her:

- *Mental Fortitude and Time Dilation or How to Think Faster*
- *Communication Through Mental Telepathy*
- *Mental Defense is More Than You Think*
- *Cognizant Recognition of Complex Tasks*
- *Familiars and Their Real Reasons for Seeing Just You*
- *Hovering as a Defense Mechanism.*

And next—there was a pause—*you require more combat spells:*

- *Ice Ages Never Apply to Ice Mages*
- *Advanced Ice and Snow*
- *Master of the Blizzard*

Make sure Cook has prepared enough food to tide you over. These books must be memorized immediately. You require these skills.

Quinn knew she needed skills, but this was a lot all at once. Still. A deep breath to recenter herself made her more willing to listen.

Milaro can guide you through the techniques you will learn from these mental aptitude books. This is of vital importance. It will allow you to absorb more, quicker, faster, and become what we need to make sure that the library doesn't suffer the same fate it did 500 years ago.

The last thing the Library said felt like an opening to ask a bazillion questions. Quinn went for it, speaking out loud this time. "Do you know what actually happened when you had to shut down five hundred years ago when Korradine quit?"

The Library usually sounded a lot like Lynx, maybe with very slight variations, but this time... the feelings through the bond she shared with the core were more substantial than usual.

We are currently unable to access all of the information in the 50-year period leading up to the shutdown. I believe we are missing certain pieces of memory that must be restored and to do that, we require a lot more power. There's nothing the Library will have forgotten completely. It's a matter of unearthing it from wherever it was buried and we will find out what reason it was buried for.

The last words had an ominous overtone, and Quinn did not want to be the person or people responsible for having made this dent in the Library's armor.

Is that all the questions you have?

"Ah, yes. Yes." Quinn paused. "For now, anyway."

You can connect more easily now you have the token. You simply need to hold it in your hand, and the connection will reach me without you having to come down to the core.

Quinn fingered the smooth stone in her hand again and nodded.

There is a list of repairs which must be addressed. Golem components are low in stock. This needs to be rectified. Some of filtration replacement devices are currently damaged and are not filtering correctly even with our slightly increased power capacity. The chaotic sludge has built up and they are in dire need of cleansing.

"How do we do that?" Quinn asked. She knew the chaotic magic needed to be filtered, so this sounded like a much bigger deal than the Library seemed to be making it.

Misha requires workshop access and will assist you in gaining the raw materials that are required for the bulk of the Library's production line. Permissions for your new assistants need to be set however...

calculating...

calibrating...

error...

error...

Too many assistants. Eight new assistants. They are not vetted. Your assistants must be vetted.

"How do I vet them?"

Have Milaro, Misha, and Malakai assist. Do not trust anybody who has not been vetted.

Quinn hesitated. "What about Narilin?

Narilin is not vetted. Aradie should be able to give you a general answer as to whether or not these people are trustworthy. Once power levels are higher, background checks will be easier.

"You told me one of them was telling the truth," Quinn pointed out.

The truth does not mean they're trustworthy. It simply means they were not lying at the point in time that they were scanned. Or else, they believe that what they have told you is unequivocally the truth, even if it turns out not to be.

"Good to know," Quinn murmured. At least she knew it wasn't a failproof way of assessing whether somebody was trying to get one over on her or not. But then a thought occurred to her. Hadn't Milaro said that he was going to be bringing some trusted people from Lynx's past? "What about that Harish and Siliqua that Milaro is bringing from his homeland? They should have arrived by now."

The parents are known to me, but much time has passed. They will also need to be vetted via Aradie and the system. Milaro may not be the best judge of character when it comes to his childhood friends.

Yet another tidbit Quinn filed away. These were actually Milaro's childhood friends. Very interesting. For just a moment she wondered who Malakai's parents were. She'd never heard mention of them. Maybe they were dead.

Correct, Malakai's parents are deceased. You need to work on your mental fortitude and keeping your thoughts to yourself when you don't mean to direct them to me.

Quinn suppressed a sigh. She really was going to have to concentrate more on where she wanted her thoughts to go, because she was getting sick of being told off for thinking too loud.

You don't have time right at this moment. Start working on it after you've absorbed the texts I listed.

Quinn pressed her second hand against the tree, wanting more of a connection to it. "Can you show me Lynx?"

There was almost a sigh coming from the branches and the orange in the tree leaves above her flickered through to yellow before returning to orange. *He slumbers. I can show you an image of what it would be like but you realize he isn't currently solid. Correct?*

"But you are," Quinn said. "I can feel you beneath my hands. So how is Lynx not real?"

Lynx is an aspect of my consciousness. He is a projection of a part of me that is me and yet is not me. I am also much more than this trunk.

Quinn digested that information and asked in almost a whisper. "He's safe. He won't disappear, right?"

Not if I can help it.

And for just a moment, Quinn thought the Library sounded very oddly like a human, like a person, like a being of some sort and not just an object or an entity. Like someone who didn't want to lose someone very precious to them.

Keep those thoughts to yourself, Quinn.

Quinn did. She locked them down as tightly as she could and thought, *I will for now.*

43

ERRANDS GALORE

As QUINN ASCENDED THE STAIRS ONCE MORE, HER MIND WAS A whirlwind of thoughts. In her hand she held the small, smooth, precious rock that the Library had given her.

She knew she had to focus on the immediate tasks at hand. Primarily, they needed to create more golems. To do so, they had to gather the necessary supplies for the golems and anything else the Library required. She also had to evaluate the loyalty and capabilities of her assistants, ensuring they were completely trustworthy.

There was just so much to do—keeping it all straight in her head was almost painful.

Although she was still unsure of how to accomplish all of it, she had a hunch that if she directed her thoughts towards the Library, it would guide her.

Stay out of my head, she warned it.

Lock your thoughts away, it countered.

Quinn came to the conclusion that Lynx was definitely just another side of the Library.

In addition to all this, she had to clean the filters as soon as the filtration system was ready, a task she didn't understand in the slightest. She didn't even know how she would find the filters, but the Library assured her that she would be informed when the time was right. The need for filter components made it seem like a less magical process, although she supposed, that to someone unfamiliar with plumbing back on Earth, it would seem just as extremely magical.

She couldn't afford to be judgmental.

Once everything else was sorted, they had to open the Library, which at this point was likely to be without Lynx. A part of her rebelled against that idea.

She stepped into the main part of the Library again, greeted by Milaro, flanked by two elves who were practically polar opposites of each other and him.

The tallest one stood about seven feet tall, as dark as Milaro was pale. He had bright white hair and fangs that just peeked over his lower lip. His ears were so spiky she was sure they would draw blood if touched. Not that she wanted to touch his ears, but it was an observation she couldn't help make. His eyes were completely white.

"This is Harish," Milaro introduced with a slight flourish. "He is one of my closest advisors and has been since I came to power. This is his wife, Siliqua."

The petite elf stepped forward, giving her own flourishing bow to Quinn. She was slightly taller than Quinn, maybe five foot five, with a deep golden tan and long, delicate ears adorned with many piercings and chains linked together in an intricate filigree that ran the length of her ears. She wore a green tunic and leggings that seemed to wink in and out of Quinn's vision, blending her with the background.

Occasionally, it looked like she didn't have legs at all, very chameleon-like. Her long brown hair was tightly braided behind her, reaching past her butt. Quinn thought she resembled closest what a wood elf might look like in Earth's fantasy fiction.

"Greetings," Siliqua said formally. "We are here to assist. How might we help investigate the cause of the current..." She glanced at the other two elves. "Malfunction?"

Quinn chuckled. "Well, that's not exactly how I'd describe it," she said.

Suddenly, a myriad of words popped up in front of her, finally slowing down to read:

Assistant access granted. Minimal visual-only access. Only for these specific elves. No one else. Due to previous history and confirmation of identity. Leniency in usual protocol has been granted for this reason.

Both of the elves raised an eyebrow, apparently having received a similar notification.

"Great," Quinn said. "You tell me what you need, and I'll let you get to it, because I have about eighty-five thousand things I need to do. It was fantastic to meet you. Thank you so much for coming and helping. This is great."

The overwhelm was real, and Quinn felt very nervous. Also, perhaps, like she was being a little rude to these people who'd come to help. A wave of anxiety washed over her. She took a deep breath, and all the knowledge from the books came flooding back. Her mind went calm, and she smiled again.

"Thank you so much for coming." She inclined her head politely, hoping they understood, and then she turned to the elf king. "Milaro, I need your help with the recruits for the assistant positions. Once they've completed training and orientation, we'll be able to open the Library."

She nodded at Siliqua and Harish and made her way over to the group of recruits. Malakai looked up from where he was directing a couple of them through certain interface options and flashed a smile at Quinn. There were only six left, which was odd. She frowned.

Malakai noticed. "Ah, yes. I apologize. After going through several of the more basic necessities that we require from our Library assistants, two of them were *not* going to be a good fit," he explained. "Not everyone, it seemed, was open to the idea of regular shifts."

Quinn pursed her lips, glad that they still had more than the required number to open. Perhaps some people just wanted a very casual part-time gig and the prestige of being a Library of Everywhere assistant. "Okay, I get that."

She was relieved to see that Eric, Geneva, and Finn were still there.

It made her feel good that the ones she'd felt a slight connection with were going to be part of the Library's entourage.

Quinn surveyed the group in front of her. "This will qualify as enough assistants to open the Library, correct?" She directed her thoughts at the Library, as she spoke.

Yes, all six of these will qualify, giving us currently eight qualified assistants including Malakai and Dottie. Milaro is an honorary assistant.

Quinn paused. This was more like the usual Library and not the more personable one that she'd been speaking to while downstairs. Then it dawned on Quinn. She'd been speaking to the more human-like Library while she had her hand against the trunk of the tree. Now, however, the Library was more distant from her, more computer-like than human. She wasn't entirely sure how that worked, but she did notice a distinction when in different locations.

"I have several things to do. Are you okay here?" Quinn asked Malakai.

Malakai nodded and cocked his head to one side. "Are *you* okay?"

She half grimaced. "Yeah, I just have a lot of information I need to absorb and go through when I already feel like my brain is drowning. It's a lot."

That was when Carty rolled into view. He had several books on the bed of his cart and he called out cheerfully "I do believe the Library sent me to bring you the exact books that you need" in that wonderful little accent that Quinn could not place, probably because it came from some other world.

Quinn wondered idly if she had her own office or somewhere she could go. Immediately, the information flashed up on her screen in front of her face, including a map that showed her the way. She glanced over toward where she thought it would be. And there was literally an arrow over a large door blinking like it was a neon sign.

That seemed entirely too on the nose, and very game-like.

"Since when can you do that?" she asked.

A sensation almost like a ripple, or a shrug passed over her. Like the Library was saying, "I can do what I want."

"I'll be in my office, apparently," Quinn said, as she realized, again, that the Library could adjust and open any room it wanted to. Considering it had the ability to create doors to and from anywhere or turn stairs into ramps, she wasn't sure why this felt like a surprise, but it did.

And that's when she noticed that Dottie was trotting alongside Carty, who was bringing the books to Quinn's office. She didn't mind the bench's company at all. But she still wasn't sure about the office. The door that suddenly appeared not five minutes ago went up about eight feet in height. It was made of what looked like heavy mahogany or some sort of dark wood. Next to it was a massive window that looked into the office but it was too dark inside to see much.

The room had definitely not been there before she thought about having an office.

Quinn took a deep breath, calmed her thoughts, and pushed into the room, the cart rolling in with her. Lights slowly undimmed until the room was lit by a soft golden glow. There were bookcases lining every single wall and they went up all the way, about twenty feet. The room was probably about twenty by thirty feet. It was a really decent size, for a massive office. She looked around it, loving the old wooden paneling with carvings all around her.

The window looked out and into the Library. It was beautiful to see the columns and levels, the people gathered together, and to feel the life seeping back into the Library's very being. While the people didn't make a huge difference, it was enough that Quinn could feel it.

She went over the books Carty had for her. There was *Mental Fortitude and Time Dilation, How to Think Faster, Communication through Mental Telepathy, Mental Defense is More Than You Think, Cognizant Recognition of Complex Tasks, Familiars and Their Reasons for Seeing You, Ice Ages Never Apply to Ice Mages, Advanced Ice and Snow,* and finally, *Hovering as a Defense Mechanism.* What a huge list.

What an amazing stack of abilities and knowledge.

The cart somehow moved them all to the desk. In the blink of an eye. Perhaps Carty also had access to dimensional pockets or something.

She sat down in the well-cushioned office chair behind the massive desk and glanced around the room.

Quinn cleared her head and picked up the first book on the pile in front of her. "Okay, I'm going to need to absorb all of these. Before that, I need to check the storeroom status," she muttered out loud. And as soon as she thought that, she decided to call Misha in to talk to her because there was a lot they needed to talk about.

And she turned to Dottie, while she was waiting for Misha to appear, who took longer than an immediate summons usually did, and asked the bench a favor. "Dottie, could you please ask Cook to make me instant energy replenishment food. I need it as soon as possible."

Dottie smiled in the way that happened inside Quinn's head. "I will do it. That will be one of my first assistant tasks." And she trotted off.

Misha appeared suddenly. "Sorry for the delay. I am very busy. These assistants are not going to train themselves."

Quinn immediately felt bad for having called Misha in, when the golem obviously had a lot to do, and it was mostly thanks to Quinn. Although she guessed it was probably better in the golem's mind to be busy, than to not exist at all.

"This should be fast. I need to understand about the storerooms and where all of the items that we allocate to construction and creation are kept so that we can allocate a golem for that and then make sure we have somebody capable of gathering all the relevant materials that we need."

"You could have just asked me to create a gatherer golem," Misha commented.

"But could I really have, Misha?" Quinn asked, suddenly a little irritated. "Look, I get it. I don't know everything I need to know yet. The initial transfer failed, and this chip has a lot less information than I find useful. I assumed, and wrongly, that reopening the Library would be an easy thing. It's taking a lot longer than I thought, considering you've all got magic and you can just wave your hands and make things happen."

Misha actually chuckled, and there was a slight metallic ring to the sound. "Apologies, Librarian. Magic is not hand-wavy; magic is knowledge, and as you know, it takes time and energy to absorb that knowledge. I apologize for making you feel less than just because I am very harried right now."

Quinn paused, and let that calm slip back over her mind. Hopefully, the more she used these mental abilities she'd learned, then they'd just become a reflex. "What can I do to help you not be harried?"

"Well, you just asked me to make a golem that will help me make more golems, so really, you have just done it. I appreciate that. I am sorry if I offended you, or hurt your feelings. And I do apologize for not bringing that to your attention sooner."

"It's okay, Misha. I'm still trying to find my own feet here. And you're like two days old, so let's give each other grace," Quinn offered, as an olive branch.

Misha smiled, in that strange way where their mouth line lifted ever so slightly. "Deal, although, I am technically both ancient and only two days old."

Quinn ignored the last part of Misha's statement. "We must do whatever is needed to get the storeroom, and the storeroom golem, up and running. Do we have enough parts to construct another golem?"

"Well, first, to answer one of your earlier questions: the dimensional storage which houses all of our supplies is kept in the storage room. It's down the hall just past Farrow's area."

Quinn nodded. It was easy to forget to follow up on things when the conversation got slightly heated.

"To answer your recent question: yes, we have enough parts to construct approximately twelve different types of golems, but a total of only six more golems. The Library, when even operating at half capacity, will require approximately twenty-seven golems total, so we are very low on personnel. And it will be necessary to replenish our supply levels, too." Misha nodded at the end of that information, as if to punctuate it.

"Okay, let's make that a priority now that the Library has been mostly cleaned up, right?" Quinn asked.

"Yes, the Library is cleaned up. Would you like Tim and Tom to begin working on the storeroom?" Misha asked, their pearl-like eyes shining.

"Yes, that makes sense, right? I assume they're already done with their Library tidying tasks for now?" Quinn said.

"Yes," Misha answered, and then glanced toward the door and back again. "May I take my leave?"

Quinn nodded, and Dottie trotted back in as the supervisory golem left, in perfect timing, with several, what looked like, little balls of food jostling around in a bowl on her back. On closer inspection, they were definitely not meatballs, and not the previous cake pops, but a variety of different grains pressed together.

"Oh," Quinn said out loud as she lifted the bowl up to her. "These are like those little energy snacks that you could get in the health food stores back home. I guess this is gonna work. Thanks, Dottie."

Dottie was already gone. Quinn assumed she had gone to help the rest of the applicants, mainly because they were all going to have to get used to the Library. Dottie had a lot more experience with it than Malakai or Milaro.

With Misha and Dottie both helping with the library assistants, Quinn pulled the first book into her lap. The most important thing, she thought, was going to be getting her mind strengthened against any potential serpensiril attacks and personally being able to manage the thoughts that she leaked through to the Library. It would be far more beneficial for all of them if she learned to speak directly to the Library on command instead of inadvertently.

She picked up *Mental Fortitude and Time Dilation*. That was an interesting title. Maybe people had a point about the whole catchy title thing.

Quinn placed the book on the desk and absorbed it. All of this knowledge rushed into her head about how to fortify her mind, how to build walls around her thoughts, how to restrict access from other people. This book was a lot more advanced than the others, and it cost

298 energy to absorb. The time dilation component addressed how she could think within her mind on complex topics, yet it would only take a few seconds in the outside world.

Oh, was she ever going to be practicing this.

Communication Through Mental Telepathy was next, but before she absorbed it she popped one of the energy balls into her mouth and watched as her now 641 energy was almost refilled. This little ball popped two hundred energy back into her system. However, she did get a Library note that popped up in front of her.

Granular Energetic Mind Balls

Energy recuperation: 200 immediate

Warning: Do not consume more than ten per day.

She raised an eyebrow at the name of the balls, but let it pass. She'd just have to make each one count.

The next book about mental telepathy was quite easy to absorb at a hundred fifty points, and it simply helped explain directional telepathy and how to make sure that your thoughts didn't reach the wrong person, or get intercepted by the wrong person. Perfect for keeping her pesky personal thoughts to herself.

Mental Defenses: More Than You Think taught her, for 187 points, just how much more she could strengthen those walls than the first book had already shown her. All of these books built upon one another with wider complexity. Quinn was super excited about the end result.

And best of all, these books didn't seem to be trying to burn her from the inside out with their knowledge.

Cognizant Recognition of Complex Tasks was just another fortifier, at 162 energy. *Familiars and Their Real Reasons for Seeing You* helped her understand why and how Aradie had been originally attracted to her as a person, and just what she could ask her familiar to do. It cost a lowly 124 energy. Quinn thought it was worth so much more than that.

Aradie had latched onto something in her affinities and decided to bond with her. Quinn reached up to scratch her neck while she moved onto the next book.

Hovering as a Defense Mechanism was another one she absorbed for 175 energy, and basically taught the caster how to hover over the ground for up to ten seconds, to escape a myriad of ground charging attacks. It was a very obscure book, and she wasn't entirely certain why the Library had given her it, but she'd take it.

Finally, popping her sixth energy ball, she looked at her energy levels.

Energy 629/681

She had 4 balls left and two more books. She eyed them both.

Ice Ages Never Apply to Ice Mages and *Advanced Ice and Snow*.

Quinn sighed, but she couldn't help the tingle of excitement that passed through her. She was going to have to eat at least one more of those energy balls, but that didn't matter.

Her ice books each cost 295 points, and taught her far more about ice magic than she ever thought she'd know.

It taught her how to be dangerous.

44

SO CLOSE...

QUINN WOKE THE NEXT MORNING FEELING MOSTLY RESTED, EVEN IF still a little drained. She pushed herself out of bed and realized that she must have simply staggered up the steps and fallen asleep after absorbing all of the books yesterday afternoon. Aradie flew down from the top of the bed where she'd been perched and hooted softly, looking up at her from where she now sat on the bed.

"Hey, girl." There was sort of a question mark in Quinn's mind, like a projection asking her if she was okay? Which was odd, since she could have sworn the bird talked to her before now.

Images easier.

"Ah." Quinn guessed that made sense and hurried to reassure her owl companion. "I'm fine this time, no dreams."

Which was sort of odd. Quinn recalled often having dreams, but she thought that perhaps the exhaustion played a part in not dreaming, or at least not recalling having done so. She wandered over to the bathroom, had a quick shower, grabbed jeans and another shirt. She paused to rifle through the bulk of them and had to admit she was really liking this wardrobe.

"Did you pick these things for me?" she asked the Library.

We scanned for popular clothing similar to what you were wearing when you arrived and we have quasi-replicated some of the designs... and you have thought a lot about jeans. Very directly at times.

"Thank you," Quinn said, popping the smooth rock into her jeans' pocket. She hoped the close proximity to her would mean she didn't have to constantly carry it around in her hand to make the lines of communication more robust. Pulling on a pair of sneakers, she made her way out of her room, where she stopped short upon seeing several people standing just down the hall from her.

It clicked. Those would be the quarters for the assistants.

And she had assistants now.

Didn't that mean that the Library conditions had been met?

"Hi," Malakai said, nodding to her in his gallant way. Behind him were Geneva, Eric, and Finn, the Firionas, imp, and Ilgonomur that she had personally interviewed, along with the other new assistants. She raised an eyebrow and nodded toward the rest of them.

"Oh, my bad," Malakai said. "Although, you could just access their information through the interface."

"I know, but I would rather be introduced to them personally. Thank you, Assistant Librarian," she said, punctuating the last part deliberately.

Malakai chuckled under his breath. "I guess I deserved that. Danio is our resident centaur library assistant."

Quinn smiled, genuinely excited to have an actual centaur on the team. "Nice to meet you."

"It is an honor to meet you, Librarian." He bent down at the waist, in a small bow.

She looked him over. His hindquarters were a bay color, beautiful chestnut-y coat with a gorgeous black tail. His hooves were especially polished and his dark red hair cascaded all the way down his back, only tied together by a hair tie at the very end. He stood easily seven feet tall making him about half a foot taller than Malakai.

Behind Danio were two aracnios. They skittered forward on their spider-like legs. Quinn couldn't help the little shiver that ran up her spine, considering that they were about six feet tall at their heads and had multiple arms.

Malakai cleared his throat and introduced them. "These are our aracnio brothers, Jim and Bob."

Quinn blinked at Malakai, sure that he was pulling her leg.

"Jim and Bob?" In her mind it sounded super cute for a spider species. Maybe their names were really difficult to pronounce.

"Yes, we—" the one she thought was Jim started.

"—are twins," Bob finished.

"Welcome to the Library," she said. And they were indeed identical, right down to the multiple eyes on their faces, and the way the hair on their legs wavered in the slight breeze that ran through the Library at all times. She pulled her eyes away from Jim and Bob and headed downstairs. She could hear the rest of them following her. Once at the checkout desk, Quinn couldn't help the excitement that ran through her.

"Well, today's the day," she said. "We're going to open."

"Ah, my dear," Milaro said. "While true, it's also not quite so."

Sometimes she wished he'd just speak plainly for once. But he seemed to enjoy the riddles. "What's not quite true?"

"We're almost there. There are just a couple more things in the orientation and then we're good. The assistants need to familiarize themselves with the Library layout, including the dining hall, book hospital, and Farrow's domain. But that won't take long. So yes, it will be fine. And everything. But it'll probably be a couple more hours, so you should work with the Library, figuring out exactly what we need to do to open the doors. I'm sure there's all sorts of fiddly things to do." He kept up his smile during the whole upbeat speech.

Quinn pouted for just a second. She'd been so ready to be fully recovered rest-wise and come down here and fling the doors open. Not that she was sure what would happen after that. "Fine, I guess I can do that."

"You guess you can do that?" Malakai asked. "Look, Dottie and I have the recruits, okay?"

"And what about me? Do I have my combat skills yet?" She double-checked her stats.

Affinity Level 7:

Defensive capabilities 7 - Combat power 7.

"Oh, wow, my skills have gone up. Well, I guess we are set," she said. She couldn't help but feel extremely proud of the amount of information she had managed to absorb lately. Even if she wasn't exactly sure how to use it all.

"Are you feeling comfortable with your power levels?" Milaro asked, his eyes oddly intense.

"You know, a little bit. But there's still a massive surge of I guess you could say nervousness, where I'm just not sure if I can handle this sort of power." It was something that constantly sat at the back of her mind.

"Of course you can," he said. "In fact, you can probably handle a lot more than most of us. There's obviously a reason the Library found you."

"Yeah, how does that work, exactly?" Quinn asked, hoping for a quick fix, maybe a brief tutorial that would clarify everything.

Milaro sighed, and then shrugged. "Your affinities are off the charts. You have all of them and are basically as compatible with the magic as the Library is. This has never happened before. Nobody else on your world has any type of magic, no affinities, nothing. Maybe the universe thought, 'Hey, there hasn't been anybody around with the Library affinities for five hundred years, how about we just make somebody with all of them so that's covered too?'"

Quinn gave him a long, hard look. He didn't seem to be joking. "I guess that's a possibility."

He watched her for a long few seconds, and then smiled, his tone reassuring. "It's not like you're *the* one, you're just the only one right now."

Quinn laughed. "That makes me feel worse and yet somehow a lot better."

"Yeah, I thought it might. Do you want to come and go through some of the orientation with us?" He asked.

"You know, I think I should stay here while I'm not being pulled in fifty different directions at once, and allow myself to get more acquainted with the way the system works." Even if she loved exploring the Library, this made a lot more sense for her.

"See, Quinn, that's why you're going do just fine," Milaro said, before ushering all of the little assistants off toward Cook's domain.

She watched Milaro go and decided that she really liked it here. Maybe it had been a mistake to always pull away from others, but hadn't that worked to her benefit now that she didn't live on Earth anymore? It sounded a little fantastical inside her head. She chuckled to herself as she watched the assistants go off on their final leg of orientation.

Aradie flew to her shoulder and sat on the still-cloth version of the protective covering. Quinn really needed to get around to having the leather one made. "What do you think, girl?" she said. "Should I just access the entire mainframe and see what it is I can do?"

Aradie shot her a look that basically said, *Why haven't you done this already?*

"I've been busy, like super busy, killing things, not dying, absorbing books, trying to get the Library repaired. Go easy on me. It's my first —well, it's actually my second week still. But that pesky time dilation thing robbed me of a day or so." She stopped herself rambling and focused. "Okay, Library access panel."

Nothing happened.

"Library, help me out here. Give me the control panel..." Still nothing. She could feel the obstinacy emanating from the Library, and, before she could get annoyed, she remembered. "The console!"

And like magic, the console appeared in front of her. "There's no need for you to be so pedantic," she muttered under her breath.

Specificity is an extremely important tool of anyone using a language, especially a Librarian.

Quinn thought for just a moment that maybe she'd offended the Library. And then she decided it didn't matter, because she had work to do. She went through all of their current stock, pulling it up, and realized just how little they actually had. There was a massive list of things the Library could do. From specific golems, carts, and helpers, to initiating new kitchen sequences, and expanding the dining hall. Not to mention the different branches of the Library.

They needed more stuff. The stock they had seemed woefully low. However, there was a stack of sixty-eight thousand fragments of malachite.

She frowned. "Why do we have so much malachite?" *Also... Malakai-t.* She wouldn't make the joke to his face, though.

The Library answered her in a way that she didn't expect. *One shard of malachite means one-dimensional door can be opened. The Library requires hundreds of thousands of these to be on hand and currently is low on stock.*

"Did it use these in order to find me?" she asked.

Yes, as previously stated, it uses malachite to open every single dimensional door. The Library did not appear to like repeating itself.

"Fine, I'll pretend to know what that means." Quinn thought she did, but you couldn't be too cautious in a dimensional Library.

It requires fuel and a focus, therefore it expends one malachite shard per door that is opened.

"Including the people coming here?" Quinn asked.

The Library repeated her, without the question mark. *Including the people coming here.*

Quinn mulled the answer over and then suddenly remembered Kajaro's ring. She pulled it out of a small drawer in the check in desk to the side of the console. She was thinking of using the ring once she'd emptied it, but its origin gave her pause.

"You know... I want a dimensional storage device," she muttered as she opened the ring up and surveyed all of the different compartments within it.

Misha can get that for you.

"That easy, eh?" she mumbled as she counted the books in the ring with surprise. There had to be at least another eighty books or so in there, but none of them were flagged as a Library book. "Not all books are in the Library?"

Of course not. The Library contains magical tomes. Magical alchemy, cooking, combat—there is always an element of magical usage in every single one of these tomes.

"Okay, so normal books don't get entered into the Library at any rate?"

Correct.

Quinn took a couple of the books out. She recoiled from the feeling of slime on the leather covers. Like it had aged badly, or been exposed to something that didn't like leather. The words on the spines didn't make sense in her mind, despite the fact that she basically had a universal translator in her brain.

Maybe only books connected to the Library were ones she would always understand. "Maybe these just don't belong here, then," she muttered to herself. She left a few of them sitting on the counter for further perusal later and leafed through the rest of his ring.

Some of its contents made her shudder, but they didn't seem out of place for the person Kajaro had seemed to be. She perused it cautiously.

That is, until Harish and Siliqua, followed closely by Milaro, ran up to the counter completely out of breath.

Quinn looked up at them. "What's wrong?" she asked.

"Well," Harish intoned, in his deep voice, "the Library was indeed sabotaged."

"We were already mostly certain there was sabotage... what's different now that it has you so out of breath?" Quinn asked, trying to wrangle the people in front of her. They were on the clock here. Doors needed opening.

"It's not easy to explain," Siliqua said. "There's information in the Library that is scattered, out of place, and degrading. Considering the way the systems and the neural pathways work, the Library should not be experiencing such degradation. It's as if chaotic magic was released directly into the system in some way that circumvented filtration. Like perhaps it was scanned in?" Siliqua looked at the other two, and then at Quinn, as if hoping they would answer her question.

Quinn leaned back. "Okay, how would that work?"

"When books are returned, they are a part of the Library. They've been produced by the Library and the production system that's contained within the bookworms and the night owls. And those books enter the system and help replenish with new waves of magic gained from the contact with the outside world." Harish reminded Quinn of one of her old English professors when he spoke. Excellent diction, and no emotion. "However, if a magical book is created outside of the Library, there are certain measures that need to be taken in order to enter it into the system as a Library book."

"That being?" Quinn asked.

"For starters, it would need to be copied into the Library format properly," Harish continued, "with the relevant quill, the correct affinity ink. Everything has a balance. And the books are created in a very specific way. It doesn't mean other magic can't be cataloged in the Library. It just means for filtration's sake and for the health of the Library system that those books must be in the ecosystem that is the Library."

Quinn glanced to the side and looked at the books she'd been considering from Kajaro's inventory. She touched the top of one again. Not only was it slimy, but some of the liquid came away on her hands. She pushed them further away from the console and backed away. "Like something that has leaked into the system?" she asked.

"Where did you get those?" Harish asked, his voice clipped.

"They were in Kajaro's ring. I thought I'd take the time to sort through them." If she concentrated she could feel an aura of unease around the books. Frankly, she was amazed this was the first time she'd noticed it.

"Put them back in. Now." Siliqua's voice snapped out the command.

Quinn did as she was told, wiping the muck off her hand onto a cloth sitting next to her.

"Burn the cloth." Siliqua sounded less panicked now.

Milaro took it and electrified it into ash. Quinn watched the ashes as they dropped to the ground. Thoughts swirling in her head. "Do you think he gambled on us bringing the ring and the books back here? Do you think the Library book he had to return was infected?"

Harish shook his head. "I don't believe there is a way to infect a powerful already established Library book. I could be wrong, though. However, someone, at some time, input multiple books into the system that were likely beginner books, or something less powerful, and tainted the Library. We will try and reverse this, find the books, reverse their cataloging, I guess you could say, and hope that we can prevent any further damage. The good news is that because the Library has been mostly shut down for several centuries, it hasn't recirculated any of the books so far."

"But we're about to open," Quinn said. "What will that do to it?"

"Well, it would speed up the degradation. However, we're localizing the problem areas and will simply hold off checking in books on those subjects until we have cleared the problem."

"And," Milaro added, clearing his throat, "this didn't just happen. This must have been planned out long before the Library even shut down, and it's only due to the fact that it was in stasis for so long that this mess didn't spread and destroy the systems completely."

Quinn glanced from Harish to Siliqua to Milaro and nodded. "But it's fixable?"

"We think so." Siliqua said softly.

Well, that would have to do for now. Quinn took a breath to steady herself. "Okay, but the doors will open soon."

"We know." Milaro reached over and patted her shoulder. "It's okay. We can do this."

With that, the three of them left and Quinn turned back to the console, and its very obvious timer.

Library system ready to open.

Commencing: 1 hour 42 minutes.

45

OPENING DAY

LIBRARY OF EVERYWHERE READY TO OPEN

Commencing: 12 minutes.

The assistants finished their orientation and filed into the main hall of the Library, chattering amongst each other. The sound echoed through the stone structure, lending it life.

Quinn wondered if the Library of Everywhere had the same rule about talking as the libraries on Earth.

Go check them over for anything that might hint they're working with the serpensiril. Quinn directed the thought to Aradie, who launched off her shoulder with a soft hoot. The majestic night owl swooped around the group, and Quinn felt, more than saw, the feed of vague images the bird shot back to her.

Nothing in their thoughts was the message those feelings conveyed. It wasn't a perfect all-clear, but it did give Quinn a little more confidence in the new assistants.

All excited. Aradie sounded amused by the last visual influx sent to Quinn's mind.

Quinn smiled as the owl settled back on her perch and hooted softly in Quinn's ear. "Thanks, girl," she said, meaning it.

All the assistants gathered around the desk expectantly, and she realized that they probably all had the countdown in the corner of their vision, too.

"Three minutes to go," Malakai said, leaning against the check-in counter on the inside, joining her as she watched the front doors. "What are you doing?"

"Pointlessly waiting while I watch the timer tick down," she said. To be fair, she hadn't been doing that for the whole two hours. She'd been scouring the system, and attempting to understand several more of its functions, and how restocking supplies worked. Not to mention how the golems that would be complete in about six hours were supposed to function outside of the Library in order to retrieve those supplies.

Why did gathering golems take so much time to make? Although it did occur that slowing down the process probably helped prolong their current power levels. Misha had likely thought of this.

"Thirty seconds," Malakai said, pulling Quinn out of her musings.

"I can see the numbers too. You don't need to count it down for me," she snapped, painfully aware of the time that remained.

"Really?" Malakai said, a smug grin on his face.

"Yes, really." But she sighed as she couldn't help noticing the fifteen move to fourteen and so on.

Suddenly Milaro was there as well.

"Well, are we excited?" he said, and immediately started counting down. "Five, four, three, two, one..."

A pulse echoed through the entire Library, hitting Quinn directly in the chest along with everybody else as she looked around. The sensation shook them slightly, not knocking them off their feet or anything, but enough that equilibrium became a problem.

The Library is open.

The words flashed in cursive script across the air in front of the door. Large enough for everyone inside to see.

Quinn watched the large double entrance doors with such anticipation that she could barely stand still.

She watched, and she watched it some more.

Nothing happened.

The door didn't open.

No one entered the Library.

So Quinn swiveled, and turned around and looked at the rest of the Library. No doors, no notifications telling her doors in different sections had opened. No announcement of any returns, any books, any people, *anybody* entering the Library who wasn't already there.

Quinn wasn't exactly sure what she was expecting when the Library countdown finished, and the doors were officially opened to everybody in the known universe who had access to the Library.

However, she did know that she wasn't expecting nothing.

She sighed. "That was really anticlimactic," she said out loud.

"The Library opened. What did you expect? People are going to A, not believe it at first, and B, have to find their books before they can return them," Milaro said, even though he grinned fondly at her. "Really, Quinn, instant gratification? It's not actually a thing."

"You've obviously never spent any time on Earth," she said, scowling at him.

Another five minutes passed in silence. Milaro's self-satisfied smile remained, making Quinn sort of want to smack it off him.

"I guess there are other things for us to do," she said, finally realizing that watched doors did not open.

"To be fair," Malakai said, crossing his arms, "I don't see how people could instantly be here, right?"

"Yeah, probably. I don't even understand how the return of books works. Like, how would they even know? What if people have died? Where are the books?" Quinn started firing off questions and then stopped herself. There were other things to do before she dug into that stuff. In the grand scheme of things, she just needed to know how to check the books in once they got here. Not to mention, she had to assign some task delegation. "Assistants, listen up."

Milaro chuckled, standing back and watching her work.

"Okay," Quinn said, clapping her hands together, she turned toward all of the assistants. "Let's send a few of you to help Narilin. I think Jim and Bob should go and help Narilin with the book hospital.

You have multiple hands; you will be able to help her get on top of the initial influx she has amazingly well."

"Righto," they yelled out in unison. Quinn couldn't help but smile. Then she turned to the others, determined to allocate them something to do, so everybody wasn't just sitting around twiddling their thumbs.

She frowned for a moment thinking up what else needed help. "Danio, Finn—you two go work with Cook. It'll help them get a jump start on their list. They need help cultivating herbs and plants, for when we open the culinary branch."

Those two only nodded before trotting and scampering off toward the kitchen area. Next, she turned to Geneva and Eric. Considering they could both fly, she felt it made sense to keep them together. "Geneva and Eric, please go assist Farrow with the worms, night owls, and silverfish for now."

Geneva raised an eyebrow. "You want us to aid with the production of tome ink?"

Quinn nodded. "I think Farrow could do with help, to make sure we can begin repairs on and recreation of tomes as soon as possible."

Eric let out a sigh. "I'll try to focus on my work." The words were begrudging, like it was going to take him a lot of effort to focus and not muck around.

"Thanks," Quinn said, and watched as the last two flew off to join Farrow.

"You realize we're going to have to let them rest too, right? We can't all work day in and day out. We'll need to organize shifts," Malakai drawled, his eyes smiling as he focused on her.

Quinn pondered that for a moment. "True. I'll get to work on that shortly." She had no idea why she hadn't thought of shiftwork in the first place. It seemed so obvious now.

She turned around and looked at the massive double entrance doors again, sighing.

Malakai piped up. "You really need to get over that. It's not going to happen immediately."

She wanted to say, "But why not? Why? Why isn't it working yet?" To be honest, she was eager to see who and what would walk through that door. What books did they have? Were they surprised that the Library still existed? She had so many questions and a plethora of things she wanted it to be.

She sighed again. "Yeah, I suppose you're right. It's probably a good idea to do something instead of wasting the whole day." No matter how hard she tried, even she could hear the pout in her voice. It wasn't the front she wanted to present to the people she now technically worked with and was responsible for.

She let out another sigh.

"You really need to stop doing that," Milaro said.

"Well, I need to do something," she grumbled. Which was true. And there were definitely things., other than sighing, she could do.

Quinn flexed her hand and willed a ball of ice into it. Theory and practice however were two entirely different matters.

"Ow," she said, as ice quickly encased her entire hand, and she had to break out of it by moving her fingers. Luckily, it had only been a thin sheet of ice. Otherwise, she would have run into some trouble.

Milaro laughed. It was a full-throated laugh, like nothing subtle about it. He was really being entertained at her expense. On a frequent basis it seemed.

"Really?" She raised an eyebrow. "Thanks."

Milaro shrugged. "You could just ask. I've been using magic for centuries. Millennia, actually. I'm quite certain I could teach you a thing or two."

Quinn paused her initial reaction, genuinely curious. "But isn't your power like a type of electricity?"

"It's called electroflame." Milaro preened a little, as if he was extremely proud of it. "It's a mixture of two magics. Became its own affinity, actually, thanks to me."

"Seriously?" Quinn said, impressed.

"Technically, I could teach you my abilities, but you have a definite water smell about you."

Quinn shrugged. "I guess that makes sense. They always say something like seventy or eighty percent of the human body is made up of water."

Milaro raised an eyebrow at that comment. "You don't say. Wouldn't you think water would be the last thing you'd want to master?"

"Ice-wise, I don't know." Quinn shrugged. "I mean, doesn't it make sense to maybe know how to resist being turned into an icicle?"

"Valid point." Milaro tapped his chin, obviously thinking.

Quinn smiled. She liked making valid points. "But aren't I supposed to have all the affinities?"

Milaro nodded absentmindedly. "Yes, but that's obviously to provide overt compatibility for the Library. It doesn't mean your body won't be more partial to specific ones."

"Well, then," she said, suddenly impatient. "Teach me."

Milaro raised an eyebrow. "Is that any way to speak to a potential mentor?"

"You're already supposed to be teaching me mind magic, which we've conveniently neglected, so you've been my mentor a while now." She crossed her arms and awaited his retort.

He laughed. "To be fair, you've been busy, and we can't exactly lock you in that time chamber you wished for, can we?"

"I swear, anime lied to me," she muttered. "Anyway, how about you go over some ice techniques with me? Or even basic techniques? Wait, if you have like electric fire, then are you even able to help me work with ice?"

"Working on basic techniques is something we need to do anyway. No matter the element or affinity, there are always basics," Milaro said.

Malakai hopped up to sit on the outer edge of the check-in desk and crossed his arms. "This'll be good. He's the worst teacher out there."

Quinn chided him gently. "I don't know. I actually think he's pretty good. He explained some mind stuff to me, and the cooking, and helped me absorb things. Like dude, be nice to your dad."

"He's not my father, he's my grandfather." The words came out clipped, and there was suddenly something off about Malakai's stance. He was defensive with the way he shrugged his shoulders up, and

Quinn made a note to never accidentally make a comment about his parents again.

"Anyway, can we get started?" She turned to Milaro to ask.

Harish chose that moment to step into view. "Actually, we need to run down a list of book categories that, when they arrive, cannot currently be checked in. We have narrowed down what we think to be most of the affected areas and should be able to get them cleansed in a few days."

Siliqua piped up, "I think perhaps a week, or two, would be a better estimate of time. I'd prefer to be finished early than have to go over time." She glanced at her husband with a little bit of irritation.

Quinn sighed. "Okay, just hit me with them."

"Fire magic, air magic, any of the related affinities or combined affinities, including yours, Milaro." Harish turned to him.

Milaro had the grace to blush slightly. "I wasn't about to get out any of the books on it. I wrote them all. I know them."

"Just checking," Harish said, before continuing. "Combat hand-to-hand, combat fire, air, and electricity masteries."

Quinn raised an eyebrow. "That's an awful lot of books…"

"But wait," Siliqua said, "there's more!"

There was no mirth in her words. In fact, she seemed quite perturbed as she continued the list. "Horticulture, specifically in-ground growth. That covers a lot. Right now, the skills Farrow has are going to have to suffice until we can cleanse that subject area." Siliqua concentrated on whatever was written in front of her with a frown on her face.

"Also the regenerative culinary recipes, which, as you know, are extremely important. Cook has access to several hundred recipes, luckily, included in his creation module, so you shouldn't have to worry about anything for the immediate future. However, do not touch the rest of the culinary regenerative magic. And lastly, ancient advanced protective spells. I don't believe you're up to that area level yet, but you can't check those in. Nor can you lend any books in any of these areas out."

"So just a few things, then," Quinn said, a hint of sarcasm creeping in despite her best efforts. "Okay, so how do people know to bring the books back? I know they'll know, but everything's been really vague. I want the details."

"Lynx probably thought the information you got would tell you what you needed to know," Milaro answered.

"The information was probably expecting me to come from somewhere linked to the Library already," she muttered, thinking it the only logical explanation. "As it is, I know less than anyone else in the universe who could have possibly been picked."

"True. I thought you'd be able to look things up yourself because everyone else has been able to," Milaro said. He seemed in a worse mood than he had been originally. Maybe it was the comment about his electric-fire magic, or the confusion about how much basic information she still needed.

"I know that an alert goes out about the book. I know there's like a pulse or something that should alert people who have the book. But what about, well, I mean, a lot of time has passed, and we've already found one dead person whose book had been handed down. So how does that work?" Quinn tried to sort through the confusion in her head.

"Well, the book itself is tuned to the Library. So when the pulse goes out, it will let the person know who borrowed it that it needs to be returned. Failing that, allows for the person to whom it was handed down through blood lineage to know the book needs to be returned. Failing that, if everybody in that bloodline is dead, which could happen," Siliqua explained very eloquently, "then the book itself will act as a beacon for the librarian to go out to fetch it at some stage, or, depending on its level of magical density, the book could try to make its way home. They aren't usually the best at finding their way back, which is why we have to go and retrieve them sometimes."

"That makes sense," Quinn said. Even though if the books had a homing signal, why didn't they just come back in the first place? Although, it's not like books had arms to open doors. "I take it it probably requires magic to come back, correct?"

"Exactly," Siliqua said, seemingly highly enthusiastic about the subject. "Because the books have been so far away from the core and the Library itself for so long, well, it basically means that their connection with the Library isn't as strong as it should be until it reconnects. The Library on the other hand doesn't have enough power to just pull all the errant books home right now. So, we'd have to locate them and then send out someone to fetch them and bring them back. If they don't have any familial connection to the original borrower anymore..."

Quinn pinched the bridge of her nose. It was way too complicated. She was about to ask another question when an alarm sounded through her head, although maybe it was just a warning message or a notification.

It rang like a trill of bells in her mind, and she realized it didn't sound throughout the whole Library, but she did notice Milaro and Malakai also seemed to have heard it because they were looking around. And then she saw the notification in front of her.

Library doors in sections A84, C95, and B7 have opened.

The Library has patrons.

46

PATRONS, PATRONS
EVERYWHERE

QUINN GREW UP KNOWING THE SAYING "ALL ROADS LEAD TO ROME."
Except in this case, it appeared all doors lead to the check-in desk of
the Library.

She gaped around as several different species, ones she hadn't yet
met, walked into the room. Given that Lynx said this was a Universal
Library of Everywhere, she took that to mean she'd likely rarely see
the same species twice, at least to start with.

The first patrons that inched their way toward the desk, wonder
written all over their faces, were small and insectoid-like—maybe
three feet tall. They had slender wings folded out behind them like a
butterfly, yet they looked very similar to a grasshopper, right down to
the multifaceted eyes and the antennae sprouting from the top of
their heads. Their hands, however, were less claw-like and more
three-fingered. Their eyes clicked in that insectoid way, flashing
through different lenses as they observed everything around them.
She could practically feel the wonderment emanating from them in
waves.

They were simply beguiled.

She had to admit the Library presented a beautiful picture to visitors. Majestic columns, rows of tidy seating and books now. She could only imagine their shock if they'd seen it a week ago.

There were four of these visitors in all, and they each held a few books. It looked like they weren't the strongest creatures, and that's when Quinn remembered she could inspect them, for want of a better word.

Schmectectoid - Insectoid-based species

Located in the: Gensha Quadrant

Library Allies for: 4,893 years

Library Standing: Good

Books currently overdue: Total 932

Quinn cocked her head to one side. This was more information than it had given her initially. Was it powering up already? Well, that meant that the Library now had enough power to figure out where all of its books were.

That would be correct. At least once someone from the species walks through the door, anyway, it then amended itself.

"Good to know," she muttered under her breath, and then flashed a smile at the newcomers. "Welcome to the Library."

The other three pushed one of them forward. This one of the schmetectoids was slightly larger than the others, and they held three books in their arms. They placed them on the counter and spoke in an oddly clicking voice. "We would like to return these books, please."

The other three came up and deposited their books quickly before backing away, bowing in the process.

"Thank you, and you are?" Quinn asked, unable to tear her gaze away from their eyes.

"I am Jasshu." The word came out a little garbled, and Jasshu was about the best that Quinn could do with it, even with the help of the Library's translator.

Still, she flashed Jasshu a smile and said, "Thank you. Would you be able to help round up the rest of the books that your species has?"

"Yes, these were readily available, and we do have more being gathered. But wanted to return what we had so far." Jasshu made to walk away, but hesitated and turned back. "We did not think the Library was still here. We have lost many to the chaos. We are glad you are back."

And with that, they hurried off to make their way back home, exiting through the massive double doors that Quinn had been waiting for people to walk through in the first place.

Quinn stared after them thoughtfully. "Well, that was interesting," she said, mulling over the last things they'd said. She knew the Library hadn't been able to fully filtrate the magic, but had assumed it kept most of it at least at bay. That some of the species had been seriously adversely affected was sobering.

There was a shuffling of feet, and she turned toward the sound. Upon seeing the approaching beings she realized it wasn't really a shuffling, more like dragging. She wondered mildly if the Library was delaying the arrival of each group of entrants so they could deal with different returns easily—so that the Librarian and her assistants could get used to things slowly.

Her assistants who she'd sent off to help out around the Library. Quinn groaned. It was fine. At some point the patrons would be arriving regularly. There was plenty of time to get used to this.

She hadn't scanned the previous twelve books into the system yet, because she had to make sure they weren't infringing on any of the groups that they couldn't yet enter into the system.

The next group was human in appearance upon first glance. They all had extremely dark hair and very pale skin, almost white. As they approached, she noticed one of them flashing a smile filled with what looked like pointed teeth. There were only three of them in total. It seemed a half smile was their natural expression and she realized all three of them had serrated teeth, sharp like a shark's. She wondered for a moment if they worked like shark's teeth and replaced themselves.

She scanned them.

Caverninon - Shark-humanoid-based subterranean species
Located in the: Menecia Segment
Library Allies for: 620 years
Library Standing: Good

Books currently overdue: Total 72

Odd. Their alliance was only about a hundred and fifty years older than the time the Library had been closed. They must have been new discoveries or simply just come into the fold late. Did that mean they could be part of the saboteur group?

"Hi," Quinn said as thoughts ran rampant through her head. She did her best to keep her expression neutral. "Welcome to the Library."

The smaller of the caverninon stepped forward and inclined their head. "Hi." They looked up at Quinn and Quinn noticed for the first time that including the sclera, the entire eye was black. So they definitively were not human. But they didn't have the double eyelids like Lynx either. She wondered what it would be like to have to live underground all the time. It reminded her of where they'd found Kajaro—although that world had been an entirely different one.

"We have six books to return. We have been trying to return them, but it appeared the Library was closed. We thought it was our fault." Their voice was stilted, like they weren't used to speaking out loud.

"Why would it be your fault?" Quinn asked with an easy smile, as she took the six books from the caverninon's hands.

"We were new to the Library. We thought we had done something wrong."

"Don't worry," Quinn said, and thought it over carefully. She didn't understand this species; their voices seemed devoid of emotion, but she thought they might be apprehensive. "I'm sure you'd know if you'd done something wrong. Besides, the Librarian would never have let you keep the books, if it was your fault. She would have come and retrieved them."

The Caverninon laughed and bowed. "Thank you for your reassurance. I am Torniette. Thank you. We would like to borrow more."

Quinn sighed, and held up a hand. "Right now we can only take returns. You are, however," she hurriedly added as she realized that Torniette's mood had sunk at that statement, "allowed to peruse what we have. We are currently trying to regain a large sum of our books. Currently, the range is not quite what it would usually be." Although...

didn't the Library always lend out books? Wouldn't this be the current state?

I'll explain that to you later, the Library shot at her, and Quinn couldn't help but think it sounded more like Lynx than usual.

"That is okay and acceptable," Torniette said. "If this is truly allowable, then we would like to partake in reading some of the books."

"Sure. Go ahead. Tim and Tom, our shelving golems, can help you if needed, and there are Library assistants available throughout the Library to help you with anything you might be seeking." She felt like a salesperson, asking them to stay in her establishment.

Quinn watched as the caverninon left and walked deeper into the library. There was almost like a sigh of relief from the structure itself. It fed through to her in an odd tinge of happiness. Books were coming back, and people were entering the Library as it always should have been.

Just as she felt like she couldn't feel more, Quinn noticed the next group. There were more of this species, half a dozen to be precise, and they looked very similar to the Salosier, except they were about five feet tall, a little denser, and had flowery hair with pinky-purple flowers attached to it. They were much more shrub-like. She inspected them with the system.

Tecopsis - A desert willow species - cousins to the Salosier

Located in the: Arid regions of Feshpa

Library Allies for: 6,800 years

Library Standing: Good

Additional information: This species travels in a pack-like formation. Often with familial bonds.

Books currently overdue: Total 128

Ah, thought Quinn. *I guess this group of six is a family.* Each of them held seven books, from what she could see. Two of them approached the desk.

"Good day, Librarian." The one in front of her radiated femininity. "I am Sabinth."

Not only did she radiate femininity, but she also had very barely contained excitement streaming from her in energy waves. She was beautiful, quite simply, just lovely. Quinn wondered if she had the same abilities that Narilin did. The ones that soothed you. Although, she was feeling more excited than soothed.

"Hello, Sabinth. I am Quinn, the Librarian. You have books to return?" Quinn kept the smile on her face, but was already feeling like her jaw hurt. She was happy to see people in the Library, but smiling took a lot of effort.

"Yes, yes, we have been waiting. We knew the Library wasn't gone. It had to still be here, because the books, well, they acted like it was still there, but like it was too far away, and we couldn't go in. We took very good care of the ones in our direct family. We realized we had taken out forty-two books. We do apologize for keeping them for so long." Her words bled into each other like a shining beacon of pure energy.

"It's okay." Quinn held up her hands, trying to stem the onslaught of words from the very excited little Tecopsis. The one next to her let out a long sigh.

"I am Taree. Sabinth was but a child when the Library disappeared, and has maintained a childlike focus and excitement for everything that the Library contains. Please forgive her over-exuberance." Their voice was deep and soothing. The polar opposite of the excitable one.

"That's fine," Quinn said. "To tell you the truth, I love books too. I get the excitement."

"I would hope you love books," Taree said, their voice drawling and smooth. "After all, we'd be very unlucky to find a Librarian who didn't love books."

Quinn filed that away. Something about what they said resonated with her. In such an odd way that she wasn't sure came from her in the first place. Maybe from somewhere deep within the core. She would address that later.

"Sabinth, Taree, thank you," Quinn said, as she took some of the books and put them on the counter, arranging them nicely. Malakai had already begun sorting through some of them. He'd only put two off to the side, and Quinn hoped that that small pile were the ones they couldn't scan in and return yet. "Thank you for coming and returning these books so promptly."

The rest of the Tecopsis remained behind Sabinth and Taree, huddling together like they weren't used to seeing other species, or being in other places.

"Would you like to stay and look at some books?" She asked Sabinth.

Her eyes lit up so much. And Taree sighed again.

"It seems we will be staying. I assume, along with the message about the opening, that we will not be able to borrow books for some time. Is that correct?" Taree practically spoke in a drawl, just without the southern accent.

"Yes, it is. I'm terribly sorry. Cook will have food and snacks if you want to stay as long as you wish. We have facilities if they're needed, and I'm sure you can doze off on a couch if you end up staying long enough. If you really want to spend that much time with the books."

Taree chuckled. "It seems that you know my niece very well."

"I swear, I was just like your niece once," Quinn said.

As the little Tecopsis broke free of her clan and ran into the Library, Taree threw a long-suffering glance at Quinn as he and the other four trailed after her.

The quiet of the Library was gone. Quinn could hear whispers in the background that carried through to the front, pages being turned as normal patrons read books in the old-fashioned way, really absorbing the knowledge and not just automatically inhaling it.

As far as she'd understood it, absorption of text was something reserved for the Librarian. Perhaps also the assistants? She pushed her query toward the Library.

Accurate. Librarians require the ability to immediately absorb and understand the knowledge the Library contains. Otherwise they will be lacking at their jobs. They must know what the Library contains and eventually end up absorbing all of the works of their respective affinities. On top of that, they must know details of each of the other books in such a capacity that they can direct patrons to the precise book they require.

Quinn blinked. That meant a lot of book absorbing in her future.

What about the assistants? Quinn asked.

They must read the books, but the information is absorbed and not just learned. It's one of the perks.

Quinn soaked up that piece of information while she picked up a stack of books that Malakai had deemed worthy of being scanned in and glanced at them to double-check that he hadn't missed any of the forbidden categories.

There were five off to the side. "Can't check those ones in yet?" she asked.

He shook his head. "Do we have anywhere to put them?" A drawer opened next to his left foot as if summoned, which she guessed, it sort of was.

"Well, I guess that's my answer," he said, looking at the massive drawer.

Quinn laughed. "Let's hope it can hold a lot of books. I've got a feeling we're gonna get more books before we fix the situation."

Each book she entered into the system allowed for the tiny line at the bottom of her vision to move just a fraction farther along. She looked at it, bemused. "Highlight function," she said, not really knowing how to direct it to tell her what it was doing. "Ah," she said, realizing that the lower end was the *critical low* that they were barely past. And every book inched towards *low, unstable, constant influx necessary.* "Okay, we can deal with that. We've started getting a constant influx. I hope," she muttered, hoping she hadn't jinxed it. That would be the worst-case scenario.

But even as she scanned the last few of them in, she got more notifications.

Library, door, C7 accessed.

Library door, D28 accessed.

So many doors opening. So many patrons filing in. It made her feel like maybe this wasn't all impossible.

Danio and Eric came out to assist with the ushering of the returnees. "You know Malakai, how about you take the next returns and I'll begin scanning them in," Quinn suggested. She felt a little peopled out. Not necessarily because she didn't like facing people, but they were the most people she'd seen in the last nine to ten days. She needed a calendar in this place to figure out if weeks were the same, what the months were...

Very unhelpfully, the Library decided to pop one up in her face at that moment, which she waved away in exasperation. "That would have been nice three days ago. Just fill one out, let me know where I am and how long I've been here. And when I last slept," she muttered. Quinn had the distinct feeling she was going to get so busy she'd need to track her sleep.

She could almost feel a chuckle wave into her soul from the surrounding Library. She didn't need to be made fun of, thank you very much.

Still, Quinn cracked a smile. She was beginning to really like the whole Librarian-Library connection.

Now, all she had to do was figure out a way for Malakai and Milaro to help her put the theory in her head into practical use. She couldn't help feeling that she'd need some of those skills sooner than later.

4 7

TOO MUCH TO DO

THE THING ABOUT THE LIBRARY BEING UNIVERSAL AND EVERYWHERE meant that the Library of Everywhere did not close.

Quinn realized, belatedly, that she should have organized the shift allocation as soon as they got the assistants.

However, she also noticed that seven assistants, if she counted the one that was pretty much permanently stuck in the book hospital right now, wasn't a whole lot. In fact, having a king elf who wasn't going to be there all the time and really was just an honorary assistant, a prince elf who was supposed to be her combat trainer and help her gain some tactical abilities, and a bench as the senior assistants didn't make manning a library this size seem possible.

It basically left her with six functional assistants, and only three supervisors between her, Malakai, and Dottie. Quinn ran her hand through her hair and decided that she was way too tired to deal with this tonight. Dottie promised she would oversee things during the night shift and stay up with Jim and Bob, the Aracnio brothers, to man the check-in desk, thus allowing Quinn to get some sleep.

Trudging up the stairs with Aradie hooting very concernedly in her ear, Quinn decided she needed a great night's sleep for once. And tomorrow, tomorrow morning, she would figure out exactly what needed to be done to sort out the roster in the Library.

The gaping hole, left by Lynx's current absence, was becoming more obvious.

It won't be too much longer, the Library whispered in her mind. But Quinn didn't dignify it with a response.

She slept fitfully, even though the bed was amazingly comfortable. She tossed and turned, and all she could do was lay and think about books, and not scanning in the incorrect books, and how many different species would be coming in every single day. So far, she'd seen about eighty people walking through the Library since they'd opened. In total, they'd only returned like a hundred thirty books. She'd check the exact numbers in the morning. She was too tired. But so many of them were different.

It was all Quinn could do to not stare.

She flopped over onto her other side and tried to get back to sleep again. Eventually, Aradie nipped at her ear to wake her up.

Quinn wanted to push the bird away, but she knew she had to get up. She opened her eyes and a calendar flashed up in front of her vision. She glared at it again. Tenth day here, really? That's all? She sighed. Yeah, that tracked, just about. It felt like an entire lifetime.

She'd been to multiple worlds, almost got killed, learned magic. Sure, just run-of-the-mill library stuff.

Dressed and showered, she decided to head downstairs and snag some food from Cook. That darling golem had another singular cinnamon donut waiting for her. She could get used to this. She flashed him a smile. "Thank you, Cook."

"Always, Librarian," they said, in that metallic-y voice that held a hint of warmth. Maybe it was like an oven. Perhaps that's where it came from.

Gleefully devouring the doughnut, she wandered into the main part of the Library, only seeing Dottie, Eric, and Geneva there. The imp and Firionas fluttered in place as they worked with the console. Quinn looked around. She didn't see Malakai, nor Milaro. "Did they leave it up to you? I thought Malakai was going to supervise this morning."

Dottie actually scoffed. "Oh, really? I'm a superellex futora. You should know that I don't require sleep. As such, I can keep an eye on these guys for you, and make sure that none of the books that shouldn't be scanned into the system get scanned into the system. Add to that, the fact that I can help them navigate the Library and proceed with their training. I'm quite invaluable!"

Quinn smiled and petted the bench on her head, or at least where she was pretty sure her hairline would be. Dottie, luckily, half purred into the touch. "Thanks, Dottie." And she really meant it. Their friendship might have had a rocky start, but Quinn found she really looked forward to seeing Dottie now.

"Shoo. You have to go train with Malakai. Milaro cannot come until later, but he has given Malakai instructions for your mental fortitude training. And right now, you have to go and do that." Her tone was soft, if a little bit chiding.

Quinn grimaced. "Fine. But are you sure you can go without sleep?"

Dottie sighed. "Well, not forever, but I can go several weeks without damaging any of my cortex. I will be absolutely fine. You require rest, sustenance, and training in a much larger measure so you don't get killed. We won't make it another five hundred years without a Librarian if you die."

Quinn paused at the voice Dottie spoke to her with. She was actually being stern and concerned. "Fine. I'll go and train, I promise. Just let me have a look around first."

Quinn double-checked the levels through the console. It seemed they'd had a hundred or so more books returned while she slept. She leafed through requesting the exact number of books returned so far. It was 382 returned, with only 348 scanned through, due to the restrictions they'd had to place on it. After some training, and more food, she'd go through and make sure she had all the numbers for the other branches included as well. But right now she had things to do.

She sighed at how long it was going to take to get eighteen thousand books back into the Library. "I guess this is better than nothing," she muttered, hoping that Harish and Siliqua would get to the bottom of the problem as soon as possible.

Being unable to scan a portion of the books in and have them returned to their rightful slots definitely put a damper on things.

~~

It didn't take long for Malakai to join her in the kitchen, where she was getting some snacks for energy replenishment in anticipation of the upcoming training session.

Quinn grimaced at him. "I guess you're going to run me through the wringer in the training room?" she asked.

"Well, it had occurred to me," he replied nonchalantly, giving her a careless shrug, "but if you're not up to it..."

"Of course I'm up to it. I just don't want to," she said. "I don't think I'm the most physically fighty sort of person."

"Oh, you're definitely not. But you've absorbed some basics, so you just need to train the muscles to follow the knowledge that you already have. You've already got dodging pretty much down, so, you know it's fast learning. It's much quicker than having to learn this from the ground up, and take lessons for years and years and years, trust me. I've been studying sword work for fifteen of them." Malakai was picking over a few small packages Cook had put out for them to choose from.

Quinn smiled at him. "Yeah, I know, you've mentioned that, and your grandfather mentioned it before that. So I know, I'm sorry for complaining. Let's grab some drinks and some food, and we can go and bash the crap out of me."

Malakai actually laughed. "I'm not going to bash the crap out of you."

"He's lying," Eric said in a sing-song voice as he hovered into the kitchen, holding up a ratty and damaged book in one small hand. "What am I supposed to do with the books that are damaged upon return? Don't you usually leverage a fine?" He seemed very put out by books being treated badly.

Quinn had to echo the sentiment, but they'd declared no fines for a bit, so she shrugged. "Yes, but it's also not their fault because they couldn't return it for 462 years or something, which means that, like, we're giving them leeway for thirty days or so."

The imp was obviously put out. "You know, I could levy fines. I'd be very efficient with them."

Quinn raised an eyebrow. "I'm sure you would be, Eric."

He harrumphed and zoomed back out of the kitchen toward the check-in desk, where Geneva threw him a disapproving glance.

Quinn sighed and motioned to Malakai. "Anyway, let's get started with some training."

~~

Oh, how she regretted those words almost immediately.

Malakai had been right about one thing though.

Dodging worked... when it worked.

She wasn't quite horrible at it now. She'd retained enough knowledge and muscle memory to successfully roll and fling herself out of harm's way smoothly. For the most part, anyway. But her inability to grasp even the most basic concept of ice control infuriated her.

"No. No. Just a sliver of it. You need to control the output of the ice. We don't have to freeze a lake right now." Malakai pinched his brow and took a long-suffering breath. "You can't just command an ice blast to form over your hand."

"But that's what I did when we fought Kajaro," Quinn said, exasperation filling her despite her best efforts. "I just willed it to hit the cephalopod..."

"... and it went completely and utterly out of control," Malakai finished for her.

"Well, it froze the lake, and I could get over to the other side. So I mean, it worked." She pouted.

"Yeah, but did you ever think that maybe that's not what the spell was supposed to do?" He leaned in. "Lack of control is not a good thing in magic. Too much energy, and you blow things up you never intended to."

"Well, if it wasn't supposed to do that, why did it do that?" Quinn flung her hands in the air in frustration. "Now that's the only way I understand to shoot magic out is to just fling it out there."

Malakai didn't have an answer for that. He simply scowled at her. "I don't know, because ice isn't one of my affinities. But I do know that to use stone, I also had to first master earth manipulation. I have no idea what my grandfather was thinking when he ordered the Library to give you ice tomes. That's like the tree before the seed. You don't even have one air book in your knowledge base, let alone water. How are you supposed to master ice?"

Quinn blinked at him because he sounded like he was making a lot of sense. "What do you mean?"

Malakai rolled his eyes. "You shouldn't just be able to use ice without any inkling of how to control water or air."

"Well... apparently I can, to freeze a lake and blast ice in some serpent's face," she shot back at him.

"You just froze his corpse, but still." Malakai then mulled over those words and nodded. "Good point. I'm just a little bit frustrated."

"That's highly obvious." Quinn took a breath and calmed herself down. "Then what do we do? What do I do, so I can harness an effective combat skill?"

Malakai frowned for a few seconds. "It's also obvious that we need to get you books on water control, on knowing how to defend with water, how to resist water, how to manipulate water, and how to create water. You have all of those affinities. Once you know how to do that with water, and with air, combining them to create ice will be a lot more controllable on your end."

"Okay, that makes sense. Why did your grandfather say that I smell like ice then?" Quinn was genuinely curious.

Malakai sniffed the air. "Probably because you do. I'm unsure why. Maybe it's your strongest element. You're really a mixed bag. You smell like every single affinity I've ever come across, and more. And all of it icy. I don't know why. I'm like thirty. Don't ask me these questions."

"You speak like that's not a long time." She grinned at him, goading him a bit.

"In my years, it's not, and very soon, it'll be nothing in your years either," he quipped right back at her.

Quinn thought about that for a moment and realized just how much her life was changing. She could deal with that. At least, she thought she could if she didn't dwell on the magnitude of the whole situation too much. "Okay then, Master Trainer, what's our next step? I can dodge, and roll, and sort of hover. What do we need to do next?"

"Well, I would like to see if we can get Misha to get us..." And that's all he had to say.

Misha appeared. "You need me, Librarian?"

Quinn did a double-take. It was the first time she'd seen Misha come to the call of someone other than herself. "Well, yes, but we hadn't yet finished discussing what exactly we needed you for."

"Books, I assume," she said, looking at Malakai with some disdain, and that's when Quinn realized that Misha had simply anticipated that Quinn would need them.

She wondered if sometimes the supervisory golem had been in charge of combat training. She was going to look that up later, but didn't need to bother because the Library answered her.

On occasion, but in rare instances. The alliance we have with the Darigháhnish here has always enabled us to pull on their long history of combat prowess. In this specific case, Malakai is the better instructor.

Good to know, Quinn thought to herself.

Malakai spoke. "We need several books on beginning and intermediate wind, air, and water manipulation. I don't know those elements well enough to think of any off the top of my head. Would you recommend some, please, Misha?"

That seemed to mollify the supervisory golem slightly. "We'll have to verify that the air books in the Library at the moment are able to be used, considering Harish and Siliqua's warning.

Quinn had forgotten some of the books were restricted. "Can you check with them beforehand?"

"Definitely," they said, nodding for emphasis, "there are several books that I can think of. I will have Tom bring them to you shortly, after I have first verified with Siliqua. Is that all?"

"That'll be enough for now. There's no huge rush," Quinn said.

"Ah, but Librarian, there is a huge rush. There is too much knowledge in this library for you to learn overnight, but we need to keep you alive because we, very selfishly, want to stay alive as well." And with that cryptic remark, Misha disappeared.

"I'm never going to get used to this," Quinn said.

"Yeah, you are. Look how much more used to this you are right now from the moment I met you," Malakai said, obviously trying to soothe her a little. She raised an eyebrow at him. "Come on. While we wait for the books anyway, let's get in some of that mind training Grandfather had you absorb," he said. The elf prince frowned, checking on something obviously in his HUD, and nodded very slightly to himself, as if he needed some convincing.

That didn't exactly make Quinn feel confident about the whole mind magic stuff. She still found it fantastical.

Finally, after another few seconds, he cleared his throat. "How about I start throwing some spells at you? You've already read a heap and absorbed books on mental defenses. So let's put some of them into practice, shall we? My grandfather instructed me in a few very specific attacks designed to test the parameters of the skills you've absorbed. Again, you should be able to use what you learn from *Mental Defense: It's More than You Think,* and *Mental Fortitude and Time Dilation.*"

"Okay," Quinn said, and she couldn't help but feel nervous. "You sure this is safe?"

"Yes. Grandfather thought so." Malakai shot her a reassuring smile as he readied himself.

Quinn took a deep breath and nodded, even though it drove her anxiety up a notch. "Ready."

The first couple of attacks Malakai threw at her were easy to fend off.

He sent what felt like a mental shove toward her, and she pushed back, making him stumble at first. It surprised her, since she hadn't expected a mental attack or counterattack to translate into a physical act.

She pulled the information she'd absorbed into herself and felt it out in her mind. It was like there were walls with bricks that she could expand and constrict. They were held together by a sort of putty acting as the mortar between each of those building blocks. The analysis felt in place, and right.

She found the harder the hit he leveraged at her, the easier it was to rebound it back using his mental energy against him and little of her own. She could return it and impact him in a way that sent him physically stumbling. Which alerted her to the fact that she needed to brace herself physically and mentally during a mental attack.

They lobbed these hits against each other for what seemed like several minutes, or maybe longer. Maybe sixteen or twenty of them even.

But the next one hurt.

It pierced through the mortar, stopped it from expanding, and exploded several of the bricks she'd been keeping intact around her mind.

Pain pierced into her memories, and it felt like somebody was driving a nail into her frontal lobe.

Quinn screamed and fell to the ground, rolling in pain.

She couldn't see anything.

She couldn't hear anything.

Nothing but darkness.

48

SUCH A CRICK IN THE...

The screaming in her own head wouldn't stop. It felt like something was ripping her brain from its cavity, flaying the skin from her bones.

And then it stopped.

Suddenly.

Everything around her became dark and soothing, at least externally. She could feel, more than hear, Aradie's panicked hooting and the soft flash of her wings against Quinn's face, as if they were open to protect her. The throbbing inside her head felt worse than any migraine Quinn had ever experienced in her life, even worse than the car accident she'd been in with her parents when she was twelve.

A concussion had nothing on this.

She could feel the bile rising in her throat, the need to expel anything from her body. She rolled over onto her left elbow and emptied her guts, before rolling back to lie on the cool mat in the training room. She could hear voices now, soft whispers. Malakai sounded guilty and Milaro was there, she thought, if she identified the voice correctly. But she couldn't quite tell through all the pounding.

What she could hear was a sibilant whisper in the back of her mind if she concentrated, telling her that not all was as it seemed and that magic was chaos. Chaos should have free rein. Chaos could help her feel no pain ever again.

It made her wonder for a moment if maybe it could. Was that really how things worked? Would it perhaps be better to simply give in to the magic and let it have its way? Sure, it might consume some who were weaker...

She blinked her eyes open as a hoot echoed around her. Encompassing and safe. Aradie stood with her beak right in front of Quinn's nose, bearing down on her, looking directly into Quinn's eyes. *Hoot,* she said again. *Be careful, be safe, protection. Thoughts, not your own.*

Quinn blinked and the blinking let too much light in, which made her grip her head as she rolled to the right side and pushed herself up onto her knees. She gasped for air, blinking more and directed the Library to dim whatever lights were in the training room. She couldn't handle the bright light all around her. It was too much.

"Quinn," Milaro rushed over to her. "Are you okay? Let me just test ." He held his hands about an inch shy of each side of her head and after an inquiring peck to his hand, he glanced at the owl and said, "I'm not hurting her. I'm healing her."

Aradie shuffled sideways and remained next to Quinn, alert and aggressive. Milaro continued to hold his hands over Quinn's head and slowly, very slowly, the migraine receded, and the pain faded into a dull stinging. She squeezed her eyes shut again.

Quinn wasn't sure how, but she could tell that Milaro had crouched down next to her.

"How are you feeling, Quinn?" he asked, his voice soothing and soft.

Aradie appeared to be on alert still. Quinn could feel a wariness radiating from the owl, and she appreciated it. It felt, ever since Lynx's absence, like she'd been more on her own, and Aradie really made her feel a little safer. Even though she was quite certain that Milaro meant her no ill will, it was still nice to know that she definitively had somebody in her corner.

"I feel like shit," Quinn said, analyzing every space of her still-pounding head, even if it wasn't in as much agony as it had been several minutes ago.

"Well, it's good that you're cohesive enough to express that," he said. "I need you to stand up, and I need you to come and sit down on a seat."

Quinn took the hand he offered and rose, blinking her eyes back open again. She felt shaky in her limbs as if she couldn't quite trust them, but she followed him obediently to the couch and sat down.

"You may not feel like it right now, but it is the best time for you to learn, and harness, your mental skills. I apologize for telling Malakai to instruct you in something that he is not an expert in. I should have thought ahead." There was genuine remorse in Milaro's words. They resonated through Quinn.

"See, I didn't mean to hurt you." Malakai sounded pretty pissed off. She couldn't see him, there were still kind of blurs in front of her eyes, but she didn't need to, to know that the elf prince was angry at his grandfather.

"I did not expect your reactions to be so instinctive, which compounded the exercise I instructed Malakai to give you." Milaro explained, his tone even and patient. "I miscalculated your aptitude. Something that shouldn't have happened."

Quinn nodded and wished she hadn't, because it made her head pound more.

"Here," Malakai handed her one of the food pouches from Cook. In it was a juice of some kind that she didn't recognize, didn't care about because she was dying of thirst, and one of those little energy balls. It tasted different when she popped it in her mouth though, with a definite sesame-seed-esque flavor to it. It was delicious.

"That's just for body recovery. It's a gem, that one. It'll help rejuvenate the body, and fight the nausea and headaches," Milaro said.

Malakai scowled and threw himself down on the other end of the couch. "How are you feeling?"

"I'm feeling much better, I think." And she wasn't lying. Quinn legitimately thought the world was ending for her, not fifteen minutes ago.

"Excellent." Milaro rubbed his hands together. "Now, you'll pull on minimal energy when you utilize your abilities, and on a lot more mana when you activate the skills that count as a type of spell casting."

At that moment, she really didn't want to learn. All she wanted to do was curl up in a ball and go to sleep. But she knew this had to be done. She couldn't keep putting this off or she'd end up getting them all killed. "Is that like when I build my walls?"

"No. That expends energy to construct and maintain. You're not casting those. That's not an immediate blink of an eye sort of ability, but it could be once you practice first, get faster at it, and then it becomes a reflex, which draws on energy and not mana," Milaro explained, into her haze of confusion.

Quinn blinked. "Couldn't they have just pooled mana and energy and made the system so much easier?"

"Well, I'm not sure who you think this 'they' is," Milaro said, a grin on his face. "But no, the universe was set up this way. It's been like that since time immemorial. Just get used to it."

"Great, so the universe doesn't even have logic," Quinn mumbled. But with the pain even farther gone now, she found that she was ready to learn whatever this next lesson would be. "Okay, boss, tell me what to do."

"I just want you to sit, cross your legs as if you're about to absorb a book, and relax. Ease your mind, close your eyes, and feel out every nook and cranny that you can sense inside of your head. Every area that thoughts enter, that actions come from, everything where your memories reside, feel it all out." He spoke in an almost hypnotic way. Soothing, and calming.

Quinn obliged him, finding that it felt much more spacious in her mind than she'd anticipated. It was an odd sensation. She nodded slowly, painfully aware of how her mind moved when she did so.

He continued on in an almost droning tone, like someone who was trying to lull her to sleep. "Excellent. Now we're going to go back into the mental blocking and fortitude that we should have been working on a lot slower. I want you to take each of those blocks and blend them with the mortar and push them together mentally. You have to feel them click into each other for the wall to work."

Quinn concentrated hard. It took a long time. The bricks kept slipping out of the mortar, and she couldn't understand how she'd originally thought it was so easy. And that's when one of them basically bent to the will of the mortar. It wasn't clicked in. It was sort of just hanging. So what she had done was constructed more of a hammock originally, and hammocks had holes, which meant that the attacks eventually overwhelmed and broke through those holes.

"Wow," she said out loud. "I was way too eager earlier."

"Yes, but that isn't your fault," Malakai said, and Quinn could practically feel the glare he directed at Milaro.

"Stop blaming me," his grandfather snapped.

But Malakai's mood obviously wasn't getting better. "Well, it was your fault."

"Stop arguing," Quinn snapped. "It's okay. I survived the backlash. I've got it now."

And finally, a brick clicked into place, and the more she did it, the faster she could click them together. The first several took a while, but after what seemed like twenty minutes, she had a nice little four-by-twenty wall going. She paused, opening her eyes.

"I think I get it now."

"Excellent," Milaro said. "Now we move on. Now that you know how to construct your own defenses, you can do so and leave them intact permanently. Tuning them up when you need to. But for now, we have to go and look at what has already been seeded inside your mind."

"Inside my mind? What do you mean?" Quinn felt a wariness at his words, but realized it didn't come from her. No. It came from something that felt foreign to her. An intrusion that didn't belong.

"Where do you think that dream with Kajaro came from? I'm not exactly sure how far forward he planned everything, but your interactions with him were no accident. He might not have thought you'd get the jump on him in the end, but he planted something in your head. He planted events for you to witness when you close your eyes and when your guard is down. We have to ferret them out, figure out how he did it, and make sure we protect you from any future onslaughts. And after that, we can figure out the why." This time Milaro's tone was anything but soothing.

It has hard, determined, and protective.

Quinn decided that she definitely liked his plan. Having Kajaro in her mind was not on Quinn's bucket list. "Okay, let's do this," she said.

Milaro sighed. "I'm going to need you to give me your hands, and I will need you to trust me enough to guide you and permit me entrance into your mind."

"But only where you need to be." Quinn qualified the permission.

Milaro nodded.

Aradie chose that moment to inch closer and onto Quinn's shoulder again. She rubbed her wings against Quinn's head and images flooded Quinn's mind. *Safety. Protection.* And basically the sensation that no harm would come to Quinn while Aradie was there.

Quinn raised an eyebrow and looked at Milaro. "You realize she's going to peck you to death if you screw up and it hurts me, right?"

Milaro chuckled. "Yes, I am quite sure she would do precisely that."

"Let's get this over with." And with that, Milaro dove in with her. At first, the sensation of someone else's thoughts, of their presence along with her in her innermost sanctum felt decidedly wrong. But, after a short while, her hesitance vanished. The aura that accompanied Milaro was perhaps a smidgen mischievous, but there was nothing malevolent about it.

He taught her how to strengthen the blocks that she'd already built. How to reinforce the mortar and allow for more flexibility so it could absorb attacks and reflect attacks without coming undone. He taught her how to concentrate. How to leverage her counterattacks using the weight of those that were flung against her mind. And how to barricade herself down like an igloo, with no entrance, or exit, in times when someone might simply force an all-out onslaught onto her mind.

That way she would be ultimately protected.

Her mind would be, anyway. And sometimes, all it took to survive, was keeping the mind intact.

Quinn wove her defenses and began accepting attacks from Milaro. His were pointed and not wild. Not like Malakai's. They were both at the same time, easier and far more difficult to deflect. But eventually, she got it down. When the point hit, she allowed it to absorb into the brick ever so slightly before catapulting it back out the other side toward her attacker. The more she practiced, the easier it would be to target that specific return.

She let out a deep sigh and looked up at Milaro. They still hadn't found anything to do with Kajaro. "Okay. I'm ready for you to dive in deeper."

He nodded solemnly. "It might hurt. I can tell it's pretty far in."

Quinn nodded. "I know. While I was out of it, I had some thoughts I don't think I would have by myself."

Milaro nodded. Whether he *really* understood, Quinn couldn't be sure. But she knew those thoughts about chaotic energy and how perhaps chaotic magic was the best way for magic to exist. She knew those thoughts weren't her own. They'd never been her own.

She could feel his consciousness sink into her own. Seeking out something. Not knowing exactly what he was looking for. Aradie's presence on her exterior was still there. Foreboding toward any enemies and yet oddly comforting for Quinn. She allowed herself to relax.

Milaro's thoughts were distinctively not inquisitive. He didn't seek any other part of her. He was simply following a very thin trail that Quinn was quite certain led to whatever Kajaro had left in her head. The elf moved in a deliberate, determined way, bypassing anything personal.

There were flashes of the fight by the lake. Of the taunts, of the cephalopod, and her ice blast. Of the way his magic had hit her. Of the way the void he had cast had clipped her hairs at the side of her head.

She hadn't even noticed that during the battle. Messy buns. Messy ponytails had always been her forte. It was easy not to notice hairs go missing. And that's how Kajaro had gotten a foothold into her mind. Through that minuscule touch, a hair follicle. He had buried in under her skin and through that seed into the very depths of her thoughts.

She shuddered.

"It's okay." Milaro's voice spoke both in and outside of her head. It was an odd cacophony of sound, of words, and of comfort. She allowed herself to relax, even if it was one of the most difficult things she had ever done.

And then she saw it at the same time that he did.

There, at the very back of her thoughts, was this tiny sliver of doubt. Doubt about everything.

About everything new she had learned.

About everything new she'd seen.

About everything she had ever been told.

Including all the information about her parents and her life back on Earth.

She paused. There was something else underlying it all. A grain of what felt like truth, but she couldn't quite grasp it.

There was comfort from Aradie very briefly, the glimpse of a soothing aura, but then it was gone. Instead, something about her parents' death wasn't what she'd known. How she would find that out now that she wasn't on Earth, she didn't know.

The insidious whispers in her mind appeared to be there to trip her up, to shake her confidence. In that instance, Quinn was grateful to be stubborn as hell.

Milaro dug deeper, pulling through. Until he finally tapped directly into the chaos Kajaro implanted in her head.

It appeared like a tiny, rotating ball at first. Hidden away in the deep recesses of her mind, like it was waiting for something.

Upon discovery Quinn felt a shiver run through her whole body, and that ball began to spin, slowly. Faster and faster as it gained momentum, until it was moving so quickly that it swirled like a vortex.

Like the vortex Kajaro had cast on her. And it began to suck everything in from all around it into a black hole.

Which included all of her memories, abilities, and their consciousnesses.

Quinn was no longer in the Library. No longer sitting on a couch in the training room. No longer surrounded by Malakai, Milaro, and Aradie.

Milaro stood there in front of her. Perplexed in his expression. But Aradie was not there. Her presence only lingered ever so faintly on the outside.

It was the only thing that led Quinn to know this was only a vision. And she wasn't alone. And Milaro was not the threat.

She took a deep breath, centered and then calmed herself. The swirling vortex slowed some, but it didn't stop or disappear.

"Well done, Quinn," Milaro said, his voice ever so slightly strained. "This is unexpected."

The bluey-black vortex enlarged in the middle of the room. Swirling and pulling everything from the edges in toward it, even tugging at the two of them now. Very slowly, Milaro inched around to stand next to her.

"This is entirely unexpected. Hold on to me. We'll get out of this."

Quinn wondered if he could sense the lack of conviction in his words.

49

PUSH BACK

THE ATMOSPHERE AROUND THEM, INSIDE QUINN'S MIND, GREW DARKER and denser, leaking negativity.

She saw cars wrapped around telephone poles, sucked into oblivion like a black hole. Funerals with open caskets, where no one had cleaned the corpses up. Tears and sobbing filled the air as it turned frigidly cold.

Milaro stepped closer to Quinn, placing a protective arm in front of her and some of the visions faded, allowing her to see what was in front of her more clearly. His face contorted with concentration as he attempted to keep Kajaro's trap at bay. Quinn couldn't tell what Milaro was doing.

Quinn hadn't even noticed there'd been a trap in her mind.

She hadn't realized her own mind could become a stranger to her.

"What do we do?" she asked, desperately trying to keep the fear out of her voice.

"We... wait. This is more complex than I anticipated." His words were forced through clenched teeth. His long sleeves fell back as he raised his hands and even his arm veins were popping with the effort, the physical and mental effort he was using. Whatever it was, she didn't understand how mind this space worked.

"The best we can do is box it in. You need to build your own mental prison around that vortex. This is not something I can build for you. I won't have the traction." His words were steady, if slightly breathless. "I will help you, but it has to be your power."

Quinn didn't even contemplate second-guessing that. She understood, integrally, how to build a wall. Why couldn't she build a cube?

She concentrated so hard she could feel sweat beading on her brow both in and out of her mind. After the first several rows, it became easier to click the blocks in together to make sure that they absorbed and retracted with the right amount of consistency. All the while, Milaro barely held the thrashing vortex at bay as its power pummeled everything she erected around it.

Laboriously, she placed each brick next to each other, on top of one another. This was exhausting work, and just when she thought she didn't have the strength left, Aradie somehow loaned her some even though she seemed so far away. Even Milaro poured what felt like energy into her. She wasn't sure how they were doing it, but didn't have time, or the spare braincells, to form the question. It meant that the drain on her own reserves was down to a trickle, and that held all the importance right then.

Finally, after what seemed like an eon, she closed the final brick around the vortex. She could hear it screaming in her mind until she did, telling her that what she was doing was wrong, that she would regret not giving in to the chaos, that chaos would consume her and everything in the universe along with it.

And then the final brick clicked in. There was a sucking sound, followed by an audible pop, and then there was silence.

Enough that she could breathe, and open her actual eyes to the training room around her, from her place on the couch.

She took in Milaro, Malakai, and Aradie. They all looked weary and tired, and then she realized she'd literally sweated buckets. She wasn't even sure if the golems could fix the couch she'd just drenched.

Not only that, but vertigo threatened to assault her, in almost the same way it had back in the library on earth.

Quinn felt absolutely drained.

"Give me one of those," she said to Malakai, her voice coming out in a raspy whisper. He threw her one of the energy balls, and she knocked it down so fast she almost choked on it.

298/762

She'd been low before that ball. Dangerously low.

Quinn took a few deep breaths, and cracked her neck from side to side as the energy recovery registered through her entire body.

"That wasn't supposed to happen, was it?" she finally asked.

Milaro rubbed the back of his neck, a rueful smile on his face. "A lot of things weren't supposed to happen, Quinn, that being one of them. I think what is a more accurate description, is that I was not expecting him to have wormed a spell into your mind so intricately. I will study up and figure out how to disentangle that cube from your mind, but it will take time, and you will need to reinforce that cube every day until I can figure out a way to get that insidious trap away from you."

"Do you think he's right?" she asked suddenly.

Milaro looked at her long and hard. "I think that *he* thinks he's right."

"For some people, that's enough, I guess," Quinn said, suddenly feeling very deflated. "Look, I'm tired. I'd like to go and wash this sweat off me."

"One more second." Malakai forced himself to stand up, and Misha walked in front of them.

Quinn looked up at the supervisory golem, blinking in surprise. "Oh, I didn't realize you were here."

"Of course I was here," Misha said, sounding almost offended. "You needed us."

"What do you mean?"

The golem's face remained passive, but their tone was not. "You were clearly in distress."

"I was," Quinn looked around. Milaro had the grace to look at the floor, as if he was embarrassed, but Quinn glossed over that in an effort to sort out what Misha was saying to her, and force an understanding into her currently very cloudy head. "And you could feel that I was in distress?"

Misha nodded once. Curtly. "While our connection is not yet as strong as it will become, distress of that level is palpable to the staff of the Library. That isn't too difficult a concept."

A brief flash of irritation hit Quinn, but she was too tired to snap. Her voice sounded defeated even to herself. "It's not difficult, it's just unusual. I'll get used to it." And she couldn't help feeling that being connected as a whole would end up being very beneficial if she got into trouble again.

"Excellent. It is neither here nor there anyway, but I have brought you your books. I took the initiative to relieve Tom of them and deliver them myself when I became aware of your predicament." Misha sounded like they were highly disapproving of the situation, and their glance at Milaro only cemented Quinn's impression.

"Oh, that's right." Quinn picked the books up. *Walking on Water: Density as a Skill, How to Create Barriers with Water, Not All Just Hot Air: That Which Doesn't Float Sinks, It's an Airy Experience: Combining Air with Other Elements, If You Can't Swim, What if You Fall In?, How to Navigate Water Control.* Despite herself, Quinn smirked at the titles. Until she got to the fifth book: *Finessing Combination Magic: How You Too Can Outlive Explosion.* Quinn frowned. "That last one isn't a very enticing title."

Misha shrugged. "Not everybody understands the necessity to title a book appropriately," they said. "Anyway, after you have recovered, you will need to learn these as well."

Quinn sighed and took the books even though they felt far heavier than she thought they should. Perhaps the weakness from her vertigo spell still lingered. "Yeah, I know, I'm gonna need to learn everything."

She checked her energy again, and even after the energy ball and some time had passed, she was only sitting at 302. She frowned, wondering what she'd missed. Although, Malakai had explained it, hadn't he? The internal wall building was a skill, and thus pulled on energy. She guessed that having to pour so much power into restricting the vortex was likely what sucked all of it dry.

She paused before turning to walk out of the room. "Did you all help me replenish energy while I was in there, I mean, while we were actively engaged?"

Milaro nodded. Malakai looked away with a scowl on his face, and Aradie firmed her perch. "Yeah, I thought so," she said with a small smile. Maybe it was good to have people in her corner.

She turned to Misha and gestured at where Aradie perched on her shoulder. "Could you make sure that I get a leather one of these? This cloth one isn't going to last much longer, and Aradie prefers to ride on my shoulder."

"Noted, Librarian." Misha had that clipped business-like tone back in their voice. "Will that be all?"

"Yes. Thank you. I appreciate you."

The golem stopped and turned. "We appreciate you too, Librarian," they said. "Thank you." And with that, Misha was gone.

Quinn groaned. "Why can't I do that?"

"Because you're not actually part of the Library. You're just linked to it integrally. When the power reserves are filled, and you've got more power available to you, however, you should be able to do something very similar." Milaro smiled.

"Like teleport?" she asked, incredulously.

"Within the Library, yes," Milaro amended slightly and then paused. "Well, I guess that depends on your physiology, but I don't believe being from a human would prevent you from doing so."

Quinn mulled that over for several seconds before nodding. Getting more books back seemed utterly imperative. "I might want to double-check that being human won't end up in a squashed mash of flesh if I teleport, but otherwise I'm excited for that." She laughed, trying to take the edge off the words.

Milaro smiled and ushered her toward the door. She thought he looked a bit worse for wear, tired, and harried. He caught her looking and grinned, but his next words reassured her he hadn't guessed her thoughts. "Harish and Siliqua have updates for us, but nothing groundbreaking that can't wait until you've regained some of your strength."

Even the way he spoke the words soothed a portion of her enough that she felt about to sink into relaxation. She nodded.

"Today's training session was harder than we expected. You must focus on your mental capabilities, on strengthening your mental protections. I don't believe Lynx would have sent you to retrieve that book from Kajaro if his memory had been completely intact. There are levels of manipulation through the system that would suggest this was deliberately set in motion." Milaro paused at the room threshold, and she could read something like pity in his gaze.

She'd never been a fan of pity. It made her stubborn. Not that she was angry at Milaro, but at whatever, or whoever had caused Lynx and the Library to lose so much, and with their loss came the whole universe. The sadness in Jasshu the Schmectectoid's voice when they'd mentioned being a victim of the chaotic magics running rampant...

Someone needed to pay for that.

Quinn nodded emphatically agreeing with Milaro. "We'll get to the bottom of it."

Aradie hooted at the end of the sentence as if to provide punctuation for it.

If he was surprised by her vehemence, Milaro didn't show it. Instead, he simply inclined his head in acknowledgement.

Just before she left the room, he reached out and caught her arm and spoke to her in a lower tone. "Also, I apologize for dropping the ball and giving you ice books first, as my grandson is heavily chiding me through mental communication right now. I simply assumed your affinities would function precisely as those I've previously had experience with. Now that you have the correct tomes, though, it should provide you with a better understanding of the elements that make up that particular affinity. Thus the ice abilities, and the way to control them, should come much easier to you, instead of accidentally freezing an entire lake, your hand, and other things."

She studied him through eyes that felt heavier than cement, grasping onto his words and attempting to understand them. Along with the mental fatigue from battling the hostile trap in her mind, it seemed she'd utilized most of her physical energy as well.

All she got out of Milaro's small speech was that her affinities were maxed out, but didn't necessarily reflect the way they usually presented themselves in others. She digested the fact and flashed a belated smile at the elf king. "Well, hindsight is always 20-20, right?" she said before gently disentangling herself and trudging her way to her quarters.

Back up in her room, Quinn decided that she didn't need more sleep.

What she needed was some more energy balls, and a long-ass, scalding hot shower.

It was the first time since she'd arrived that Quinn really took stock of the majestic bathroom she now found herself in.

The walls were tiled in a pale terracotta shade. She didn't think the actual tiles were terracotta, but the color was very similar. It gave off soothing vibes, as did the steam, as it billowed out of the oddly modern plumbing fixtures she'd taken for granted until this moment.

Surely the plumbing here had to be done by magic? Although, perhaps engineering was a sort of magic if she thought about it long enough.

Sighing, she leaned forward and let it wet her long, dark hair, aware the whole time that Aradie was perched at the top of the shower keeping a watch over everything. Not for one moment did Quinn doubt that Aradie could use her beak with lethal force.

The heat eased muscles she didn't realize needed it, and unsurprisingly, helped clear her thoughts. Rejuvenating as she'd hoped, the shower was everything she'd wanted it to be.

After she was done, she toweled herself off with a huge, plush bath sheet and rifled through the closet for something comfortable. To her surprise, she pulled out a soft pair of sweatpants and a large hoodie with one of those front pockets that went all the way across.

Hadn't she only just thought about that sort of comfort?

"Do you, like, create stuff when I think about it?" she asked the Library.

Not in the way you mean. But yes, sometimes. It's more fleeting thoughts you've had about things that would make you more comfortable in your new life. We never intended to steal you away from the things you loved. Being a Librarian is supposed to be beneficial for you, too.

"Thanks," Quinn said, genuinely excited to have something fleecy and fluffy to sit down on the bed with. "No time like the present to get stronger."

She grabbed the two packets of food she still had left over from what Cook had given her, and pulled the books onto her lap, ready to absorb information that could likely save her, the Library, and the universe's existence.

50

CURIOUSER

THE NEXT DAYS PASSED IN A WHIRLWIND. FROM MORNING TILL LATE AT night, Quinn worked on mental fortitude, learning how to defend herself, how to seal away offensive attacks, and how to reflect those same attacks back at her assailants with extra force. She learned how to combine her combat magic and make the most out of her abilities with ice, learning to generate and manipulate water for both defensive and offensive purposes.

It was amazing how powerful water could be, let alone air. Air was one of the most destructive forces she'd ever seen. She literally broke three of their training dummies by not quite understanding what she was trying to do the first few times.

After training, she spent the afternoons and evenings in the Library, returning books, speaking to new returnees, and working with Cook on some of the items she would need for the future.

Day leaked into night, knowledge became power, and Quinn started to feel a sense of comfort as if she was finally settling in properly.

Then on the afternoon of Quinn's twelfth day in the Library, Narilin came to see her. The willowy beauty that still astounded the

Librarian every time she saw her, moved with lithe floating grace, almost hypnotizing in its allure. She was, quite simply, breathtaking.

Quinn did a double take as she stacked the "do not, under any circumstances, enter these books into the system yet" pile, and steeled herself to face the book doctor.

The Salosier reminded her so much of a walking weeping willow, except that she never exuded a sadness of aura, only quiet confidence and grace. It was easy to forget that Narilin was almost three hundred years old.

"Librarian," she began, as soon as she reached Quinn's side, executing a flawless bow. "I have received word from my family about the books they will be returning."

Quinn's interest piqued. "They're coming here to return the books?"

"Well, of course." The Salosier paused, a brief line of consternation crossing her brow. "Where else might they seek to return them?"

Quinn had to bite her tongue to stop herself from laughing. Despite the fact that she had put her own foot in it, Narilin's response was simply priceless. "Sorry, that was a little facetious of me," she said. "Now, you said your family has uncovered all of the books?"

"Yes. The two hundred sixty-seven that I had correctly recalled would be returned to the Library have now been gathered, along with another hundred seventy-two from one of the neighboring clans to us." Narilin's speech, as always, was flawless, just like the beautiful, almost vine-like leaves she had running down her entire back. Quinn always felt like Narilin was a relaxing soul. There was always something different about her that Quinn couldn't quite place.

Quinn cleared her throat. "Well, that sounds fantastic. So we should be getting, what, four hundred thirty-nine books returned?"

"Precisely." Narilin seemed very happy that Quinn was capable of basic addition. Quinn wasn't sure whether she should be offended by that or not. She chose to ignore it instead.

Which brought her to the more important question, perhaps. "Fantastic. Do you have any idea what sort of books there are going to be?"

"Oh, as discussed, a hundred eighty-seven of the books that we will be returning came from my grandmother's wish to open the culinary establishment that she has been running for the last hundred years. Those books will go toward the Library's specifically culinary branch opening number and should mean that we get to open the culinary branch that much sooner." It was the first time that Quinn had seen Narilin be truly excited when speaking about something other than taking care of books. She had observed her being excited about repairing books, cleaning them, creating them... but this was the first time her excitement was directed elsewhere.

Quinn hesitated. She wasn't sure if she should mention the check-in issues to the Salosier. "We may be unable to check some of those books in quite yet, though we can keep them here and make note that they were brought back."

"What do you mean?" Narilin asked. "Is something wrong with the system?"

Quinn wasn't quite sure how to take that tone of voice. There was an edge of panic to the tone. Did Narilin know something, surmise something? Was Quinn just suspecting everybody all around her now? Aradie cooed in her ear and she got an overall sensation of calm from the bird. Perhaps she didn't need to be so worried right now.

"There is just a minor hiccup in the system with certain subject matters. We have to put those books aside until such a time when we can return them all." Quinn decided partial truth was better than outright avoidance of mentioning the issue.

Narilin cocked her head to one side as if she was digesting the information. "The system will not allow these books to be returned quite yet?"

Quinn shook her head. "No, it's more there is a problem with returning specific subjects. The books may not escape being damaged."

Alarm spread across Narilin's face so quickly that Quinn was taken aback. "The books will get damaged by being returned to the Library?" She sounded horrified.

Quinn held up her hands in a placating gesture. "They're not going to get damaged. We are taking steps to make sure that doesn't happen.

That's why there just may be some of those books that cannot be cataloged yet, though bringing them back to the Library is fine."

Narilin scrunched up her face. "May I see this problem? Is there perhaps a way that I might assist so that no more books get damaged?" She sounded genuinely distressed. Even the tiny leaves at the end of her hair were curling up.

And Quinn remembered the absolute piles and piles of books that she had to repair. Yeah, she could understand where the Salosier was coming from. Not only did she dislike seeing books harmed, but she also already had enough on her plate.

And Aradie's aura seemed to imply that she could trust the tree-like lady. Quinn sighed, shrugged her shoulders, and decided to just go with it. "I guess you could help, have a look into the system, see if we can understand where it's coming from or why it's happening."

Just as Quinn was about to take Narilin to link into the console, Harish and Siliqua showed up.

Quinn raised an eyebrow at their impeccable timing. "Haven't seen you two for a couple of days."

They looked drained, paler than she remembered, with shadows under their eyes. She could sense the exhaustion coming off them in waves. Glancing at the returned books meter, Quinn realized that the Library was still a long way off from having enough energy to do any, let alone all, of the things they needed to do. But the Library was definitely making headway.

It was gaining more than it was losing, which meant her attunement to it was strengthening as well. Though it was still pulling on some of her own energy reserves. She bit into a piece of sweet bread Cook had made for just such energy consumption and mulled over the current situation.

Maybe she'd eventually feel everything everybody who ever entered it could feel. That might get a little overwhelming. Right now there were simply so many possibilities. "Narilin has offered to see if she can help identify the problem in the system." Quinn left it there, hoping she hadn't just put her foot in it.

There was a very pregnant pause by the elves who exchanged unreadable glances with one another.

Quinn could feel it in the pit of her stomach and the way Aradie tightened her grip on her shoulder. Neither of the elves were happy with the information they were bringing, nor inclined to share it with someone they didn't know. She got it, she did, but at the same time, they were all a part of the team.

They all needed the Library to survive.

Everyone did.

And the Library, as far as it could right now with Aradie, had all vetted the people in it.

Could they have missed something? Sure? But if they let themselves be paralyzed by mistrust and indecision, they'd never get anything rebuilt.

Quinn eyed the almost overflowing drawer that held the books they couldn't yet scan into the Library. Over the past few days, they had amassed 1,283 returns in total. That was a lot of books, and 179 of them couldn't be entered into the system properly.

That was enough to propel her to make a decision.

"What's the problem?" she asked, trying her best to leave her irritation inside her head. "We have to work together to get everything back to where it needs to be. Trust might have to be earned, but we must believe we can fix this or why are we even trying?"

Siliqua sighed and nodded once, abruptly, as if she'd made her own mind up. "You make a good point. I will get right to it." She glanced over at Narilin. "You understand the fundamental function and process of the Library's systems, right?"

Narilin gave a gracious bow of her head. As if she was swaying in the breeze. "Return, glean excess power gathered while absent, adjust for any chaotic stickiness to re-enter the filtration system. Balance them out, recharge the Library and its own filtration system, lend the books out again. Continue the cycle."

"Precisely." The wood elf seemed suitably satisfied.

Quinn wished she knew exactly what they were talking about and directed all her attention to understanding the rest of the conversation.

"The sludge, I guess we will call it, for want of a better word," Siliqua began, "is lodged in several very delicate parts of the system."

Narilin's eyes narrowed almost imperceptibly. Quinn wouldn't have noticed it if she hadn't been so intent on the whole conversation. "What type of sludge?"

Siliqua hesitated, but finally spoke, sounding defeated when she did. "Chaotic remnants."

The Salosier sucked in a breath with a hiss, her expression twisting momentarily into one of distaste. "Could it, perhaps, be from a part of the filtration system not working correctly?"

Harish shook his head and took over. "It might be exacerbated by the fact that the filtration system is in need of maintenance, but that's not the cause. The remnants are very deliberately placed around specific subject matter. Some of these are needed to increase power in the individual and the Library, others that are essential to opening the Library in its entirety. You get the picture."

"Sadly." Narilin let out a sigh that rustled her leaves. "May I perhaps take a look?"

Harish and Siliqua looked over at Quinn immediately for guidance. She shrugged. "I don't see why not? I mean, what's it going to take to clean these areas out?"

"That will depend. There are many purification magics my brethren and I have access to that can help. They have been developed out of necessity. Many planet dwellers do not work well with the nature around them. I fear, however..." Narilin hesitated ever so slightly.

Quinn pounced on it. "Fear what?"

"There might be more to this. It's original aim might not have been to infect the Library itself, but to bog down the filtration system in a way that would cause havoc if you weren't being vigilant." Her large eyelashes batted every so softly.

Quinn's gaze, however, narrowed. "So basically, the aim was to push the sludge so far that it breaks the filters."

"Exactly." Narilin seemed proud of Quinn's comprehension. Even Harish looked on with approval. "Or it could have been one of the aims. But if the current state of the filters is perhaps exacerbating the situation, I would surmise that this was a very deliberate choice."

"So why don't we just go and fix the filters, then?" Quinn asked, not understanding the big deal. A HEPA cleaner needed new filters every six months or something. Maybe it was less, but surely the principle of the thing was the same. It wasn't something she'd ever been in charge of.

"That's exactly it. Without the manifestation to guide us, without a specific number of intermediate books in the return... there are only limited options available to us." Siliqua's voice held a small note of panic that she seemed to be doing her best to squash.

"Oh," Quinn said again, this time without enthusiasm. She knew what this meant. She didn't like what this meant. But that didn't mean she didn't know exactly what this meant. "So you're telling me that I'm going to have to go out and retrieve more books, right?"

"It's a likely outcome," Harish said, and then grimaced. "Actually, an almost definite one."

Quinn squinted at him. "There's something you're not telling me about the whole filtration process, isn't there?"

Harish half shook his head before shrugging. "It's not necessarily something I'm not telling you, just that I don't believe you've even seen schematics of the filtration chamber."

She shook her head, because she indeed had not. The Library flashed up an overlay of very unhelpful blueprints over her vision that she waved away. It wasn't going to help her unless she had a chance to study them and understand them.

"That is not what should be concerning us right at this..." But whatever Narilin had to say died on her tongue as she watched a point past Quinn's shoulder.

She turned to follow the Salosier's line of sight and couldn't help the massive grin that overcame her. "Lynx, you're back." She smiled, receiving an immediate message from the Library.

I thought you could do with a welcome surprise. He is fully functional again, but has restricted access to areas that could potentially infect him and thus more of our systems. He will not have full maneuverability yet.

Quinn took the note under advisement and knew implicitly that Lynx was also aware of the situation. "What does this mean exactly?"

"It means," Lynx said, taking over as he usually did, "that you no longer need to do everything on your own. You can boss me around too." He leaned forward peering at her, like he was scanning her. "My, my, dear Librarian. You haven't wasted any time getting stronger, have you?"

"Couldn't very well slack off while one of us was having a four-day nap now, could I?" she quipped, secretly so glad he was there again. She hadn't realized quite how much she'd missed him. With his supervising the new assistants, it gave her so much less to worry about when it came to the unified front the Library presented to new patrons. Granted, he could sometimes be very blunt.

But they'd have to deal with that.

Lynx smiled. "Nap, shmap. It was my first period of resetting myself in over five hundred and eighty years..."

"Did you say five hundred eighty years?" Harish interrupted him, a flash of panic entering his gaze.

Lynx studied him before answering. "Yes. I did."

"Why did you need to reset at that point? There's nothing in the log history that implies you would have gone offline?" Harish pressed the subject with a deep hint of urgency, his brow furrowed with consternation.

"Korradine was already talking about retiring, and we decided before she initiated the sequence that I should take the time to..." His gaze drifted back into that mode where he both was there but also wasn't. Quinn promptly picked up a writing pad and balanced it on his head.

She'd missed this. Even though she couldn't deny the gravity of the situation. Nothing said she couldn't try and provide a glimpse of levity.

A darkness flickered through Lynx's eyes before he blinked them rapidly, opening them again, moving rapidly enough to dislodge the writing pad. "Son of a..."

He focused on Quinn, as the notepad clattered to the ground. "Change of plans."

Damn it. She hated it when that happened. With a resigned sigh, she crossed her arms and leveled him with a partial glare. "What is it now?"

"With chaotic remnants leaked in through the system, and the filtration system underperforming, not to mention the fact that I now realize my previous reset was... very conveniently timed." Lynx glanced at Harish who gave him an almost imperceptible nod. "It seems that we are missing a few very important, items."

Quinn just knew that we, meant her. "Spill."

"There are four more books you need to retrieve, and we need them as soon as possible." Lynx flashed her half a hopeful grin.

Quinn suppressed a groan. She knew it. At least this time she felt more confident about protecting herself.

51

DÉJÀ VU

THERE WERE SO MANY THOUGHTS THAT RAN THROUGH QUINN'S MIND AT the prospect of having to go and retrieve more books. But there was one thing she needed to know immediately. "When does this mean we need to leave?" she asked.

"Well, it's not as dire as it was the first time. This time you don't have to get me those three books within a seventy-two-hour period," Lynx said, flashing her a grin, as if that would somehow make the frantic scramble for the last three books feel any better.

She raised an eyebrow, digesting that piece of information. This should mean that she could head out far better prepared than they had been for the initial round. "Okay, give me a ballpark number. What are we looking at here? And why do I suddenly need to go get four new books that the Library didn't realize I needed before?"

"Well, you are the Librarian. You're kind of supposed to go get books." Lynx's smile grew bigger as he spoke. It was like he thought this was one big joke. Perhaps his little slumber had simply rejuvenated his mood too.

"No, technically, a librarian—if you're going on Earth's definition —stays in the library and people bring the books to her. That's how it works. I'm not a swashbuckling Indiana Jones. I'm a Librarian. People should bring the books back to me." She crossed her arms and leveled a glare at the manifestation. "I promise I'll even say 'thank you' when they return them."

Quinn paused and amended her last statement. "As long as they do so in the thirty-day grace period. Otherwise, I'm fining them."

"You seem very focused on the fines." Lynx raised an eyebrow.

Quinn felt a bit defensive. "Well, you haven't seen the state some of them came back in."

Lynx coughed away a laugh, then cleared his throat, and continued. "These books aren't like the ones you retrieved first. Their subject matters make them highly confidential codices. They're not just borrowable by anyone. In fact, they're from the restricted vault. It's a much more stringent process to remove them from the Library. They were borrowed for a very specific purpose." His tone was hesitant like he didn't want to tell her, but he knew he had to.

"And you *are* going to tell me what that is, right?" she asked, trying not to lose the temper that she was barely holding on to. It felt like now that Lynx was back, he had yet again taken over and was playing that whole game of keep-Quinn-in-the-dark.

You realize you can just ask, right? the Library spoke in her mind.

True, she'd always been able to ask. Even in her foster homes, she'd been able to ask. But that was never something Quinn had been good at. So this wasn't completely Lynx's fault. It was probably also a little on her total inability to confront people. She was determined to get better about that.

She took a deep breath and said, "I'm not walking into another Kajaro situation, right?" When Lynx shook his head, she continued. "What *am* I walking into?"

Lynx looked decidedly uncomfortable. He wavered very slightly, in and out of vision, before settling and propping himself up on top of the desk. "The books you're looking for are books about chaotic magic and how to control it."

"Didn't you say it can't be—" But that's all he let her get out as Lynx held up a hand to stop her tirade of questions.

"Magic is naturally chaotic. There are theories on handling it in its raw state, theories on filtering it, cleansing areas and people who have been affected by it." He gestured sweepingly with his hand. "All the possibilities and probabilities are endless."

"Okay, that sounds great," Quinn said, not meaning it in the slightest. "What does that mean?"

Lynx rolled his eyes. "I should have known you wouldn't settle for just my word."

"Good. Then we're on the same page. Fill me in. Explain it to me." She crossed her arms tighter. "I can wait, you know. I've been told I have a long time to live now."

He chuckled, even though he didn't appear to want to. "A while ago, about seven hundred years ago, the Dabilia—an amazing, close to primordial race—contacted me. Their homeworld was being overrun with chaotic energy, and while their magic was able to keep it at bay for a while, they'd spent a few millennia trying to fight it back, and it was slowly encroaching on their main city. They requested access to the restricted texts."

"There are restricted texts in this library?" Quinn asked, leaning forward slightly.

"Yes, there are. They're in a vault, and we rarely let them out. I wanted to call them forbidden but the Library insisted they're only restricted. They can only be accessed for specific circumstances, and for dire reasons," Lynx paused, a look of wistfulness spreading over his face. "In this case, it was a very dire reason. Saving a planet, saving a species, who can't live off that planet, is, to me, one of the paramount reasons that the Library even exists."

"When you say forbidden," Quinn interrupted, because she needed to wrap her head around the concept. Was the Library really gatekeeping? "What exactly do you mean?"

He shrugged and no one else spoke up, so after several seconds Lynx tried to explain further. "We don't restrict the vast majority of books. Not for any reason. Sometimes, if your fine was earned in the pursuit of narcissistic design, then your fine will reflect the gravity of your transgression... but generally, the Library lends everything to anyone."

"As long as it won't be directly used to harm the Library or like fuel genocidal tendencies?" Quinn asked.

"Precisely." Lynx nodded. "Except for these books. They are dangerous, insidious sometimes. If you let their magic get into your head, chaos has a way of pulling you to its side."

Quinn nodded, not liking the shivers that passed through her body at his words.

Lynx waited a moment and then continued. "We dug through all the books, researched the ones that could be applicable, and I allowed the Dabilia to borrow them. To continue the research on their own. I couldn't go with them. We couldn't spare any librarian assistants at the time. We didn't think we needed to. The Dabilia are exceptionally adept at all types of magic, but even though I was fully aware that their world was experiencing difficulties, the Library began running into its own problems shortly thereafter. We didn't have anything left to help them once the Librarian was gone."

He sighed, and the sound echoed through the foyer with a hint of melancholy. "Now that I've been able to scan the area correctly, and even though I'm not fully functional yet, it appears that the Dabilian homeworld is no longer fully in existence. It's no longer capable of sustaining their lifeforce and hasn't been for a few centuries now. It is mostly burnt out."

"Do you mean it exploded?" Quinn asked, horrified. Even though she'd never met these people in her life, she could feel the connection the Library had to them, to the magic, and to the books from the moment Lynx mentioned them. It wrenched at her soul in a way that she hadn't realized she could feel in conjunction with the Library.

"Exploded isn't the right word." He paused, thinking.

"Are they extinct now?" Quinn pushed the subject.

"Well, that's just it. Chaos leaches everything from everyone. It pulls your energy in, it makes you its own until it devours you from the inside out. Everything, and everyone." Lynx's voice sounded a little lost.

"Is that what it did to their homeworld?" Quinn asked, horrified.

"Yes, and that's putting it as nicely as I can," Lynx answered finally.

"Are the books gone?" Quinn was confused. "I don't understand what I'm supposed to retrieve."

"No," Lynx said. "These books are a different breed to the others of the Library. There shouldn't be any force that can damage them. Unless they were literally torn apart by chaos, which I doubt, they'll still be there. While I can't sense the books themselves, I can sense their protective casings. It's just a matter of braving a chaotic dead zone, to retrieve them."

Quinn took a deep breath, settling herself. She hadn't thought about the extent of things, she guessed. Hearing "chaotic magic is bad for you", versus "oh this world was torn apart by chaos"... those two things seemed on such opposite ends of the scale.

"Are you okay, Quinn?" Lynx asked, leaning in close to check. Perhaps he could also feel her emotions through her connection with the Library.

"It's a lot to take in, Lynx," she said, her voice small.

He studied her. "I would imagine so. Do you have questions? What can I answer?"

"You're saying chaos was already running rampant before the Library went away. It just made it worse when it did?" she asked, straight up.

"Precisely. It wasn't as bad back then. Not nearly so. With the filtration system running at peak capacity, it was difficult for chaos to break through the leyline thresholds. But chaotic magic is always there. There's no getting away from that. It is part of the universe, and that's exactly how the universe exists in the first place," Harish said, taking over the explanation in a very professor like manner. "Magic is chaos. Chaos is magic. In order to harness it as a living being, we have to filter it, because if we don't, it will consume us and tear us apart."

"What about the people who want chaotic magic to reign?" Quinn asked, getting everything straight in her head, "Those people, have they already been infected by chaotic magic?"

Harish sort of shook his head and shrugged, and Siliqua put her hand up as if to speak and thought better of it. It was Narilin who decided to speak instead, in her soothing voice.

"That is a simplification of the fact. You have to realize that chaos is here—even right now. It is an intrinsic part of the magical world, but it requires a level of understanding that most creatures are incapable of perceiving. For good reason. It will insinuate itself in you, like a parasite, and worm its way inside and through all of your systems, until it has become a part of you, and is already devouring you whole before you realize it." Narilin's crisp way of speaking made the harsh truth undeniable.

"Like rot from within," Quinn said. The Salosier shuddered at the thought. Quinn realized that rot and trees were probably not the best combination.

"That is a very apt description, Librarian," Narilin said with a small bow.

"I'll get to 'however else the rest of this works' later. I've got a basic understanding. Tell me what I need to do. I'm guessing we have to go and prepare, right?" She glanced around at them all. "At least I've got a couple of combat texts up my sleep, although a healing one wouldn't go astray. I'll be taking Malakai with me, I take it?"

Aradie hooted in her ear, as if offended that she wasn't Quinn's first thought. "Well, of course, I'm taking you."

"I'm not sure if you can take your owl or not, Quinn," Lynx said. "We'd have to make sure."

But he cut short when Aradie flew up into the air, hooting directly at him. To Quinn's ears it sounded like very angry punctuation, especially if the images that flowed through her head were anything to go by. There were flashes of history, of fights, of weapons and gunfire and magic fire. The bird flung thousands upon thousands of images every few seconds directly at Lynx. Quinn had to scrunch her eyes tight until Aradie landed softly on her shoulder and pushed her ruffled feathers behind her, with a definite aura of self-satisfaction.

"It seems Aradie will be absolutely fine to go with you, and it was remiss of me to think otherwise given her vast history with the Library," Lynx said. Even he sounded a little bit out of breath.

"Explain to me what she just did," Quinn said.

"Suffice it to say, Aradie is one of our oldest night owls and has made it a matter of her pride to keep you safe. With the amount of history she has with the Library, it was foolish of me to second guess her. She is fully up to the task and is far stronger than you might think," Lynx said.

"Oh, good," Quinn said, and absentmindedly reached behind Aradie's head and scratched her. The bird leaned into the touch and Quinn felt better already. "I'll take Malakai and Aradie with me and we'll go."

Eric chose that moment to fly up directly in front of her and cleared his throat. She hadn't noticed it before, but when he hovered, his wings let out a distinct low humming sound. It set her teeth on edge ever so slightly, more anticipatory and definitely the opposite of the soothing Firionas.

"What's up, Eric?" she asked the imp she'd grown oddly fond of.

"I would like to accompany you to the Dabilian planet," he said, his voice clipped and serious for once.

"You want to come to a chaotic dead zone?" She raised her eyebrow.

"I'm an imp. I can go anywhere. I can breathe any air. I can do anything." This time the pride leaked out of the words and she didn't doubt him for a second.

Quinn glanced over at Lynx and a message shot up in front of her, defining the imp and its disposition and its ability to survive literally any terrain.

Imp

Gates of Halschius

Number 7

Survivability: Eternal. Will not die. Even when you wish they would.

She covered her laugh with a cough at that last comment. The Library, always surprising her with definitions when she least expected it. "As long as you do as you're told."

Eric raised an eyebrow. "I'll do as I'm told, as long as you understand that I will be more expert than any of you there."

"Okay, we'll listen. Then I guess it'll be Malakai, Aradie, myself, and Eric," Quinn said, slightly mollified by the fact that she'd practically be leading an expedition, and definitely wouldn't be alone in what sounded like very scary, chaotic, torn-apart portion of space with a high likelihood of corpses lying everywhere.

Her mind was slightly overactive with the thought that there were probably going to be bodies floating in space. She felt like the Library chuckled.

That's nothing like what a chaotic dead zone world is like, Quinn. It's okay. It's not going to be that sort of scary.

It was like the Library thought it was making her feel better.

5 2

PREPARATIONS

QUINN'S FIRST STOP, AFTER THE NOT-VERY-REASSURING COMMENTS BY the Library, was the kitchen, where Cook was already preparing bags of provisions. She assumed Misha had observed the conversation in the lobby and simply informed Cook of what was needed. Malakai stood leaning against the door, his arms crossed and a definite scowl on his face.

"What's your problem?" Quinn asked as she settled in next to him, watching Cook work their magic.

"Chaotic dead zones are not somewhere I like to go. Frankly, they're not somewhere anyone wants to go." For just a moment he sounded like a pouting five-year-old.

Quinn fought back a nervous giggle. "Why not?"

"It reeks of my mother's domain, okay?" The look he shot her could have killed lesser beings.

She would have taken a step back if the wall hadn't been there. "Your home life is a lot more complicated than mine was, and I had some really crappy teen years."

He raised an eyebrow at her. For a moment, irritation and curiosity warred in his expression. "Well, maybe one day, when all we have to do is check in books and leverage fines, we can sit down and have a cup of tea and talk about how crappy our lives were."

"Ouch, Malakai. That was catty." She pushed away from the wall, oddly irritated by his mood. "Anyway, I believe we're here for some protective food?"

Cook glanced her way. "Yes, you require food that allows you to breathe while repelling chaotic dust. It cannot be permitted to enter your lungs. If it does so, the tar will build up, allowing it to infest your tissue and blood paths. Little can save you, once pure chaos has infected you."

Quinn gulped, involuntarily scanning herself to make sure that none of what Kajaro left behind might have done this.

Cook paused while they meted out several scoops of something decidedly black in appearance, eerily similar to a ball of poppyseeds in a Danish. Once those were done, Cook continued speaking. "These have a three-hour limit each. I have sixteen of them for each of you, although Aradie's are modified. Set timers, take them without fail. I advise you not to spend more than two days there." Cook upended them in bags that locked and sealed with a hiss, sucking all the air out of them like a vacuum.

Quinn nodded. "Eat one every three hours. Got it. Thank you." She added the last as an afterthought. She really enjoyed Cook's company; being polite was the least she could do.

Cook offered a smidgen of a smile, or at least, that's what the slightly upturned corners of their mouth indicated. "The next ones heal. It is of vital importance that you consume one should you become injured in a way that breaks your skin while in a chaotic dead space. These will allow for the wounds to stay fresh and not gather any chaotic dust. It will repel anything already on it, as long as it is taken within five minutes of being wounded. You must apply these healing salves quickly. Paramount importance."

"Got it." Quinn nodded, liking the prospects of this trip less and less with every single word Cook spoke.

"Energy and mana regeneration will work very similarly to what you are used to; however, every single one of these bites has a chaos-expelling component. Take these if your energy or mana feel sluggish. You cannot risk being tarnished with too much chaotic energy or it will impact you negatively."

Quinn stared at Cook. She had never heard them speak so much since they'd been created. "Thank you for all of this."

"Thank me once you have returned safely. I have used what stock was on hand and must now replenish my stores. I will be unable to make this same selection of foods for a while unless we can procure delivery of some more of these ingredients. Do I make myself clear?" They sounded oddly stern. Much like her fifth-grade teacher back on Earth.

"Understood," she said, gathering the food up. Malakai reluctantly assisted her.

Cook paused and turned to face her fully. "Return safely."

"That's the plan," she said, forcing a grin as she turned to leave. Armed with their bags, Quinn tried to fight down the nerves and made her way toward the storage room where Misha stood directing a couple of new golems who seemed to be very basic and clay.

Quinn frowned at the scene. "When were they ready?"

"Approximately twelve hours ago," Misha said.

"Well, I need to name them." Quinn moved over to them, looking them over, trying to get a feel of them through her connection with the Library.

Misha let out what sounded like a long-suffering sigh and flashed a golem smile at Quinn. "Fine, what would you like to name them?"

"They're storage golems, right? Not shelving." Quinn had an idea for the shelving golems and wanted to keep their name trend on point. So this was an important distinction for her.

"Storage, gathering, and recollection, yes." Misha confirmed.

"How about Hunter and Hank?" She wasn't sure what made her think of the latter, but Hunter felt appropriate for the position.

"Sure, let us call them..." But even as Misha spoke, the golems transformed ever so slightly, turning from claylike hulking brutes into one tall and gangly, and a slightly sturdier one who was a little bit shorter.

"Hey, Hunter and Hank." The golems simply waved, while organizing the storeroom, but their connection to Quinn through the Library flared briefly with life and a trace of gratitude. As if they'd somehow come home. "That'll do," Quinn said.

"It is quite remarkable," Misha commented before turning back to the Librarian.

"What is?" she asked.

"That they take on the name immediately, and identify as an individual as soon as it is assigned." Misha's moonlike eyes swirled briefly. It reminded Quinn of when Lynx was communicating with the system differently. Then their eyes went back to normal and they blinked. "Anyway. I have had clothes prepared for you. The Library has fabricated these with stock that we already had on hand. You will be required to wear treated leather garments. They will repel chaotic dust from settling on your skin and entering your system through your pores."

She glanced over Quinn's shoulder and amended her last statement. "For those of you that have pores anyway."

Eric let out a grunt, but didn't actually say anything. Quinn thought, knowing him, he showed admirable restraint.

"This material also prevents chaotic magic burns should you come into contact directly with a live stream of chaotic magic," the supervisory golem continued.

The more Misha and Cook went on about chaotic magic and its drawbacks, the more anxiety Quinn could feel welling up in her gut. Don't let it touch you. Don't breathe it in. Don't slip and fall into a vat of it. Talk about the makings of a super villain...

It'll be okay, the Library tried to soothe her. But right then, Quinn wasn't exactly up for the soothing. Still, there was more to listen to. Misha's tirade didn't seem to have an ending.

"You must keep the outfits on and sealed as much as possible. I have access to several magical excrement pockets. They will be programmed into the suits. Just if you really have to go, you'll be able to, okay?" Misha kept plowing straight on, while Quinn did a double take over these pockets that were mentioned. "There are two buttons you'll have to push in order to activate it. Clear so far?"

"Sure," Quinn said, wishing she really wasn't.

Misha nodded and pulled out what looked like large satchels. "These four bags here are specifically for the retrieved books. Once you acquire the books, each one must be placed in a bag and sealed. You must seal the bag so that it begins the cleansing process and avoids any chaotic leakage that the book has gathered over the last few centuries. Do you understand?"

Quinn understood, but at the same time, she was so overwhelmed, she didn't know why she was even contemplating this. "Yep, I get it," she said, wishing she didn't. Both Malakai and Eric took their packs.

"What about Aradie?" she asked.

"Aradie is stronger than any of you. She's impervious to chaotic magic," Misha said simply.

Eric harumphed. "Sure, she is. Her and all her soft feathers are super impervious to chaos." He rolled his eyes for effect.

Aradie, not to be outdone, let out a series of trilling hoots that frankly would have won any argument.

Eric scowled, and Quinn clapped her hands to divert attention.

"That's good to know," Quinn said, wondering again what that whole interaction earlier with Lynx had been about. She found herself wanting some downtime with her owl to get to know this mysterious magical little creature that somehow managed to keep both the manifestation of the Library and imps on their toes.

"And this." Misha pushed a book into Quinn's hands.

It was a plain brown leather binding with faded stamping on the cover. Strips of leather dangled down from where they'd bound the book closed. She looked up at Misha questioningly.

"You mentioned a healing book earlier. This is the best one I could find that you should be able to learn straight away and have some chance of activating on this journey, without having to practice for days before utilizing the methods inside." Misha's eyes swirled. Quinn was beginning to learn that they did that when excited. "Healing is a highly complex field."

She felt the leather of the book and how soft it was. Either worn by age, supreme quality, or perhaps a little of both. It emanated an aura of wholeness, of keeping things together. *Taliar's Guide to Self-Regeneration: How to Stave Off Death*

"Absorb it now, so it has time to settle before you head out," Misha commanded, and gestured to a small couch in the corner of the storehouse.

Quinn eyed it suspiciously, not having noticed before when she came in.

I'm a Library filled with magical tomes. Creating a couch isn't exactly what you'd call rocket science. Which, by the way, neither is rocket science.

The Library's voice drifted through her head with an odd hint of amusement at the end of the sentence. Quinn could feel the small communication pebble and how it got warm in the pocket of her pants. She liked the deeper connection. Even if some tidbits of information in her head still felt a little odd.

Sitting herself comfortably, Quinn did the usual routine. Open the book, palms face down on the pages, and breathe it in.

Magic swirled around her in a golden dusting. Almost like glitter, it reflected the light in myriad colors and swirls. It guided her through her entire body, as if inspecting her like a dexa scan. Only this was much faster. It felt as if someone was running a feather duster throughout her entire body. Lightly enough that it didn't quite tickle, only just started the process.

Taliar's Guidance - learned

Taliar's Regeneration - learned

Taliar's Resistances - learned

Basics acquired

Quinn blinked her eyes open. None of the other books had done that before. She'd simply gained all of the knowledge without any acknowledgment.

You can find the spells and abilities you have access to. The Library sounded sort of hurt.

But this is different than those times, Quinn ventured

Healing is a part of formation and creation magic. It has its own rules.

Stretching, Quinn picked herself up from the couch feeling rejuvenated. Like she'd slept for weeks. "Wow, that is amazing stuff."

Misha raised an eyebrow at her, or at least that's what the expression resembled most. "Do you feel more prepared than the previous trips to recover books?"

Quinn cracked her neck from side to side and grinned as she formed a small ice ball in the palm of her hand. "Most definitely. Thanks, Misha," she said, before leading the rest of her team out of the storage room.

Now all they needed were the names of the books and some weapons.

No weapons for you, the Library said. *Hand-eye coordination is not your best feature. Use magic firepower. You've become adept enough at it, and you're not fighting bookworms this time.*

Quinn took a deep breath and went to get changed, before heading back to the check-in desk. When the Library was right, it was right. She stopped and looked at the gathering that still inhabited the lobby. "Well, tell me what books I'm looking for."

"*Laws of Chaos, Upside Down; Chaos Theory, Myth and Legend; Reality Combined, Chaos Fever Dream; Mastering Your Reality Through Chaos.*" Lynx rattled off the list while completely ignoring the glare Milaro was shooting his way.

"Okay," Quinn said, wondering what the new beef between them was. Their friendship might have spanned millennia, but they also disagreed a lot. "Sounds easy enough, right, Malakai?"

"Yeah, really easy." The elf prince scowled, and it only made her really want to understand where he'd come from all the more.

"Remember," Milaro said, crossing his arms and fixing her with a serious look. "Your direct connection to the Library will likely be sporadic. Jump back when you can, but keep a close eye on the timers for your protective food."

"Got it." Quinn nodded emphatically. She wasn't about to try and stay in an inhospitable environment for too long.

"Do *not* let the books come into contact with your skin before you've had the dimensional cleansing pockets purify them. Keep your gloves on." Siliqua's tone sounded urgent, and her smile seemed forced. "You can do this."

Even if the wood elf didn't sound as if she believed a word of it, Quinn still appreciated the effort. "We can do this."

"What she said," Eric grumbled. Malakai glared, and Aradie hooted.

And without giving it a second thought, so that she didn't run up to her quarters and hide, Quinn willed the Library to let open at the Dabilian homeworld.

The double doors swung outward, revealing an inky darkness beyond, punctuated by the odd flash of reddish light. Taking a deep breath and biting into her breathing food, Quinn stepped over the threshold and into the darkness.

53

INTO THE DIM

As Quinn stepped over the threshold, her foot hit the ground. Even beneath the thick boots, she could feel a solid, yet spongy sensation as her foot sank against the surface. It had a gritty feel like fine gravel, yet visually, at least, it appeared to be smooth.

The darkness around them was inky, punctuated by flashes of red and white, with hints of purple and blue lighting up the sky. She reached into her pocket and pulled out a torch, or more accurately, a glow stick. It cast a dull golden light around her, extending about four feet in every direction. She could sense Malakai off to her left, Eric hovering behind her right shoulder, and Aradie perched where she always perched, on Quinn's left shoulder.

Then, the Library doors swung shut behind them with a resounding whoosh, and she could feel absolutely nothing.

Light panic set in for a moment, and she had to remind herself to breathe deeply, not fast, and to not let anything distract her from the path. Aradie shot calming visions into her head: an ocean at the shore, the moon at night, trees bowing gently in the breeze.

Quinn breathed in deeply and spoke. "Okay, let's head towards the lights, I guess."

Malakai didn't respond. He'd been grumpy for days now, and she wasn't sure how to approach him about it. She turned her attention to the imp instead. "Any contribution, Eric?"

"None. I have excellent vision. I will lead the way. I will make sure nothing attacks you. Or at least, if it's dangerous, I'll warn you." She could hear the grin in his words.

"Why wouldn't you..." She paused. He was an imp. "I get it," she said instead. He flashed her what she thought was an impish grin in the low light and pulled in front of her to lead the way.

They moved slowly, testing the ground as they walked. Luckily, Eric wasn't so mischievous that he forgot the human and the elf with him needed to walk on the surface. They didn't have hover packs, although, next time, she was going to find a book on hovering that wasn't just for defensive maneuvers. She didn't know the terrain well enough here to hover over it anyway.

"Do you see anything up ahead?" she asked Eric and he shook his head. Her eyes were acclimating to the darkness and had started picking out rock formations on either side of them. The light in her hand illuminated the rocks very slightly, and she realized it looked sort of like that volcanic rock when it had dried. Igneous rock, perhaps? It was very unusual. A question occurred to her suddenly. "Does chaotic magic burn?"

Eric, ahead of her, shrugged. "It depends on what the chaotic magic is being used for."

Malakai laughed. "Chaotic magic is pure destruction, and it can take any form that will destroy everything around it." He sounded bitter. His words were clipped. Quinn really wanted to know what the hell his problem was. They were, however, limited on time here. They might technically have three days... but she didn't want to be in this cloying air for any longer than she absolutely had to.

"It's only chaotic if it runs out of energy and needs to consume energy to reconstitute its ability to create," Eric muttered absently. "Of course, it's been eons since it had the energy to create."

"Like I said," Malakai snapped this time. "It's pure destruction."

Quinn knew the air here was thicker, even if she hadn't been told. It felt dense as it pushed around her, and each step she took required a lot more effort than she would have had to exert on Earth, or on either of the other planets she had previously visited.

As they moved farther into the darkness, Quinn reached for the Library on a whim, but she couldn't feel it properly, even with the stone pressing against her leg. It felt as though she was trying to reach it through a bowl of pudding. The sensation was thick, viscous, and difficult to penetrate. She stopped trying, just as she felt a headache sparking, and hoped that when they had to return the connection would work properly. She didn't like leaving so much to chance.

They continued, cautiously stepping over the rough terrain. It rose and lowered in ever-slight inclines and declines. Rocks around her looked more and more as though a volcano had exploded here a long time ago and left abstract formations in its wake.

"How does chaotic magic attack?" she asked.

This time, Malakai sighed and Eric snorted. "I think it's better that Mr. Elf tells you about that," he said in a sing-songy way that sounded almost mocking. She caught the scowl Malakai threw at the imp.

This should be good, she thought.

"Chaotic magic doesn't attack. It's insidious. It will gather, expand, and devour once you can't fight it off anymore," Malakai explained as if it all made sense.

"How do you fight it off?" Quinn asked, not dwelling on the fact that he looked like he was going to throw up. Maybe the golden light in her hand made his skin pallor different than it truly was.

Malakai didn't speak for several seconds, so long that Quinn actually thought he had decided to stop speaking to her. They slowly moved a dozen more feet, and the silence grew uncomfortable. Just as she was about to ask a question again, he finally spoke.

"You don't really fight chaos magic off. You build up immunity to it and you purify it. You turn it from something that is dangerous and deadly to something that can be used for good, and I guess bad as well, depending on the individual. But you turn it into a force that isn't going to try and devour the person from the inside out." Malakai's voice was barely above a whisper.

Quinn blinked. She didn't have any spells that could purify chaotic magic. Yet. That didn't seem like a very good thing to her. Why hadn't anyone thought to give her a skill like that? And why was the Library not able to answer her out here, even though she knew why the Library couldn't intervene in her thoughts and answer her questions right now? She didn't like being cut off from it. She'd been so closely associated with it for such a short, yet long, time that she'd sincerely grown used to having it there, popping into her thoughts and answering all of the queries and questions that she had about this new world.

"Don't panic, Quinn," Malakai said, suddenly standing perhaps a little too close to her.

She took a step back. "Don't crowd me."

"Oh, sorry," he said, stepping back himself and glancing away. "You just didn't answer me when I spoke to you."

"I get it," she said. She had got a little caught up in her own thoughts and spaced out somewhat. "Anyway, I'm fine."

"No, you were very obviously stressing about the fact that you don't have any abilities that can purify chaotic energy. That's what the suits are for. That's why we're basically wearing chaotic armor, so that it can't, in any way, impact you and affect you. That is why we have to make sure that we take these bites every three hours, that we attend to any cut or any wound immediately. We just have to be careful and we can do this," he said. His tone was very reassuring and as Quinn watched him, she realized that perhaps he had lost his extremely bad mood from the last few days. At least she hoped he had.

There was an impatient snort from Eric's direction. "Enough dilly-dallying, you two. Come on, this imp hasn't got all day."

"No, you've got almost two days," Quinn said, unable to help herself. She let out a small chuckle at her own joke.

"Stop being so pedantic," the imp said, but he definitely cracked a smile.

With a much better mood, despite the extremely gloomy and dark area they were traversing, the group continued on. They moved through the area slowly and cautiously. Quinn half expected writhing monsters to jump them from behind every igneous rock formation.

There was nothing. No sounds but their footfalls, soft as they were, and the whirr of Eric's wings as he kept himself in place, slowly scouting the territory in front of them.

The golden light did little to expand their visual circle, and every piece of rock reminded her of flowing lava. From the atmosphere, Quinn felt like there should be so much more. Why weren't there evil-looking monsters jumping out to attack them?

"This would not make for a very interesting video game." She sighed softly to herself. She probably shouldn't be wishing for a very interesting video game, considering the fact that she would have to be one of those who fought the monsters off, and suddenly she liked the peace and quiet of walking through the murky stillness.

"Up ahead," Eric said, suddenly. "Do you see those shadows up ahead?"

Quinn paused, looking beyond the Imp, and there, in the light that was sparking reds, whites, and blues, with the slight yellow glow of her stick for back up, she could see them.

Buildings.

The silhouette of dilapidated, long-defunct buildings.

"I guess that's the best place to head," she said. The three of them picked up their pace slightly, now that there was some light emanating from the area where the building silhouette stood. It reached toward them. She could make out shadows now, playing on the igneous rock. The rock formations all around them cast long shadows that moved in strange ways as they passed them. It reminded her of creatures from nightmares.

She still couldn't hear anything except for their footfalls, nothing around them but silence and darkness. The flashing lights would remind her of fireworks, if they weren't so ominous in the way they lingered and flickered out.

Quinn pushed down on her nerves. She shouldn't be afraid of the dark, even if she was walking across a desolate planet that had been ravaged by the chaos of magic and wiped, apparently, every other living thing from the face of it.

"What's there to be nervous about?" She breathed out the words.

Malakai nudged her shoulder, and she felt a little better. Aradie hooted low and soft and showed her pictures and images of what the city had once looked like, bright and beautiful. Parts of it reminded her a little bit of the Mesa Verde in Arizona and Colorado, where the houses had been built into cliff faces, except somehow more majestic. And then there were beautiful sandstone buildings and wonderful arches. It didn't look anything like what she could see in front of her.

Well, maybe it did. Maybe now it just looked like somebody had put a bomb in it and exploded it and all that was left were some structural elements that had been reinforced by igneous rock. Yeah, that's what it looked like.

About twenty feet from the closest building, they stopped.

"This seems too easy," Eric said very slowly as he scanned around. "I'm going to go and scout. I will return to you. Nothing will befall me. I promise I'm not going to give anything the satisfaction." And he fluttered off before Quinn could say anything.

"Just you and me, kid," Malakai said in a very deep voice that did not suit him.

"Don't do that again," she said.

"Yeah." He coughed, clearing his throat. "That was not a good choice."

They moved toward the building and entered through what must have been a doorway. The Library stone pulsed very faintly against her. Doorways it was, then. There were remnants of the buildings all around them.

"All this happened in under five hundred years?" Quinn could have sworn there were better ruins in Rome.

"Yeah." Malakai's tone was cautious as he navigated the room. "You don't understand. Once chaos hits, everything's gone."

"Oh, I'm beginning to understand," she said, not liking that she did.

The first room they stepped into was probably a living room in whatever sort of dwelling this had been, maybe a house or a lower-floor apartment. There were remnants of what might have been a chair and a box. Maybe some balls on the floor. The glow of the lights outside and in lit everything up in such a surreal manner. It was like the whole area had been frozen in time.

Just beyond the chair stood a body. It looked like a statue at first, like maybe Medusa had come and paid a visit and turned a person into stone. Somehow it stood there with a hand reached out toward something on the ground that was no longer there. It's face held a shocked expression, the mouth open in an O, like a stolen moment in time where they'd hesitated and were now transformed into that stony shock for eternity.

She examined the statue closely. "Is this?"

"Yep, that is a Dabilian." Malakai didn't even need her to finish her question.

Quinn looked at frozen figure. They reminded her of a large scarab, except they had little legs and four little arms to either side. Their heads were just a tiny bit more humanoid and they stood upright. "Wow, they look fascinating."

"Fascinating is a great word for them. They are no more." Malakai flashed her a sad smile.

Quinn sighed as she looked around the desolate room. "Yeah, I got that much."

They kept looking around, walking through that first room to a second where the remnants of what must have been a baby's crib sat encased in the rock like a stone statue all by itself again. The table had broken and sat unevenly on the floor, leaning against a stone chair. It almost looked like somewhere she could have lived. Any of them could have lived. The air felt thick. She checked her timer.

Still thirty minutes to go.

She had to make sure she didn't breathe in any of this. If all of this was anything to go by, there was no way she was letting chaotic magic consume her.

Slowly, her skin began to crawl, like something was worming its way inside her. She kept looking over her right shoulder so as not to disturb Aradie. The bird hooted once softly and launched herself into the air, sweeping around, finally coming to stand very lightly on the edge of what had been the crib. She hooted low and long and Quinn shivered at the sound.

It was more like a warning, like something was coming.

She turned, listening. There was a noise, a skittering, something soft and low and stealthy. She could almost feel vibrations through the floor through to her feet, but they just didn't quite reach. She looked up at Malakai, whose face showed just as much confusion as she felt. Not to mention that hint of fear in the tightening of his eyes.

"Do you feel that?" she whispered.

He nodded, holding a finger up to his lips to silence any further conversation. They stood, unmoving, listening intently.

With a low pop right next to them, Eric was there, his voice low, urgent, commanding, "Get outside. Move, we're about to be attacked."

54

OBSTACLES

QUINN DIDN'T NEED TO BE TOLD TWICE TO MOVE. BEING INSIDE A building, even one as open to the elements as this one, felt too restrictive if they needed to maneuver.

They wasted no time exiting the room they'd entered, and running past the spot where Eric had initially left them. Aradie flew overhead, her wings spread out as she soared through the sky, a wide beacon of hope.

"What can we expect?" Quinn asked, trying to get her nerves under control. Thinking about battling monsters had probably caused the monsters to—no, even Quinn knew that was nonsense. She wasn't manifesting thoughts out here.

"Centipedes," Eric said.

Quinn squinted at him. "What? We're running from little centipedes? We can just step on them."

"No, Quinn. These can step on you with *one* of their feet." Eric's tone held no sign of mocking her.

She gulped and could practically feel the color draining from her face. "Oh no. Are they like the bookworms?"

"These are far worse than the bookworms," Eric said. "These are chaotic-fueled centipede-type creatures. I believe that's what you'd call them in your world. They have a much more complex name here."

"Doesn't everything," she muttered under her breath. Quinn attempted to scan the area. She tried to pull up her HUD, and while it came into view, it couldn't seem to focus on anything. She shuddered.

"Are you telling me we don't have access to our display here either?" She hadn't even thought about that. She thought the system spread everywhere.

"You should have some access. It's just not the most reliable when chaotic energy is this thick. You have to remember your skills yourself and use them. That's why I drill them into you," Malakai said.

"Okay." Quinn refused to get upset. Instead, she used the mental training she'd absorbed to calm herself. Compartmentalization for the win. They just needed to get this fight done. She had to be in control.

"I'm ready," she said, and determination practically flooded her mind. When they got back to the Library, she wanted to devour as many mental fortitude books as possible

"Pop one of the food balls first," Malakai said, just in time. She'd barely shoved it in her mouth and bit down, extending the timer to three hours again from seventeen minutes when the first centipede burst through the igneous rock about two meters to her right, causing the ground to shudder convulsively and make her stumble.

Quinn almost went down and only managed to save herself by crouching. The creature reared up, little legs dangling from each side of it as it towered above her, probably about ten feet. She dropped her light stick and it lay on the ground, casting ominous shadows over the creature as it flailed in the air.

It had pincers up where its little head would be, and when she said *little*, she meant the body was approximately two feet wide and its tail was still stuck in the ground. She rolled back defensively, activated her hover dodge, and pushed herself away, just in time to avoid the face as it came crashing down toward her.

The click of the pincers rang in her head like bells.

She breathed deeply, trying to catch her breath after the exertion, and pushed out ice, aiming it with her hand. She barely scratched the side of the creature as it twisted away from her. Malakai and Eric were unable to come to her assistance. They were dealing with their own monsters.

Just as Quinn readied another ice blast, holding a hovering escape in her mind, Aradie swooped down toward her assailant, letting out a screech that would have deafened Quinn if it had been aimed at her. The centipede rose up, this time thrashing, all of its legs aimed towards Aradie and that's when Quinn realized it was actually casting something at the bird.

Tiny tendrils of red laser light shot towards Aradie, who expertly maneuvered around them in the sky. Her sleek dark form darted and rolled to the sides, sometimes only visible by the sparks of color in her feathers illuminated by the dim light. She hovered briefly, shooting another sonic burst down at the creature. Quinn decided not to stand there gaping at her bird's capabilities, and shot a gust of wind to unsettle it followed by three icicles in quick succession.

She aimed at the segments of its body, three different ones, all the way down. Two of the icicles even appeared to stick in the joints. Finally, the creature squealed loud enough and pulled itself completely out of the hole in the ground. It must have been at least twenty feet long in total. Its body moved in segmented ways, adjusting and rushing over the rocks.

Quinn wished the light around her was a bit brighter, but didn't trust herself to use her light spell that, she realized now, she'd never truly practiced. She dodged carefully around, focused only on the creature's movements, timing her own avoidance with its movements like a dance of cat and mouse.

She definitely didn't like being the mouse.

Behind her, she could hear Malakai's exertions as he and Eric fought the other one. She didn't dare look back, but she could smell burning. Eric's power was fire and brimstone. She guessed the centipede they were fighting was learning a lot about how to be cooked.

Cracking a small smile to keep herself mostly grounded, the creature turned suddenly straight towards her, completely deviating from its previous attack pattern. It dove almost on top of her in the blink of an eye. She pushed herself to the side in the nick of time, but even so, felt the razor-like sharpness of one of those tiny legs impact through her leather garments. It might only have been her left calf, but it stung so badly she thought she'd been stung by a million wasps all at once.

Quinn screamed out in pain and reached forward with her gloved hand, ripping the leg off the creature and out of her wound before rolling away in a desperate plea of not getting skewered again. She knew she needed to hurry up and kill this thing, so she could treat the wound before chaos got into her system. Logic helped her, the clarity of mind from books that she'd absorbed the energy explanations from, all allowed her to separate her mind from the rising panic inside her at the poison that just entered her system.

She stood up, leveraging herself to hover over another tail swipe that attempted to get her. That's what she hadn't been looking out for, the tail. "Damn it, rookie," she said to herself, lashing out with icicle after icicle. She expended them into each segment of the creature's body. She could feel the mana and energy as they left her own body and knew that while not infinite, she had a fair few shots in the tank and wasn't about to run out.

Not in this fight, anyway. She would definitely make it.

Aradie's screeches grew frantic. She attacked left and right, honing in on the head, exploding several of the legs off with a sonic blast. Quinn also began working on the legs, shoving ice at the creature, freezing it. Suddenly, she heard a massive crash behind her and a groan. She couldn't turn to look, but the next thing she knew, where she had frozen the creature, there was now an explosion of heat. The two temperatures collided so badly that the centipede began to lose whole chunks of its joints that she had previously frozen when Eric attacked it with the pure heat of his hellfire.

"Sorry to keep you waiting. I guess you were almost a centipede lunch just now," Eric said, a hint of humor in his voice.

"Don't try to wisecrack. You're not good at it," she retorted, flinging more ice at the centipede. Eric matched her strike for strike, hitting the same spots with his hellfire that she froze. The creature squealed, rising up again, curling in on itself before moving so fast Quinn's eyes could barely follow it to try and get away from them. With its partner dead, it had obviously decided that these people were not the easy lunch it originally thought they'd be.

She breathed and summoned a massive ice block directly in its path. But because it had moved so fast, it ended up freezing the entire middle section of the creature inside of the ice block. Several legs were severed as the momentum it had impacted the sudden stop and she could hear it stretching to such an extent that flesh ripped, just before an agonized squeal began.

She stumbled to the ground as both Aradie and Eric finished the creature off. Malakai stumbled to her side. He looked pale despite his usually darker skin. He flashed her a very weak smile.

"We did it. Encountered a centipede dolificus or whatever you were calling them," he said, slightly out of breath.

She raised an eyebrow. "Really, that's their name?"

He grinned at her. "No, and I can't remember it off the top of my head. I was just trying to make you laugh."

She glared at him a moment before shaking her head. "Yeah, I need to put something on this," she said, reaching for the salve from her backpack. She grabbed a fingerful of it, immediately pushing it into the rip that had formed in her armor from where the centipede leg cut her, and made sure to spread it all around the wound and the skin inside. The stinging and pain began to recede.

"God, I hope I made it in time," she said.

"You did. The fight seemed a lot longer than it was." Malakai ate something from his pack.

"Yeah, it's the way, isn't it?" she said, still rubbing the salve in, making sure that any trace of the chaos was wiped out of her system. It began to ooze through the cut and she ripped the leather armor a little more to make sure that she didn't leave that lying against her skin. After doctoring up the wound, she noticed that Malakai had been doing the same to his hand. "What happened to you?"

"Yeah, I wasn't paying enough attention when it first came out. I'm fine," he said.

She raised an eyebrow but didn't comment any further.

"Okay," she said, looking at the healing salve. The skin had already knitted back together, and it expelled a nasty black sludge. It reminded her of something—the sludge that had been on the cover of those tomes that were in Kajaro's inventory. Wow, he hadn't just been a proponent of allowing chaotic magic free rein; he had literally been partaking of it. She locked that thought away to address once they got back to the Library.

Right now, they had more urgent things to attend to. She slapped some tape over the rip to seal it up and keep chaotic dust out, and she was good to go. "Okay, I'm good. Eric, wounds?"

"I'm impervious," he said, flashing her a grin. "Don't worry. I'll keep you safe."

She gave him a curt nod, wondering where she could get a bit of that imperviousness.

He took that as a sign to continue speaking. "It was good team-work, really was. Ice works well with my hellfire. You are all right. I think I'll keep you around," he said, flashing a little grin, showing a tiny hint of fang.

Quinn decided she really liked the little imp.

Aradie was still soaring. She was barely a blip in the distance before she began coming back. She sent safe pictures to Quinn as if saying, *It's okay. I've made sure that there's nothing else that's going to attack you while we do what we came here to do.*

Quinn heaved a big sigh of relief, but she wasn't stupid enough to think that this was the last possible fight they'd have while here.

This time, they moved as one. Eric, Malakai, and Quinn moved in triangular formation as they made their way back into the city. Even twenty feet outside of it felt so different, so devoid of anything. Once they crossed the threshold of the burnt-out building, however, an underlying melancholy seemed to pervade the air. It was as if remnants of a life that had been cut short when chaos interceded were frozen in time.

The sight genuinely made Quinn's heart ache.

She steeled herself, focusing instead on finding the books.

"Can you feel them?" Malakai asked.

She shook her head.

"Seriously, just close your eyes. We're here to watch out for you. Aradie's still scouting. Just try and sense them." He used that soothing version of his tone. "Your connection to the Library might be faint, but those books aren't separated from you by solar systems. Focus."

Quinn frowned, reached into her pocket, and pulled out the pebble. She shoved it into her glove to give herself permanent contact to it. Now, just behind her eyes, she could feel the Library's presence. "Wow, that stone really helps," she murmured. Her sense of relief surprised her. Just being able to feel it closer again, made her feel safer.

Suddenly, she opened her eyes and pointed off to the left, where several buildings were more or less intact, certainly more so than the very open one they were currently in. They made their way over, jumping over remnants of furniture and what looked like a horse cart, although Quinn knew it must have been a hover vehicle or something similar at some stage. There didn't seem to be somewhere to harness a horse. She got the feeling they hadn't ridden horses on this world.

They entered what looked like an old warehouse. The windows were blown out, and it was just like everything else—frozen in time. Just like Pompeii had been, so many thousands of years ago. She could feel the pulsing of the book, as if it was telling her that it was there and needed to be retrieved.

They pushed through the rooms until they came to what must have been an office. Crumbling desks and something that might have been an office chair, as well as entombed cabinets and shelving decorated the room. Quinn found what looked like a safe and groaned. "Does anybody know how to crack a safe?" she asked.

Eric smirked at her, flew down until he was actually touching the ground, and then walked right up to it. The safe was just as tall as him. She thought maybe he was going to use a brimstone to burn through it or something, but instead, he took hold of the handle, pushed it down, and yanked the door open.

"Nothing is holding this together anymore," he said. "Like we said, everything chaos touches rots—and that includes internal door mech-anisms unless it's got magic protections against such things."

She could tell he was trying not to smirk or be too sarcastic toward her. He was failing quite abysmally.

Quinn opened the safe, and Eric stumbled back. She could feel the power emanating from the book, even from where she stood. That's when she remembered that imps had been freed by the Library from their chaotic origins. It made Eric's accompanying them on this little mission so much braver than she'd realized.

She reached in and grabbed the book.

55

GATHERING

The book felt surprisingly light in Quinn's gloved hand. Even as she touched it, she could sense there was something about it that was drawn to her—an eagerness, a feeling akin to coming home. The power emanating off it didn't feel threatening, or particularly chaotic to her, but she wasn't about to chance anything.

She closed her eyes and held it in both hands, oblivious to what anybody else was trying to say to her. It was almost as if the book was trying to speak, as if it wanted to be kept safe, as if it needed her to—

Oh! It needed her to put it in the bag.

Opening her eyes, she grabbed one of the satchels, shoved the book inside, and sealed it shut. With the last whisper of air sealed out of it, she felt as though the book actually sighed with relief.

"Well," she said, "I guess that's *Chaos Theory: Myth and Legend*, all nice and locked up." She made her voice sound a lot brighter than she felt. Nothing about this place made her feel good, and she knew without a shadow of a doubt, as she clutched the petrified pebble given to her by the core in her hand, that retrieving the next few books was probably going to be a lot more difficult.

However, twenty minutes later, standing a good half mile or so further into what had once been the city of Dabilia, she stood in front of a desk. In the desk's drawer was the next book: *Reality Combined: Chaos Fever Dream*. She looked at it and couldn't help the overwhelming sense of uneasiness stemming not only from the simplicity of this retrieval, but also from the overall atmosphere. "This seems too easy."

"Don't say that, Quinn. I thought you learned that lesson with Lynx back at the Library," Malakai said.

She raised an eyebrow at him. "You're very superstitious."

"I'm an elf. We're all very superstitious," he said, as if it was a well-known fact.

"Oh, you're back in the bad mood again." She leveled a stare at him.

"I wasn't in a bad…" Malakai paused and his shoulders sagged a little. "Yeah, you know, you're right. I am. I'm back in the bad mood, but I will try to get back in a better one, okay?"

Quinn grinned at him. "Yep, perfectly okay."

She placed her gloved hand on the book ,and this one also felt like it was trying to whisper to her again. The power that pulsed from it felt a shade different to the previous one. She wondered if the gloves blocked the words out or if it was all in her mind. Was there some sort of chaos in the book now, making it more than just a book about chaos? Is that why it allowed them to learn how to manage and filtrate the chaos?

Quinn sighed. She was probably never going to know. She pulled out a second satchel so she could lock this one away too. "That leaves just two more," she muttered.

She still couldn't shake the feeling that this was way too easy. But maybe this was really all it was—a dead world with a few invertebrate remnants of insects and creatures that had started to flourish while the world stayed frozen in its stony time lock. She shrugged, grabbed the satchel, pushed the book inside, sealed it shut, and felt yet another sigh of relief.

The physical sensation of a sigh coming from a satchel was actually very disconcerting. The books were sighing, or she was imagining that the books were sighing…

Either way she wasn't sure if that was a good sign.

Eric raised his head from where he'd been studying one of the other desks in the room. "Did you hear that?" he asked.

Quinn paused, having heard nothing before he spoke, and listened. Unable to hear anything else, she shrugged. "I can't hear anything. There's no skittering. There are no vibrations. There's no sound. Oh, have the lights stopped?" she asked, looking around, not seeing any of the white, red, blue, and occasionally purple flashes of light they had grown really accustomed to.

Malakai frowned. "Now that you mention it…"

She shivered. It wasn't that she was cold. It was that this couldn't bode well. "Okay, we only have two left to get. Let's not waste time." She wanted to get out of here five minutes ago. She popped another ball into her mouth.

Aradie hooted, coming in to land quite roughly on her left shoulder this time.

Quinn grimaced as she had to brace herself against the weight distribution and then reached up to scratch the back of the owl's neck. "What? What's wrong?"

Images flashed as Aradie hooted very softly. There were images of buildings nearby, of what looked like a completely imploded portion of the settlement, and beyond that, another room with another desk.

"Is that where the next one is?" Quinn asked her familiar. It was good that the bird was so attuned to the Library signature, since Quinn was still having some difficulty with it herself. While she could tell what general direction something was in, her owl had an easier job of locating the precise area before they got there.

Aradie hooted, but in a way that seemed more like a question than an affirmation.

"Well, guess we're going to get it." They made their way over across the spongy type of ground, making sure that nothing skittered after them.

They had to circumvent holes in the road, test ahead to make sure the ground was stable, and circle around a few of those strange collapsed vehicles. After a short while they came to a warehouse almost identical to the first with another desk in the main office section where the book lay.

Quinn took a deep breath, reached out and pulled the drawer open immediately jumping back just in case.

Nothing happened.

She frowned. "Oh, well, I guess there's just another book in another drawer." But even as she spoke, she felt a weird sense of unease.

It prickled at her skin like someone had just pulled masking tape off.

First of all, before picking it up this time, she looked at it long and hard. She couldn't see any wires attached, she couldn't see any hairs that might trigger a trap, nothing. She reached in, grabbed the book, clutched it to her chest and closed her eyes.

Nothing happened.

"Were you expecting something to happen?" Malakai asked.

"Well, yes. Weren't you?" She didn't repeat again that she found this far too easy, because, well, that was beside the point. But she *really* did. She glanced at the cover, noted that the book pulsed in the same way that the other two had, that sort of welcoming, luring, interested, and yet "put me away so I can become myself again" sort of vibe that she'd had from the other two.

She shrugged. "*Mastering Your Reality Through Chaos*," she said. "I guess this is the next one."

Quinn pulled out the appropriate bag, shoved it in, sealed it shut, felt the sigh that ran all the way through her and heaved a sigh of relief herself.

"I guess... I guess we've only got one more left to go," she said hesitantly.

"There, there, princess," the little imp said. "Don't you worry your pretty little head about it. We'll get that fourth book, get right out of here, back to your Library."

The thing was, she'd spent enough hours now with Eric, as they were on their fifth air filtration food, that she knew the imp was using bravado right now. He was just as nervous as she was about where the next one would take them. Not that she could blame him, but it was definitely an interesting turn of events that all of them, approaching the retrieval of the fourth and final book, all felt that this was just somehow far too easy to do.

"I mean, Cook prepared enough food for a couple days, and we're sure there is no temporal displacement right?" she asked Malakai.

He shook his head. "No, not here, not in this world. It's just the same as any chaotic dimension, which is exactly the same as the chaotic filtration system. And just so you know, having misaligned temporal disturbances is actually a very rare thing. There are only, I don't know, like..." He paused in thought.

Quinn laughed. "Like what, a handful of worlds?"

"I guess that depends on your hands... but no, more like maybe a hundred fifty that are different time-displacement scenarios." Malakai made the statement sound so matter-of-fact.

"Only?" she said, almost choking on the word.

"You did absorb that book I gave you, right?" Malakai paused and made an exasperated noise with his tongue. "Oh, no, I need to give you the other one. Don't worry, when we get back, I have another book for you to absorb. Probably should have given it to you before we started training, I guess. I'm just not used to being around people who don't already know all this stuff."

"Yeah, I get it," Quinn said. And then she frowned. She clutched the stone in her hand, and tried to locate the next book. "Huh, I'm not getting an immediate reading or even direction for the remaining one right now," she said.

Aradie hooted and pushed off from her shoulder. Quinn had to adjust her stance as the familiar took off. She was not yet used to how heavy the bird was. They had to find *Laws of Chaos: Upside Down*. It had to be somewhere here.

She positioned herself outside the other side of the warehouse this time, in the middle of what seemed to be an abandoned street. There were those odd cart-looking vehicles everywhere. "I mean, they looked like a cart, but they don't have horse bones in front of them.

They probably also don't have horse bones because they were massive, humanoid scarabs to begin with," Quinn muttered to herself.

She faced north, south, east, and west by her best estimates but couldn't get any flash of where the book might be. "It can't be destroyed, right? Do you think maybe this one got destroyed?" she asked.

Malakai shrugged uncomfortably. He shrugged his shoulders like he was flexing them and looked around. "I'm not sure, but…"

Aradie dove down toward them, landing on the top of one of the solidified carts. She hooted.

"Oh, off in that direction?" Quinn asked with a frown. She looked up at where Aradie's images showed directed her, toward one of the larger buildings several blocks over. From what she could see, it sort of looked like the rafters of a steeple might. From a place of worship.

She wasn't sure how long it'd take for them to get there, but there was no time like the present. "Okay, then," she said, "I guess we're headed there." She checked her timer, twelve more minutes. She popped her sixth ball wondering how they'd already managed to meander around for over half a day.

~~

Quinn did not like tromping through the remnants of a dead society.

This time on the way, she saw a mother Dabilia, and a child, frozen in a running motion. Maybe that's why most of them were dust, particles, or broken. They'd been caught unawares, running for their lives.

Their facial expressions were an enigma, considering the tiny insectoid-like heads they possessed. Still, though, it didn't look to be a slow jog but more of a frantic dash.

Quinn sobered up and continued on her way after looking at them wistfully for several seconds. She sighed, not trying to spread her sadness, but just trying to rid herself of it.

Before them was a massive stone staircase that, indeed, led up to an awe-inducing structure. Or it would have been, in its heyday. Before portions of it fell into ruin.

She climbed the steps. There had to be at least forty of them. Some were wider as if she was approaching a grand entrance to some amazing building. The air felt heavier here, but she knew popping another ball wasn't going to help her. She still had two hours on this one, as it was.

"I don't like the feeling of this," Eric said, grimacing.

"If you don't like it, it must be horrible," Malakai quipped.

Eric glared at him. "Stop it, elf. Bite me."

"Can't, you're impervious. I'll break my teeth."

"Damn it, I was hoping you didn't know that."

Quinn thought they got along charmingly. An idle thought occurred to her and she really hoped that the Library was doing okay.

"Hey," she said, "we need a doorway to return to the Library. Maybe that's why I couldn't reach it when I tried while we were in the middle of nowhere."

"Sounds like a very plausible explanation, Quinn," Malakai said, but didn't offer anything else up.

Finally, at the threshold to the entrance, they stood before massive double doors that, in an eerie way, reminded Quinn of the Library's main entrance. Even though to the sides of them most of the walls were missing, it still felt right to enter through them.

Quinn gasped once she pushed them open she saw the interior of what had once definitely been an amazing cathedral of some sort. There were pews, most of them broken down, but she could see hundreds and hundreds of the Dabilia kneeling in prayer. Some of their stone bodies were broken, so many of them crumbled, but it was obvious that everybody had been here, either trying to pray to some god they believed in, or perhaps trying to pool their power if they were the primordial species as Lynx had mentioned.

She felt tears brimming in her eyes and sniffed them back. She couldn't get emotional about a species that died centuries ago. Could she?

"Must be in here," she said. "Maybe this was their last stand."

She inspected every row as she walked past, frowning, still not finding what she was looking for. The book was nowhere to be seen.

Some of the Dabilians were holding each other's hands, holding their children, or had devolved into a complete and utter pile of ash in some cases.

But nobody was holding a book.

She felt like maybe the chaos was still eating away at these long-dead husks. That was sobering thought.

Aradie flew around, searching, Eric too, while Malakai and her each took a side of the pews. She was getting extremely frustrated, until right at the top, where usually there would be a lectern, was a chest. A massive chest that she'd first mistook for a table.

There was a familiar type of power emanating from it, even though it felt weak.

"Do you think they locked it in the chest?" Quinn asked, very confused. It didn't look like the safe. This thing looked impregnable.

Eric shrugged. "I don't know, but this isn't like the safe was. I won't be able to just pull this open."

"Yeah, I got that already," she said.

Aradie too, gathered around the massive container that had probably once been a golden chest, when it wasn't turned to igneous rock.

"Well," Quinn said concentrating for a moment through her Library connection with the petrified stone against her palm, "it's in there. I can sense it. The signal is just very weak. Could it be so corrupted by the surrounding chaos that it needs repairs or it just really needs its bag?"

Malakai shrugged. "I don't know. I haven't done this before. Couldn't they have sent us with somebody a little bit more experienced?"

Eric cleared his throat. "I have experience, just not with retrieving texts like this. That could be it. Just be careful as you open it," he warned, his voice trembling ever so slightly.

"Why me?" Quinn asked. "I'm the least experienced adventure person here."

"Because you're the Librarian, which already affords certain protections against the book and the chaos," Eric shot back.

She sighed and reached out to try and push the lid up. It gave a lot easier than she expected. So much so that the weight she'd been pushing into opening it redistributed too fast and made her stumble.

Which was very lucky, because where she'd been but a split second before, the lid and the rest of the chest smashed down with a loud toothy snarl.

56

MIMIC

THE MOUTH... LID... OPENED AND CLOSED SO FAST, SO MANY TIMES, Quinn scrambled further back barely registering that it wasn't actually moving toward her yet. The bloody chest table she had been about to open and retrieve the book from was a mimic.

"A freaking mimic."

"What did you say?" Malakai asked, yanking her arm and pulling her further away from the monster.

"It's a mimic," she said, able to hear the close to freaking out tone starting to emerge in her voice. "A bloody mimic." Maybe it had heard her curse that there weren't any monsters like in video games. This was definitely the last time she was ever going to mention that.

"What do you mean a mimic? That's a... mishiminaghakufrepil," Malakai said, somehow twisting his mouth around that name.

Quinn spared a second to flash him an irritated look. "Yeah, like I said, it's a mimic. Trust me, just use my word. It's a lot easier to pronounce and retain."

That was about the length of conversation they got, before the mimic somehow morphed its massive lid to reach over with its jaw that was filled with, oh, about four lines of serrated teeth and chomped down just where they'd been standing. If Quinn hadn't used her hovering as a defensive technique abilities to push them out of the way, they would have been toast.

Or... like a midday snack.

She racked her brain trying to think, trying to gather all of the magic and knowledge she'd absorbed to work for her in this position. As it was, she simply shot out an icicle and hoped for the best as she ran further away.

The massive chest heaved itself and opened its lid, for want of a better word, and growled out a massively challenging roar. If it had been a lion, it would have been the leader of the pack. Slobber and drool ran down the sides of its lips, or lid, Quinn was getting very confused about its anatomy, and dripped onto the stone floor where it sizzled and began to burn holes in the floor around it.

"That's not good," Malakai said, freeing his sword from its scabbard, glancing at it, and then diving into his storage to pull out a completely different one that looked like it was made out of a golden material. Which was silly, it couldn't be gold, it wouldn't be hard enough to be a sword. She trusted him to know what he was doing.

In the meantime, she glanced around trying to find Eric, who had flown up and was quite literally casting what looked like a brimstone pillar to drop on top of the mimic.

"It's not going to do anything, Eric. It's just going to absorb your power," the elf called out, despite not appearing to look in the Imp's direction.

Eric stopped, glanced down at Malakai and cursed under his breath. Quinn was happy she couldn't understand what he said from down here. Instead, she simply tried to freeze the mimic. She shot out a plane of ice, leveling it to hit in between the open mouth and the bottom jaw. But it was far quicker to react than she'd anticipated, and it closed its mouth, making the ice only shatter a few of the front teeth.

It roared in pain and challenge again, the sound making the ground beneath her tremble.

Quinn couldn't help her limbs from shaking. The flashing lights that guided them toward this city suddenly made sense as they became more and more intense all around them. In fact, it felt like she was standing in a 70s disco or at a fireworks display inside this Cathedral of Death. The lights kept moving more frequently, pulsing like they were trying to confuse them with the colors, to mislead their minds.

Really, if you want the book, just go up and take it. The voice that sounded through her mind sounded an awfully lot like her reasoning tone. And really, wasn't that what she needed to do?

Quinn blinked. No, it was a mimic. It was an actual real live monster standing right in front of her. She couldn't just go and take the book. It had internal organs in there.

It's only one more book. We've got to get back to the Library, her calm mind voice insisted.

Quinn stopped, took a steadying breath, and felt the stone in her hand inside her glove still there. She could feel the soft ebb, the soft pulse of the Library's presence with her. She knew she had to get the book back, but they'd have to kill the mimic first.

There's not enough time. You need to ignore the mimic for now. Just get in, get the book, and get back to the Library.

"I can't dive into the mimic," she said, like she needed to reason with herself.

"What are you talking about?" Malakai snapped at her. "What is wrong?"

She blinked, looked around, and realized that she must have missed something. The stone floor next to her had a whopping big hole in it that wasn't there before, and she looked around trying to find Eric, who was darting in and out, and stabbing the creature instead of using his magic. She turned and saw Aradie, who flapped her wings and screeched with her sonic power at smaller chests that surrounded their rear escape route. The bird was barely keeping them at bay.

"Quinn, snap out of it," Malakai's voice barely penetrated the fog in her head.

Just come and take the book, her not-voice said again to her.

And that's when she realized that the damn mimic was in her head.

It was trying to get past her defenses and convince her to do something utterly stupid.

"It's in my head. Be careful, it can get in your heads," she cried out.

Already in yours, my dear, it said with this slimy whisper, letting her know it had given up all pretense of trying to be her own voice. In fact, it sounded far too like Kajaro for her liking.

She gathered all of her mental energy, everything she had learned from Milaro, everything she had gathered from the damn core. She was not going to let this bastard play with her thoughts. And when it taunted her the next time, it encouraged her.

Just come on in, Quinn. You know you want the book.

"I don't want it that much," she said. "Get out of my head."

And with the last word, she pushed against every single thing the creature had thrown at her. Against every single tendril that was foreign in her mind. And she shoved them all straight back into the mimic's face. With so much force that this time, she made the ground and walls around them began to tremble. Several windows that were still partially intact exploded outwards with the force.

The mimic roared in pain. Debris from the building's framing scattered around them all, like ashes in the wind. Quinn pushed back the dizziness she felt and focused on the creature again. Icicle after icicle, she aimed this time into its gaping mouth.

Stunned, it couldn't seem to move. Malakai let arrows fly. Eric took that moment to fire torpedoes of earth into its gaping maw. It wasn't as effective as his fire, but that was next to useless against the creature.

After a couple of seconds, it regained its wits, shook itself, and somehow leveraged itself up onto a multitude of tiny, tiny legs. The massive chest began moving toward them.

This was not what Quinn had been aiming for.

The creature was struggling. She could see part of the lid hanging limply to the side on the right. Several of the legs were completely immobile, being dragged by the force of the others. She had to stun it again. She needed to follow the train of thought that had been in her head back to its origin and attack it just like that again.

"We need to stun it," she said.

"Well, what are you waiting for?" Malakai said. "You did it once, do it again."

She bit her lip. "It might take a bit."

She wanted to ask if they could keep an eye on her while she prepared, but she knew that he, Eric, and Aradie were already doing everything they could do right now anyway.

"Okay, I can do this." She shot ice onto the floor, making sure it stuck and readied some water creations to make it extra slippery when the time came. She hoped that the little legs would lose their purchase and send the mimic sliding in the wrong direction.

Then she dove in.

In her mind, she looked for anything foreign and found one tendril left. It was clinging, sort of like the little feet that were carrying the mimic on the bottom of the chest. It reminded her of them. She grabbed onto it, took a deep breath, focused her mind, and sent another repulsion down the line, mimicking herself from earlier, as best she could. This wasn't something Milaro had taught her.

She could feel the power whoosh out of her. It wasn't quite as angry and as vehement as before, but she hoped it would do the trick, especially since they'd already weakened the mimic slightly. It raced into the creature, just as the little feet found the ice she'd laid out for them. Not to mention the constant barrage of earthen bricks being rained down into any opening the mimic gave and the arrows hitting the precisely correct spot, because Malakai's aim was perfect.

If Aradie had been able to help them, instead of fending off the little army of other pieces of furniture, they would have been fine. Just as the mental pulse hit it and stunned it, the feet lost purchase on the ground and slid.

It was excellent, almost poetic timing. As the mouth stunned open and allowed Malakai the opening he needed. He grabbed his sword. He leapt into the air, and with speed and sheer force, he drove the sword into the side of the hinges and decapitated the mimic.

When it was three quarters of the way through the ice, it was obvious the stun had worn off. The mimic flailed, little legs and lidless gaping maw working overtime.

That's when Malakai leapt in with his sword drawn and hacked away at the rest of the mimic. Each slice of his sword made a grating sound, followed by an anguished squeal from the creature. Goldish-black blood spurted all over the otherwise pristine elf, but he didn't stop. He hacked his way through the last quarter of that jaw and mouth area, until the mimic finally flopped to the ground, amidst an onslaught of ice and earth.

For just a few seconds, complete silence fell over the area, punctuated only by the dripping of blood from the mimic corpse as it hit the icy floor. Slowly, its body began to transform into a blob that reminded Quinn of playdough. Moldable into anything.

And then, the little mimics began to squeal.

"Get it, get the book," she cried out.

"No shit," Malakai said.

Then Quinn received multiple images from Aradie. She turned to face all of the small chests that Aradie had been keeping stunned with her sonic screeches. They were morphing, transforming through a glob-like sliminess into creatures that had legs.

"Oh no," she gasped, rushing toward the mimic corpse that was now just the same as what the globs had gone through to transform. "I guess they can just shift into any shape?"

"Yes, of course. They're a shape-shifting species," Malakai snapped at her.

She wanted to point out that there was an entire species that looked like furniture, and that an entire species of chest mimics wasn't out of the realm of possibilities, but they were under a time crunch here.

"Quick, grab this, help me." Malakai handed her a dagger, oblivious to her inner diatribe, and together they literally tore the remnants of the glob apart, digging deep to find the book.

"Ow!" Malakai exclaimed.

"Did you cut yourself?" She whipped around to see, not caring that the tail end of her ponytail was now covered in goop.

"It's okay, it'll be fine. We just need to get back now."

Quinn didn't like the sound of that. "Put the salve—"

"I'll put the salve on when we're done," he snapped with urgency.

She couldn't force him to do it, but she did make sure that she remembered that he needed it. And she could also be glad that the caustic attack the mimic had didn't seem to survive its death.

"I've got it." Her hand closed around the spine of a book. It was thick and she could feel the pulsing welcome it gave her. Pulling herself back from the massive slime, she shoved the book into the final satchel, sealing it shut so that it could purify.

The sigh of relief wasn't as prevalent this time, but a feeling of calm did suffuse her.

Meanwhile, Aradie was only having so much luck buffeting the rest of the creatures who could now walk back. What had kept them in their chest forms while the mimic was raging, she had no idea and could only be thankful for. Maybe they had to follow the big mimic's lead or something.

"Run, we've got to go," Eric called out.

"Where to?" Quinn yelled.

Eric literally stopped and hovered in front of her face. "To the doors. We need doors to get back to the Library. That is how this whole thing works. Remember?"

Without a second thought, she turned, yanked Malakai by the arm, and sprinted toward the entrance they'd come in through in the first place. Yanking the doors closed so she could place her hand on them took a lot longer than she thought it would.

"Library, open a door now." Nothing happened. She put her hands in front of her, gripping the rock she'd been given by the Library tightly. "Don't fail me now," she said, willing herself not to turn around. She couldn't look, she couldn't see how close the other mimics were.

"Come on, sometime today," Malakai called out to her, his tone urgent. She pushed her hands flat against the doors, willing her whole consciousness to reach through the thick gel-like substance that seemed to be blocking her and find the damn Library. A pulse resonated through her whole body.

"Library, open," she said, as she pushed.

The doors pushed forward, and they didn't open onto the desolate stairs in the darkened, stone-like countryside they'd just come in off.

It opened to reveal the front desk.

"Run!" Quinn stood at the doors, motioning the others to run through. "Quick, quick!" And only when Aradie, Malakai, and Eric were on the other side did she slip through herself, pulling them closed, even as she saw the mimics rushing toward her.

Lynx was already there, looking over her in concern. "Are you okay?" he asked.

She partially ignored him, panting from the exertion. "Malakai. Malakai needs—needs healing," she said, pushing down that frantic sensation that elevated her heartbeat. Her mind felt foggy too. She couldn't believe they'd made it. But they were back, back at the Library and she was covered in slime, entrails, and oddly black-gold blood.

It took a little while to get everyone settled and Misha was already applying salves to Malakai's wounds.

Quinn hovered for a few seconds. "Is he gonna be okay?"

"It was very close to the limit," Misha said, "but part of his heritage has the appropriate constitution to fight chaos in ways I wish we could replicate."

That was another hint. Quinn was dying to know more about Malakai's history, but this wasn't the time. She took in a deep breath as she toweled the mucus from the corpse of the mimic off her.

"I have erected a sanitizing shower to get anything out of, off you, and out of your armor. It's equipped with chaos purification. You should go through it," Misha said, without any inflection at all in their voice.

Quinn tugged the four satchels out of her storage belt and handed them to Lynx. "I don't know how long they need, but we've got them."

There was invisible relief when Lynx sighed. "Thank you. That took a lot less time than I thought it would."

Quinn looked at him. "Trust me, it was longer than it had any right to be."

Lynx grimaced. "Thank you for getting them."

She gave him a tired smile. "How long do they need?" At his questioning look, she elaborated. "You know, to stay in the pouches?"

"Oh." He frowned and activated the console, tapping each of the satchels in turn.

Quinn grimaced at the display.

Laws of Chaos, Upside Down

95 hours remaining

Chaos Theory, Myth and Legend

89 hours remaining

Reality Combined: Chaos Fever Dream

82 hours remaining

Mastering Your Reality Through Chaos

86 hours remaining

She shrugged. "Guess we've got some time on our hands."

Lynx smirked. "Well, if you count taking care of the Library, checking in books, and getting your skills and abilities up a few notches as time on our hands? Then yes, we do."

Quinn laughed. "I think I'm going to take my time in that decontamination shower first and then rest up a bit."

"You deserve it," Lynx said, his voice quiet, but the thanks echoed through his double-lidded purple sclera eyes.

She took that sincerity and went to wash all the gunk off.

~~

Later, Quinn was showered, degunged, and completely and utterly comfortable in a nice pair of fuzzy sweats, slippers, and a big hoodie with somewhere she could shove her hands into. It was the perfect popcorn and movie night outfit, except she didn't have any popcorn and was pretty certain they hadn't been hiding televisions from her since she got here. Her bedroom ceiling wasn't quite the level of entertainment she was looking for.

She made her way back down to the foyer and paused from her spot on the winding staircase.

It gave her an overview of a Library that was no longer dilapidated, no longer a wasteland of ruined books and torn pages, and no longer completely broken.

A soft, golden glow permeated the entire area. Books no longer littered the floor; instead, they lined perfectly organized shelves all the way down as far as she could see. Even the upper level held its own magical glow. Furniture was perfectly placed throughout to allow patrons room enough to visit the stacks and collections, but also a place to peruse, sit, and discuss their findings.

And the light that shone through the windows at the very top was dark, like a moonlit night.

She smiled as she looked down at the desk and saw Lynx, Geneva, Eric, Finn, Narilin, Malakai, Milaro, and Dottie all milling around it.

It all seemed so peaceful. Simply beautiful.

Sure, there were problems with the power source, the filtration system, and still almost seventeen thousand books to retrieve. But they'd get there.

Quinn watched her newfound coworkers, some she'd even consider friends now, from where she stood on the stairs and thought, *Maybe, just maybe this whole Library thing might work out.*

TO BE CONTINUED:

Don't want to stop reading?
Patreon has rough drafts of books 2 & 3
RR has rough drafts too!
Otherwise, book 2 will be releasing soon!

ABOUT THE AUTHOR

Born in Australia, K.T. Hanna met her husband in a computer game, moved to the U.S.A. and went into culture shock. Bonus? Not as many creatures specifically designed to kill you.

KT creates science-fiction, fantasy, and LitRPG, with a dash of horror for fun! She is a member of the SFWA and NINC. Her hobbies include gaming, reading, and lake time!

No, she doesn't sleep. She is entirely powered by caffeine, Chipotle, and sarcasm.

ACKNOWLEDGMENTS

I have a lot of people to thank. Even those who don't contribute directly through the writing craft keep me going and help me write my best stories.

Love of my life, Trevor, and my little Bria. It's his fault I found the genre, and her fault I never give up on writing.

I wouldn't be here without the following friends:

SSODA

Crown

Eric Ugland

Quinton Shyn

Andrea Parseneau

M Evan Matyas

Daniel Schinhofen

Michael Chatfield

Luke Chmilenko

Tao Wong

Geneva

Jess

Ino

And of course my family:

Mumskin & Papilie, Tracey, Jett, & Robbie.

The entire Coteh server

My Legion Family

And every one of my Patrons, not to mention my FB Group and people in my discord.

Thank you

You all help me maintain a level of sanity.

ALSO BY K.T. HANNA

Printed in the USA
CPSIA information can be obtained
at www.ICGtesting.com
CBHW020003100924
14328CB00031B/261